DARK FUTURES

Visit us at:

www.darkquestbooks.com

DARK FUTURES

EDITED BY JASON SIZEMORE

Dark Quest Books
Howell, NJ

Dark Futures

Cover Art "Fairy Tail for the Night" © by Alexey Andreyev
Cover design by Justin Stewart

Dark Quest Books
www.darkquestbooks.com

ISBN: 978-0-9826197-2-8

For the consigliere

TABLE OF CONTENTS

TABLE OF CONTENTS

INTRODUCTION

Let's not kid ourselves. The first ten years of the 21st century hasn't been the best of times. Terrorism. War. Pandemics. Environmental disasters. Political fallacies. Human rights atrocities. I'll stop there before I run the risk of sounding like a Billy Joel lyric, but I think you get my drift. Worldwide angst is at a high level.

In turn, the world of speculative fiction has taken a darker turn the past few years. Much has been made about this by the genre community. Some go so far to treat this trend as *bad*. These people posit such desperate questions as "Why are writers so black and blue? Why can't they write about the great things in life?" This shallow reactionary attitude points to many individuals missing one of the most important aspects that writers, editors, and publishers perform in society.

We serve as the voice of the people.

I'm not only talking about novelists and short story authors, but this applies to anyone in the creative arts: filmmakers, playwrights, artists, sculptors, and so forth. We digest the world around us and produce work that functions as a mirror of society. Others view this work as a means of coming to grips with the world they fight through day to day. It's voyeuristic escapism. It's a twisted form of schadenfreude—I've got a crap life but at least *that* didn't happen to me. It's entertainment.

Happy endings and pleasant entertainment will always rightly have its place in the world. But the human race seems to like things that comes in pairs…night and day, left and right, and good and bad. People like variety. Need variety.

And I hope that the following stories fill that dark niche hiding in your personality.

Jason Sizemore
June 25th, 2010
Lexington, KY

MEMORIES OF HOPE CITY

Maggie Slater

I

Father says Hope City is a utopia. He's always high when he tells me this, lounging on the couch, tripping on moondust or cosmo or maybe just drunk. When I ask him what a utopia is, he stares at me through glazed eyes, smiles a bit—like he's getting a blow job from a girl he finds ugly—and then he laughs in my face.

I don't usually spend time around Father when he's like that, and often I don't have to because someone needs to be guarding the door to the house from K-2s and the pigs. On nights like this, when Father's stoned, I sit by the door with the taser and my shiv until BJ comes home.

"Shove off, Rion," BJ always says, taking the taser and slumping down onto the front step. If I don't move fast enough, he'll scowl at me and tell me to buzz off before he hits me.

BJ never hits me.

He's threatened to lots of times, but I know and he knows that he never really would. We know it's just a game we play, even though we're both too old for games, him nineteen and me thirteen.

It was BJ who waited for me at the edge of our territory, right next to the stinking Hope Canal, after my first sex trade. The Agros had needed fresh water—a lot of fresh water, since they grow most of the plant stuff—and as a price, Father had worked it out for me to have sex with one of their daughters. That and the battery stash, two more tasers, and five kilos of the plant he makes moondust from made for a fair trade.

I was twelve at the time, and still a little scared of Ming. She was so pretty, and at least fifteen. Unlike my sister, Bee, she had breasts that wobbled when she walked. I never told anyone this, but once I had a dream about her long before I had sex with her, and when I woke up, the bed was sticky.

I was tired and a little embarrassed after that first sex trade, but I was glad to see BJ waiting for me.

"So what'd you think?"

"Ask me tomorrow," I said, and he laughed and ruffled my hair.

But I know that tonight BJ isn't coming home to take my place guarding the front door. I know this because I can see him floating in the trash cloud between the north and south poles of Hope City, where everything rotates so slowly there isn't any gravity. It's pretty far away, but I can make out the dark spot of him between me and the other hemisphere of the city.

I guess I shouldn't say I can see *him*. I can see *it*.

The corpse, I mean.

I haven't really paid attention to watching the door, so when Ariel says, "What are you looking at?" her voice makes me jump. Ariel is my other sister, the older one. She and BJ are twins.

She stands next to me, squinting up at the junk cloud. She has blood on her legs—splattered blood, not her own blood—and a dripping sack of raw pig meat in her hand. It's because I'm looking at the blood on her legs that I see her knees shake a little when she says, "Holy shit," really soft.

She drops the bag, and it hits the ground with a heavy, wet thump. "Holy fucking shit!"

Then she's gone, running into the house, yelling for Father.

There isn't any point in telling Father. He already knows. He knows because I'd run in, just like Ariel, screaming for him. It's embarrassing, but I was so scared my eyes were watery and I was shaky all over.

Father hadn't been high then. He'd been checking the battery supplies of our tasers. One by one, he popped them into the charger, making a note of the green or yellow or red bulb color. We can charge the batteries for about a year, but after that, they don't hold a charge for very long.

When I came running in, he had just yanked out one of the batteries and thrown it against the wall with a curse. "What the fuck is it?" He glared at me, eyed me up and down.

"BJ! I think he's—I think—"

Father just watched me, the glare fading to boredom. "Shit," he said and turned his back on me, picking up another battery. "You scared me."

I stood shivering in the room. The air was real thick, and I couldn't catch my breath right. "But BJ—"

"He's dead," Father said, not looking up, not turning around. He paused, squinting at the battery in his hand to figure out which end went into the charger.

I didn't know what to say, then. I just stood there—the shakes gone—dazed and lost on what to do next. Then I said, "Who killed him?"

Father scoffed and looked at me over his shoulder. He was smirking. For a long time he didn't say anything, and then he pushed his chair back with a grunt and walked past me to the cabinet. He pulled open the drawer he kept his moondust and needles in and handed me a roll of dust and a syringe.

"Come on," he said, motioning to the couch.

I followed and sat down next to him. He took the dust, took the syringe, and began mixing up a dose. I watched him, but I didn't speak. On the coffee table, he dumped some of the dirty clothes on the floor and grabbed the rubber tube he used to find his vein. Only he didn't tie it around his bicep like usual.

"Here," he said, motioning for me to give him my arm. I did, and he tied the tube around it. "You're old enough to have some fun." He smacked the inside of my elbow until a vein stuck out.

I didn't want to get high like he did. Moondust makes you sleepy and boring, and once you've had some, you'll always want more. BJ used moondust a lot, and he always ignored me when he was high. Later, when he crashed, he'd curl up in a ball in his bed and cry like a girl, sobbing softly to himself. It scared me when he did that.

The only time he really almost hit me was when I asked him about why he cried; he made a fist and swung at me, but at the last minute he turned and punched the wall instead. It broke his hand and he cursed a lot while Song bandaged his bleeding knuckles. The hand never really healed.

And he told me, looking me dead in the eye, "You shouldn't ask about some things."

But I couldn't tell Father any of that, and BJ was dead. So I just watched as Father slid the needle into the vein and pushed the plunger down, sending all the foggy grey-red stuff into my blood. Then the world went slow and blurry and I didn't care much that BJ was dead. I only remember Father saying, "Feeling better?" and hearing him laugh as he got up and left me on the couch.

I'm coming down off it now, and the shakes are coming back. My head aches, and my stomach feels greasy and filled with dirt. Inside the house, I hear Ariel screaming at Father. Their voices ring in my ears until I hear a thud, and then another thud, and Father cursing her. Then everything goes quiet, and a few minutes after that I hear someone climb the stairs and slam a door.

It's really cold, or it feels like it. I know it can't be lower than sixty-seven degrees, because it's always sixty-seven, so the cold must just be in my head, coming off the moondust.

I look back up at the trash cloud, trying to find the corpse, but it's drifted over a dark patch of the opposite city, so I can't see it. But in the twilight, I do see the Commandant's lights at the south pole switch on. I check my watch: nine o'clock. Right on time.

And somehow, that makes me feel a little better.

The door beside me opens and Father steps out. He stares up at the junk cloud, too, but he doesn't say anything. I figure now is as good a time as any to mention what's been bugging me for the last hour.

"Father?"

He grunts to let me know he's listening.

"I think we should go up there and get BJ's body down. It's just going to rot up there and then eventually it'll rain back down on the streets, and even later, the rest of it will fall, and then the pigs'll eat what's left."

Father looks down at me. He isn't smirking, and he isn't scowling. "I want you to listen to me very carefully, Rion," he says. His voice is soft, and he says my name, so I know he's saying something important. "I don't want you to talk about BJ anymore. I don't want you to go anywhere near that body. Fuck him. You hear me?"

But that doesn't make any sense to me. We never display our dead, and Father told me only the K-2s let the pigs eat their dead, but they fuck the pigs too, because they aren't any better than pigs themselves. But we—the Quids—we aren't savages like them.

When I don't answer right away, Father kicks me. He doesn't kick me very hard, just hard enough to knock me to the ground. "Are you fucking deaf? Answer, you little shit!"

"I heard you," I say, and he looks like he's really going to hit me, but when I flinch, he smirks and heads back inside.

No one relieves me tonight, but that's okay. I don't want to go inside where I can't see the speck of BJ floating over my head. Besides, I know I won't be able to sleep, knowing he might fall back down to the city. The one time I doze by accident, I dream the pigs are eating me, and I wake up. I must have cried out, because I hear footsteps on the stairs and a second later, Bee stands there, taser in hand.

"What's going on?" she asks, glaring into the darkness.

Bee's fifteen, like Ming, but smaller. Her stomach bulges because she's pregnant from the last sex trade. She's still a little mad at Father about that. The pregnant part, not the trade part. Father's traded her lots of times; she just hates the morning sickness.

"Nothing," I say. "Just a bad dream."

Bee turns her dead-eye look on me. "You fucking scared me, you know that? I thought it was the K-2s again."

I apologize and she shrugs, glancing at her watch. "I was going to come down and take your place in an hour anyway. Go in and get some sleep. You're useless when you're tired."

I obey and she takes my place. The house is dark and quiet; only Leo and Thom are still up, playing cards on the back step leading to our garden. On my way up the stairs to my room, I hear soft female voices coming from behind Ariel's closed door. One's crying—I hear her voice crack when she speaks—and the other murmurs gently. I pause on the landing to listen, but I can't make out the words.

Then the door opens and Song steps out. I see Ariel curled up on her bed inside, but only for a second before the door closes. Song has two used needles and her eyelids droop.

"Why aren't you in bed?" Song asks.

Song is Father's whore. She was originally one of the Agros, but that was before Kam killed Patya. They gave Song to Father to keep him from killing Kam to make up the difference.

"Rion. Did you hear me?"

I don't like Song much. She's always high, and when she's mad she slaps me and screams at me until her face turns red. She curses at me, and sometimes I don't even know what she's saying because she doesn't always speak English when she's that mad.

Song takes a step toward me, and I back down the top stairs. "I was on post," I say.

"This late?"

"No one took my place."

I don't want to talk to her about BJ, and she doesn't ask. Instead, she nods slowly and then drifts down the hall to Father's room. I wait until she closes the door behind her and I don't hear her moving anymore. Then I go to my room to sleep.

II

The Hope Canal smells like shit. The moment you touch the greasy, thick water, you can just imagine some nasty worm parasite burrowing into your skin, making you sick. You can't drink the stuff, and you can't swim in it. There aren't any signs that say so; everybody just knows.

Ming leans way over the railing of the Hua Dao bridge, her fingers scrabbling for the thin metal wire knotted loosely just under the edge of the road. I stand in the middle of the narrow bridge, trying to watch for anyone who might have followed us, though I'm getting distracted by Ming's small, tight shorts and the strip of blue underwear I can see peeping out at the crotch.

"Come on, you fucker!" she mutters, and then her fingers snag the line. "Hey," she says to me as she starts hauling it up. "You want it, you help."

I hurry over, grasp the slick wire line, and start pulling. Below, the algae-slimed air tank rises to the surface.

It doesn't take us too long, but raising the tank makes a lot of noise, which makes me nervous. Once or twice I lift my head to glance around at the canal-side streets, expecting to see someone standing there. I feel like we're being watched.

The tank falls with a clang on the stone of the bridge, and Ming stoops to unwind the length of wire from its circular valve. "It's not totally full or anything," she says. "It's just what I've siphoned off some of the others. Little bits, you know? Don't want Baba asking questions."

Baba is the head of the Agros. Father's missing his left ring finger because of him.

"There." Ming stands up, pulling the wire free. "One air tank. Payment please." Ming flicks the fingers of her open palm at me.

I pass the small container of moondust to her, and she immediately holds it up to the light and sighs, a small smile spreading across her face. "My own private stash," she whispers, and then, with a glance at me, she shoves the vial into her pocket.

"So, we done here? We good?"

I stoop down next to the air tank and check the gauge. Half full, at best. I'll have to use it very carefully when I go up into z-g, but it's better than nothing. If I wanted a full tank, I'd have had to get Father involved to negotiate. As it is, I don't know what he'll do to me if he finds out I've been bargaining with Ming behind his back.

But since he won't help me get BJ down, this is the way it has to be.

Ming starts tapping her foot on the ground. "Kid, you deaf? We good or what?"

"Yeah, we're good," I say. I hate the way she calls me Kid, like I'm a five-year-old, or a stranger. I can still remember the smoothness of her skin, the curve of her uplifted chin, the squeak she made when I'd actually gotten her to orgasm that first time.

But Ming doesn't leave.

"Why you going after BJ anyway? After all the trouble of putting him up there in the first place?"

"He's my brother," I say, hefting the tank. Her last words linger in my ears an extra few seconds, then, just as I start walking away, they sink in, and I stop. "What do you mean?"

"I mean, why are you going to pull him down when Father put him up there?"

I stare at her, the weight of the tank dragging my arms down. "Father didn't put him up there."

Ming glances around us, like she's feeling the same skin-prickle that makes me think we're being watched. "Look," she says, moving close to me. She hunches, her black hair tickling my cheek as she whispers in my ear, "I don't know what you've been told, but Father was the one who put BJ up there. I saw him do it. He asked Baba to help. They traded a tank of water for it."

"That's bullshit." I shake my head and try to walk away, but Ming follows.

"I just thought you should know. You know? Father's going to be pissed if you get BJ down. He wanted him up there."

"We don't display our dead," I mutter, shrugging off the hand she puts on my shoulder.

She doesn't follow me anymore, and for the first time, I'm glad. She's nothing but a dirty Agro. What do they know about us Quids? They're really just one step up from K-2s. I wonder how I never realized that before.

Halfway down the street, I still feel her watching me. But when I glance back, there's no one around. The skin on the back of my neck tingles. With a shiver, I heft the air tank and pick up the pace.

III

There are really only three kinds of people in Hope City: those who think the Commandant's lights are automated; those who think they're not; and those who swear they've seen Him walking around the city at night.

Those who think the lights are automated also think the real Commandant who lived in his sealed-off house either died a long time ago or left with the rest of the able-bodied Hope citizens. They point out that the lights go on and go off with perfect regularity at dawn and at dusk every day. People aren't that regular. Plus, no one's even seen so much as a shadow pass between the source of the light and the frosted windows. No one goes in, and no one ever comes out.

Those who think the lights are switched on by hand don't have all that much proof, really, except that there are stories, old stories from people who died a long time ago, that when the sickness first arrived at the station and people started dying, the Commandant refused to abandon Hope City. He'd sealed himself off to keep from getting sick, but he stayed. The people who think he's still there don't like talking about specifics: How could he eat? What would he drink? How old would he be now? They just grunt and wave off the questions. I think people—even people like me—just like thinking there's someone there.

Then there are those who swear they've seen the Commandant wandering around the city at night. Every clan has one or two people who say they've seen him cross the street ahead of them, or who've called out to a man they thought was a friend only to realize they didn't recognize him. He doesn't say anything, and he always disappears without a trace. They describe him wearing a dark uniform, but the details about his hair or face are always different. That's how you know it's just in their heads.

But there is something lurking in the city. About a year ago, BJ came home shaking all over, and when I asked him what was wrong, he shook his head and said he'd seen a thing. He told me it walked on four long, slender legs, and had one blue-green eye—like a lens—and that it was made of metal. He'd just turned a corner on his way home when he saw it standing over a pig corpse in the open street. He wasn't sure at first if it was real, because he'd been on West Orchard Street, and all the streetlights are busted up except one at the far end by the canal.

BJ said he froze and it stood up, and the two of them just looked at each other. Then the thing stalked away, its legs clicking on the street until it turned down Paulson Road and disappeared.

IV

The tingling doesn't go away, even after I stash the air tank in a safe place and go home. I get back in time to take Leo's place watching the back door. Bee brings me food after a few hours and I eat on duty. It's a quiet night, but I feel edgy. I jump when someone inside starts yelling and a fight breaks out. I almost zap Joc and Wend when they come back from patrol, slipping around the garden wall.

Even the steady blinking of my taser's yellow-red battery light makes me nervous.

It's late by the time my watch relief comes and takes the taser, letting me get to bed. I lie for almost an hour, itchy and twitchy. With every creak of a footstep on the stairs, my eyes fly open in the dark and my heart hammers against my ribs.

At last, almost near morning, I get up and creep downstairs to my father's moondust cabinet. It's almost totally black inside, but the floodlights out front and out back cast bold columns of light across the floor. My hands shake as I slide open the drawer with the needles and the containers of dust.

Just a little, I tell myself. *I just need enough to sleep.*

The rubber tube looped around my arm, I slink back up the stairs to my room. There, I prepare the dose just like Father does, and stick the needle into my vein. Within moments, the itching fades away and I sigh, lying back on the bed. The little crack in the corner of my boarded-up window shines bright white, catching the floodlight.

Somewhere far away, a door opens and I hear the shuffle of soft, sneaking footsteps. I close my eyes. *I bet this is what it'd feel like to float in the canal.* The thought makes me smile. Can't remember what I was so worried about. I feel fine now.

When my bedroom door creaks open, I turn my head and open one eye to see who it is. Through the crack: a slender black eye, a coil of black hair, a pale crescent of cheek.

"Rion?" The voice is soft, and for a second I think it might be Ming, but then the door pushes open and Song steps into the room. The latch clicks closed behind her. "Rion, are you awake?"

"Yeah, I guess."

She stands in the darkness, completely shadowed. "I wanted to talk to you about something."

I sigh and close my eyes again, turning to the wall. "I'm tired."

The side of the bed sinks a little and I feel something at my back. A cold hand touches my shoulder. Smooth. "Are you high?"

"Maybe." I shrug off the hand and pull the blanket up to my chin. "Who cares? I couldn't sleep."

Song whispers something I can't understand, and then she says, "Gavin told me what you wanted to do."

Gavin is Father's first name. No one calls him that, though. I don't think even my own mother called him that. It's weird to hear it aloud.

"Go away," I say. My skin is starting to crawl again, though this time, from the spot where she touched me. Who gives a shit what I wanted to do, anyway? I just want to sleep.

"There's something you need to know."

"Go fuck yourself," I mutter and pull the blanket over my head.

A second later, it's torn away from me, and I'm slapped across the face. Hard. I lie shivering in the pale floodlight; Song stands, gripping the collar of my shirt, looming over me.

"I'm trying to help you, stupid!" she hisses. "You think your father is going to let you go up there and pull BJ back down? After what he did?"

"Leave me alone!" I gasp, trying to pull away from her. My shirt tears and I scramble back into the corner, the buzz gone.

Her hand snakes out at me and strikes me again before I can block it. I wince and she grabs my chin, forcing me to look at her. Her fingernails cut into my cheek. "Shut up! You want him to hear? You want him to come in here and find out that you traded with Ming behind his back?" She laughs bitterly, her black eyes glinting in the floodlight. "Oh, I know all about that. About the air tank, too. So you shut up and you listen. Got it?"

I can't nod, can't do more than squeak, "Okay."

She releases my jaw and takes a step back, smoothing back her hair, soothing her expression with a huff. Again, she whispers to herself in another language, but I understand it because she's used those words before to call me stupid when she's mad. Then, in a softened voice, she says, "You wanted to know who killed BJ, right? Well, no one did. BJ did it all by himself. I was the one who found him." I see the silhouette of her slight chest heaving in the light, hear her voice roughen. "I'd come up to bring him something to eat. There was blood everywhere. Puddles of it."

She turns her face to the window and licks her lips. The bar of light from between the boards on the window frames her eyes, and there's a wet shine to them. Her breathing wavers, and I realize she's trying not to cry. "He was alive when I found him. Barely. He blinked. He smiled at me. So much blood...like he'd torn a pig to pieces with his bare hands."

My throat starts closing up. "Bullshit. BJ wouldn't—he didn't—"

Song looks down as she slips something out of her pocket. "He told me to give this to you. He said, 'Tell him: this is what a utopia is.' I don't know what's on it. He died before he could tell me any more. I had it in my hand when Gavin came upstairs and found us."

When she turns to me, hand outstretched, I swat it away. Something small flies out of her fingers and knocks against the wall, skitters under the bed. Her hand stays outstretched, and she gazes at it like she's never seen it before in her life. Then she looks at me, and the blank gaze hardens.

"Get yourself killed, then," she mutters, turning to the door. "Gavin will rip you apart if you take BJ down. BJ deserves to rot up there. Only cowards kill themselves."

It's like every muscle in my body was waiting for this moment, this trigger. In the split second between her turning her back to me and reaching for the door, I launch myself at her. Her teeth click as her back slams up against the wall. There's so much white in her eyes. A gasp. I have her by the throat, and I squeeze as hard as I can. Her fingers claw at me, her mouth gapes, squeaking for air. But in that quiet moment, a cry from outside catches my attention and she breaks my grip. I fall back and she slides to the floor, her hands at her neck, glaring at me like she could kill me if I hadn't almost just killed her.

Another cry from outside and the first twanging zap of a taser. I scramble to my feet and run to the window to look down through the boarded cracks at the street. Darting shadowed bodies—human bodies—race by.

K-2s. *Shit.*

I turn back to Song. She hasn't moved, but she's watching me carefully.

"Stay here," I mutter, grabbing my shiv from under my pillow before ducking out of the room and into the crowding hall.

Bee brushes past me with the others, two feet of rusted pipe in her hands. "Go out the back," she says, and then she's gone, rushing down the stairs with Leo and two others whose faces I don't get a chance to see. I hurry in the opposite direction to the broken window at the end of the hall overlooking the garden. Sure enough, someone has smashed the floodlight, and in the darkness I see two hulking shapes pulling up whatever growing things they can lay their filthy hands on. I climb out onto the window ledge. It's a relatively short jump, just one story, but the thump I make when I land makes the figures look up.

I jump on the nearest and smallest, driving my shiv right into the gut. It shrieks in a voice that sounds almost like a pig and falls back, writhing. I stab once, twice more, and it stops moving, its blood splattered on my hands and face.

The blood makes me slippery, so when the second figure catches me and wrestles me to the ground, I wriggle out of his grasp and knee him hard in what I hope is his face. I can't get a good grip on the shiv, though; my swipes are weak. I must nick the guy, because I hear him hiss and pull back for a moment before his fist slams me in the chest.

My vision spirals. I'm on the ground. The mud is warm. Just over the edge of the roof, on the other side of the city, the Commandant's lights swirl. A big hand grabs my shirt, and there's a flash of light on the blade of a knife.

"Don't you touch him you sonofabitch!"

A taser crackles, and the hand immediately lets go of my shirt. The figure falls back. My sister Ariel stands over him, zapping him again and again, till his scream isn't more than a squeak. The arching fingers of electricity leave tracer shadows in my eyes. Then she twists to me and fumbles for the shiv in my hand. "Give it to me, damn it!"

She makes sure the guy won't stand again. From where I lie, I see only the flash of my little knife and hear the squitch, squitch, squitch of the blade in flesh as she stabs him to death.

There's a far-off shout, followed by pattering, running footsteps, and then everything's quiet.

A flash of light. Leo stands at the back door, his face bruised and bleeding. "They're gone," he says, helping me to my feet.

Ariel crouches by the body of the K-2 she killed. He's a brawny guy, maybe a little older than she is. A few feet away from him is the one I killed. A girl. Maybe nine. My face burns, and I wipe the blood from my lips.

"How many?" Ariel's voice is soft. Tired.

"Three," Leo replies. "Bee, Thom, Joc."

My heart takes a double, twitchy beat that makes me sick to my stomach. I hear Ariel curse, her voice breaking. I don't stand around or watch when Leo stoops down beside her, his hand on her back. I go inside, where there's light. Some of our people sit, nursing wounds and broken bones. Father's slumped on the stairs, his jaw set, his eyes glaring forward, while Song, hands covered in blood, sews up the gushing cut on his brow. He catches my glance for a moment, but his blank expression doesn't change. Song doesn't look at me.

When he glances away, I turn and see Roger lift Bee from the floor by the sofa. Her eyes watch me with the same dull gaze as Father's, but the long purple gash across her throat smiles at me.

V

The whole city spins slowly around me as I twist the nozzle on the air tank. With a hiss, it pushes me a little further out along the z-g column, a little further from the north pole of the city. The smoke and smog up here make my eyes sting and water. The taste of vomit sticks to my tongue. It's hard to breathe and my head aches. My nose is stuffed up, though, so at least I can't smell anything.

An empty food tin bounces off my head as I drift forward. At least it's quiet up here, away from the streets and the fighting and home. I might even like it, if it weren't so full of trash. The tin spirals away, falling faster and faster until it drops out of sight into the city below.

I have to be really, really careful. It wouldn't take much to push myself too far to the outer edge and start falling.

BJ's corpse is way out in the middle, and it takes me almost an hour to get near it, pushing through the garbage. Behind me, I stir up a little storm, and I watch things fall back down to the city where they came from, thinking about the lurch of the gravitational pull and the friction of condensed air.

I had hoped the corpse had stayed close to center where I could just grab it and head back, but it's drifted toward the outer edge, the invisible, lurking line I don't want to cross. To get close enough to grab it, I'll have to boost out a few yards, deliberately getting close to that point of no return. Then, hopefully, I can just boost us both back to center.

I want to, I remind myself. *This is what I want to do.*

It takes a lot of effort to start pushing myself out to the corpse, but once I do, it's only seconds until I can grab the arm. BJ's rotting face is slack-jawed, and tiny liquid spheres ooze out of him when I touch him. I twist, feeling a spike of vertigo as I boost back to center. The corpse drags on me, grinning, leaking.

The arm's already coming off, and when the body bumps on my foot, it pops loose, spraying pearls of corpse juice behind it. BJ's head lolls back as his body spins away from me, falling, falling—

VI

He lands not far from the bridge where Ming and I made our trade. By the time I get there, the pigs have already moved in, greedily lapping up organs, shreds of muscle, and the overabundant puddles of rot juice and blood. They're everywhere, these pigs. Most are bristled and tusked, like wild pigs. It only took a few years of being out of their pens and on their own to do that. Just a few years to revert to wild things, like the things they were on Earth.

A boar lifts his dripping snout at me when I step onto the street, his beady little eyes watching my every twitch of movement. His sows lounge around him, rooting in BJ's shattered ribcage, tearing at the flesh left on the bones of his scattered legs. The boar grunts, letting me know that they've claimed this feast, and if I want any, I'll have to fight him for it.

I don't even have a taser.

The moment BJ's arm returned to Earth gravity, the skin slipped off and it became too difficult to carry. I left it behind, with the spent air tank that ran out on me halfway back to the pole. I had to swim through the air, the disembodied arm spraying me with fluid. It got in my mouth and in my eyes and up my nose.

It's getting dark in this part of the city, save for the Commandant's lights reflecting on the stinking canal water. Soon, it'll be night, and I'll return home to Song and to Father. BJ's corpse will be gone by morning—a quick snack for hungry snouts.

I'll never be able to eat pig again.

The boar, understanding that I'm no threat to him, returns to rooting, and I leave him to his meal. There's nothing I can do here, anyway, and there never was.

The memory stick I'd picked up from my bedroom floor, the one Song had tried to give me, presses cold against my skin through a hole in my pocket.

I shouldn't have watched the videos on it. Even telling myself it had to be fake or something doesn't make the images of green trees, clean water, and smiling faces go away.

I walk without paying attention to where I go or whose territory I cross into. It doesn't matter to me. I smell like blood and death, but that's what home will smell like, too. Maybe it's always smelled that way, and I just never noticed.

A streetlight snaps and buzzes, its sickly white-green light flickering on. It makes the rest of the street look dark and mean.

But when I turn the corner, I see it.

It stands near the end of the road, its legs fully straightened so that it's taller than anyone I've ever known. The light from the streetlamp glints off its metal frame. Its eye swivels to look at me, and I freeze. It is exactly like BJ described it. For a long time, we just stare at each other, its lens dilating, trying to see me, focus on me.

How long has it been watching us? At least a year, but probably more. Maybe forever. It watched BJ when he was still alive, and it watched Father put him up in the trash cloud. It watched the K-2s attack us and kill my sister and my friends. It watched me trade with Ming, and it watched me fail to bring BJ back.

Maybe it made all those videos of the old Hope City, the ones that made BJ cry when he came down off moondust.

But I'm too tired to be afraid of it. It's only a machine. An eye. A lens.

"What are you?" I ask.

It only watches me in reply.

"Did the Commandant send you?"

Still, it stands, listening.

Before I realize what I'm doing, I walk up to it and kick out one of its legs. The thing tilts, but it balances itself gracefully. Unfazed.

My face burns as it stares down at me. What do I look like to it?

Am I just another video clip? Will someone watch me someday? What will they see?

I grit my teeth. "How can you just watch all this? Why don't you help us?"

It does nothing. Says nothing. Then, without a sound, it turns and starts walking away.

My vision blurs and I clench my teeth so hard they squeak. "Why don't you do something?" I snatch up a brick from the street, and before I even know what I'm doing, I throw it as hard as I can. It hits the thing in the corner of its giant eye, and it stumbles, trips, and falls to the ground with a crash. The lens shatters, sending fragments of glass skittering across the pavement.

It doesn't get up. Doesn't move. And after a while, shaking, I go home.

NOSTALGIA

Gene O'Neill

Retro Level—San Fran Shield

Galen Chacon arrived early at the Ferry Building at the foot of Market Street, excited about a shipment recently arrived from an antique book dealer in San Barboo

Shield—rare hardbound books produced in China, all notable classics from the last century. With his mind on the unpacked shipment, he hurried into the garden plaza on the main floor of the shopping mall, hardly noticing the riot of color, the perfume of blooming flowers heavy in the air, or the handful of people waiting for the place to open.

As Chacon reached the middle of the plaza, a strange man, wearing an eco-mask and dressed in a long grey overcoat, approached him. The old-fashioned attire, functional years ago, before the Shield protected against environmental hazards, was rarely seen now, reminding Chacon of Freemen garb from Outside in Cal Wild—except the coat wasn't decorated with an assortment of silly good luck charms or amulets.

Opening one side of his coat slightly, the stranger spoke in a whisper, "Smoke, mister? Ten grams, a hundred, kilo?" There were different-sized bags attached to the lining of the overcoat.

"Or pre-rolled packs," the man added, waving the sweetly pungent playing card package under Chacon's nose.

Oh, no! Chacon thought, reeling backward from the bundled-up man, as if the masked stranger carried a rare but obvious disease. He's a tobacco dealer!

The prohibited substance was grown and smuggled into the Shield from Cal Wild, at great risk for the smugglers—an automatic judgment of color, dying, and banning to wander the wastelands Outside as a pariah. A Dyed Person.

Chacon was shocked that the man would approach him openly in one of the busiest shopping areas under San Fran Shield. The dealer was obviously deranged. Glancing about, Chacon realized there were actually only a few other people roaming the plaza, the shops not opening for another hour or so. No one was paying any attention to him or the tobacco dealer.

Still, the dealer was taking a tremendous risk.

Movement caught his eye.

Beyond the handful of people, Chacon was startled by the sight of two metallic creatures with burning red eyes bounding through the Market Street entryway; several strides behind the creatures was a pair of men wearing skintight modtrend, transparent from the waist up, their bodies and shaved heads brightly tattooed mosaics. *Yakuza*, of course. Their fearsome appearance made him gasp for breath.

The dealer had noticed the direction of Chacon's startled look, and after turning and spotting the hounds and yakuza, he roughly brushed Chacon aside and took off running across the plaza in the opposite direction.

The yakuza must be bounty hunters working for the Company, thought Chacon, recovering his balance and poise. But after a lowly tobacco dealer? What kind of bounty would he possibly command?

The two creatures hurtled by him, a pair of silver blurs in hot pursuit of the dealer, who was scrambling through a bed of blooming iris, clumsily stamping purple, yellow, and black flowers flat as he headed in the direction of the waterfront view exit at the far side of the retro-level of the Shield. Chacon had never seen the bio-electronic hounds in action, but he knew they were equipped with acute olfactory apparatus, rumored to be able to detect a person's or organic substance's pheromones—tobacco in this case—even the smallest sample, at up to a hundred and fifty yards.

The bio-electronic creatures caught up to the fleeing man in the overcoat, and one ripped into the back of the man's leg, shredding his pants and apparently hamstringing him, driving him to the ground, the jarring impact knocking off the eco-mask.

For just a moment, Chacon got a clear view of the dealer's face and head— grey-streaked hair, a deeply wrinkled brow—and he was stunned.

Oh my God, the man was obviously an illegal—an aged person!

Of course that would explain the rarely seen bounty hunters' interest; illegals commanded numerous Shield credits from the Company. It would also explain the aging man's high-risk occupation and behavior. Chacon shook his head in dismay. But he didn't even consider intervening. He just watched.

The pair of silver monsters circled the downed illegal, snapping, making tinny-sounding growls, and keeping the man curled up in a defensive fetal ball for a few moments, groaning and clutching his bleeding leg, until the two bounty hunters caught up and called the artificial hounds off. With a practiced motion, one of the yakuza slipped a come-along stun over the still-prone illegal's head, then the other provided some kind of quick first aid to the tobacco dealer's torn leg.

In a few moments the orderly group passed back by where Chacon stood, still frozen in place in the middle of the plaza, the two brightly-tattooed yakuza leading the limping illegal, the wary silver bio-monsters bringing up the rear. They departed the plaza out onto the street, all boarding a waiting Company hummer. He could easily imagine their eventual destination. The deep sub-surface level of the Shield and the rumored sen-dep tanks. Probing...and perhaps other unpleasant things. The Company would want details of the illegal's clandestine existence, the source of the banned tobacco, and who knew what else. Chacon shuddered, sympathetic toward the aging man's tragic fate.

Then, they were gone, leaving the half-dozen stunned witnesses behind.

Sucking in a deep breath to gather himself, Chacon finished

crossing the plaza to the bank of upchutes. By the time he reached his second floor shop, Nostalgia, he had forgotten the illegal and the dramatic capture, his thoughts again drawn to the remarkable shipment awaiting from San Barboo Shield. He unlocked the place and hurried to his storeroom.

Of course he stocked a number of other old books, pages yellowed and brittle, in a small section of Nostalgia, the establishment offering all kinds of pop culture artifacts of the last century and a half—DVDs and music CDs were the most popular items, but these twenty-six books, in addition to being rare editions, were all well constructed and in remarkable condition. In fact, Chacon marveled at the pristine condition of the texts as he carefully unwrapped each one—even the slipcovers clean and unmarred—and flipped through the snow-white pages. They were all exquisite!

He turned his attention first to the manifest:

Rob Roy, Lmt., San Barboo Shield
Collector and Purveyor of Antique, Fine Books
Invoice for Nostalgia, Lmt., San Fran Shield
Payment required on acceptance: 1350 Shield scrip

Chacon carefully scanned each of the twenty-six precious items. He loved the heft, the grainy cover texture, the smell of the inside of the fine books—

"Galen, I'm sorry to disturb you," a disembodied voice said, interrupting Chacon's enjoyment.

"It's okay, Albert E," Chacon said, responding to the voice of his AI assistant, smiling self-consciously. "I haven't been doing any serious cataloging of the books anyhow. Just unpacking and daydreaming. What is it?"

"You have a high priority message on hold," Albert E said. "Print or audio on your wrist Viz?"

"Print it on my desk computer screen," Chacon instructed, moving over to his desk at the rear of the little shop's storage room.

The message appeared on the antique PC screen:

Mr. Galen Chacon
Nostalgia, Ferry Building Shops

Mr. Chacon,

   We regret to inform you that you have failed your post-test after the Kenjo-Hayflick Procedure. You have until 6:00 p.m. today to put your affairs in order. At that time you will officially become an illegal, required by law to report in here at the department for processing.

Regretfully,
T. S. Yoshihira,
Senior Medtec, K-H Procedure Testing
SF Shield Health Department

"Oh my God!" Chacon blurted aloud, shocked. He'd completely forgotten about the test, taken almost two months ago, naturally assuming he'd passed like almost everyone else. The impact of the message slammed him like a kick to the groin: the first Treatment hadn't worked! "No way," he murmured, struggling with the reality of the message.

It must be true.

He would age past thirty-five, grow wrinkled and old…be *disgusting*, like the illegals on the Shield infomercials on holovision, or the tobacco dealer he'd just seen apprehended. Everyone under the Shield took their first Treatment at thirty-five, and he had expected positive results, like all of his friends. He'd dismissed the test from mind shortly after completion. Feeling still dazed after a minute or so of staring dumbly at the screen, Chacon took a deep breath, sighed, and read the message again carefully, lingering on the final word, *processing.*

What exactly did that mean?

The official line by the health department was that those who failed the Treatment—a very small number, supposedly less than one half of a percent—were put on ice, the aging process suspended until new research developments could identify and correct the defective sequence of DNA or whatever suppressed the Kenjo-Hayflick Procedure's longevity effect. But Chacon didn't know if he believed that or not. How many really failed? And suppose it was only a half of a percent, did the Company have the capacity to store fifty thousand corpsicles? Also, it was commonly rumored that those who failed had their habitation contracts immediately revoked, were rendered a color judgment, and were actually banned from San Fran Shield to wander the polluted wasteland of Cal Wild like the untreated and aging color-coded criminals. All he knew for sure was that you never saw anyone who looked over forty or so on the street under the Shield, and from the holovision news he knew that bounty hunters contracted by the Company—yakuza recruited from Japantown—and their bio-electronic monsters relentlessly tracked down *all* illegals who did not turn themselves in to the health department. For an aging person, there was no place to hide under the Shield.

He shivered and swore again under his breath. *"Jesus."* Albert E remained respectfully quiet. Then, Chacon glanced at the time: a little after ten. Only eight hours remained before he was required to turn himself in.

There were a dozen things to do here at the shop, instructions to leave for Albert E, including the hiring of a human replacement for himself. Chacon's eccentric customers wouldn't deal with a computer voice, regardless how efficient and honest. No, Albert E would need someone human as a front man. Then there were all his financial affairs, and there were at least a dozen other things needing his attention before six that night.

But Chacon couldn't focus on details. He was too overwhelmed with the desire for human contact; he wanted to go see someone, tell them the startling bad news—his ex-wife, Marilyn, whom he saw often still, or his folks recently back from Japan, whom he'd seen for the first time last week after two years, or, of course, his brother, Peter, whom he rarely visited, but saw and spoke to occasionally on the Viz.

Abruptly, Chacon got to his feet, saying to the computer as he left the shop, "I'll be back soon, Albert E."

"Take care, Galen."

Chacon programmed the 'shaw for Precita in the Mission of the surface retro level, where he'd been raised; a few minutes later he dismounted the self-guided electric vehicle near the site of old Bernal Park.

Of course the open space, which had been over two blocks long in the original city, was gone, replaced by wall-to-wall conapts, like all the old neighborhood parks, even the great Golden Gate. In place of Bernal Park, one small building site had been reserved and a bio-electronic NuPark—a kind of virtual reality illusion—constructed.

Bernal NuPark—San Fran Shield

Chacon entered the NuPark, planning on taking a direct path across the lot and exiting in a minute or so in front of his folk's building. But he found himself in an unmaintained wild forest of dense growth; once inside, it seemed much larger, all sound and sight of the surrounding Shield Level screened away. A strong smell as-sailed his nostrils, rich organic decay, like the smell of...*death*. After a few moments stumbling along a barely distinct path, Chacon found the heat and overwhelming smell stifling. Despite the muggy discomfort, he shivered, feeling an increasing sense of claustropho-bia. There was something else disturbing about the place, an instinc-tive feeling, like he was being stalked or watched by someone or something. His pulse raced as he envisioned being stalked by a wild animal, a tiger even. A tiger! The old poem by Blake flashed into his head.

Jesus.

He gasped, sucking in a deep breath of humid air, almost chok-ing on the pervasive sickly-sweet smell.

Nervously, he sped up to a jog, trying to hurry along the narrow path and escape the nightmare but slowed by roots, vines, and other debris littering the once-graveled trail. Yet, despite having to focus his attention on the obstacles in his path, Chacon was unable to shake the creepy sensation of being watched, followed. Twice he stopped abruptly and glanced about, but he saw no tigers, nothing else stalking him. Obviously no one used this dark, smelly, muggy, foreboding place. He wondered about the other NuParks. Were they similar? Places to be avoided by the residents of San Fran Shield? He didn't know the answers. But his suspicion made him shudder.

No matter that he seemed to have easily covered a mile, the damned virtual park seemed to go on and on forever. How could it be so endless—an old lot, 80 by 120 feet deep at most? So real. So sinister.

He stumbled along for what seemed like another ten minutes, his apprehension beginning to turn to genuine panic—

Retro Level-San Fran Shield

Then, suddenly, Chacon emerged into light, noise, fresh cool air, all in sharp contrast to the muggy, overgrown, depressing NuPark. He just stood there, gasping and letting his racing pulse return to normal, feeling an overwhelming sense of relief.

Across Precita was a row of grey conapts, including his folks' new place. He wiped his sweaty brow, then turned and stared back into the dark growth, remembering how different the old real Bernal Park and the neighborhood had been back during his childhood:

A long, narrow strip of open green space, lined with trees and picnic tables, surrounded by quaint little Victorians, each divided into apartments, many painted in gay colors, influenced by the mostly Latino residents. His folks, both struggling artists, had lived there by necessity; cheapest rent in the city. And the park, like others around the city, had been a refuge by day for older people, also living in the nearby Victorians, who sat in groups around the tables in good weather, playing card games, checkers, chess, dominos, reading the Chronicle, or just visiting....

One summer, when Chacon was thirteen or fourteen, an older Black man sitting by himself at one of the picnic tables had looked up from his chess board and asked, "Want to play, boy?"

"I don't know how," he had admitted shyly.

The older man had nodded and grinned, a full gold tooth glittering in his mouth. "Well, I certainly do feel like a game. Guess y'all just have to learn. Sit down."

He spent every afternoon that summer and weekends in the fall over in the park with Jess—that was the older man's name—who taught him the game. During those games, he'd learned a lot from discussions with Jess about life in general—especially about his companion's abhorrence for Company policies. Jess believed the Treatment was a crime against nature. "Everything has a time, boy, a time to live and a time to die, like it says in the Book...." It had been a wonderful ten or twelve weeks for Chacon. But one overcast weekend in early winter, Jess hadn't shown up with the chess set. A few days later, Chacon learned his friend had run into trouble with the Company, actually refusing the Treatment, becoming an illegal by choice. A rare demonstration of principle. Over the years, Chacon had often wondered what had happened to his friend.

As he stared absently back into the NuPark, remembering those discussions with Jess, Chacon wondered if now was indeed a better time. Every available building spot under the Shield, at least down on the retro level, was occupied. Company prohibitions governing behavior proliferated, Tattletales often blinking on over the crowds, blaring out the latest pronouncement. And, indeed, crowds everywhere now, but absolutely *no* children, and everyone appeared the same age, looking exactly alike...except for the illegals.

Thinking back, he knew the old people in the park hadn't been disgusting, like the infomercial propaganda on holovision suggested. No indeed. They were wrinkled, moved slower, talked softer than younger adults, but they weren't disgusting. Not at all. Jess had been a friend, a good friend to Chacon, when his folks had been too busy. Maybe, after the Company developed the Treatment, they'd actually banned a valuable resource, the old people.

Chacon sighed, turned back toward the wall of conapts, and

watched a large group of people come out of the entry of his folks' building. They'd just moved in after successfully displaying their latest collection in a number of galleries in Tokyo. The people were talking and laughing, all dressed in gala modtrend—the one-piece, skin-tight garments an array of shimmering pastels, cobalts, limes, and cocoas—but the people all appearing exactly the same, androgynous and interchangeable. Involuntarily, Chacon shivered with dread.

He retreated a step back from the group, back toward the park of his past, coming to a conscious decision: Jess had been right. He needed to stand on principle, like his old friend. It's *not* a crime to grow old. And I'm *not* turning myself in to be dyed, banished, frozen or whatever. "Fuck the Company," he said, speaking aloud a rare vulgarity.

He watched the crowd move up Precita, probably headed for the RapTrans station on Cesar Chavez Boulevard, realizing it might be wiser to not visit his folks, now. He'd only be putting them at risk, if he were really going to be an illegal in a few hours. And Marilyn either. No, he couldn't visit anyone. But what was he going to do, Chacon asked himself, walking aimlessly toward downtown. He was only a meek little shopkeeper. Really insignificant. Not a revolutionary. A fugitive, an illegal—an *old* person, his wrinkling face programmed to disgust and alarm others into turning him in. How could he stay out of the grasp of the yakuza?

The reality of his decision sank in.

He remembered the pathetic illegal this morning, trying to hide behind an eco-mask, dealing tobacco to make a living. He couldn't do that. Chacon would have to secure some of his Shield credits before six tonight. But where would he go then? Where would he live? And his family and friends? Of course he would be giving them all up. He was really on his own now.

Alone.

Maybe not quite yet—he wasn't illegal for a while. He needed some help, and he decided to call Peter. If anyone could help him, it was his brother. Peter knew how to solve problems, get things done, sometimes working with or around the Company.

Chacon had laughed when he'd first heard about Peter's newest project from his parents last week. His brother was the point man for a Company-approved consortium involved in bringing the Statue of Liberty to Alcatraz. An additional attraction for the adventure tour of the Bay outside the Shield, which would feature a wild hovercraft trip exposed to the environmental hazards of Cal Wild like the ever-present UV, giving the appropriately dressed tourists a good, close look at the remnants of the Golden Gate and Bay Bridges—only towers were left of the former, and the latter ended at Yerba Buena Island now, no span into the Shield—and perhaps they might spot some of the Freemen squatters on Treasure Island, and then physically visit the Statue of Liberty atop the Alcatraz ruins. Apparently, it wasn't so nutty, because he understood Pac Rim tourists were already scrambling to sign on for the tour.

Anyhow, he called Peter on his wrist Viz.

The *Grinning Skull*, in the Haight, was packed.

After paying the admission fee, Chacon worked his way through the crowd to the bar area, but found no place to sit. It was early and he glanced around, knowing Peter probably wasn't there yet. The marquee outside had announced the *Skull* was presenting two showings of "One Day in Dallas," a holoplay of a presidential assassination in the mid-20th century. The line was already forming into the theater, everyone dressed in black or indigo modtrend, their faces white, eyes lined heavily—a kind of gothic cult, obsessed with death.

Chacon moved into a space at the end of the bar and ordered a metabolic fizz from a waitress. The air in the bistro was muggy, the contrasting scent of sweating bodies and heavy cologne making his nostrils itch.

There were at least six of these deathplay bistros located on different levels of the Shield, all apparently quite popular. Strange, he thought, studying more carefully the faces in the crowd, sensing a kind of electric tension in the air. The successfully Treated were fascinated, obsessed even, with death. What did they actually get from this morbid curiosity? He wasn't sure. It all seemed so perverse and counterintuitive. Sipping his drink, he decided this was probably a good place to meet his brother. They weren't likely to see anyone they knew.

At that moment, Chacon spotted Peter working his way down the bar. His brother was dressed in conservative modtrend, dark blue, his hair trimmed stylishly short, but no jewelry or makeup. A low profile.

"Ah, there you are," Peter said, offering his hand. "Been awhile." Peter was ten years older, but with his successful Treatment, they both appeared the same age—mid-thirties—as did most of the others in the club. A few looked slightly older, but no one really aged in appearance.

Chacon clenched his brother's hand. "I've been meaning to call, get a hold of you, but you know how it is? I've been busy at Nostalgia."

Peter nodded, glancing about. "Lot of people here tonight," he said, a slightly concerned expression on his face as he scanned the crowd, probably looking for a familiar face.

"Don't think we know anyone here," Chacon said, trying to sound calmer than he felt. Ever since leaving the NuPark earlier in the day and making his momentous decision, his anxiety had continued to increase as six o'clock drew rapidly nearer.

"Good," Peter replied, relaxing slightly, and ordered an eyedropper of rush at the bar.

"Well, what about my problem?" Chacon asked impatiently.

Peter nodded, his expression businesslike as he produced a card from his pocket. "See this guy; he can help. I'm not sure what he does...actually I don't want to know. But I hear he's helped a lot of his own people with your problem. They apparently continue to live somewhere here under the Shield in relative safety and anonymity. Although there is a rumor that some have been smuggled Outside and actively aid the Mojave Resistance Movement."

Chacon nodded. He'd heard of the MRM from holovision and Tattletales. A supposedly rag-tag bunch of renegades. But he'd thought the Company had suppressed them. Apparently not. He glanced at the wrinkled old card. It read:

Dr. Kats' Tats
interactive full body art

Interactive full body art? Some kind of tattoos? The address was in Japantown out on Geary. He turned the card over. A name was freshly scrawled in longhand with dark green ink, but he couldn't quite make it out—Samuel or Samantha *something*?

Peter explained. "A friend. The signature means this guy will listen seriously to your problem. But you may need as much as 10,000 credits for his solution. Okay?" He eyeballed his rush and shivered as it almost instantly hit his system.

"No problem," Chacon replied. "But what do you mean, he's helped a lot of his *own* people?"

Peter blinked and glanced about nervously, then leaned closer and said in a low whisper, "It's ironic that one of the developers of the longevity procedure, Kenjo, is Japanese, because most of the small percentage of failures of the Treatment are actually Japanese. It's not commonly known. Anyhow, this guy Kats is Japanese, may even be hooked up with the MRM. I know little about him…don't want to know."

"I see what you mean," Chacon replied, slipping the card into his pocket, then finishing his drink. "I better meet with him as soon as possible." He glanced at his wrist, tapping the time on his Viz. "I'm illegal in about twenty minutes."

They shook hands again. "Thanks, Peter, I appreciate your help and I'll see you…well, who knows?" Chacon shrugged.

Peter nodded and smiled encouragement.

Chacon left the *Grinning Skull* and hailed a 'shaw, cut across town, then rode up Geary into Japantown, watching the increasingly gaudy display of green, red, blue, and yellow neon holos blinking on as controlled twilight on the level changed to night, the holos advertising everything from a guy jerking on the Wire to sushi bars and pachinko parlors. On the retro level under the Shield, Japantown had expanded beyond its former western boundary at Webster and Post, with the business district following along Geary Street, clear to the numbered avenues toward the ocean side of the domed city.

The 'shaw stopped.

He spotted the address on the card, a plaza set back off Geary near Masonic Avenue. But after dismounting from the vehicle, he wandered around a kind of cul-de-sac several times, passing a cluster of small biotech labs, finding a teahouse and a massage parlor at the far end of the little circle of establishments, but no Dr. Kats. He was stumped, looking about the various businesses—

Then Chacon spotted a sign, stenciled in white on a blackened window below a holo of some kind of Japanese demon or gargoyle:

Art by Katsumoto

Maybe this is it, he thought, pushing open the door and entering a dimly lit small reception room, the scent of burning incense heavy in the air.

There was no one at the small desk, but an Asian man poked his head through an open door.

"Oh, may I help you?" he asked in a mildly accented voice, bowing slightly. The man wore conventional modtrend attire, but his black hair was shiny and long, coiled in a kind of bun at the back. He also wore a mustache and goatee. His expression was pleasant, bushy eyebrows raised inquisitively over alert dark eyes. He looked last century.

"Yes, please," Chacon said, resisting the impulse to bow back. "I'm looking for Dr. Kats."

"Oh...?" the man said, moving to meet Chacon, a guarded expression on his face.

Chacon dug the card from his pocket and handed it to the man.

The man glanced at the card, making a kind of dismissive shrug before saying, "Ah, I see," then chuckled. "It is a very old card, you see, one printed just after I came to Japantown in the Shield, many, many years ago, when I still did full body tattoos. Lots of Japanese immigrants then. But now...."

Chacon felt a slight sense of elation. This had to be Dr. Kats. He said, "Please, turn the card over."

The man did, a smile creeping over his face, softening his features as he read the name under his breath. "Ah, my old friend, Ms. Samantha Kandiyohi." Then he looked up at Chacon, the guarded expression and hedging voice gone, and nodded, all business now. "Your problem?"

Chacon briefly explained about the message from the health department, that he had been an illegal since six that evening, and his decision not to turn himself in.

"Ah, I see," the man said, apparently not surprised by Chacon's declaration. "Okay. You call me Dr. Kats. And you are?"

"Galen Chacon."

"I think I can help you, Galen," Dr. Kats said confidently. "You need to be like a chameleon, or maybe a tiger in jungle. Move around, but not be seen. Right?" He grinned, then added, "You put yourself in my hands."

Chacon nodded his cooperation. He had nothing to lose.

Dr. Kats led him into the second room, crowded with a work bench and table bearing instruments, beakers, Bunsen burners, and other lab equipment. Many tools were strewn about, along with partially assembled electronic gadgets, and in the corner stood a mysterious piece of equipment—the room was a cross between a cluttered 'shaw repair shop and a biochemistry lab, not like any tattoo parlor Chacon could imagine. Dr. Kats led him to the strange piece of equipment, really a kind of coffin-appearing box hooked up to a lap console.

"This look like the iron maiden, right?" Dr. Kats said, grinning wryly while opening the lid of the coffin, revealing an interior lid lined with thousands of tiny, needle-like glass lenses.

"These like lasers," Dr. Kats explained, "and take place of tattooing needles." He turned to Chacon, patting the piece of equipment. "Get undressed completely."

Chacon took off his clothes as Dr. Kats produced a syringe. "This dull the slight pain, make time pass fast." He gave Chacon the shot, then helped him into the coffin-like apparatus. "You will hear me clearly as I program your interactive body art on console." He indicated the lap device on the bench. "Ready?"

Chacon nodded as the drug began to take effect, drying his mouth and numbing his skin.

Dr. Kats closed the lid, and Chacon was in the dark, floating in space.

"Okay, Galen," Dr. Kats said, "you will notice a series of minute burning or tickling sensations all over. But the procedure won't last long. Okay?"

Chacon worked up some moisture and said in a slurred voice, "I'm ready."

"We begin. Now, first, a little twilight." Tiny fingers danced across Chacon's back.

"Some shadows," Dr. Kats announced, and Chacon felt more tickling across his back and chest.

"Green indigo." Prickling along his neck and face.

"Ah...lots of shade." Coolness spread down his back and across his buttocks.

"A little deep space." Colder, almost icy all over his body.

"Night."

"Ink...."

Chacon drifted, no longer listening to the voice in the dark or the probing fingers dancing across his body, Dr. Kats' expressions only an unintelligible background mumble....

The coffin was open.

He was sitting up, and Dr. Kats was explaining about his special cloak of camouflage. "You go anywhere at night, now, you invisible. But must stay in shadows and wear these programmed glasses to see better in dark." He handed Chacon a pair of very ordinary-appearing dark-framed spex.

Then, Dr. Kats hit a toggle on his lapboard, and the lights dimmed, the room turning heavily shadowed around the walls. He led Chacon to a mirror in the shadows. "Galen, say hello to the tiger."

A dark, blurred reflection, not even a human figure, really. It was incredible. He was indeed almost completely invisible.

Abruptly, the lights turned up again, and Chacon stared at his naked self in the mirror. The mystical full body art wasn't apparent anywhere on his skin.

Dr. Kats was grinning. "Good, right? Put on your clothes."

Chacon fumbled with his clothes, realizing he still hadn't shaken off the effects of the numbing drug.

A few minutes later, Dr. Kats gave Chacon more instructions. "If you get in bind with yakuza bounty hunters, remember two things."

He held up a finger. "First, to stop pheromone hound trackers, you hold up palm like this." He demonstrated the stop signal. "And say, *ma-te-o*." Dr. Kats nodded. "You say."

"Ma-te-o," Chacon repeated the apparently Japanese word, holding his palm up.

"Trackers have been surreptitiously programmed by good friend in other bio-electronics lab to obey that command; then you able to get away," Dr. Kats explained. He held up another finger. "*Two*, if you need sanctuary, go into a NuPark. You be safe there. Okay? Repeat, please."

Chacon nodded, his thoughts still sluggish from the drug. "*Ma-te-o* and NuParks."

"Good," Dr. Kat said, smiling again. "Oh, remember to keep programmed glasses on all time now, you find them especially helpful in NuPark. You see."

After paying, Chacon shook hands with Dr. Kats and left the biotech cul-de-sac.

It was night, and Chacon walked the streets of Japantown, kicking the effects of the drug, feeling elated by his tiger-like camouflaging tats. The crowds of people paid him no attention as he carefully utilized the shadows of the buildings along the streets. Hungry, he even swiped a bowl of noodles from a soba cart parked near an alley on Post without anyone noticing. He was giddy.

But as the days went by, the novelty of being invisible—able to take almost anything he needed with impunity—wore off.

Chacon was alone and terribly lonely.

A week or so after his visit to Dr. Kats, Chacon found himself not far from his folks' place and the old park. Keeping in the conapt shadows, he was indeed invisible; passersby didn't even look at him. But the effect did nothing to lift his depression.

So what? he thought, stopping across the street from the Nu-Park. I can move about the Shield now at night with impunity, but I can talk to no one. *I am truly alone.*

Alone. Jesus!

The thought chilled him, and he shivered.

At that moment, he heard a sound, and after half turning, he was struck in the chest and knocked off his feet.

Lying on his back, Chacon stared up into the glaring eyes of a pair of the bio-electronic hounds, hovering over him. They'd obviously locked onto his pheromone scent and stalked him. Even with his tattooed camouflage, he was caught. The hounds circled him and growled as they waited for their yakuza handlers, the bounty hunters. They would turn him in to the Company as an illegal. And then what? The question made him feel sick to his stomach.

With a growing sense of panic, Chacon considered jumping up and trying to escape, taking his chances at being torn apart by the silver monsters before the yakuza hit him with a come-along stun. But then, in his mind's eye, he saw Dr. Kats holding up one finger. What the devil was the special word?

Ma, ma…M something.

Think, think, he repeated silently, staring up into the red, glowing eyes, the tinny growls raising the hair along the back of his neck, making his pulse race—

He had it! He first held up his palm and shouted, "Ma-te-o!" as he cautiously eased to his feet.

As Dr. Kats had suggested, both creatures locked up immediately, their eyes dulling to ordinary glittering glass, and Chacon slowly backed away.

Now what? he thought, checking back up the dark street.

He was sure the yakuza would be following along shortly. They'd fix the dogs—reactivate them. He had to find somewhere to hide, and quickly. Just the shadows along the street wouldn't suffice. Not with those hounds' sensing devices....

Again, in his mind, he saw Dr. Kats holding up the second finger.

Bernal NuPark—San Fran Shield

Chacon left the two immobile hounds, crossed the street, and stepped into the sanctuary of the NuPark, expecting the humid jungle to close in around him like before—

He froze.

At first he thought he'd somehow traveled back in time to the old Bernal Park, back when he was a teenager on his own in the Shield.

The NuPark was light and spacious. People sat at benches and tables; some strolled around. He shook his head, knowing it must be a hallucination. But they were there...and they were all illegal, some grey-headed, some men even bald with white beards. And they were *all* wearing spex like his. Most of those close by had turned to look at him as a tall figure approached him from the side.

"Hello," she said in a gentle voice. "You must be Galen. We have been expecting you."

Chacon just stared at the speaker, a tall, middle-aged Japanese woman, slight breasts and hips contouring her athletic figure. She wore the programmed glasses, too.

"Hello," he finally managed in a hoarse whisper. "Yes, this is my first time looking at the park wearing spex." Then he remembered the pursuing yakuza and gestured back the way he'd come. "But they're after me. The bounty hunters."

She grinned, taking his arm and walking him by the nearest table of people, who were playing the old-time game of bridge with greasy, worn, homemade cards cut from poster board.

"It's all right. You are safe now," she explained. "If they follow you in, they will only see the overgrown forest—hot, smelly, scary, uncomfortable. They won't be able to leave fast enough." She patted his arm, like a parent comforting a frightened child. "My name is Keiko. We are all illegals, but friends, here." She paused, reaching another table, where two people were playing Go on a beat-up wooden board using grey and white pieces of gravel from the park path. "Just like you, all friends of Dr. Kats."

Keiko walked him around, introducing him to many others, the names a blur. She pointed out the little cabins back in the forest, explaining that he could live in one. Or, in a few days after he caught his breath and got his bearings, he might like to think about becoming part of the MRM, perhaps even eventually joining the Family in the Mojave Desert Outside down south.

Finally they stopped, and Keiko allowed him a few minutes for it all to sink in.

Not nearly so stunned by the revelation now, Chacon realized that he was indeed safe...and even more importantly, he was not alone. He was just like all these other people. None of them really illegal or in danger of being picked up just because they were aging. And apparently part of a greater resistance to the Company. He would have to learn more about this MRM, which was apparently alive and well in Cal Wild.

At that moment he spotted two old Black men playing a game under a nearby oak tree.

The oldest one waved, as if he knew Chacon.

My God, it couldn't be, he thought, shaking his head.

Keiko released his arm.

Chacon moved closer to the table.

The man with snow-white hair grinned broadly, exposing his golden front tooth, and nodded at Chacon, as if aware of his thoughts; in a soft voice from the past, he said, "Hello, boy, it's good to see you again. You're all grown up now."

Of course it was Jess.

Looking twenty years older…as he should.

Chacon shook the old man's hand.

"You still play?" Jess asked, pointing down at the tattered board, pieces adapted from common items, like pawns made from black and white buttons.

Chacon nodded. "It's good to see you. I often wondered about you," he said. After a minute or so more of chatting, he waved goodbye, letting the two return to their game, and he beckoned Keiko.

"The people here still play the old games like they did originally in the park when I was a boy?"

Keiko nodded. "That's right."

"But the games and cards are old, worn out?"

She smiled. "Well, we don't often leave the NuPark during the day to shop. Anyhow, there are probably no businesses under the Shield that carry cards, games, books, and such from the last century. Shield residents all have newer pastimes and hobbies now. Like FunLand and such, you know."

He said, "Oh, really?" knowing there was *one* place that carried the antiques. Yes, indeed. He glanced down at his wrist Viz. He would have to make a call to Albert E, see if the AI could round up a few items from Nostalgia and have them secretly delivered some place close to the NuPark.

Then, Chacon glanced over at his friend Jess, smiled wryly, and visualized the antique chess set in his shop with the beautifully carved stone pieces.

It would last a lifetime.

PERSONAL JESUS

Jennifer Pelland

Welcome, new citizen of the Ecclesiastical States of America! We are proud to add you and your fellow New Yorkers to our nation. With God on our side, we will soon breach the defenses of the Godless states of California and New England and once again be one nation, under God, indivisible, from sea to shining sea!

We understand that decades of living under secular rule in close proximity to homosexuals, Jews, and Papists will have made it difficult for you to live under God's laws, so we are happy to provide you with your own Personal Jesus to guide you. Simply press Him to the bare skin over your heart. He is fully waterproof, so don't worry about taking him off, ever! Failure to apply your Personal Jesus is a federal offense, and if you do not apply Him within twenty-four hours of receipt, a Higher Power officer will assist you with His application.

When you find yourself having questions about God's laws, touch your Personal Jesus and ask your question. He can guide you in matters pertaining to, but not limited to:

- Modesty codes for dress, language, and behavior
- Rules of dating, marriage, and childrearing
- Appropriate societal behaviors and norms for men and women
- Mandatory daily church attendance, including directions to the church closest to you at any given moment
- And more! Personal Jesus is always there to help.
  Like our true Lord in Heaven, your Personal Jesus is always

listening to you. If you slip in words or in deeds, Personal Jesus will gently correct you with a mild electrical shock. The shock is merely enough to startle, not enough to hurt, and is done with love. Your Personal Jesus only wants you to be a good citizen of these Ecclesiastical States, and understands that our newest members often take time to adapt to Godly living. Your Personal Jesus also understands that some people take longer to adapt than others, and if you exceed a certain number of corrections, He will alert the Higher Power that you require more rigorous instruction. Don't worry about reporting to them—Personal Jesus will lead them to you.

Your Personal Jesus also cares about those around you. He is all-seeing, but unlike the true Lord, He is not all-knowing. If you fear that your neighbors haven't fully embraced the Lord with their hearts, and that they are perhaps still harboring thoughts of secular humanism even while dutifully reporting to church every day, touch your Personal Jesus and confide your fears to Him, and He will send Higher Power officers out to help. Your confession will be completely private, and your neighbors need never know that it was you who assisted them. (For those of you who were Catholics before being liberated by the Ecclesiastical States of America, do not call this confession a "sacrament" or your Personal Jesus will correct you.)

There will be times in your life when the presence of your Personal Jesus will feel like a burden. Please rest assured that even the most devout of us suffers from moments of doubt. But please remember, your Personal Jesus wants to be there for you, even in your darkest moments. In fact, once applied, He forms a permanent bond with your skin, much like the bond the true Lord has with all of us, His children. If you attempt to remove your Personal Jesus, He will sadly and reluctantly administer a disabling shock to you, and any Personal Jesus in your vicinity will do the same, just in case you have any accomplices in your attempt.

Here are answers to some commonly asked questions about Personal Jesus:

Question: How does Personal Jesus get His power?

Answer: Just as the real Lord does—from his followers. Your Personal Jesus instantly becomes a part of you, and He draws energy from your body much the same way your pinkie does. However, unlike your pinkie, He never grows weary, no matter how much He works. If you receive repeated corrections, He may be forced to exhaust you with His need for sustenance, at which point He will summon Higher Power officers to ensure that you receive adequate rest and nutrition to recover.

Question: I know that cleanliness is next to Godliness, and I also know that masturbation is against the law, so how does Personal Jesus tell the difference between innocent grooming in the shower and masturbation?

Answer: Your Personal Jesus is close to your heart for good reason—so He can see into it at all times. If your shower activities produce an increase in your heart rate, He will know what you are doing and correct you.

Question: How can Personal Jesus really know what I'm doing? He can't have a camera in Him, can He? He's almost always under my clothes—the decency laws won't let me show my breastbone in public.

Answer: Personal Jesus keeps a watchful eye on you in two ways. Firstly, He's in constant communication with the Personal Jesuses all around you, so He knows who you're with at all times. Secondly, your Personal Jesus is also a GPS device, so He knows where you are at all times. This powerful combination allows the network of Personal Jesuses to deduce when a person is straying from the path of righteousness and determine whether the situation requires a simple correction or a correction followed by a call to a Higher Power officer.

Question: Personal Jesus keeps people from hurting or killing other people, so how will I be able to fight once I'm conscripted into the war with New England and California?

Answer: Your Personal Jesus only stops you from harming people with Personal Jesuses of their own. In our Crusade to reunite the United States, you will be fighting the unsaved. Your Personal Jesus cannot see them, as they have not yet come to Him. So don't worry about being corrected accidentally while doing the Lord's work!

Question: Isn't Personal Jesus just a Pavlovian training device? I thought Christians were opposed to science.

Answer: This question contains two common misconceptions. Pavlovian conditioning involves a neutral stimulus. Personal Jesus is actually operant conditioning, in that it involves punishment. Remember, if you spare the rod, you spoil the child! And we are all children in the eyes of God. The second misconception is that Christianity and science are in opposition. This could not be farther from the truth. We, like all true Christians, embrace the scientific curiosity that God gave us, and are eager to use that curiosity in service to Him. Your Personal Jesus is the perfect example of that.

Again, we welcome you to the Ecclesiastical States of America, and hope your Personal Jesus will aid in your transition from secular rule to Godly rule. He will protect you from your weaknesses, stop you from transgression, and put you solidly on the road to salvation, whether you want Him to or not. Why? Because He loves you and only wants the best for you.

And so do we.

The Monstery of the Seven Hands

Natania Barron

Brother Bell steadied himself over the steel sink, bracing for another wave of nausea. His stomach convulsed and he gagged. In spite of the effort, nothing but spittle and a streak of bile fell into the sink. Cold sweat trickled down his back, and when he glanced back into the mirror again he noted the broken blood vessels in his left eye.

No. He was not acclimating well this time.

The drugs usually worked better; the transition had never been so difficult before. The host had been screened and approved by all the highest levels of the monastery. But a week of this sleepless, vomiting hell? He'd had enough. He would have to schedule a discussion with the Master Hand before the day was out.

If he lasted that long.

Splashing cold water on his face, Brother Bell smoothed his cheeks with the palms of his hands, turning his head to the side to get a better view of his new appearance in the mirror. He was still getting used to this body, so young and fresh. He had forgotten the feeling of limber muscles and joints, had become accustomed to the pain and discomfort of his last host. Part of him missed it.

While he knew he should be grateful to the Masters of the Hand, he could not help but find the flaws in the body. He knew it was growing more and more difficult to find unspoiled hosts, but this freckled, red-haired creature? It was a mockery compared to his first—that glorious, pale, long-limbed angel. The face in the mirror was still a stranger, even if the eyes had remained the same. Green. They were always green.

At least there was one mercy the gods had given him: for the first time in a week, he had not awakened to the host's voice screaming at the back of his mind. Vomiting was one thing, but that horror was intolerable. Perhaps the transition was not going so badly, after all.

"Brother Bell," the voice on the intercom said. It was the lisping voice of Sister Mint.

"I live to serve," Brother Bell said, the host's voice awkward in his ears. He had not had much occasion to speak over the past week and the voice sounded hollow, distant, like he had silt in his ears.

Brother Bell turned toward the intercom, a dark circle on the smooth grey walls. The sink, the intercom, the writing tablet desk and the bed—these were the only points of interest in his drab cell, meant only to help his mind ease into the host process. He missed his old room.

It had been nearly a century since the last transition, and much had changed in the Monastery of the Seven Hands, not the least of which had been its removal to below Abbassus City. Before, he'd at least had a decent view. Of the library, if he recalled.

There was a pause at the intercom and Brother Bell imagined Sister Mint tucking in her chin, the hairs at her throat bristling. "Of course you do," she replied at last. "It's been over a week and you have been absent at every prayer. We were expecting a day or two, of course—"

"I have been indisposed," Brother Bell replied, standing as straight as he could, arching his back and filling his fleshy lungs. He could picture himself on Sister Mint's screen, pale and stiff in his silver robes. Every one of the brothers and sisters were on surveillance at one time or another. Especially the ones in new hosts. He recalled the destruction of Brother Calis, flailing in his cell, clawing at his own eyes and eventually bleeding to death on the spongy grey floor. Brother Bell supposed his own acclimation could be worse.

Another long pause.

"Your host was sent through an arduous screening process, Brother Bell," Sister Mint said, her words clipped with irritation. "One of the best specimens we'd seen in three decades. He was free of mutations, diseases, influences, addictions…why, Sister Greene had a reformed vapor addict as a host, and she was out of healing in three days."

"Sister Greene should be commended—"

"Yet you, one of the oldest among us, have dallied a near week. It took the gods seven days to craft the firmament—perhaps you are looking for a bit of poetic metaphor in your healing? I know you do so enjoy that," Sister Mint said.

Brother Bell did not want to provoke her. He had seen her wrath, decades ago, when one of the citizens above had broken into library. She had taken her flail to him and not stopped until there was nothing left of the man that couldn't be wiped off the walls.

He would please her, though he hated himself for it.

"I will attend prayer today," Brother Bell said, softly. "I live to serve."

"What was that?"

"I will attend prayer today," he repeated, reining in the indignant tone that bubbled beneath the surface.

Do you remember that night when we held hands in the tunnel while the bombs fell around us?

The voice. Old Name. The one he had fought for this body; the one who had died in the shell of his old previous form. But damn the memories.

The body remembered.

The words rang in his head, making him grit his teeth. He could not let such weakness be visible to Sister Mint. Brother Bell bit against the inside of his cheek as the words repeated again and again, echoes whispering, an endless cadence in his skull with flashes of images behind his eyes: the Abbassus City skyline illuminated by the glow of detonating bombs; broken buildings like jagged teeth against an orange sunset; smooth white shoulders streaked with shadows; her lips, her widow's peak; hands fumbling with the zippers while the whole house shook; screaming children; the old man playing the cigar-box guitar, unseeing eyes white with cataracts.

Not his memories; not his dreams. He didn't want them.

Brother Bell chewed on the inside of his lip until he felt a gush of blood and saliva run across his teeth. He swallowed, repressing the wince.

Old Name went silent. The pounding in his temples began, insistent and sweet with pain. *There is no life without pain,* he thought to himself, quoting the Scripture of Raas. *Sacrifice the soul, sacrifice the body. Bite the body, bite the soul.*

If Sister Mint had any idea of his inner turmoil, she said nothing. There was a distant, garbled voice on the other end of the intercom and she let out a long hiss. She had been distracted; she had not seen him. Someone had interrupted her.

"No. No prayers for you today, save those you ought make on your own," she said. "We have a new arrival. And I want you in charge."

"Monastery or asylum?" asked Brother Bell, automatically; once, he had been in charge of admissions, but it had been years since he was asked to do such minor work. He would take it, if it would keep Sister Mint at bay.

The shuffle of fabric came over the intercom, and then the grinding reverberation as the microphone adjusted. "We're not sure. That's for you to discover," Sister Mint replied. "We're sending her file to you now. May the Hands guide you, Brother Bell."

"And also you," he said as the intercom buzzed and clicked off.

He rushed to the sink and threw up blood, shivering as the slot in the wall to the side of his bed beeped and began printing out the documents profiling the new arrival. Brother Bell took his time, stuffing a wad of cloth ripped from one of his clean socks into his mouth to staunch the bleeding; he turned away from the camera lens, just in case Sister Mint was still watching. But he doubted it. She sounded far too occupied. She had always been a lazy pig.

Brother Bell grabbed the dossier, the thin sheets of plastic paper
sticking to his fingers. He pressed his thumb into the small green
box at the bottom of the blank page and the ink swirled into form.
He was surprised to see a strikingly beautiful woman staring back
at him when the picture settled. Her headshot was very clear, her
head turned to three-quarters, a dime-shaped mutation under her
ear. Other than that, she was flawless. Her eyes were soft blue, her
hair so blond it was nearly white—perhaps another mutation, but
lovely nonetheless. She looked like his angel.

He scanned over the rest of her file. Her credentials were im-
pressive: she leaned Orange politically and had advanced degrees in
philosophy and nature—which he hadn't thought was still taught
Above. Her name was Malina Cresp Hamden; she was unmarried
and thirty-eight years old.

Old Name remained silent, and as Brother Bell navigated the narrow hallways down to the receiving room, he continued to stare
down at Malina Hamden's face, contemplating the delicate angles of
her jaw, the curve of her earlobe. He'd once had a face like that.

Past the round doors in the healing wing, through the infirmary,
down the lift to the mess hall, and through to the now-empty prayer
vault he moved. One more door and he'd be through; he would see
her, this angel.

I whispered promises to you I knew I couldn't keep. Old Name's
voice started up again, just as Brother Bell was about to open the
last door. He only had to hold up the cuff of his habit, information
woven into its very fibers, to gain access to the receiving room. His
mouth went dry and he staggered to the side, propping himself up
against the soft black walls.

*If I do this I'm gone forever you know that but I'll be free of you free of
love that's all I want.*

Brother Bell gasped as his head spun again, pressure com-
pounding the pain, and he dropped the dossier to the ground. More
visions:

The great library reduced to a pile of rubble, rats scurrying through torn books; up on the dais, the great Liberator draped in orange robes, throwing paper flowers to the crowd below; sweaty palms shoved into dirty pockets; vapor, passing from hand to hand in small glass globes; her back arched in ecstasy; the gun pressed to her stomach.

"Bite the body, bite the soul," muttered Brother Bell, feebly lifting his arm and planting his teeth into the soft rise of his forearm. He let his teeth sink through the skin, drawing blood until the voice ceased and Old Name—what was left of him—sank back into the shadows of Brother Bell's mind. He tired of the images, facing the realities of the world above. He had worked his long life to keep it from him, and now he could not escape it.

Brother Bell pulled off one of his socks and wrapped it around the bleeding bite on his arm, pulling it taut, "Need I remind you," he said, "that this was your decision."

He was not sure whom he addressed.

Brother Bell wiped his brow again, collected the dossier, and stuffed his foot back into his boot, his toes slipping against the sweaty bottom.

It was time to meet the angel.

The receiving room had been set up to provide comfort and information even in the absence of one of the brothers or sisters. So it was that, as Brother Bell entered the room, he found Ms. Hamden sitting comfortably in a plush red chair, watching the initiation reel play out on the wall. He caught only the cascade of her hair, curling and slightly brittle at the ends. She was wearing a red cardigan, patched a few times, and she turned to see him immediately.

Beautiful, still, but worn. Far more worn that he had hoped. Ms. Hamden's face was practically sunken, the full lips in the headshot dwindled down to lines of worry in her mouth. Her chest was sunken, and her legs were sinewy and pale, sticking out from the bottom of her short black skirt.

But still…the lines. The lines of her face spoke of an angel. He wanted her. He wanted the body. While it might be risky to make a transition now, so soon after the last, did it matter?

Old Name flickered and Brother Bell pushed on the wound at his arm, sending the voice away—for a moment, at least.

Ms. Hamden was looking at him, curious. The hair at her brow was darkened and stuck to her forehead with sweat.

"Ms. Hamden," Brother Bell said, his voice raspier than he would have liked. He sounded uncertain, which had not been his aim.

"Brother—"

"Bell," he said, linking his hands together in the greeting of the Monastery of the Seven Hands—the three central fingers crossed, the thumbs and little fingers touching. He had to be composed; she could not suspect him. "Brother Bell."

She shifted her gaze to the film, then back to him again. As she did so, Brother Bell caught something off in her movements. When she slipped her fingers under her knee to adjust her leg, that was when he realized the issue: she was paralyzed.

There had been nothing in her file about that. He felt the momentary hope of possessing her body fall away as he tried to remain passive, welcoming. He hungered for her beauty, but he did not want a life in a broken body. That was worse than no life. Brother Bell had languished long enough in his last decrepit body, and he had no desire to revisit it. Even for the face of an angel.

"Shall I call a wheelchair for you?" he asked as tactfully as he could. Every word spoken brought his tone closer to the one he recalled, and he felt a flush of excitement in knowing he was that much closer to overcoming the current host's resilient nature. He was looking forward to resuming his regular duties in the scriptorium.

Ms. Hamden shook her head. "Not yet. It's not necessary. I've just been resting here."

"You...took the lift?" Brother Bell asked. "Down, I mean—how did you—?"

She extended her arms, rotating them at the wrists. "Good upper arm strength," she said.

"You crawled."

"I did," she said. "I was engrossed in your...." she flicked her fingers toward the wall where the instructional film had been playing. It had automatically stopped when they'd begun speaking. "Not exactly art, but it has been so long since I've seen one of those films—any film, really. I was quite invested in it, I suppose."

"You come here looking for refuge, then? From the broken world above?" asked Brother Bell. He had once had a much more descriptive opening question for new arrivals, but he had since forgotten it. This would have to suffice.

She gave him a coy look; she was not a believer, he didn't think. Not with those eyes. A seeker, perhaps, then. "Refuge? I suppose. I seek something."

"What is that, may I ask?" Brother Bell allowed himself a rare smile. Sometimes smiles unsettled people, but he would risk it in this case if it meant establishing more of a connection.

"I wouldn't have said 'something' if I knew what it was, now would I?"

It was just like Sister Mint to drag him out of his cell in such a state and demand that he work with someone so challenging. She was beautiful, she was mysterious, but Brother Bell had seen enough women like her in his long life and had no particular desire to play games. He had far more important things to be doing about the monastery than indulging this woman. And if her body was broken, she was no good to him.

Ms. Hamden was smiling at him as if she had everything figured out, as if the broken world Above had done nothing to darken her spirit, to tax her soul, to take the very fight out of her. But Brother Bell knew what it was like up there. Not from personal experience, of course, but from his years of working with her sort of people. He had known generations of them. Mostly eager, mostly claiming they were seeking—mostly broken and willing already.

He licked his lips, the peeling skin rough against his swollen tongue. "It only seems to me that you have traveled a great distance to get here, quite literally by your own hands—it would only make sense that you had a particular reason for coming so far, something specific."

The room had a satiny quiet to it, and in the silence Ms. Hamden closed her eyes and folded her hands before her.

"I lost a friend," she said softly. Her teeth were not straight but very white. "She died by her own hand. The situation unsettled me enough that I decided I'd had enough of scraping by up there. That I wanted a chance at something greater. Something more." Ms. Hamden opened her eyes slowly, like a great all-seeing goddess. Her lashes were long, but light at the roots. "I was told once that the those who live here in the Monastery of the Seven Hands need not worry about the sting of death, of pain, of useless bodies dying around us."

Brother Bell nodded measuredly. "For some; for a few. For those willing. For those worthy of knowing our secrets."

"You mean the story of the gods Raas and Eael," she said, measuring him for a reaction. He could tell that she expected him to react in surprise, but she was far from the first to have guessed the secrets of the monastery. One only needed to read a few pages of the Scriptures for that.

"Certain truths have been made clear to us," Brother Bell admitted, willing his unfamiliar face to remain passive, unaffected. Nausea crept its way back, twisting in his empty stomach. He cleared his throat. "But that is for another time, another conversation. For now, we must decide where you are headed. The calm of the asylum or the discipline of the—"

"I think I'd like the wheelchair first, if you don't mind," Ms. Hamden said gently, looking away from Brother Bell entirely. He was glad of it; he did not enjoy her lingering stare.

He went to the intercom and rang the infirmary. He waited for the code to pulse, then entered the request in kind. Three long beeps indicated the message had been received and was being processed. A moment later, a high trill: the chair was on its way.

Glancing over at Ms. Hamden again, Brother Bell caught the long lines of her legs, the dark emptiness below the skirt on her lap, and felt the forgotten flicker of lust in his loins. There were many parts of his new body he was not yet accustomed to, but this was welcome. Though he would not stare long, it was enough to remind him of the possibilities this new body held. He supposed he had been a bit harsh in thinking so ill of the gift before. He would have to write Sister Mint a personal message of thanks.

A slot in the wall opened up and a metal chair rattled out. It had two green lights on the arms, pulsing in time like a heartbeat. Thinking the sooner he was done with the woman the better, he donned another smile and brought the chair near to her, swinging it around so it would be easier for her to make the transition.

She looked at him, blue eyes flashing, and he backed away. Clearly, she was of a mind to do this herself. Engaging the brake, she lifted herself from her seat, then hissed out a long breath and pulled herself over to the wheelchair. It swayed a little with her weight, but it did not roll away as Brother Bell had worried. She pulled her legs up at the knees, arranging her feet on the flat metal platforms below. She had no shoes.

"Let me just—" began Brother Bell, coming around to hook up the chair to her hand, where it would monitor her heart rate and vital signs; this was particularly important if she was to be taken to the asylum, which Brother Bell was considering most seriously. At least there she'd linger only a few years before being taken by one of the brothers or sisters—if anyone wanted that broken body of hers, that was. Still, good bodies—in any form—were hard to come by. Perhaps he would see her face again. He nearly laughed to think of Sister Mint behind Ms. Hamden's eyes.

But Brother Bell did not finish his sentence, as he felt Ms. Hamden's long fingers wrap around his forearm with unyielding strength.

"Tell me why you are allowed such secrets while we fester above—tell me why you collect us, the best among us, to live in this underground prison," she whispered harshly. She pulled him down toward her face, and Brother Bell could not refuse; her words were like poison darts, paralyzing him. He could feel the points of her nails pressing into his flesh.

Brother Bell was aware she was no longer simply playing games, but the part of him that was sensible was already fading away, drowning in the voice of Old Name. *Every morning after you left I wished I would wake up dead and that somewhere in between sleeping and waking a terror would come out of the night and take it all away from me every last memory every last thought that had you in it....*

"Did you think we'd never learn? Did you think such knowledge would remain within your dank walls forever?" she asked.

"The gods...have gifted us with...the knowledge," he said. "Only those at the Monastery of the Seven Hands know how to—"

And then Ms. Hamden was whispering in his ear. "When Raas courted Eael as his own, he thirsted for her like the sea to the shore. But she would not have him. So he came to her when the moon was new, and slipped into her bed, and took from her the only thing she had kept for herself. Her body was broken, mangled, when he was finished with her. He shook the very center of the earth, but yet she lived. One of her hands was so broken she had to cut it off to save herself. The one-handed goddess. She slunk to her cave, her limbs still twisted and covered in sores—a sick creature, formless and unloved," Ms. Hamden said. "She waited...and she learned."

There was nothing left for me nothing left of me I did it because I loved you too much because I couldn't live without your face because I wanted you to be proud of me for something.

The tumbling spire; the screams of the damned; faces pitted with mutations and sores; mother's voice in the other room; the feeling of concrete under his fingernails as he scraped like a rat to get out; the sound of footsteps above; the face of an angel.

"She sent word to Raas, through the god Baya, and he came to her, flushed with his victory still, after so many eons. Eael hid in the darkest corner of the cave and waited for him to come."

"And when he came to her at last, she wove a spell, a glamour. Eael brought Raas' face to hers, breathing softly, and grasped him firmly. And at last, when they were close enough, she opened her gaping maw, her teeth like jagged mountains."

Bite the body, bite the soul, thought Brother Bell distantly, like a half-remembered melody.

I could never take back those words you were my love always love always angel love.

"Sacrifice the body, sacrifice the soul. When Eael opened her eyes again, she was standing in Raas's body, strong and resplendent, while he languished in her broken form. She trapped him in that prison of ruined flesh."

Brother Bell's eyes dimmed, old eyes that had seen so much.

Old Name was laughing. Leaving.

Never thought it'd end never thought….

"Bite the body, bite the soul," said Ms. Hamden, blood trailing from beneath her nails down Brother Bell's forearm, falling to the soft floor. She tilted her head forward, her tongue reaching out, lapping the blood like an eager cat.

Then she smiled and bit down, through the flesh, laughing and moaning.

I promised you one last time…one last time….

"Brother Bell, is everything alright? There was a power surge and we lost contact for a moment—"

The intercom was buzzing and a watery voice continued.

"Brother Bell?"

The word slowly came back to him. He had blacked out for a moment. He never should have left the quiet of the healing cell. He should have refused Sister Mint.

But now he was sitting, he was—

"I am quite fine," said the voice that had once been his. But he hadn't spoken.

Her body. The broken angel.

She had trapped him in it.

Ms. Hamden looked out at Brother Bell from the body of Old Name, a flicker of a smile on her lips. Brother Bell tried to move the body she had imprisoned him in, but it was unresponsive. He could blink, but that was all. Horror washed over him, but a silent horror. Even his mind felt broken.

He tried to scream, but there was nothing but a low whistle of wind in his throat.

"But I'm afraid the new arrival suffered something of a stroke. She's gone quite catatonic."

My angel. My broken angel, thought Brother Bell.

From behind the eyes of Old Name, Ms. Hamden grinned, leaning down to look her old body in the eyes. The hands that had been his, so nimble and long, caressed the face he now wore. Lingering, almost longingly. The eyes were brown, the sclera flecked with a blossom of brilliant red.

"We'll put her with the rest of the shells," said the voice on the intercom. A pause, an electric sizzle. "She won't last long, likely."

"A shame. She had such potential."

My broken angel. My broken angel body....

"Bite the body, bite the soul."

BEAUTIFUL GIRL

Angeline Hawkes

I was a beautiful girl. Before the war. Before the bombs fell and peeled back the flesh of youth like so much curling, silver-aged paint on the clapboard side of an old farmhouse. Back then, my first husband told me, "Girl, you could walk into any bar in this country and pick up any man you want." I didn't put much truck in those words until the day I walked into a store and never went home again. Wasn't no bar, either. I had way too much class to sink that low. I was never a whore to sell my wares to any man who flashed money and a cheap smile. No one would think you'd find the love of your life in a bookstore; no one but me, I guess.

But that was a long time ago.

Oh, women still say I'm beautiful, but they say it in a non-threatened kind of way that says, "You're too old to steal my husband." Because that's how women *are*. Even back when men were a dime a dozen women were threatened by a beautiful woman. Oh, don't get me wrong; women will ogle a gorgeous woman just like a man will, but not in a stirring of the loins kind of a way. We recognize beauty amongst our own kind. Recognize it and instantly feel defensive. A beautiful woman will feel the same way in the presence of another lovely woman, just as a homely woman will. Triggers a primal defense mode that motivates you to protect what's yours: mainly, the man.

Things are different now, different in the way that there are no lipsticks or perfumes or flower-strewn fabrics with bits of frilly lace and whatnot to dress yourself in. Different because a cruel joke was played on nature. Seems the power men created to maintain their power came and destroyed the very thing that created it in the first place. Women kept having babies, though nothing like the numbers born in the past centuries, and in some races not at all; but the babies just kept on coming up girls. Girls, girls, girls. Until men became a product to barcode and barter. Reduced to pets and breeders, much the same way early civilization did women. Funny how things happen sometimes. Comin' full circle like that.

"Cass?" Reni asks me.

"Yeah?"

"Tell me some more stories 'bout the cowboys again."

Reni loves to hear about the cowboys. Back in the day when men were really men. When men wiped sandy hair from their eyes and sweat on the backs of their sleeves—pushed broken straw hats out of their sunburnt faces so as to see the cattle strollin' by. Back when men were strong and slid under cars, tinkered and souped'em up until they'd go really fast.

Reni came to me as a little one. I'd say he wasn't much more than nine, maybe younger. He didn't know how old he was. I found him wandering on the beach, hair grown past his waist. Thought he was a girl at first, till I came closer and caught sight of the unmistakable gangly gait of a skinny little boy. He spoke mostly Mexlish. Lucky for me, I knew a spattering of Spanish from before the war, back when English was English and Spanish was Spanish. I was afraid for him and lured him with a roasted apple into my cave before anyone could see him and claim him as her own.

When I stood him in the cave pool and washed the caked dirt from his lithe body, I saw there was no barcode or brand anywhere on his flesh and was amazed at his good fortune. Reni's name was Rendel. But that's all he knew. He had a vague recollection of an older sister, maybe a mother, he wasn't sure—but that had been a long time ago, and all he really remembered were soft hands rocking him and a smile on a face he could no longer see.

He'd been alone ever since. Wandering the world like a lost cub seeking his mother. He settled in with me like it was meant to be, like it always was. Was hard for me at first. Hard for me to let my-self love this motherless child. My heart ached for my own children lost in the war, lost forever. I didn't want to risk that condition again, that feeling of love and loss. Didn't think this old heart could take it.

This old heart. That's another funny thing. Before the war, doc-tors told me the old ticker wasn't so strong. And here it is still tick-ing, long after those healthy men have been churned under the earth. I don't say buried, because when the cities fell, no one was buried, 'less they got buried by falling rubble. Mostly the bodies, the human refuse, just got left behind, abandoned.

So, here's Reni asking me about the cowboys again.

"Reni, how many times can you listen to the same old stories over and over?" I laugh.

"I never get tired of listening. 'Sides, someone has to 'member."

I sigh. "Think I'm gonna kick the bucket, do you?"

This time Reni laughs. "I bet you're the oldest person on earth."

"Could be. Probably the smartest too."

Reni laughs again. "When you were young, I bet you were toast."

I must look puzzled. "What's toast?"

"You know, hot bread."

I shake my head.

"Good looking?"

Now, I laugh. "Where I come from, *toast* means you're in big trouble." I realize that now food is such a commodity that it's be-come more precious than gold or diamonds or flashy cars or any-thing we used to think was valuable before the bombs fell.

Reni smiles his big, radiant smile. "You was toast, I know it."

"Well, some said I was." I laugh again. "But that was a *long* time ago."

"How old are you anyway?"

I have to think. I don't know that I remember exactly. Some-where along the way it became a trivial piece of information. Age was something you kept track of only when you didn't have to worry about starving or freezing or dying from heat. Something we celebrated with birthday cake and candles in neat little rows demonstrating how many years we owned. "Don't think I remember."

"I think you're a hundred!" Reni says, pretty sure of himself.

"You think so, do you?"

"Well, yeah, you were like fifty something when the bombs came, weren't you?"

The kid's pretty smart. I've done a good job teaching him everything I know. "Yeah, something like that."

"Well, the way I figure, it's been at least fifty years since the bombs came. So I numbered up that you're a hundred."

"You could be right."

"How you think you got so old?"

I laugh. "Kept my ass in this cave, I guess."

"It's a good cave."

"Yeah, it *is* a good cave." I look around. The sun's going down over the jagged horizon. I can remember when the horizon looked straight and steady. The bombs came and blew half the planet away, leaving behind a huge crater filled with lava and later with cold stone. Nothing grew there. No one went there. I think it used to be Africa and some of the places around there. Can't remember exactly anymore.

"We need to get inside." I say and hobble up, leaning on my stick that Reni's engraved with the faces of his nightmares and the faces of his dreams.

"Wish we could stay and look at the stars."

I shuffle toward the entrance and look back at his long form stretched on the warm ground. He's almost a man now. Bit skinny, but that's to be expected on what we call food. My heart gives me a tremendous kick, just thinking of Reni's impending manhood. The older he gets, the more I fear for him. The more I fear losing him just like I lost my own son.

Back when we threw away our boys like used newspaper. Like something we were sure we could pick up on the next corner the next morning. More wars. More machines. More casualties. More. More. More. And then....

And then. I don't like to think of *and then*. I miss my babies. Babies. That's what children always are in the hearts of their mothers. Aching arms yearn to hold my babies once more.

Reni. *Who was your mother? What happened to her?* How many times have I stared at him and wondered these questions? And how did he manage to escape the Man Collectors? How did she keep him from the barcode?

How much longer could I?

"Inside now. You know we've got no choice." I wave my arm toward our cave. Our fortress. I notice the skin that hangs loosely from my skeletal arm. Shriveled, wrinkled, like old fruit. *God, I'm old.* I laugh inside, but don't feel the laughter because I'm afraid Reni will stay out too late. That the time will come—one night—and he'll defy me and sneak out. Out there where the patrols pace the borderlands. Where they'd snare him and brand him and parcel him out to the women that run the new world.

My Reni.

He pulls himself up from the ground and goes inside. I hear him moving aside his stone to go into his hole. That's what we call it: his hole. It's really an inner cave that's reached by traversing a narrow rocky tunnel, mostly on your stomach. There's an inside stream and we keep dried foods in there, just in case the patrol ever finds my cave and me.

I can't access the hole any longer. I used to stay in there most of the time. Back when the sun was too hot because the ozone had been stripped away. Over time, I acclimated to the heat and could go out for short periods. Not like the new generation that had been born under the radiating rays of the sun and walked around with skin weathered into leather and hair the color of dried straw.

Reni had dark black hair and eyes that reminded me of chocolate. Chocolate was another story with which I'd entertained the boy. A long ago treat that my mind could still smell and my tongue could still savor if I concentrated hard enough.

Inside the cave, I settle onto the pile of dog furs that I call a bed. I hear Reni looking through the books. I used to scavenge in the city and bring back food and all the books or magazines I could find. I have a whole cave full now.

"Have you found something for us to read?" I ask him as he pokes his face out of the hole with a smile to stop the band.

"I was thinking we should go out on the mountain of metal and watch the stars."

"Reni—"

"I know, I know, someone might see us. But we could use the guns."

"No. You know we can't use the guns. Someone might hear them and come."

"What good is it to *have* the guns if we never get to *use* them?" he asks.

How like a man to ask such a question. I laugh. I've taught him well. "The guns are there in case we ever need to use them. For protection."

Reni makes a face. He's bored; I know it. The same thing day in and day out. This cave. The beach. The same books over and over again. He'll leave me some day, unless I leave him first. *That* scares me. Not me leaving. God only knows I made peace with that possibility a long time ago. Back when I cowered in the bank vault, there by coincidence, pushed in by my husband, the love of my life, with a few other women who were employees. He'd gone to find our daughter, our beautiful girl with her own daughter, who'd gone to the restroom only minutes earlier, when the world was as it had been every day before. The door had slammed before he could return. And with it, the door had slammed on my life.

I feel like I might cry.

No matter how many years go by, the pain is still as fresh. Still pierces my heart. I still long for my love. Long for my children. Faces I see perfectly. They've not aged like I've aged, forever young in my mind's eye.

But Reni. If I leave, if I die, I leave my Reni. What will become of him, my man-child? I start to sing an old Disney song. "I wanna be a man, man-cub—" A smile creeps across my face.

"Whatcha singin'?" he asks me.

"King Louie's song."

He laughs. But then he's serious again. "Cass?"

"Yeah?"

"Tell me 'bout the cowboys again?"

I sigh. "How 'bout I tell you about Tarzan?"

He shakes his head no. "And not about Robinson Crusoe, neither."

"Why not?"

"I don't wanna hear no more stories 'bout men who are all alone."

I sigh, a long, tired, *I've-been-alive-for-longer-than's-natural* kind of sigh. "You figured me out, huh?"

Reni laughs. "I appreciate what you're trying to do. But it's depressing."

Now I laugh. "I know. I'm sorry."

"Do you think *all* the women have white eyes?"

"What makes you think of that?" I feel a little scared that he's been thinking of the world beyond our cave.

"Well, I was just thinking that maybe there's someone out there that looks like me, you know, with brown eyes."

"Maybe. Dunno. The older people of course. Like me, with blue, brown, sometimes green eyes. But the younger ones, like you, mostly just have the white eyes. Or," I shudder, "none at all."

Reni makes a face. "Like the cat?"

"Yeah, like the cat." We found a cat once, with a litter of kittens. Only one out of the bunch had eyes, or even eye sockets. The mother, too, was eyeless. Adaptations to the sheer intensity of the sun. Evolved to exist with the other senses instead.

"When's the last time you went to the Borderlands?" Reni asks.

"When you got sick that time."

"That was a long time ago."

"Was it? Doesn't seem like that long to me. I was so scared. You were so sick." I remember the anguish I felt, the fear I had to swallow to make myself go into the Borderlands. I sold a stack of my precious books to an artifacts dealer to get the medicine I needed to combat Reni's fever. I was afraid I'd been followed home to my cave. Was afraid for days.

"How come you never went to the Borderlands like everyone else? How come you stayed here in the cave? Weren't you ever lonely?"

"Always. But I have my memories."

"Of your husband and kids?"

"Yeah. And now I have you."

Reni smiles really big. "I won't ever leave you, Cass."

"I know you won't, pumpkin." My name for him, though he's never seen one. A real one anyway. We found a plastic jack-o'-lantern once, under a block of cement fallen from a building. He played Halloween for days after that. "But some day, I'll have to leave you."

"I bet you live a hundred more years!" He laughs, but I can tell he's sad, thinking about what's inevitable. Fear grips his face and he suddenly looks older than his youth. I see a glimmer of the man he'll one day become. The man he'll one day be in a world where men like him no longer exist. Free. Intelligent. Brave and full of love.

I sigh.

"Tell me 'bout the cowboys?"

"Oh, Reni—"

"*Si*, then tell me about when you were young." He crawls out of his hole and over onto my dog furs. He pulls up his long legs and rests his stubbly chin on his knobby knees like he has since he was a little one.

I smile, letting my mind wander to the other side of the bank vault door. I feel my hand engulfed in the warm, strong hand of my husband, my love. I search for a story.

"One time, a *very* long time ago, I was a beautiful girl—

Do You Want That in Blonde, Brunette, or Auburn?

Glenn Lewis Gillette

—1—

The last human on Earth heard a knock at his door.

"Who's there?" popped into Arun's mind, but he shook off the question. *No point hoping.* Odds predicted that an overlooked human stood outside.

Arun glanced at the door monitor, screen dark for many years, but he shrugged that off, too. *Best get to killing whoever it is.* Get it done so he would truly be the last human on Earth against the time ET came calling, if they ever quit dragging their asses around the solar system, so he could save humanity.

Setting aside his darning, he stood and hefted his shillelagh, never far away. Then, just in case, he grabbed up his SIG SAUER® in its holster with the last of his hand-loaded cartridges and clipped that onto his belt. He glanced through the back window of his trailer and nodded respect to the simple grave markers there. *Soon another.*

Two steps and Arun wrenched open his front door and thrust his left foot forward to give leverage to his shillelagh from where it hung at his right knee.

A robot stood there, a delicate and alien figure with an oblate spheroid for a body supported by two slender, articulated legs, all surfaces shiny with no markings. Its rounded top reached to Arun's chin and canted as if looking up at him.

"Good afternoon, sir!" a resounding baritone voice exclaimed, direct from the spheroid's equator, no speaker grill apparent. "I have come from the stars to offer you the chance of a lifetime. May I impose for just a moment?" It spoke in broadcast American dialect.

Arun cocked his head in appraisal. Not exactly what he had expected, but it would do. *Not human engineered or built,* he concluded subvocally. Something about the lines, and the gleam, and the smell, screamed extra-terrestrial in origin.

Its opening lines, though, followed classic cold-call technique. *What sales call could be colder than interstellar?*

A robot, though? he wondered. *Interstellar travelers wouldn't send robots as their Away Team. Not to the last human. Must be their enviro-suits. Cyborg at the very least.*

"Sir? May I impose?"

"Huh?" Not used to having his thoughts interrupted, Arun stammered. "Y—ye—yes!" Panic touched him. Eleven years, two months and eight days of planning, yet he was flustered. He glanced around at the long shelves that lined the walls of the Airstream Panamerica trailer: journal after journal, plotting scenarios against this moment.

What's my current plan? He longed to lunge for his latest journal, back by his chair.

"Sir?" the ET pestered.

Oh, yes, a long-con. Get them *to ask* me *for something, something I can trade for what I really* want.

Arun settled both feet at shoulder width and hefted his shillelagh to keep it ready. "All right, yes! Impose away!"

"May we build you a mate?" the ET said.

Arun had to grin. Close to what he wanted. *Only more; a lot more. How'd they know?* And he recalled his earliest days in sales training, before he gave it up for computer science. "We don't sell drills," his mentor had said. "Our customers don't want drills. They want holes."

These ETs really know their business. What else would the last human on Earth want besides a mate? He sniggered at the question, not for the first time, and answered it with, *A whole new race, that's what.* But he'd wait on saying that aloud, wait until he'd sprung the long con on this ET.

What do I say now?

Arun cleared his throat, hoping to push the next line out of his memory. "'What do you want in return?'" Arun asked himself, not so subvocally.

"You seem curious about our price. Will your final decision be sensitive to price?"

The price: what *they* want, what *they* ask for. *For a long con,* Arun scolded himself, *they ask...no, I get them to ask for what they want; no, what I trick them into thinking they want...right? Is that it? Yeah...but what was it I'm supposed to trick them into wanting?* He'd figured something out. Even though psyching out a being—not a *human* be-ing—when he didn't understand its psyche, even if it had a psy-che—*Even a* real *con man couldn't do that, could he?*

Arun remembered, then, how to psych out an unknown psyche. What he wanted it to ask for would stay secret till this ET de-manded to know, demanded to pay for it even before it knew what it was or what the price was. He just had to get this ET to infer that such a secret existed.

"Yes, I am sensitive," he admitted with histrionic reluctance. "Some prices are too high." He hoped this ET had studied human beings enough to read inflection and body language. What else could it have been doing for all these years while decelerating from near-lightspeed?

"Contributing membership in our interstellar consortium."

Arun trotted out Coy Line #1, "That—if that's all you want–that, I might be able to swing.'"

Wait, that didn't sound like much.

"And what else?" Arun peered and squinted to emphasize his skepticism.

"That's it, sir. Contribute something we've never seen before, and we'll deliver you a fully mature, ready-to-procreate mate."

Arun forgot his script and demanded, "How could I possibly surprise a whole 'interstellar consortium?' You ask too much!" *That fit, sort of.*

"You do still follow biological imperatives, do you not?"

"Uh, yes...."

"May I confide in you?" It actually leaned toward him, a shiny ball chumming up to him, accelerating beyond cold-call protocol. This close, its metallic odor bit his nostrils slightly.

"Uh, yes...."

It leaned further, but somehow those skinny legs held it upright. "Some time ago, we upgraded our personality-transport mechanisms beyond the organic."

Curious, Arun jumped into the slight pause. "Just you or your whole race?"

"We *do* enjoy certain advantages now, the only way interstellar travel is practical, even for salesmen," it rattled on. "However, we have also come to appreciate the *creativeness* bestowed by DNA-based imperatives. We're sure you have a lot to offer us."

It straightened. "Do we have a deal?"

Oh, Lord, don't close the sale yet! I should've rehearsed more. Arun scrambled for a resistance line. *It's all coming down to me, just me.* He gulped painfully. *I arranged it that way, remember?* Grief welled up in him, squeezing out unplanned questions.

"Am I really alone?"

"Yes, that is correct. We have scanned the entire planet, cataloged all life-forms above and below the aquatic boundary. We paid particular attention to artificial habitats, regardless of location and structural integrity."

"Not another person alive?"

"No, sir. Condolences on your loss. However, we offer you an option for personal recovery."

Personal considerations are not my concern here, gadget. *My race killed itself, a one-car crash, nobody's fault but our own.* That fact shamed Arun. His old-country father had taught him: if you do something stupid, don't take anybody else with you, and if you crash and nobody else is there, then you must've done something stupid.

Arun shouted at his father, this ET, and the universe, "I want a second chance!"

"What's that, sir? I'm sure our feature-rich offering can provide that benefit. If you could just help me understand—"

I've done it, I think. Close enough for apocalyptic work, anyway.

He couldn't keep this up. He'd never been good at bartering, part of why he'd left sales, to stop dealing with people, deal just with machines—dumb, human-built machines, not a nightmare like this from the stars.

So, the finale! It didn't have to make sense, he'd decided. It just had to slam the door in their faces.

Arun flailed the shillelagh. "Get out of here!" he screamed, starting to get into it. He pulled the pistol and fired point-blank.

No effect. He heard no ricochet whine, saw no spark of impact even though he couldn't have missed.

The ET quirked. A wave of pressure, not hot like a shock wave but just as abrupt, swatted Arun, flinging him backward into his trailer. His next step, anyway.

With a glance of regret at his journal and his darning, he plowed head-first through the vinyl shelf-paper covering his escape chute. He grabbed the swing-bar installed there—*that* he had rehearsed enough—and plopped onto the slide that took him down, down and fast, into the mine shaft he'd installed his trailer over.

A mine shaft that would spell mystery to ET. A mine shaft that he'd spent years working on, installing electromagnetic (and every other kind of) baffles, layer upon hodgepodge layer of every coating he could dredge from the remains of human civilization. All to keep ET from seeing where he went and what he was doing. *"Captain, long-range scans detect power sources and pimples on their asses."*

But how long should he wait before ending the squeeze period of his con?

—2—

Arun wandered, trailing his hands along the tops of cabinet after cabinet, down tunnel 873, up tunnel 874, trudging on and on, biding his time, his miner's helmet throwing a feeble yellow light. He'd slept a little on a pallet set up in an old explosives niche. He'd eaten his fill of K-rations, which wasn't much. He'd taken a long, well-deserved shit in a chemical toilet cached just for this occasion. He'd dozed again, snacked, tried to read the first edition of "Robinson Crusoe" he'd set aside. After three hours, waiting overflowed, much too soon.

He distracted himself to stretch ET's wait, guessing how long to make the ET cool its heels, though it really didn't have any. Psyching a non-psyche?

He'd envisioned a long con revolving around a great unknown. Interstellar travel and marvelous detectors had to go hand-in-hand—or tentacle-in-tentacle. If he could hide something—it didn't have to be anything, really—from the ETs, they would want it, surely. *The mine will baffle it, right?* Any and every shield, no matter the spectrum, he'd rousted free and dragged back to this mine and added it on. He'd resisted his urge to smooth. He'd dappled it with chaos. *It* will *work, right?*

He called it a long con to give it some class, but was it any different really from the drink under a hat, that cheap bar trick? Cover a drink with a hat, then bet the chump you can drink it without touching the hat. Chump agrees, and you duck under the bar, make glugging sounds, then re-appear wiping your mouth and burping with satisfaction. When the chump grabs the hat to see for himself, *then* you drink for real, and the chump pays for it.

Long con or cheap bar trick? *Either way, there ain't no drink. No "there" there. What'll this ET do when it figures that out? Will it pay up anyway?*

Another tunnel. *Which?* "Nine-oh-four," he read, and wandered on, wasting time, burning rotation, sawing off the branch he sat on.

Overhead, Earth tracked through a quiet night. He had planned to let dawn crack on the impatient ET, hoping it was as hard on it as himself.

He was just wasting his time now, working this close encounter, no longer preparing for it, no more thinking, just the *doing*....

He'd never conned anyone, except his parents once or twice. He'd only read about con games or watched them in films. He didn't really understand how they worked, how a grifter lured people to destruction with their own flaws, so how could he expect to fool ET?

A rationalizing quote rose in his mind: "A pigeon needs a bit of larceny in his heart," con men said, because "you can't cheat an honest man." Others disagreed, but they just wanted to blame the con man, pawn all the bad off on the "gypsy." In his turn, Arun wanted to ignore those moralizers, yet this whole caper, all his preparations, the groundwork he'd laid, felt grimy, furtive, criminal, *wicked*—

Like the cabinet top under his fingertips: suddenly slimy, revolting–

Arun snatched his hand away. Slowly, gulping to tame his revolted stomach, he faced the stack of five drawers, recalling hour upon hour of cramming them full of DNA extracts. Right next to it, on either side, stood another cabinet, and after that, another, and another, tunnel after tunnel. Précis of every human, dead or alive-then-dead-by-his-hand, everyone he'd encountered since civilization had collapsed and he'd ventured forth in a maniacal attempt to ensure that the spacecraft he'd spotted entering the solar system came to him and not some fool human who would blow the only second chance their race would get.

A chill climbed up his spine, erecting every atavistic follicle he possessed. Creeped out, he lunged for the closest of the eight escape hatches he'd built for the mine after blowing its main entrance into a solid plug of rubble.

—3—

Arun clambered up through a rocky pocket, pulling himself into fresh morning air atop a scrubby hillock under a huge, deep blue-again sky that welcomed him, the lone survivor. He breathed deeply and smelled only natural odors, no more artificial anything seeping or drifting or spewing.

Global warming hadn't overwhelmed the planet after all, despite humanity spending itself into oblivion to prevent it...or maybe because they did. *"The operation was a success,"* the doctor declared, *"but the patient died."*

Picking his way down the slope, Arun wondered how long until ET found him again.

"Good morning, sir!" the ET called from Arun's trailer's stoop across the alpine meadow. Repeating that cry, it approached quickly. This time, though, another machine ran alongside, their long legs crossing the raggedy, grassy surface, glinting and crimping like galloping scissors.

Both ETs closed to American conversational distance and halted abruptly with no swaying nor any of the panting Arun expected after such a run.

Remember, Arun instructed himself, *these beings are not organic nor are they robots. They...*he scrambled to formulate a theory about his opponents, important in an extremely important contest. *They no longer have the urges or caprices of an organic brain; neither do they have the rigid structures or code-based algorithms of a programmed machine. Set protocols, probably, that sometimes cross-link.* Like yesterday when ET mixed sales protocols. *"Beyond the organic,"* he remembered. *They don't think human.* Arun shuddered. *So, how am I to beat them at this critical game?* The answer came from an old show about advertising. *"Change the conversation."* He vowed to remember that.

"Did you pass a good night, sir?" said Junior ET, the one from the previous day.

"What do you mean by that?" popped into Arun's mind, but he smothered the retort. *Still, it was a suspicious question, yes? Or am I only hoping it is, that my sting operation is working?*

"Tolerable," Arun blustered to cover his reaction. Surely his face and posture gave away his poor night, but maybe age and wear camouflaged that. "And you?"

"Busy, busy," Junior ET answered. "We are still cataloging flora and fauna for our report back to the consortium, a report that awaits your initial contribution."

Arun waved away the closing gambit with both hands. "We do not have a deal yet."

"Do you want her in blonde, brunette, or auburn?" More assertive closing.

Arun's aging body stirred with the possibilities, but he shook his head and made to turn away. The ET did not call him back. A glance showed them leaning slightly, silently toward a common center. Arun felt something wiser, shrewder, in the second ET, despite the identical chassis.

Junior ET straightened, its attention once more focused on Arun. "My boss here has authorized me to offer all three models."

The boss, as I suspected. Arun prayed its presence augured a higher level of negotiations. *Time to settle on payment.* Something big, so ET was obliged to deliver big. *I wonder what it'll be?*

Smiling slightly at the joke on himself, maybe on everybody, Arun asked, "What do you want from me?"

Junior ET answered, "Our asking price yesterday was fair."

"That was for one mate, not three."

Senior ET said, "Three for the price of one, on sale. More than fair, wouldn't you agree, sir?"

And just like that, they were down to it: humanity's final bargain, where a single man had to think himself out of a jam, a giant step after mankind had failed to make the grade.

He wanted what they offered, only millions-fold, and on different terms, so Arun turned coy, testing how hooked this pigeon was. "What makes you think I can contribute anything to your consortium? My biological imperative is pretty well moot now."

"We think you can," said Senior ET, archly, Arun thought.

Say "No" to a human and often you spike his desire, but do ETs work the same? "I don't know...." Coy again.

"How about a demonstration, then? A trial run, let's call it. I'll let you look up something *out of this world*. What do you say?" A trial close.

See what these ETs really want? "Might as well."

"Let's step into my office."

* * *

The office came to them. Nary a whistle from either ET, yet a shadow appeared on the meadow grass beyond. Arun looked up.

A flying brick angled toward them. Blurs on four corners implied airfoils working. No flying carpet. No anti-gravity. But it flew quietly and quickly, settling short of the rocks under their feet, sparing the deeper grass and the meandering stream working there. Sides flared open, revealing a chair, desk, screen, keyboard, and mouse. Junior ET ushered Arun to his place in the scenario.

Nicest chair in a decade.

The screen sat blank, its flat, dark grey emptiness almost vertiginous. Arun wondered where it would take him.

He waved at the workstation—"An ansible?"—testing how well the ETs had studied their prospects on the way into town.

Junior ET stiffened ever so slightly. "That is not our ansible." Bristling?

"Rather," took up Senior ET quickly, "our version of your Internet." It reared, invoking everything above it, including the day-cloaked stars. "Nodes all over this part of our galaxy."

Arun scoffed. "Interaction at those distances?"

"No need to go ask for data. It's here now at your fingertips." Perfect place for an expansive gesture. *How do they get along without gestures? How do they get along without arms and hands, for that matter?*

So Arun asked them.

Without warning, the cheap keys on the board—picked up from human jetsam?–riffled, while another invisible hand twitched the plain mouse beside it.

"We manage," said Junior ET. Smug?

Arun remembered how Junior ET had swatted him the day before. *No pity for these armless ETs, then.*

Ignoring the interruption, Senior ET continued, "Our interface device—we translate its designation as 'churn'—mixes your queries with the consortium's signal—"

Arun scoffed again. It felt good, especially since he knew a lot about this subject. SETI analysts knew their business. "There's no signal out there."

"Connect the dots," said Junior ET. Patronizing?

Again, Senior ET spoke over the other's words, almost covering them. "Modulation by frequency and chrono-sequencing. Information encrypted within the data thereby conveyed. All within the cosmic microwave background. I am sorry, human, but there *is* a signal out there."

"Entangled photons?" The guess made Arun feel especially geeky after all these years alone.

"Those logistics are too complicated," started Senior ET, but Junior cut him off this time.

"Holographic encoding of micro-probability virtual particles. Happy now?"

Arun waved a shaky hand. "Sure...."

"*However*," continued Senior ET, "only our churn enables you to find the signal and read it and search it—and contribute to it. Which brings us to our demonstration.

"Please," it instructed as something soft and insistent nudged both of Arun's arms. "Ask us something."

"Like what?" Arun said.

Both ETs paused; not long, but Arun had gotten used to their too-quick replies, so this almost-normal gap meant they were chatting out of his earshot, but right in front of him. Rude!

Ignoring them, Arun settled himself to the task and his rusty computer skills.

"How many worlds?" leaped into his mind, but again, he pinched off his random thought.

Instead, with a self-punishing "Duh!" Arun typed "stop global warming" and tapped the Enter key.

The screen washed with ripples for a few seconds, then flooded with a list, flowing from top to bottom, one, two, three...to twenty, pages maximum of items, then it added page numbers on the right: 2, 3, 4...on and on. Glib, smug, cruel.

First item on the list linked to something about personal vehicles that could glean CO_2 during trips.

Arun leaped again, straight at Senior ET, his hands reaching for a neck that wasn't there, his voice screaming to frighten an id that wasn't there. "Where were you? Why'd you take so long to get here?"

An invisible pillow caught Arun, stopped him cold, set him back down in the chair, like a child in a tantrum.

Gasping, hurting, Arun muttered, "Long con, here I come." Then, more loudly, "Do you guys want a deal or not?"

Listing slightly, only Senior ET answered, "Yes."

"What if I want more than one mate—or three?"

"How can you pay for more?"

Arun sucked in air, clearing his head, and blew it all out, showing off his biological-ness. The con man's bluff still seemed his only choice. "Whatever I've got—" he tilted his head toward the ground beneath his trailer "—down there, I'll throw that in. *And* I'll wear my fingers to nubs—" he nodded at the workstation "—contributing data, information, knowledge, maybe even some wisdom if I can come up with some, though a voice interface would be nice." He held his next breath, then used it, "What do you say?"

"What do you want?"

Arun practically shouted, "Cultivate a whole new race of humans. If you can make three, you can make millions. I've saved seed stock."

Silence emphasized the ETs' tilting. Seconds ticked by. *Good.* Arun imagined circuits whirring, volatile storage churning, persistent storage screaming, as they tried to assimilate a unique request. Time stretched further. *Not so good.* Gloom oozed from the sewers of Arun's mind, a gloom he had always beaten back before, but only narrowly the last few times. Waiting for the ETs to knock had given him hope. Now....

"We must say no to that scope of effort. It exceeds our traveling resources." The ETs straightened, pulled apart. "However, we *can* sweeten our previous offer. Let us say *twelve* mates in exchange for contributing membership in our interstellar consortium, provided you do *contribute*."

Arun sagged. "What good will that do us?" he whispered.

"Reproduction for you, your genome; the purest definition of survival."

"Starting over? Arun and his dozen Eves?" Wives. Kids. *I couldn't do that before the collapse.* "I'm too tired."

Junior ET canted its body as though confused, but Senior ET said, "We're sorry you feel that way about our offering. Have we misjudged your need?"

Arun protested, "You've come a long ways to just walk away. You must want something from Earth."

"We stop at a promising world. We sell the concept, set up a churn, and start a subscription. We move on according to our set schedule. The rest is up to you and the consortium."

Feebly, Arun clung to his plan. "My offer of—" he could barely tilt his head "—*you know* —isn't worth your while?" Had he hidden something else down there? More than the file cabinets full of dead-people extracts and a hysterical attempt to hide it? Surely, he could offer more, but what? Surely….

"We regret that we cannot. It's just the two of us. Our ship is mostly engine and fuel with minor room for support and maintenance."

"Okay." Arun bent his mind to accept that an interstellar consortium hadn't sent its best and brightest, only its representatives, *sales* representatives. What should he do next? What had his mother done at a store that hadn't given her what she wanted? Escalate. Boy, could she escalate. He stood and marched up to get in its face, or at least the shiny surface that Senior ET kept pointing at him.

"Let's talk to *your* boss. Get out that ansible Junior mentioned."

"That's very expensive, and we must stay within our budget."

"But you've failed here. Surely, he'd want to know that. There cannot be enough intelligent species—" he twinged at the irony, considering how matters had come down to this, him, of all people, the last human "—out here in the galactic boondocks for you to dismiss one."

Unpromising territory out here. How'd they screw up to get sent here? And screw-ups don't think outside the box, particularly when they're just boxes.

On Arun's right, Junior ET said, "We cannot fulfill your request. Efficiency dictates that we move on."

Good, another nerdy topic. "What's more important?" Arun demanded. "Effective or efficient?

"Effective," Junior ET snapped.

"So you'd give up a lot of efficiency to get to effective?"

"Yes."

"Then work with me!"

Senior ET said, "Do you make a new offer?"

"All right, all right! I'll *give* it to you, what's in the mine." Believing would make it so. He hoped believing would make it so.

Senior ET nudged Arun's attention back to the desk. A laptop computer—more jetsam?—emerged on a moving shelf.

"Take that into your mine. Make a down payment on your contribution."

Arun gladdened. "We have a deal then?"

"We must have proof that you can pay," said Senior ET.

"Cash in fist!" declared Junior ET.

Bluff busted, Arun could only push for commitment *before* payment. "Shake on it!" he demanded.

Senior ET stepped back, Junior a split-second behind him. Disengaging.

"We regret that we cannot," it said and kept walking, not backward because it didn't have a back.

Desperate, Arun followed, waving his arms, trying to pump fresh ideas out of his ass. *Need a sure thing right now.* He'd read a book titled "Games You Can't Lose," from which he'd learned the drink-under-a-hat trick. *For real, then. Better make it a coin instead of a hat.*

"I'll bet you!" Did they pause? "Yes, yes."

Arun kept talking to keep the ETs attentive. "Betcha I can grab a coin covered by a hat without moving the hat." He patted his pockets, empty. *No coin.* He glanced around the office, but it was gone.

The ETs had lured him away and closed up shop. The chair had been rolled out onto the meadow, canted on a tuft of grass, the laptop sitting there. Behind it, the flying brick was all buckled up; only an oblate hatch at waist level remained open. The ETs angled that way.

"Scanned the book," Senior ET said over its shoulder.

"Seen the movie," Junior ET added snidely.

"Take them with you!" Arun pleaded. "Take my people with you. Back to your home planet, whenever you get there. It doesn't matter if they're resurrected here and now or a millennium from now halfway across the galaxy. Take them with you!"

The ETs paused on either side of the chair. Somehow, they indicated the laptop.

Arun followed the gesture.

Senior ET said, "The churn will take your submissions. Contribute something new and it will notify our home office, which will approve your access to search our info-base. *Ansible at work.*"

"Reading improves your mind," Junior ET said, continuing its mechanical derision. It squatted and leapt backward, disappearing neatly through the open hatch.

Arun protested, "What about the women you promised?"

"We regret that we must withdraw that introductory offer. Further examination of your prospects reveals a poor return on that investment. While the entire human population at its heyday might have produced an idea new to the galaxy, we now doubt that you, just one of you, will ever produce such a thing, despite the promise of the dark mine. You're welcome to try.

"Good luck on your endeavors." It squatted, leapt, and disappeared.

The hatch winked shut. The flying brick started its rotors, lifted off the meadow, and flew away.

The last human on Earth raised a hand as if to wave goodbye, but shrugged it off. He peered into the bright sky, so quickly empty, but could find no trace of humanity's last hope.

—4—

While all about him were losing their heads and blaming it on every god and devil ever invented, Arun hid in plain sight and kept working his job, searching for extra-terrestrial intelligence. His Wal-Mart generator and the building's emergency cache of gasoline, supplemented early on by raids on abandoned vehicles, kept the equipment in the back office running. He turned off extra lights and never appeared in public areas.

He couldn't feed others or cure the pandemics that spread eve-rywhere in the last days of commercial flight or quiet civil unrest. Nor could he restart the global economy or lead the resurgent tribes into stability that might promise the return of civilization. Hell, he couldn't even convince the last desperate woman in the office to stay with him instead of running off into Denver as it collapsed around them.

In time, riots quieted, and the stink of decaying bodies seeped in through vents despite the immobilized HVAC. In time, that too passed. Quiet descended. Beasts returned, but they didn't make much noise.

Meanwhile, Arun just kept watching satellite feeds, hunkered down and watching the stars, *hoping*. As controllers for other obser-vation spacecraft, LEO and beyond, lapsed into silence, Arun as-sumed their duties, minimal housekeeping mostly. His favorite channel became the sun, provided by the six Inti (Mayan mythology was big the year they were funded) spacecraft that bracketed the star, an oddly comforting magnificence reduced to a 21-inch flatscreen monitor. He didn't do anything with the data pouring down from the spacecraft, but he came to love the silent inferno on the screen.

Naturally, he flipped to the specific feed when a solar-flare alarm sounded and flashed. The alarm message started with "Anomaly," and he didn't have to study the picture at all to see the long, narrow spike of plasma that erupted from the sun, not ra-dially, but tangentially. A spurt unlike he'd seen live or via archive. It seemed at that time—this prescience gave credence to his per-ceived revelation when it came—that the flare was more an ejection than a spit, as if someone had driven a spear through the sun's love handle, leaving not even a flesh wound, but a mere splash that quickly melted away.

By then, Arun loved distractions; chasing down minutia in petabytes of data kept him from thinking about people dying in droves all around him, all around the world. He went looking through all the other detectors aimed at that part of the sky, plus any data he could find about the other side of that trajectory before it—whatever it was—hit the sun.

Arun tracked the object across the planetary orbits of Venus, Earth, and Mars—skipping extraordinary distances to find it—and calculated its velocity: 0.8137c, and that was *after* it had blasted through the sun.

He also initiated a search of solar archives for any flare with a similar signature—and found something, almost fourteen months before; a different vector, even larger, but even then priorities had afflicted data reduction: if it didn't directly impact human lives on Earth, nobody looked at it. Exit velocity of the object then: 0.9376c.

Net-net: a huge, thin shaft of an artifact doing a significant but dropping portion of the speed of light, ripping free of solar fluid. Any technology capable of approaching lightspeed ought to withstand a plunge through a star. *Why not?* Arun shrugged. Deceleration? Probably. Re-fueling? Possibly, if such a ship used something as mundane as hydrogen for fuel. How did they turn? He didn't care because they obviously had. How did they survive such helio-braking? How did...how did.... All he came to know was that the ETs did it somehow and they were coming to Earth. Why else slow down?

He hoped.

—5—

The chair had proven awkward to move, its castors balking at the tufts of grass and the sandy soil in between. In the end, he made two trips: the laptop portal to the ETs' cyberspace first, then the chair. At least he'd gotten a good chair out of it.

After he'd re-settled his living area with the new chair and a shelf for the laptop, Arun got practical. He finished his darning and made some sandwiches—enough for a few days—filled the water cooler, cleaned out his toilet, changed his underpants, and brushed his teeth.

He settled at the small keyboard and pondered the abyss of a screen and the single prompt at the bottom: submit.

One offering after another: rejected.

Arun tried to relate to the ETs, to the interstellar consortium. *Never could relate to people, but these aren't people; they're part machine, So, are they all that different from the idiosyncrasies of compilers and opsys and network protocols? Not really.*

So he talked human tech to the churn: nothing new, not even UNIX.

Arun pissed, slept, ate, crapped, and walked outside to stare after the ETs, blue-skying under the bluest sky in decades.

Why would anybody want traveling salesmen to come back? He remembered a joke that sparked the thought, *What would exiled salesmen not want their boss to hear?*

He threw his meager reserve of caution to the wind and typed, "Have you heard the one about the traveling salesman and the farmer's daughter?"

The small screen swirled for the first time. Eight minutes and forty-seven seconds later, it displayed, "No. Tell us."

Rather than risk relying on his poor memory for jokes, Arun dug up a book and typed its first entry.

A horizontal bar split the screen in two. At the bottom, it displayed "Submit," but the top half prompted, "Query."

Arun smiled and sighed and cried, rivulets of tears and snot. Unabashed, he let the storm run its course. Then, he washed his face, grabbed a cool tall one—nothing but well water for years—and started looking up starship specs.

—6—

The last human on Earth heard a knock at his door. Arun rushed to fling it open.

Senior and Junior ET stood there. Wary and belligerent, both of them.

Arun canted his head, waiting.

Senior ET said, "What would it take to close this deal?"

Followed quickly by Junior ET's bitter, "Good thing we hadn't built up much velocity. Budget. Schedule."

Arun glared at Junior. "You'll make up for blowing budget and schedule by restoring an intelligent race who made just one little mistake. Many points for effectiveness, remember? Now, stow it." He turned to Senior. "I've got some ideas. What hull are you flying?"

"Mark 4529." Lean and mean, the traveling salesmen's kit.

"What superstructure?"

"Point fifteen." Plenty of support and maintenance, though, keeping them out working the territory.

Arun didn't bother to invite them in. "What happens when you—your *box*—breaks?"

A pregnant pause of silent comms, then Junior ET said, "Last backup of personality core downloads to a new box."

Arun asked, "So your ship stores more boxes?"

"Yes."

"How many?"

After a slightly longer pause, Senior ET took over. "39,420 in stasis, 8,006 in cannibalization, 642 unrepairable."

Arun pounced. "Activate them all, and you could husband our race. Restore one with your download and repeat. If you can make twelve humans, you can make millions." Selling as hard as he could.

"Even by the hundreds, there are things we cannot do. Machines have their limits, as we have discovered a long time ago. We cannot do everything required for that scale."

Arun drew the deepest breath he could manage. Every centimeter of his skin tingled. *Not writing a check my body can't cash, I hope.* He reached out both hands to shake on the deal.

"I can provide those features," he promised posterity.

Terra Tango 3

James Reilly

—1—

"Terra Tango 3, this is Overlord, come in."

Jarrett yawns and grabs the headset off of the dashboard.

"This is Terra Tango 3, go ahead," he croaks. He rubs his eyes and stares out at the derelict slabs of concrete that used to be Wall Street. Now it's a ghost town of waist-high weeds, cracked side-walks, and blankets of ivy masking the weathered façades of what was once the hub of capitalism.

Welcome to Manhattan; the world's biggest sound stage.

There's a brief silence followed by the sizzle of static.

"Change of plans, Jarrett." The voice is deceptively warm and as soothing as hot chocolate, but Jarrett knows better. Devon Kincaid is as warm as an ice water enema. Her call sign is Overlord, and noth-ing could be more appropriate. As the show's creator, executive producer, and director, Dev personally lords over every facet of Dead Heat from the Network sub-orbital, looking down onto the action with a view rivaled only by that of God himself. Then again, after five years with the series, Jarrett's learned that as far as Dead Heat is concerned, there is only one God, and *she* is a stone-cold bitch.

"Make sure the sector's lit, 'cause we go live in thirty. Net-work's got something special lined up for this week, and I don't want to miss a beat of it, understood?"

"Yeah, got it. Tango out."

Jarrett climbs out of the cab and into the cramped confines of the editing bay. A few strokes on the keyboard bring the system online, linking the three thousand-plus closed circuit cameras to Network's satellite. Within minutes, the two banks of monitors surrounding him are cycling through live feeds from Battery Park to Empire State Boulevard.

The studio feed is running through highlights from last week's episode. The petite grade school teacher from Arkansas planting the business end of a spiked baseball bat into the skull of a deader; the lawyer from D.C. looking on in horror while a mob plays tug-of-war with his large intestine; the art dealer from Kalamazoo being dragged down through an open manhole cover by an unseen horde of cellar dwellers. The highlight reel gives way to footage of Dead Heat's first and only winner, Marcus Denton, a former Marine drill sergeant from Cedar Rapids, carving a deader in two with a chainsaw. The recording slows to a crawl, freezing on a close-up of Denton's contorted, blood-spattered visage, and then fades into a live shot of Denton and Dead Heat's ingratiating analyst, John McCarver, back in the studio.

"Amazing stuff, Marcus, just simply amazing," McCarver gushes. "Rarely do we see such poise and raw determination in this game. You know, I've watched this footage at least a hundred times and I've always wanted to ask you, what was going through your head right…at…*that*…moment?"

Denton smiles and runs his hands down the lapels of his meticulously pressed suit. "Well, John, I think the *real* question is what was going through *his* head."

"Oh, mercy." McCarver slaps the desk and laughs. "Boy, did I ever set myself up for that!"

"No, but seriously, my training as a marine, as well as my faith in the Lord almighty…."

Jarrett tunes the rest of it out. He's seen enough of Marcus Denton to last him a lifetime. Since his victory three years ago, Denton has grown into a bonafide celebrity, with his face plastered on everything from cereal boxes to women's underwear. He'd become both an inspirational figure and a cult hero to the masses, but to Jarrett, Marcus Denton will always be the opportunistic asshole who threw a 58-year-old housewife from Chattanooga down a fire escape to distract the horde of deaders who stood between him and the finish line.

The wailing guitars of Dead Heat's faux-metal theme song buzz through the speakers as Denton and McCarver sign off. Dev comes over the master channel and addresses the crew.

"The shuttle is thirty seconds out. I want aerial to get some sweeping passes of the ship as it descends. Tango 3, get me a few good angles of the hatch as it opens. Last week the fucking guards blocked almost all of the good stuff. I *don't* want a repeat of that."

"Roger that," Jarrett says. "I've got two down shots and three at ground level. As long as they land on their mark, you've got coverage."

"Okay, you should have visual in five...four...three...." Dev's voice is drowned out by the deep rumble of the shuttle as it hovers above. Jarrett steadies himself as the rig rocks violently in the ship's wake. Rocks and debris pelt the armored exterior of his vehicle with a barrage of metallic pings. The monitors flicker from scanlines to static to the blinding white of the shuttle's landing lights, until, finally, the ship settles on its mark and fires down its engines.

"Tango 3," Dev's barking voice is barely audible above the ringing in Jarrett's ears. "What are you waiting for? Get me on that hatch!"

"Yeah, roger that," he says, his teeth still vibrating from the shuttle's landing. He brings the cameras online and the monitors display five different angles of the ship's steaming bay doors. "We're go."

"Alright," Dev shouts. "Let's open her up!"

There's a dramatic pause before the rear door folds open. A thick spiral of smoke and a shaft of blinding white light spill out from the cargo bay as Jarrett brings up the network feed. The tail end of the opening credits theme crossfades into host Wink Magnenson's patently solemn voiceover.

Welcome, America, to another exciting episode of Dead Heat. The

lottery has been drawn, and this week ten more competitors will take to the
deadly streets of old New York, where they'll not only be fighting for their
lives, but for a chance at the ultimate prize: lunar citizenship and a spa-
cious new luxury home at Earth View Estates in the gorgeous Daedalus
settlement.

Jarrett laughs, just as he does every time he hears Magnenson's description of Earth View Estates. He's been there; hell, he shot the commercials for the place. Save for the ultra-high-end digs already occupied by the lucky few who could afford them, the majority of the "family" units didn't amount to much more than tastefully decorated prison cells, hardly bigger than Jarrett's cramped quarters back at Network. Still, when you've spent the better part of twenty years sleeping ass-to-elbow in the rat-infested cargo bay of an over-crowded space trawler, even a shithole like Earth View might be an improvement.

Shadows dance in the glow of the bay door as a dozen guards in full riot gear march down the platform six to a side. They stop and face each other and shoulder their weapons in well-choreographed unison as the contestants—each in handcuffs and leg irons—appear in the doorway. Jarrett zooms in as the first of them—a trembling Asian man dressed in a wrinkled three-piece suit—shuffles down the ramp.

Our first contestant is a 57 year-old former banker from Los Angeles,
Mr. Tony Fong!

The network feed cuts to a live shot of the auditorium inside the California orbital station, where thousands of Fong's fellow west coast survivors are holding up signs and cheering him on. The camera pans to a hysterical Asian woman flanked on either side by her weeping children. A flashing caption below reads *The Fong Family,* and the audience erupts into chants of "Tony! Tony!" There's a brief pre-recorded interview snippet with Tony himself. The interviewer asks him what he will do if he wins Dead Heat. An obviously terrified Tony looks into the camera and screams in broken English.

"Please! I do not want to die!"

There's a collective "awwww" from the audience, and then the camera pans back to his family. His wife is now unconscious, and the two children are fanning her face with their collector's edition Dead Heat episode guides. The audience howls with delight.

Our next contestant is Sheila Joy, a 62-year-old former nurse's aide from Palisades Park.

Sheila apparently has no family, so the audience is given a wide shot of the Tribeca Orbital's cafeteria. Dozens of Sheila's "fans" hold up signs urging her on, but Jarrett knows that those signs are provided by the network, and the people holding them are doing so only so they can see themselves on television. Sheila's interview is the polar opposite of Tony Fong's. She looks positively serene, and when asked if she's afraid to die, Sheila shakes her head.

"I died a long time ago," she says.

The profundity of her statement is compromised by the animated zombie that shambles across the screen followed by a flashing, blood-spattered caption reading "DEAD MEAT."

Next up is Kimberly Rivet, a 19-year-old student born and raised on the Dixie Orbital station, making her both the first native non-terrestrial and youngest contestant in the show's history. She's also the only person ever to smile during the interview segment. "It's my favorite show," she giggles. "I can't believe I'm gonna be on the TV!"

Kimberly is followed by an obviously sedated 46-year-old accountant from Aberdeen named Ken Pierce, hulking 32-year-old maintenance man Blake Peters, 51-year-old former soap opera actress/infomercial pitchwoman Shelly Briggs, diminutive 39-year-old karate instructor John Alves; 48-year-old one-time Michelin chef and current cafeteria manager Elliot Gordon, and 56-year-old self-described anarchist Dirk Ryder, who's sporting a homemade T-shirt that reads *Nuke the Moon* and waving his middle fingers at the camera.

The tenth contestant is still standing at the top of the ramp, bathed in shadow and swirling smoke. The show's dramatic music swells in the background as the network feed cuts to a close-up of Wink Magnenson staring grimly into the camera.

"Tango 3, give me a static shot of the shuttle bay," Dev says. "Here we go."

And, as a reminder that none of us are safe from the hand of fate, we give you our tenth and final contestant, Magnenson says. The backlighting behind the trio of silhouettes at the top of the ramp intensifies. *And he is one of Network's own.*

The contestant's face is revealed. Jarrett feels his heart sink. "Oh, fuck me," he whispers.

Milledge Hawkins begins his descent down the ramp, his arms folded neatly in front of him, his head bowed forward, staring somberly at his feet.

Less than twenty-four hours ago, Jarrett and Hawkins were throwing back beers in the Network commissary, celebrating the kid's promotion. Jarrett had been training Hawkins to do remotes for nearly six months, and next week's episode was going to be the kid's first solo outing, as well as Jarrett's first day off in six months. Now Jarrett's young protégé is being paraded past the other nine contestants, his eyes glossy and distant, his lips quivering.

Jarrett pounds his fist on the console and picks up his headset. He's about to radio Dev when he notices the guards escorting Hawkins out of frame. He switches cameras and sees them marching toward the rig, and he suddenly realizes that, unlike the other contestants, Milledge Hawkins isn't wearing restraints.

"What the hell...?" Jarrett whispers. He's about to start cycling through the cameras again when the monitors are suddenly awash with static. The lights in the rig flicker momentarily and a chiming alarm rings out, alerting Jarrett that the perimeter defenses have been breached.

There's a series of loud thumps on the rig's rear hatch.

"Dev, what's going on?" Jarrett asks.

There's another round of pounding on the thick metal door, followed by the buzz and clank of the release mechanism override.

"Dev, what the *fuck* is going on?"

The hatch swings open. The guards step inside. One holds a set of restraints; the other leverages a pistol at Jarrett's head. Hawkins follows close behind, unable to look Jarrett in the eye.

"No way," Jarrett shakes his head. He brings the mic so close to his mouth he practically swallows it. "No fucking way this is happening, Dev. This is *BULLSHIT!*"

"No, Jarrett," she replies. Her voice is no longer confined to the headset. It pours in through every speaker in the editing bay. "This is *good television*. You, of all people, should appreciate that."

Jarrett's horrified expression fills every monitor as the guards descend upon him and drag him to his feet. Hawkins slips past them toward Jarrett's station as they slap on the wrist restraints.

"I'm sorry," he whispers.

"You knew?" Jarrett lunges toward him. Hawkins winces and raises his hands defensively as a sudden blow to the back of the skull sends Jarrett to his knees.

"Go easy on the kid, Jarrett," Dev says. "He only found out this morning. I've been sitting on the lottery results for a whole week. I mean, fuck, you know how hard it is to keep a secret like that?"

"How could you...I...I've got friends. *Family.*"

"And I'm sure they'll all be rooting for you," she says.

"Umm...I'm logged in now," Hawkins says. His eyes meet Jarrett's and then dart away. "I think...I'm ready to go when you are."

"Alright. Get him to the starting line, boys," Dev says. "We've got a show to do."

"This isn't over, Dev!" Jarrett digs in his heels as the guards drag him out of the editing bay. He jams an elbow into the facemask of the guard to his left, eliciting a trebly grunt, before the other one trips him up and sends him tumbling down to the base of the ramp.

Jarrett sucks in a lungful of fetid air–a stomach churning mixture of sulphur, shit, and decay–as he lies writhing on the concrete. He had forgotten how bad it smelled, having not stepped foot outside of a production rig since his rookie season, when he'd made the mistake of climbing onto the roof to adjust the vehicle-mounted cams without taking his anti-rads. He'd spent the next two months bald, blistered, and pissing neon.

"Are you gonna behave now, or am I gonna have to use this?" The guard produces a baton from his belt. A flickering white-blue arc dances between two small electrodes at its tip.

"You know what?" Jarrett grumbles, rising on his haunches. "Why don't you kiss my—"

And with that, the baton grinds into Jarrett's ribcage. There's a smell not unlike burning hair as 5000 volts course through him, and, in the throes of a full-body convulsion and what feels like a million needles piercing his flesh all at once, Jarrett slips into unconsciousness.

—2—

The shots they give them are a cocktail of anti-rads, high dose stims, and concentrated testosterone. The anti-rads are a formality, given in case of the unlikely event that a contestant actually finishes the race. This was legal's idea. After all, you can't have someone successfully run the gauntlet only to succumb to cancer three weeks later. That would be bad for ratings.

The other stuff is purely for entertainment value. Dev started using them three seasons ago after sponsors complained about a lack of fight on the part of the contestants. The cocktail of stims and testosterone made grannies fight like gladiators, and—according to the focus groups—the audience loved it.

The contestants are lined up in a row along a magnetized rail that keeps their ankle restraints firmly anchored to the ground. The Network physician administers the last of the shots and then retreats back into the shuttle, followed by the bulk of the guards and crew. A tingling sensation builds at the base of Jarrett's neck as the drugs go to work on his nervous system. Before long, any residual effects of the beating he took at the hands of the guards is replaced by a welcome numbness and a sense of urgency unlike anything he's felt before. He's seen what the drugs can do, but he's never experienced it first hand until now. It's powerful stuff. Powerful enough to make him think he can do this.

Hell, he *knows* he can do this.

One of the P.A.s drops a flimsy circular mat in front of the contestants and points to Jarrett's old rig. The mat glows, and suddenly the shimmering hologram of Wink Magnenson appears before them, his finger pressed to his ear bud as he shouts at no one in particular.

Just try to give me a little color this time. Last week I looked like a god-damn green goblin, he says.

The production assistant crouches in the midst of Magnenson's flickering visage and adjusts a set of dials on the mat. Magnenson puffs away at his cigarette and runs through his lines, his image shifting from pale blue to a warm crimson. The P.A. gives the thumbs-up and then twirls a finger in the air, letting everyone know it's time to clear the set.

Magnenson tosses his cigarette and smiles at the contestants.

Good luck to all of you, he says with well-rehearsed sincerity. *Now let's get out there and give 'em a good show!*

—3—

Jarrett loads fifteen rounds into the Mossberg, fills his pockets with the rest of the shells, and takes his place beside the others in front of the twenty-foot-high mass of steel and barbed wire that represents the starting line.

"You got gun? Is no fair." Tony Fong holds up the antique mace he found in his pack. "What I get? Is this joke? This not funny!"

At the start of the race, each contestant is presented with a box with his or her name on it. For nine of the contestants that box can contain anything from a rocket launcher to a machine gun to a machete. One unlucky bastard, however, gets what Dev calls "the laugher": an item so completely and utterly useless as to not qualify as a weapon at all. Jarrett's seen people run off into battle wielding everything from an egg beater to a rubber chicken, so, all things considered, Tony Fong got lucky.

"Look, just...just stay behind me, okay?" Jarrett says. "You watch my back, I'll watch yours, deal?"

Fong nods. "Yes, deal," he says, nodding and smiling emphatically. The chain rattles as he lets the heavy spiked ball drop by his side. "Is still not funny."

There's a commotion at the other end of the line. Kimberly Rivet is squatting on the sidewalk, slamming the butt of her P90 submachine gun against concrete, and Ken Pierce is trying to wrestle it away from her.

"Give me that, you stupid cow," he shouts. "That's not how you load it!"

"Back off, asshole," Kimberly cries. "It's my gun, and I'll load it however I—"

There's a short, percussive burst, followed by a communal gasp as the top of Ken's head is reduced to a fine red mist. Ken teeters there for a moment, catching bits of himself in his trembling, upturned hands, before collapsing at Kimberly's feet.

The young girl laughs, her eyes bulging as she wipes the spatter from her face. "Holy fuck! Did you see that? I mean, seriously, *holy fucking fuck*...." She crouches and gingerly retrieves her weapon from the pool of blood and brain matter forming around it. "Yuck. Anyone got a towel?"

"You think they give me his weapon?" Tony Fong stares up at Jarrett with chemically dilated eyes. He gives his mace a whirl, and then doubles over in a fit of laughter. "Because this no good!"

Jarrett laughs, too. The drugs are going into overdrive. There's a tickle running from the pit of his stomach to the center of his chest and an oddly pleasing tingling sensation in his scalp. His muscles pulsate in sync with his racing heart. He turns down the line to see that the others are laughing too, the muscles in their faces twitching, eyes as wide as saucers, seemingly sharing the same rush of euphoria and invincibility that's coursing through him.

They're all still laughing as the massive gate yawns open before them.

—4—

Deaders are slow and as dumb as fuck. They're only effective in mobs, when they can surround you and take you down with brute force and numbers. The secret is to stay out in the open, stay together, and never, under any circumstances, let them back you into a corner.

Kimberly Rivet learns this lesson the hard way.

Once they enter Zone One, the mobs pour into the street from gates on either side. The contestants split into three groups–Jarrett, Fong, and Kimberly take the right side, Blake Peters and Elliot Gordon watch the center, while the rest cover the left flank.

The first mob goes down easy. It's been twenty years since Jarrett's fired a gun, but in the years following the outbreak he had more than his fair share of practice, and it all comes rushing back with disturbing ease.

Peters and Gordon aren't faring as well. They retreat to the left side, leaving the middle of the street wide open. They're balls deep in deaders when Jarrett notices Kimberly wandering off from the group. She's spraying and praying, egging on the mob in front of her, when she suddenly runs out of real estate near the entrance of the old AIG building. She starts to cut left, but there's another, smaller mob moving in. Jarrett and Fong aren't more than twenty feet away, but it may as well be miles, and all Jarrett can do is pray she can land enough head shots to cut a swath through the throng.

Problem is, she's a terrible shot.

"I can't hit shit with this fucking thing," she cries. The P90 is riding up on her, sending out a harmless volley of fire above the heads of the encroaching horde. Just as she seems to compensate for the kick, they're on her.

Jarrett fires off a couple of rounds from the Mossberg, hitting a deader center mass with the first shot, vaporizing its head with the next. Jarrett stops to reload and Fong charges forward, proving surprisingly competent with the cumbersome mace. He caves in the skull of the deader closest to him, and when that one falls, he takes down another.

"Tony, get out of there." Jarrett forces the last round into the chamber as Fong retreats from the scrum and falls to his knees beside him. Jarrett rapidly fires eight more rounds into the pack, reducing the remaining deaders to little more than a twitching pile of viscera.

"Wow," Fong says as he gets to his feet. He points his fingers skyward and flexes his thumbs. "You like *cowboy*!"

Jarrett cracks a smile, but it quickly fades when he sees Kimberly leaning up against the base of the building. She gives them a half-hearted wave and then rests her hand on the ragged gash in her shoulder. Her other arm hangs limply by her side, the flesh on her wrist chewed down to glistening bone.

"It's okay," she says. "I didn't expect to make it past…the first zone anyway."

"You did good, kid," Jarrett says. He steps in close and brings up the barrel of the Mossberg. "Now you know I gotta to do this, right?"

Kimberly nods. "I'd do the same for you." She laughs. "Then again, I'd probably miss."

Jarrett gives her a weary smile as he pulls the trigger.

Fong kneels beside Kimberly's body, folds his hands and whispers something in Mandarin, and then picks up her gun. He pats Jarrett on the back. "She no suffer now. You good man."

Jarrett nods and turns back toward the others as the shuttle hovers overhead. A large green crate is lowered into the center of the street, signaling the end of the first round, as well as the first commercial break. As the other contestants rush toward the crate, Fong looks to Jarrett, as if for approval.

"You go ahead," Jarrett says. He's not in any rush. He knows the contents by heart—ammo, energy bars, and bottled water spiked with assorted pharmaceutical pick-me-ups; as much as he can use all three, there's something else he needs to take care of first. "I'll be along in a minute."

Fong nods and jogs off to join the others as they circle the crate like keyed-up kids on Christmas morning.

Jarrett walks the perimeter and tries to look inconspicuous while he figures out which gates opened and in what sequence. It's all very familiar, and this fact brings a smile to his face. He had his suspicions when the deaders were first herded into the zone, but now he's sure of it.

They're still running *his* program.

Either Milledge Hawkins was too green to issue a simple override, or his guilt-ridden protégé was doing him a favor. Either way, knowing what's coming and when gives him a huge advantage going forward. That is, so long as he isn't obvious about it.

After all, Dev is watching, and something tells Jarrett he's got her undivided attention.

— 5 —

John Alves is the first to go down in Zone Two.

Refusing to carry so much as a jack-knife, the martial artist opts, instead, to go into battle wielding only the weapons god gave him. When the first wave of deaders hits, Alves downs at least a dozen of them, shattering skulls and snapping necks with a dizzying array of kicks, punches, and jaw-dropping aerial acrobatics. For a while it appears as though the agile martial artist will be able to clear the zone all by his lonesome, but when a kick to the abdomen of a surprisingly obese deader results in Alves' left leg becoming hopelessly lodged in the creature's rotting belly, things turn ugly quickly. A mob converges on the portly deader and his newly acquired protuberance, and as Alves struggles to free himself, a tug-of-war ensues. After a sickening symphony of snapping bones and shrill cries, the mob disperses, each deader shambling away with a piece of Alves in tow.

Simon Elliot performs a hasty sign of the cross for his fallen comrade as he bounds toward a cornered Blake Peters. A screaming Shelia Joy is hot on Elliot's heels, waving her blood-soaked machete over her head in a berserker rage, hacking her way through the throng.

Shelly Briggs lays waste to a trundling wall of dead flesh with her AK-47 while Tony Fong, proving much more adept with the P90 than Kimberly had been, cuts down the few who manage to avoid Shelly's arc of fire.

Jarrett calls the shots from the roof of a burned-out SUV, methodically picking off stragglers as he counts down the seconds before the next batch of deaders emerges from City Hall Park. He does his best to act surprised when they come into view and he announces their presence to the other contestants. Shelly and Fong rush forward, taking up a position behind an overturned Mini Cooper. Dirk Ryder takes a more adventurous route up Broadway and flanks the deaders near the park entrance. Ryder breaks out the game's first power-up–a Soviet-era rocket-propelled infantry flamethrower he procured at the World Trade Center monument checkpoint–and launches a napalm-filled shell into the heart of the oncoming horde. The resulting fireball incinerates more than half of them; the rest shamble forward, slathered in liquid flame, until fire devours their flesh and the undead collapse into heaps of smoldering bone.

Framed by tendrils of black smoke and lapping flames, Dirk Ryder tosses the spent weapon aside and pumps his fists in the air. A wave of heat and smoke dries Jarrett's eyes, and he blinks the sting away. When he opens them again, Dirk Ryder is gone.

—6—

Cellar dwellers aren't nearly as predictable as deaders. One can't simply round them up with bait and expect them to mill about in holding cells until show time. They're too smart to be baited, too quick to trap, and no one's made an enclosure that can contain them. Jarrett knows this because he's tried. Dev's been obsessed with the mutants since they made their surprise debut back in season two, and since that time has tried everything short of flooding the sewers to goad an appearance out of them.

Living off of dog-sized sewer rats, algae, and the occasional Dead Heat contestant, these remnants of the hundreds of thousands left behind during the Great Evacuation of 2130 are fast, cunning, and, unlike their undead counterparts, very much *alive*. Well-adapted to their irradiated environs (courtesy of the Great Incineration of 2131), dwellers rarely emerge from their subterranean abodes, opting for stealthy snatch-and-grabs and the occasional manhole cameo.

They're also notoriously camera shy, which is what makes this atypical above-ground appearance all the more unsettling.

Jarrett had warned the others at the end of Zone Two, after Ryder went missing. He'd told them to be careful around manhole covers and gutters and steer clear of shadows and alleyways. They had stared at him wide-eyed, hunkered around the supply drop like a bunch of kids sitting around a campfire listening to ghost stories.

Then Blake Peters broke out in a fit of laughter and the rest fell like dominos.

"This is serious," Jarrett said. The drugs had peaked again, and even he was having a hard time keeping a straight face. "You don't know these things. They only show up when they're hungry, and by the time you see them it's already too late."

"Sounds like my ex-husband," Shelly Briggs said.

Simon Elliot threw his arm over her shoulders. "Oh yeah? Maybe we could introduce him to my ex-wife?"

Tony Fong said something, too, but between his drug-induced cackling and his poor command of the English language, no one seemed to understand a word of it. They all laughed anyway.

Well, everyone but Sheila Joy. Sheila sat cross-legged on the pavement, sharpening her machete with a chunk of singed bone. Jarrett tried to get her to drink some water, but she didn't acknowledge him. She just moaned and stared off into the distance, her eyes bloodshot, her face molded into a permanent scowl.

While the rest of the challengers had become fearless and carefree, the drugs had had a completely different effect on Sheila.

Sheila had become pure, focused rage.

She is an absolute monster in the early going of Zone Three. While the rest hold firm, adhering to Jarrett's orders to let the deaders come to them, she chops her way into the thick of it, leaving a trail of severed heads and detached limbs in her wake. As the third and final wave approaches, the old woman tears off her blood-soaked shirt and bra and charges down the block toward Crosby Street, her enormous sagging breasts slapping against her belly like war drums.

Thwap Thwap Thwap.

Jarrett takes up a position on the first level of a rusted-out fire escape overlooking the intersection of Bleecker and Broadway. He has Fong and Shelly Briggs set up below him facing east, while Simon Elliot and Blake Peters watch the west toward Mercer. Jarrett knows nothing will be coming that way, but he has to make it look good.

The deaders are within a hundred yards now. Jarrett watches Sheila Joy dive headlong into the front of the ranks, and when she vanishes in a blur of steel and crimson, he orders the others to open fire.

And, with that, the dwellers come out of their holes.

Jarrett peers out from the basement window of the brownstone. Three of the smaller dwellers–either kids or runts– are fighting over what looks like Simon Elliot's liver. One manages to tug it away and scurries off on all fours, leaving the other two to pick over the well-stripped remains. Twenty or so warriors, decked out in rudimentary armor consisting of everything from hockey pads and football helmets to vests made up of strung-together beer cans, march up and down Bleecker Street, bashing their clubs against garbage can lid shields and hooting and hollering.

"What are we hiding for?" Shelly Briggs asks. She holds up her AK-47. "We can *take* these *things*."

Jarrett shakes his head. "These aren't deaders. They're not just going to stand there and let you shoot them," he says. He taps the magazine of her rifle. "Besides, how many bullets you got left in that thing?"

"How the fuck should I know?"

Jarrett sighs, tips the gun forward, and points at the exposed slit running up the back of the magazine. "You've got ten shots. I've got maybe six or seven." Jarrett nods toward Tony Fong. "How about you?"

Fong holds up the P90 and pulls the trigger, eliciting a loud click. "No more."

"So what do we do?" Blake Peters whispers. "We can't just sit here all night. I say we get to the checkpoint. At least we can rearm there."

"We're at least seven blocks from Washington Square," Jarrett says. "You want to try to outrun them? Be my guest."

Peters frowns. He stands and tucks his Desert Eagle into his jeans. "Who said anything about running?"

—7—

The bullet whistles past his ear, close enough that he can feel it displace the air. For an irradiated sub-human, the dweller's a pretty good shot.

Jarrett has Shelly Briggs by the wrist, practically dragging her up West Third toward Washington Square Park. Tony Fong sprints ahead of them, turns, and fires off a few rounds from the AK-47. Jarrett can tell by the horrified look on Fong's face that the dwellers are closing in fast.

Peters had bought them some time with his foolish heroics. Once the hungry dwellers saw the big meal that presented itself to them, they were too enthralled to notice Jarrett and the others slip out of the brownstone's basement window, making their escape under the cover of Peters' surprisingly shrill screams.

They only make it as far as Lafayette Street before the dwellers notice them.

"You guys just go," Shelly says, grinding her heels into the pavement. "I can't run anymore."

Jarrett tugs her toward him so hard he feels her shoulder pop. "It's only a couple of blocks," he says. "You can do this!"

Another round from the Desert Eagle whizzes by, hitting the wall just over Jarrett's left shoulder with a deafening ricochet and a shower of sparks and shattered brick.

Fong gets behind Shelly and gives her a shove. "You rest later!"

Jarrett can hear the bare feet slapping against the pavement behind them. There's no chance of outrunning them now. They have to make a stand.

"Tony, in here!" Jarrett guides Shelly around the corner into a narrow alleyway between two brownstones. They rush toward a dumpster at the end of the alley, and Jarrett pushes Shelly behind it. He crouches down in front of her, and Fong takes up a position on the other side.

"Dead end!" Fong says.

"Yeah, well, at least they can't get behind us, right?" Jarrett shoulders the Mossberg and levels his sights at the alley entrance. He knows this is a bad idea, but he'll be damned if he dies without taking at least a few of them with him. "Let them get close. We can't afford to waste a shot!"

The dwellers slow their approach as they enter the alley. There's ten of them; at least ten that Jarrett can see. The one with Peters' gun is front and center, his sinewy frame draped in a tattered Irish flag, cinched at the waist with twine and leather strands strung through what appear to be dozens of rotting fingers. He's wearing a Jets football helmet, the facemask removed, replaced by sharpened bones on either side that jut forward like tusks. The thing smiles, its teeth filed into jagged points. It raises its hand. The others stop dead in their tracks.

"Yoooo caaaaaaaaaah hiiiiiiiiiiiiiiiide." Its voice is throaty and percussive, like a death rattle. The thing wags its finger and sniffs at the air. "Nooooooo waaaaaaaaaay tooooo goooooooooooooo." It starts forward slowly, scraping the barrel of the Desert Eagle against the brick wall. Two of the dwellers move in around him, crouching low to the ground. Another silently scales the ladder at the mouth of the alleyway and scuttles along the underside of the fire escape above them.

"Now?" Fong's voice is tremulous. The AK-47 is rattling in his hands

"Wait for it," Jarrett says.

The leader fires off the last two rounds from the Desert Eagle. The first shot glances off the dumpster; the other takes out a chunk of wall a few inches above Tony Fong's head. With the weapon spent, the leader tosses it to the ground, reaches over his shoulder, and unsheathes a massive serrated blade.

"Wait for it," Jarrett repeats.

The remaining dwellers flood into the alley behind him. The one on the fire escape creeps closer, then freezes, then creeps closer still.

"Wait for it...."

The two out in front weave in and out of overturned barrels and rubbish bins. They're not more than twenty feet away when the leader lets forth a rallying cry.

"Now!"

The dweller closest to him leaps just as Jarrett gets off his first shot. The blast caves in the thing's chest, sending it flying back up the alley. The dweller on the fire escape launches itself over Jarrett, kicking off of the wall behind it and landing on his shoulders. The dweller squeezes Jarrett's neck between its thighs and pounds on his head with its bony fists. Jarrett brings up the rifle and buries the muzzle into the soft flesh beneath the dweller's chin. He pulls the trigger and a geyser of blood and brain matter erupts from the top of the creature's shattered skull. The dweller goes limp and tumbles forward over Jarrett's shoulders, knocking the rifle out of his hands just as the next two come bounding toward him. Jarrett wriggles out from under the dead dweller and recovers his weapon, but before he can get off a shot, their heads explode like gore-filled piñatas, drenching Jarrett and Shelly in a warm, sanguine mist.

"Yeeeehawwww!" Tony Fong shouts. "Who cowboy now?"

Jarrett wipes the blood from his eyes and gives Fong a grateful thumbs-up. Shelly scurries past Jarrett and grabs one of the fallen dwellers' weapons–a rudimentary cleaver that looks to have been fashioned from a piece of sheet metal welded to the handle of an aluminum baseball bat–and scrambles up onto the dumpster. She swings the weapon from side to side, taunting the remaining dwellers.

"C'mon you skinny fucks! Come get some!"

The leader smiles and, as if on cue, a torrent of dwellers pours into the alleyway behind him.

"Oh shit," Shelly groans.

The leader raises his jagged sword. "Keeeeeeeeeeeell Demmmmmmmmmmmmm!"

The creatures move forward as one, a roiling wave of flesh. Jarrett and Tony climb atop the dumpster with Shelly and unload their weapons into the writhing mass. Each dweller they kill is replaced by another as the things clamber over their dead, undeterred.

Jarrett turns to fire on one scrambling up beside him. He pulls the trigger, and the forend snaps forward with a heart-sinking metallic clank.

"I'm out!" Jarrett shouts. He grabs the Mossberg by the barrel and slams the butt of the rifle into the dweller's forehead, splitting it down the middle like a ripe tangerine.

A gnarled hand grasps Shelly's ankle, knocking her down. She hacks at the thing's wrist with the cleaver, chopping out a wedge of muscle clear down to the bone, but the thing holds fast and drags her into the churning sea of ashen flesh.

"No!" Jarrett drops to his belly and reaches in after her, jerking his hand back when he feels a set of sharpened teeth dig into his forearm.

Shelly surfaces moments later, bloodied and barely recognizable –a slab of meat in tattered rags. The dwellers make short work of her, tearing her apart with brutal efficiency.

Fong cries out and empties his clip into the heart of the scrum. Once he's out of ammo, he drops the gun at his feet, looks at Jarrett, and swallows hard.

And then Jarrett hears it; a distant whirring sound that gives way to a high-pitched whine.

He knows this sound.

It's a fan favorite.

And he knows what comes next.

The dwellers turn toward the mouth of the alley. Jarrett grabs Fong by the shirt and drags him back over the dumpster. They hit the pavement hard, and Fong gives him a dazed, slightly annoyed look. Jarrett wraps his arms around him.

"No matter what happens, keep your head—"

The rest is drowned out by a percussive barrage of lead, muted screams, and an avalanche of brick and mortar that pours down on

Jarrett and Fong as the wall behind them is reduced to rubble. Bullets perforate the steel trash container, showering them in sparks and superheated shards of metal. Fong is wrapped around Jarrett so tightly he can hardly breathe.

When the hail of fire finally subsides, Jarrett peels the trembling Fong off and peeks over the decimated dumpster.

Sheila Joy—as bloodied and naked as the day she was born—sloshes toward them through an ankle-deep slurry of dwellers. She lowers the barrel of the XM214 Minigun–this week's Zone Three power-up–takes her finger off of the trigger, and smiles as the whirring motor winds down.

"Fuckin' A, is this thing *neat* or what?"

—8—

"What are you doing here, Dev?" Jarrett asks, throwing the empty Mossberg to the ground before him.

The Washington Square checkpoint is the staging ground for the fourth and final zone of Dead Heat. But, instead of a crate of ammunition and supplies, Jarrett, Fong, and Sheila find a Network shuttle surrounded by a sextet of guards. Devon Kincaid sits cross-legged on a rotted picnic table, decked out in a glossy white leather trench coat, black leather pants, and her signature skinny red tie Her spiked blonde hair dances lazily in the updraft from the shuttle engines. Against the burnt orange sky, it reminds Jarrett of lapping flames.

She takes a quick nip from a silver flask, stuffs the flask back into her coat, and stands, arms outstretched.

"Sorry folks," she smiles. "Technical difficulties!" Dev hops down from the picnic table and waves a pair of the guards over to her. "And, due to circumstances beyond our control, I'm sad to report that this week's race will not be completed."

"So what this mean?" Fong asks.

"Well, it means that the race is over, my tiny friend," she says, staring down at him.

Fong looks to Jarrett. "And we win?"

Jarrett smirks. His eyes lock with Dev's. "I don't think so, Tony."

"Always such a cynic, Jarrett." Dev frowns. She turns to Fong and Sheila and the plastic smile spreads back across her face. "You're *all* winners! Just not grand prize winners." She holds up her fingers and makes little quotes around the words "grand prize," as if to suggest that it's no big deal. "But we do have some lovely parting gifts for you," she says, nodding back toward the shuttle. "And, if you go with these gentlemen, they'll tell you all about it."

The guards raise their rifles and start to usher them toward the ship when Dev pulls Jarrett aside. "I just want a minute with this one," she says.

The lead guard nods and moves the others along.

"I really hope it's a new microwave," Sheila Joy says. She smiles blankly at Jarrett through a mask of dried blood. "I'll let it be a surprise, though. I love surprises."

Fong frowns. "This no good, Cowboy," he says. "This smell bad!"

"Walk with me, " Dev rests her hand on Jarrett's shoulder and guides him through a thicket of gnarled bushes and dead trees to a clearing far from the shuttle. "You think you had me fooled, don't you Jarrett?"

"I don't know what you're talking about," Jarrett says.

"Oh, cut the shit, kid. I was on to you from the beginning." She stops and spins him toward her. "But you know what? I didn't care. I wanted to let you keep going. I mean, fuck, you guys were putting on such a great show!"

"So what's the problem?" Jarrett says. "Why not let us finish?"

"The problem is," Dev stops and turns him toward her, "you made it look *too* easy."

"Nothing about what I just went through was—"

"Shhhh," Dev puts her hand over his mouth. "You got sloppy and you got obvious and you made it look too fucking easy," she whispers. "And that raises questions, Jarrett. Questions about the integrity of the show. Questions about *my* integrity. And I just can't have that. So…I had to pull the plug."

"That's bullshit, Dev," Jarrett says.

She grimaces and points a long, bony finger in his face. "No, Jarrett. You want to know what bullshit is? Bullshit is when the Network president calls me halfway through *my* fucking television show to ask if tonight's episode is *fixed*. The *Network president*, Jarrett. If that half-blind fossil noticed something was up, what do you think the rest of the audience saw?"

"So what happens next?" Jarrett asks. "To them? To me?"

"Yeah, that...." Dev shrugs. "Well...it's a shame about the Chinaman," she says. A single shot rings out from behind the shuttle. Dev flinches. "He tested through the roof!"

Another shot. "The old lady, eh, not so much."

"No!" Jarrett lunges past her, back toward the shuttle. As he does, a third shot echoes through the park.

This time it comes from behind him.

Jarrett stumbles. A searing pain spreads across his shoulder blades; something warm and wet trickles down his belly. His hand brushes against the frayed flesh of the exit wound in the center of his chest as he turns back to Dev and falls to his knees.

Dev lowers the pistol as she walks forward and crouches beside him. She holds him to her, gently patting him on the back. "You made me look bad, Jarrett. An you should know that's something I just won't tolerate."

"You're...a fucking cunt, Dev," Jarrett says. He can hear the footfalls of the guards as they approach.

She smiles. "I am what God made me."

"And...you know what..else?" Jarrett whispers.

Dev rolls her eyes. "Oh, do tell."

"You're infected."

Jarrett lunges forward, biting into her cheek. He feels his teeth snap through the skin, tearing flesh from muscle, the bitter tang of salt and copper on his tongue. Dev pulls herself free and scurries away from him, eyes wide, a bewildered half-smile on her face.

Jarrett falls back and laughs. He rolls up his sleeve and shows her the ragged bite on his arm.

"I was a dead…man anyway," he says.

It's a lie, of course. A dweller bite is harmless, really. Nothing that some industrial-grade antibiotics and a round of chemotherapy won't take care of.

But there are no cameras in that alley.

And Devon Kincaid doesn't *know* it's a dweller bite.

Neither do the three guards who rush into the clearing.

"She's infected!" Jarrett yells. He scrambles to his knees, holds up his wounded arm, and flashes the guards a bloody smile. "That…bitch is…fucking…infec—"

A shotgun blast to the stomach hurls Jarrett back into the base of a burned-out oak. His head lolls forward and he stares down at the cavernous wound in his belly. The contents of his stomach spill out into his lap, and as he feebly tries to stuff them back in, he lets out a weak laugh.

"No, you idiots! Wait!" Dev shouts. She charges toward them, one hand pressed to her bloodied cheek, the other still clutching the pistol.

The guards open fire.

Jarrett gives up on wrangling his slippery guts and lets his head fall back against the tree to enjoy the rest of the show. He only wishes the cameras were on for this.

It would make for some seriously good television.

Tasting Green Grass

Elaine Blose

Calvin should have heard from her by now.

He sat surrounded by an array of mismatched video screens, watching images flashing and reflecting past his sad black cow eyes. Information was broadcast on a twenty-four hour feed: news footage from a broken world left to die. His interest focused on the stream of incoming messages from the generation ships that had left Earth. Until that message arrived, he could not—would not—tear himself away to watch anything else.

On a screen to his far left, a pundit on some news talk show caught his attention. "We're not sure where the creatures came from. Too much data has been lost through the ages and in the war. Hell, we don't even know where we came from. Some say evolution, others say religion, but really, how sure are we of either belief?"

A second man spoke up. "It has been said that at one time there were people and animals, not people, animals and creatures. Many believe mankind has created the various creature species, and if this is so, then we have brought this destruction on ourselves."

"There is no evidence to support that!" interjected the first man. "Besides, not all creatures are bad. You're stereotyping again. We could have achieved peace with them if—"

Calvin had heard enough.

He closed his eyes and sighed. Calista should have sent her message by now. Naturally, the response time became longer and longer as the ships traveled farther away from Earth, but even taking the delay into account, receiving her communications had never taken this long. He opened his eyes and found himself unable to concentrate on the feeds.

Calvin's body ached from sitting in wait for so long. He stood up and stretched out his body as he walked around his tiny home — a forgotten fabricated building in the middle of a small, deserted country town. The only light came from the tower of glowing monitors. Going over to one wall, he looked again at the aged photograph of a green pasture with grazing cattle and snow-capped mountains looming majestically in the background.

Was the photo of a real place? Calista had always insisted it was. Could Earth ever have looked like that? Often, he wondered what that green grass would have tasted like; the thoughts prompted his bovine gene artifacts to make his mouth water.

Blood flowing again, he went back to his patched-up office chair in front of the monstrosity of screens. Despite the break, his eyes watered again after only a few minutes. Calvin needed to sleep, but instead he scanned the news feeds once more. More of the same doom and gloom talk he'd heard for over a year now: scientists predicting how much longer the planet would last, others who thought things were getting better, and the vocal minority who thought it was a mistake for the rest of the populace to head for the stars.

The war between humans and creatures had taken its toll on the world. Both sides had taken heavy losses. After the war, half of the human populace had fled Earth for a new planet, leaving the rest behind to fight.

As he browsed the news feeds he caught a report about a recent creature attack on a nearby human city. Attacks were happening more and more in recent months. But what had grabbed Calvin's attention were the reptile attackers. This wasn't the first time he'd seen this particular squad on the news. He paused and zoomed in on the reptiles one by one. When he got to the last one, he froze.

Calvin jumped at the sudden pounding at his door. Grabbing a gun, he looked at the surveillance screens that showed the grounds outside his hovel.

It was Dragyn.

Calvin set the gun down and switched the frozen news image to another channel before opening the door.

"I didn't wake you, did I?" In walked a reptilian humanoid creature covered with hard green scales and leathery bat-like wings that were folding in behind him.

Calvin noticed the sun rising above the horizon before he shut the door. "No, I was up."

"I was going to come later, but it's already hot outside. Besides, I figured you'd have things you'd want to do today." Dragyn held up a bag while making a face. "I brought some food...well, vegetation."

"Thanks." Calvin took the bag and set it down on his tiny kitchen table.

"Are you still watching all this crap?" Dragyn stood in front of the video screens, appraising the scene. "Honestly, I can't figure out what it is you watch. You need to get out of this dumpy shack." Dragyn looked at Calvin. "Have you been watching this all night?"

"Not sure."

"You look like hell. When *was* the last time you slept?"

Calvin shrugged.

"What's wrong with you?"

Calvin didn't answer.

"Have you had any progress finding the rest of your species?"

"I gave up."

"What? When did this happen? And more importantly, why?"

Calvin slumped into a chair by the kitchen table. "I've searched for years and have come up with nothing. If they're out there, they don't want to be found." Calvin frowned. "What if they were all killed in the war and I'm the last one left?"

"Oh come off it. You're not the last one."

"You ever wonder—what are we?" Calvin asked.

Dragyn rolled his eyes. "Not this discussion again."

"Do you think the humans made us? Or was it really evolution?"

"Calvin, I honestly don't know, and if I did I'd tell you. You need to pull yourself together. You weren't like this when we served in the war." Dragyn's wings expanded behind him. "I remember the fierce warrior who fought in the military with me. What's happened to you?"

"I need some sleep."

"It's more than that. You were already holed up in this hovel when I found you. Too afraid to leave. More interested in watching this crap," Dragyn motioned at the wall of monitors, "than anything else. And while we're at it, you never did tell me why you changed your name to something that sounds so...*human.*" Dragyn's wings retracted toward his body. "I worry about you."

"I know."

Dragyn shook his head. "Well then," he said as headed for the door, "I'll leave you to your sleep. I'll be back in a few days to check on you." A hot, dusty breeze rushed in when Dragyn opened the door. He glanced at Calvin. "TV rots the brain, you know." Then he was gone.

Calvin sighed. Going back to his video screens, he brought up the paused image of the reptile warrior. Dragyn. He let the image go. Unable to stay awake any longer, he went to his cot and lay down.

He fell asleep instantly, only to be awakened an hour later by a loud alarm.

He leaped out of bed and dashed to the monitors and fumbled with the controls. An image of a teenage girl with tousled black hair and lots of blue and black eye makeup, holding a white teddy bear, appeared on screen.

"Hey Calvin." She held up the bear and made him wave at the camera, then lowered him, "and anyone else who gets this. First off, I miss you sooooo much. Also, if it seems like it's been forever since I sent you something, it's because my parents found your messages to me.

"They freaked out and told me I wasn't allowed to talk to you anymore. We got into a major fight over it. In the end, I told them that I've known you for years and that we hung out together on Earth all the time and that I tried to help you find your people.

"Then I explained to them that you're on Earth and I'm on this stupid ship and there is nothing wrong with us talking. They finally caved. Since I no longer have to sneak to send you messages I can send you something whenever I want now." The smile on Calista's face made Calvin's heart ache.

"Believe me, as bored as I am, I'll be sending you stuff all the time. I have to make time count, because my parents told me during our fight that I might not be able to communicate with you when we get to the planet because we'll be too far away.

"What will I do if I can't talk to you? I should have stayed behind with you like I wanted to. I hate this boring ship.

"It gets worse. They explained to me it will take years to reach the planet. They said they lied to me about how long the trip would take just to get me off Earth.

"Can you believe it? Guess there is nothing I can do about it now. Parents!

"Enough about my problems. You have to tell me everything that's going on with you. Any new friends yet? You promised you were going to make some new friends at that creature town by your home. What about finding your people, any luck there? You have to tell me *everything*.

"Anyway, I gotta get going. I just got my message privileges back and wanted to send you something before I went to bed. I miss you Cal and I love you. Oh, and Beeker loves you too." She held up the bear and made him wave again. "Calista signing off."

The screen went blank, but Calvin quickly replayed her message. At least now he knew why Calista had taken so long to respond and was relieved to hear that she was all right.

He couldn't believe how big Calista had gotten compared to when he had met her—a little tyke who loved everything and trusted everyone. She was a rebellious teenager now, and he still loved her just as much. He wondered if she'd told her parents that Beeker had been a gift from him. How much longer until she thought herself too old for that stuffed bear?

As Calvin replayed her message he thought about Dragyn. He had never told Calista about Dragyn—or Dragyn about Calista.

What would she think of him hanging around someone he had served with in the military? Calvin had told her he'd fought in the war and had been forced to do horrible things. He hated that part of his life, but Calista didn't care. She told him he was a good person and that the war was over.

Calvin also wondered what she would think of him for giving up on trying to find his own kind. He couldn't lie to her; she always knew when he did.

Finding his people had turned into such an ordeal. When he'd first sent out a message looking for them, thieves and scavengers were the only ones who sought him out. Calista had helped him to reroute the signal and showed him how to use a constantly changing variable so no one could find his location, but they would still be able to use the contact number to send a message to him. After Calista left, the search became monotonous. He had nearly given up when Dragyn had found him, but his efforts had only renewed for a short time. Finally, he'd faced the fact that he wasn't going to find them.

Then there was the creature town. Calvin had promised her that he would go and make new friends. Shame washed through him as he thought about all these things.

Calvin went to the kitchen and began to put away the canned vegetables Dragyn had brought. He thought again about what Calista had said about not being able to communicate when she got to the planet. How much time did they have left? When would the ships be too far out for the communications to get to Earth? Then he realized that Dragyn was all he would have left.

Something on one of the cans pulled him from his thoughts. On closer examination, he realized it was a speck of dried blood.

Calvin put the can down. He marched over to the monitors. Deep down he knew he shouldn't be relying on Dragyn. He glanced up at the monitors to see the broken world that lay outside his door. Everyone, humans and creatures, lived in disease, poverty, and violence. The outside frightened him.

Yet Calista had befriended him. A pure flower among the

savage weeds. He remembered when she had stumbled upon him in an old barn where he had already begun hiding from the world. A complete coward.

Calvin knew what he had to do. He moved in front of a screen and began recording a message for her.

"Calista, I got your message. I swear you've grown even more since your last one. I still haven't had any luck finding my people." He figured it wasn't a complete lie. "I'll let you know if I do. I miss you more than you know. I wish you were still here with me. You were never afraid, always brave." He paused. "Not like me, a complete coward. I haven't gone to the creature town yet, but I'm going to right after this message. I'll take that big ax you found and go. What you must think of me for not going. You're right, I need to make some new friends. Someone good like you.

"You take care and don't be giving your parents a hard time. If they find this message, I want them to know what a wonderful child they have who I am proud to have as a friend. I miss you and love you so much. Calvin out."

Calvin sent the message. He went over to the trunk where he kept armor and weapons and withdrew a three-foot-long round metal stick. He pushed a small button and it extended and formed a nasty-looking ax head at the top.

Calista had found it one time when they were looking through an abandoned building and had insisted he take it for protection. He smiled in remembrance at the way she always fussed over him.

He retracted the ax and went to the video screens, only instead of watching everything going on in the world, he began planning a trip to the nearest creature town.

Two days later, he stood facing the door to the outside, trying to work up the nerve to open it. Calvin knew he had to do this. He had routes mapped and had come up with visuals of the town he was going to find.

Taking a deep breath, he opened the door.

A warm blast of wind hit him. His hands shook as he locked the door behind him. He fought the mounting urge to turn around and go back with each step he took toward the building where he kept a small hover vehicle. He got in and set a course in the computer. His heart raced as he started the engine. The building doors opened automatically and he pulled out. He noticed that a couple of small buildings next to his home had caved in and wondered when that had happened.

The vehicle increased speed as he got past the buildings. Calvin absorbed the landscape around him. There was not much to see other than sparse vegetation and dust. He thought back to the picture on his wall of cattle grazing and still couldn't comprehend how Earth could have ever had such a place.

Again, thoughts of fresh green grass made his mouth water. Like his distant kin, he was a vegetarian, and it had been said that if not for that fact, his kind would have been the most feared fighters on the planet due to their sheer strength and power. However, without the bloodlust, the drive to commit violence was dampened. Personally, Calvin couldn't stand the sight of blood. Perhaps this was why he was such a coward. He'd had his fill of everything violent during the war.

Calvin's thoughts were pulled away when the remains of a domed city came into view. As he drew closer, he saw the shards of the shattered dome sticking out of the ground like broken tombstones in a forgotten cemetery. He was currently receiving broadcasts from the city, which meant humans still lived among the rubble. He kept his distance, and soon it was out of sight.

Forty-five minutes later he arrived at his destination—a small town in the middle of a wasteland. Dust blew across the streets; pavement was of no use in a place like this. His vehicle slowed as he entered the town of fabricated buildings that bravely stood up to the wind and dust that left them colorless and drab with only lighted signs to give them personality. Few people were out, and no one seemed to pay any attention as he came to a small tavern bearing a weather-beaten sign stating "Food and Spirits." His research had told him this was a friendly place with good food.

As the evening light faded, Calvin wondered what came out in the darkness. Pushing such thoughts aside, he took a deep breath and got out of his vehicle.

A couple, their species unknown to Calvin, stopped and stared at him. He ignored the rude gawking and stepped inside the tavern.

The smell of food hit him hard, sending his twin stomachs into growling fits. Hunger temporarily washed away his fear. He took a seat at the bar, even though few people sat at the serving tables. Calvin felt huge in his seven-foot frame, which caused him to slouch unconsciously.

The bartender stepped up to Calvin. He looked human, except for a set of pointed ears and green cat-like eyes. "What can I get you?"

"A menu."

The man nodded to something in front of Calvin. Calvin didn't understand and felt embarrassment flush his face.

The bartender said, "Push here." He pushed on the countertop in front of Calvin and a menu appeared in bright colors on the counter's surface.

"Thanks," Calvin muttered.

"Don't worry, you're not from here. Can't remember the last time I've seen one of your kind."

Calvin stared into the bartender's eyes. "You've seen my kind before?"

The bartender shook his head. "It's been many, many years. Didn't think there were any more left." He pointed to the menu. "Just push for your selection and I'll get it right out to you." The bartender walked to the other end of the bar and poured a beer out of a tap for another customer.

Calvin made his selection and entered his credit code. The menu disappeared and soon after the bartender brought his drink.

Calvin chanced a look around. Tables and chairs took up most of the floor space. A few people were playing a card game of some sort in the corner. Off to the side of them was a small area reserved as a dance floor. In front of him, behind the bar, was a mirror that showed his reflection of dun-colored cow-like features and horns sticking out from either side of his head. The mirror also showed a man with a long face and even longer black hair walking up behind him.

"Where did you crawl out from?" the stranger asked as he strolled up beside Calvin.

Calvin tensed.

"Easy now, I ain't lookin' for trouble." He sat down next to Calvin. "Name's Dancer." He held out a hand.

Calvin hesitated. Then, not knowing what else to do, shook Dancer's hand and said, "Calvin."

"Calvin is it? Odd name for one of us. That's more of a human name. Is that what your parents really named you?"

"No." The bartender brought Calvin's food. "Had a friend who said that Calvin sounded a lot like cow."

Dancer laughed.

Calvin wanted to flee, but the sight and smell of the large vegetable salad kept him planted.

Dancer's laughter died down. "So you stuck with it? That's all right. Where's your friend?"

"Gone." Even though he didn't get out much, he knew to never tell another creature he had a human friend. So Calvin just sat there digging into his food.

"I'm sorry. I didn't mean to be nosy. So where ya headed?"

"I, uh, just came to get something to eat."

"I'm curious why you're not with the rest of your kind."

Calvin stopped with his fork halfway to his mouth and looked at Dancer, "I have no idea where they are or if there are any more like me left. Have you seen others?" Calvin asked anxiously.

"Well," Dancer hesitated, "actually, I haven't seen any around here...but I know you guys stick together and I must admit I've never seen a lone wanderer of your species before." Then Dancer glanced all around him, and in a low voice, he said, "Best be careful. You stand out, and if the reptiles find you, no tellin' what may happen."

"Reptiles?"

Dancer's expression grew serious. "Lots remember when your

kind was around and the type of fighters you were. Powerful group, your species. If a reptile found you, they would try to recruit you to their cause. They're trying to get rid of the rest of the humans. Once they're gone, many of us fear the reptiles will come after us next."

Calvin's heart sank to his stomach.

"You all right?" Dancer asked. "Didn't mean to scare you or nothin', just tellin' ya to watch yourself. Then again, if you've survived this long on your own, then you've nothin' to worry about."

Calvin glanced around him and saw the place was filling up. People eyed him and whispered to one another. He looked at his plate, and since his food was nearly gone, he got up. "I have to go."

"Hey now, you okay? Like I said, I didn't mean to scare ya or nothin'."

"No, I...." he looked around again. "I don't like crowds." He headed for the door.

"I'll walk out with ya."

Calvin's heart beat like a frenzied drummer, and his breathing came in short gasps.

As he got to his vehicle, Dancer's voice called out. "Calvin, wait a minute." Dancer caught up to him. "You sure you all right? Look, if I said somethin' I shouldn't have, I'm sorry."

Calvin grabbed onto his vehicle to steady himself.

"Listen, don't know if you're staying in the area, but here." He handed Calvin some sort of holographic card. "This is where you can get in touch with me. Come back around. I'm usually here every night." Dancer glanced around him and then whispered, "Maybe I can help you find your people."

He seemed so sincere, like Calista, and then Calvin remembered why he had come. "I'll come back."

Dancer smiled, nodded, and went back to the bar.

When he was out of sight, Calvin hopped into his vehicle and tore away from the town. He tried to calm his tattered breathing in order to concentrate on where he was going. He knew Dragyn and his friends had been causing trouble, but to hear someone else say what the reptiles were doing suddenly made Calvin feel ashamed. If

Calista knew any of this...but he couldn't think about that now. He stopped a few miles out of town and calmed himself before setting the computer with the course for home.

As Calvin watched the night landscape go by, all he could think about was his conversation with Dancer. Was that why Dragyn had been pushing him to find his species? Calvin had just figured Dragyn was tired of looking after him.

A part of Calvin refused to believe any of this about Dragyn. They had been friends since the war, and Calvin enjoyed his company. All these thoughts swirled in his head as he rode back past the ruined city. A spectral glow radiated above the center of the city, and it made Calvin wonder how much longer any of them had left.

Dragyn came around the next day.

"You look better," he said when Calvin let him in. "Got some sleep, then?"

"Yeah."

"Brought a bit more food for you." Dragyn handed Calvin a bag and said,"I have also brought some great news."

"What kind of news?"

"It's rumored that one of your species was spotted last night. The details are sketchy, but isn't that great?"

"And?" Calvin wondered what Dragyn was going to say about him going out.

"And? Is that all you can say? Come on, this could be a sign. You might be able to find your people at last. You need to send a message, maybe this one knows something."

Then it hit him—Dragyn didn't realize that it was Calvin who had been out last night. Calvin never left his hovel and Dragyn knew it, so why would Dragyn think the creature was him?

With this in mind, Calvin asked, "Why are you so intent on me finding my species?"

"Because I worry about you, why else?"

"I don't know, you just seem so adamant about it."

"I'm adamant about it? I do believe it was you, when we were fighting the war, who kept saying that when the war was over you were going to find your people. Was it not?"

Dragyn had a good point, but Calvin pushed further. "I've seen you and your friends on the news."

"What do you mean?"

"Saw you attacking the humans." Calvin looked him in the eye. "War's over, you know."

"Of course I know that. Believe me, killing is the last thing I want to do. But honestly, where do you think your food comes from? The humans tried to drive us to extinction. Now *all* of us struggle for survival. You should know this from watching TV." He waved at the monitors.

Calvin sighed. "You're right."

Dragyn changed the subject and was going on about something else, but Calvin wasn't listening. Maybe Dragyn wasn't involved. Calvin didn't know what to think. Dragyn stayed a while longer, then left. As much as Calvin wanted to believe him, he couldn't shake the nagging feeling in his gut that he needed to put distance between them.

A couple of days later, Calvin worked up the nerve to go back to the creature town. In that time, he had seen Dragyn and his friends attacking the ruined city not far from him. The news reported several human causalities, and as Calvin drove past, smoke still spiraled up in several places. All Calvin could think about was what Dancer had said about the reptiles.

Calvin was more at ease when he entered the tavern this time. He sat down at the bar and pushed the counter for the menu. The bartender smiled and gave a nod as he passed by. When he brought Calvin's drink, he said, "See you came back."

"I liked the food."

Dancer's voice came from behind. "You must be eating somethin' pretty terrible to think this food's good."

"Or maybe he has better taste than you," the bartender replied.

Dancer sat down next to Calvin. "Was beginning to think I wasn't goin' to see ya again." He, too, ordered a drink. "Figured you'd moved on. How long you been on the road?"

Calvin took a deep breath and said, "I haven't been wandering. I live not far away."

"So why haven't you been around before?"

Calvin looked away and down at the scratched-up bar. "Because the outside scares me."

In a soft voice, Dancer said, "It scares all of us these days."

"You said you haven't seen any of my kind around here. But you've seen them somewhere else, haven't you?"

This time Dancer looked away. "A long time ago. Who knows what's happened by now."

Calvin got the feeling Dancer wasn't telling him everything. "I've tried to find them. Sent out messages looking for others like me, but so far I've come up with nothing."

"With the reptiles looking for them, I doubt you'll hear anything."

Calvin sighed.

"Don't you worry. Didn't I tell ya I'd try to help you find them?"

The bartender brought Calvin a big plate of mixed vegetables, and the aroma instantly caused his mouth to water.

"I'm curious, and tell me if I'm being too nosy," Dancer took a drink, "but if you live around here, why come out now? I mean, granted, I can understand the scared part, but still, why now?"

Between mouthfuls of food, Calvin answered, "I promised a friend that I'd get out more."

"The one that named you?"

"Yeah."

"Well don't you worry, ya got friends now."

Calvin couldn't wait to tell Calista about all of this. He had finished up his meal and was about to order another drink when the place suddenly fell silent. In the mirror behind the bar he saw reptiles entering the tavern and noticed that both Dancer and the bartender had uneasy expressions.

"Who do we have here?" a familiar voice asked.

Calvin's heart sank. Dragyn came over to the other side of Calvin.

"What a surprise to see my old friend getting out and about."

He sat down and ordered a drink. "In a way, I'm hurt. I've been supplying you with food for how long now? And not only have you left your hovel for the outside world, but you came out for food. I'm hurt, Calvin. Why didn't you say anything?"

Dancer glared at Calvin. When the bartender came over with Dragyn's drink, he also glared at him. Suddenly, Calvin knew he'd never be able to come back because of Dragyn.

Without a word, Calvin got up.

"Where do you think you're going?"

Calvin said nothing.

"Not so fast." Dragyn got up, his wings spread slightly. "Let me buy you a drink. I mean, come on, the first time you've been out in how long, the least you could do is let your best friend buy you a drink."

Calvin clenched his fists and could feel everyone's eyes on him. "Should have come earlier, then," he said and continued toward the exit.

Once outside, dust hit Calvin in the face. He was almost to his vehicle when Dragyn yelled, "That's it, run home! After all, I doubt anyone wants to be your friend here. Go back to your TVs. I'll stop by later and we can have that drink."

Calvin got in his vehicle and drove at breakneck speed all the way home.

Once there, he bolted the door and made sure the surveillance cameras were working properly. After that, he slumped into his chair in front of the video screens.

Calvin knew he would never be able to find his people or make new friends now. He'd have to leave. Leave his home and never come back.

But where would he go?

He saw something shiny at the base of the monitors; it was the card Dancer had given him. Calvin flipped it over in his hands and decided he had nothing to lose. He inserted the card into his communications array. Disappointment engulfed him when a message service came up, but helpless to do anything else, he left a message.

"Dancer, I'm sorry about what happened. I...I should have told you that the reptiles had already found me. I don't want nothing to do with them. I, uh...look, if you get this, please call me back."

Calvin sighed and doubted he'd hear back.

He sat there and stared at the screens but didn't see any of the images that passed by him. Instead, Calvin's mind thought over what few options he had.

A message alarm brought Calvin out of his stupor. He thought Calista must really be bored to send something so soon.

When her face appeared, his first thought was that she was trying new makeup. Then, to his horror, he saw blood on her face. "Calvin." She glanced behind her. "We're under attack. It's creatures—reptile creatures. We don't know where they came from or how they got here." A noise, like an explosion, caused Calista to jump. Tears streaked down her cheeks through the blood. "I knew I should have stayed on Earth with you. I don't want to be on this stupid ship anymore." Another explosion, only closer this time. Calista shrieked. "I don't know what to do. I'm scared." A louder explosion this time. Calista threw her arms over her head and ducked. She came back up hysterical. "I don't want to die." She glanced behind her. "They're coming for me. Oh God, Calvin, why? If you don't hear from me again, I want you to know what happened to me. You've gotta keep on. I love you, Calvin." Calvin saw Beeker lying next to Calista; one arm was missing, bits of white fur were singed, and he was spotted with blood. As Calista reached a shaky hand to send the message, something entered the room from behind her. Then the screen went blank.

Calvin couldn't believe what he had just witnessed. He replayed the message. When it came to the end, he paused and zoomed in on what was coming from behind.

A reptile creature.

A very large one, different from Dragyn, but a reptile nonetheless.

Calvin replayed the message again, and again, and again, until realization finally set in.

Calista was gone.

Another transmission caught his eye on a screen to the right. A soldier on one of the ships informing Earth of the attacks.

Calvin's breath came in short gasps until it turned into snorts of rage. Red filled his vision. He stood and let out an ear-shattering bellow.

He sat back down, taking deep breaths, trying to calm himself.

Then came the horror.

All his monitors were alive with messages from the ships, visions more horrific than anything he had seen during the war. People with blood on them making desperate pleas and being cut down by the reptiles. People fighting for their lives. It was like the screens were showing different parts of the same horror film.

Calvin couldn't watch anymore as the tears rolled down his face. He went to his cot and curled up into a ball.

He was all alone now.

Calvin wept and wept until he settled into a numb trance. He came out of it when someone pounded at his door.

The surveillance screens showed Dragyn. Movement flickered on a screen to the right, then a different reptile figure came into view on a screen above that one.

Dragyn had brought his friends.

Calvin went to his trunk and pulled out his old military armor. The banging on his door grew louder. Calvin's breath came faster as he suited up and armed himself. He took up position in front of the door with a rifle. He watched Dragyn on the monitor.

Did Dragyn know about the ships? Again, he thought back to what Dancer had said about the reptiles wanting to take over. It was then that Calvin realized he shouldn't have stayed in his shack after Calista left. He should have been out making friends and finding his people.

It was too late for everything now.

He saw Dragyn rig something to the door. Calvin was ready.

An explosion sounded. When movement came through the dust and smoke, Calvin opened fire. He took down two for sure. Then there was nothing.

The surveillance screens showed four more outside.

"Calvin, we should talk," came Dragyn's voice. "I know those creatures probably filled your head with lies about us. I'm your friend, Calvin."

"If that's true, then you won't shoot me when I come out?"

"Of course not." He saw Dragyn give orders and everyone lowered their weapons.

He went outside and saw that dawn was breaking.

"What's this?" Dragyn asked when he saw Calvin. "What are you doing? Oh, this is ridiculous. There is no reason why we should be fighting."

"You started it. You blew up my door."

"I'll get you a new one." Dragyn stepped closer. "Lower the gun, Calvin."

"Did you know that the ships carrying the humans to the new planet have been destroyed?" Calvin felt the rage bubble through his veins as he said it.

A smile started at Dragyn's lips. "What? You're not serious." He tried to look surprised, but wasn't successful. "Who would do that?"

"Reptiles."

Dragyn's eyes narrowed. "Whatever the other creatures told you—"

"What would they have told me about you?"

Calvin caught movement out of the corner of his eye. He turned and fired at a reptile who had raised his gun.

Everyone opened fire then. Calvin took them all down except Dragyn.

When Dragyn saw he was the only one left, he took a step back. "Surely you don't think I knew about the ships? What's it to you, anyway? Why are you always defending the humans?"

"I had a friend on the ships."

"A friend?" Dragyn started laughing. "Creatures and humans are not friends. Believe me, this human was no friend of yours."

"Yes, she was!" Calvin's vision was red with full-blown rage.

He threw down his gun and withdrew the ax. It extended out in a flash, and the ax head gleamed in the early morning light.

Dragyn's eyes widened. He shot at Calvin and it pierced his armor, but nothing could stop Calvin in full rage. He ran head-on toward Dragyn, bringing the ax up over his head. He swung down easily, slicing through Dragyn's neck. The head flew to the ground, and the body fell like a marionette whose strings had been cut.

Calvin let out a bellow.

Looking up at the remaining stars, he yelled out "Calista!" and then he fell to his knees and began sobbing all over again as he hugged the ax.

He noticed the blood draining out of his wounds as the sun's first rays hit him. Lying down on the ground and rolling onto his back, still hugging the ax, Calvin noticed the clouds in the sky and thought back to the photo of the cattle grazing on green grass. He wondered if there would be green grass in the afterlife.

Then he knew it wasn't the green pastures he wanted—he wanted to see Calista again. He smiled at that as he watched the clouds drift by and squeezed the ax even closer, as if it were Calista herself.

"Well, if this isn't a right old mess," came a voice out of nowhere. "Hey guys, he's over here, and he ain't lookin' too good. Better hurry."

Then Calvin saw Dancer's long face and knew it was his voice.

"Hey Cal, don't worry, we got ya."

"How...?" said Calvin.

"Easy now." Dancer knelt beside him. "Some friends of mine have been looking for ya for some time. We've seen all your transmissions, but could never find your location and it was too risky to use the contact number. That card I gave ya had a tracker in it. Got here soon as we could."

Calvin turned his head and saw other creatures. His vision was fading, but if he didn't know any better, he'd think they had horns and faces like his.

"By the way," Dancer said. "Sorry about Calista."

ENDANGERED

Robby Sparks

"I heard about what you do," Zahra said, reaching out to touch Jack's shoulder.

He recoiled as if she were a leper. "I stopped that years ago!"

The woman stood by the bungalow, the same place she had been when Jack had pulled the dory up from the calm water of the inlet, returning from a day of fishing at sea.

"But I thought you could help me."

"Does it look like I can help?" Jack shouted, motioning at the trees and surrounding jungle. "Look where I live!" Wind rustled through the palms. Coconuts littered the ground. The sound of insects filled in the air. "I haven't used my generators in years. A couple of decades, in fact. They've probably eroded away. Junk on the ocean floor, home to sea urchins, sharks–God knows what else since the last mutation cycle. Damn polluted water," he grumbled.

Zahra wrung her hands against her tattered tunic shirt. "But you know what they'll do when they find out I'm pregnant."

The man steamed past her, up the makeshift steps and through the bamboo door of the hut. Zahra pleaded as she followed. "They'll either force me to have an abortion or they'll take my baby as soon as it's born."

Jack slapped a string of fish on the table and proceeded to strike a fire. "Answer me one question, then," he said, moving away from the kindling flame and stopping inches from Zahra's face. Sweat dripped from his shaggy white locks and deep wrinkles creased the corners of his eyes like a series of tributaries from the river Nile. "Why did you get pregnant?"

Zahra glanced at her sand-crusted toes.

"I...."

"Were you raped?"

She snapped her gaze up. "No!"

"Are you a whore?"

Without hesitation, she landed an open hand hard across Jack's bristled cheek. She stiffened her back and stared him down with a piercing glare. "I wanted a baby, okay? One that wasn't an issued clone! One that wasn't a cyborg. A real baby." Her face flushed as red as the jewel on her forehead, her eyes bulging with tears.

Jack backed away, rubbing his chin. "Then you should have gotten a dog." He shuffled across the room and fell backward into a hammock. "Hell, you should have gotten two."

Zahra bit her lip in an attempt to restrain her emotions, but failed miserably. Burying her face in her hands, she began to sob. "I don't know why I even came here," she cried. "They said that you'd help. That you were a kind and compassionate man." Looking up, she gathered her composure, wiping her nose with the back of her hand. "But now I see they were wrong."

Jack ignored her as his body rocked steadily from side to side, staring beyond the mosquito netting that covered the windows of the hut. "They sure were, honey," he grumbled. "They sure were."

Zahra's head dropped in despair, her hope shattered on the wooden floor. She hadn't expected to be turned away. Not in her wildest dreams. This man's colleagues had placed him on such a high pedestal she hadn't thought it possible for him to be anything other than a saint, a considerate scientist, a prominent humanitarian, a mentor and friend to all. But that must have been another time and another place, she thought. Or maybe another person altogether. The only things she had found here were a dilapidated shack and a cynical, loathsome hermit.

Turning, she made her way through the door and down the steps. "What will I do?" she asked herself. She couldn't go home. The monthly weigh-ins mandated by the government to ensure people weren't overconsuming food supplies would eventually re-veal her condition. Then her life and her baby's would be over. "There's got to be someplace I can go."

Desperate, she started rationalizing that if Jack could live in the jungle all by himself, maybe she could, too. Maybe she could have the baby right here. It wasn't as if babies weren't born hundreds of years ago in more strenuous conditions and harsher environments. It just might be a feasible thing to do. Maybe. Returning to so-called civilization certainly didn't appear to be an option.

She pondered her fate, walking away from the thatched-roof hut, crushed and defeated, when an arm snatched her from behind. She attempted to scream, but a large hand clamped over her mouth. Struggling to get free, she wiggled about until her captor's face came into view.

It was Jack.

"Shhh," he whispered, urging her to be quiet, but she didn't lis-ten. She continued to kick, hit, and scratch, trying everything to break loose from his grasp. But even at his age, Jack was strong as an ox.

Glancing back to the bungalow, Jack nodded his head. As he did, what looked like a small rusted trash can cocked sideways in the sand suddenly sprang to life, sprouting arms and hovering to-ward them with eyes blazing like fire. At the end of one arm spun a thin metallic probe.

Zahra shuddered.

Extending the probe, the robot produced some sort of electrical field, blue in color, that swept across Zahra's entire body. As the field passed over her thighs, something sizzled, and she winced in pain. A burning sensation warmed her side. She bit down, praying that whatever was happening didn't affect the child she carried–praying that this man who held her wasn't the devil himself, with the robot as his minion.

Then the blue light disappeared, and the robot's eyes turned a soft green.

Jack let Zahra go.

She squealed, gasping for breath that had been restricted by Jack's fish-ridden hand, reeling away aimlessly. "What did you do to me? What did you do to my baby?"

"Nothing," Jack said. He reached down and picked up a small pack Zahra had dropped in the sand. He seemed oddly calm. Sincere.

Zahra tugged on the lip of her pants and checked where a dark spot smoldered against her mahogany skin. "Don't you lie! You did something to me. What did you do?" She launched out at Jack with fists swinging, but he caught the punches, wrestling her arms down.

"I cleaned you," he said.

Zahra tried to kick him in the groin but missed.

"You had a bug," Jack explained. "A chip buried underneath your skin. We had to sweep you with a disruption field."

Zahra thrashed her knees about, punching Jack in his abdomen and causing him to grunt.

"Listen. A health official probably injected it during one of your physicals, you just didn't know it. It's one of the many liberties the government takes with citizens these days. Through it, they may have been tracking you, or even listening."

At this point, Zahra was convinced Jack was insane. One minute he was insulting her, the next minute, attacking her. Now, for some reason, he seemed concerned, albeit paranoid, talking about bugs and secret injections and people listening. A Dr. Jekyll and Mr. Hyde complex, for sure, she thought. A paranoid schizo-freak.

"How would you know if I had a bug on me?" she asked.

"Oro told me," Jack said, releasing Zahra's arms and stepping away from her kicks. The stumpy little robot beside him beeped and returned a sturdy salute. "She gave me the heads up when I saw you waiting for me. I'm truly sorry about the insults earlier. For making you cry. I hope you understand that your reaction was critical in determining whether or not you were sincere about needing help, or if you were sent here to extract details about my work or locations of the babies."

Zahra's heart leapt. "Babies?" She immediately dismissed her concerns about Jack's mental condition, her skepticism and anger replaced by hope and need. "Did you say 'babies'?"

"Yes."

Zahra fumbled with her hands for a moment, rubbing them together anxiously. Her mind seemed to drift, as if an unheard voice were speaking to her from another dimension, and her gaze turned inward. She began to think about all the things she had endured since becoming pregnant–the panic attacks, the increasing paranoia, the fear of being captured–and about the hope she had so desperately clung to. It had shattered a few moments ago, but was reforming into a new entity that shone brighter and more spectacular than before, flooding her soul.

"Does this mean you'll help me? That you'll help my baby?" she implored, almost panting with excitement.

Jack tossed the hair out of his face. "Of course. That's what I do. But we'll discuss that later. First, let's get you back inside and washed up. I'll cook some fish."

Jack led Zahra into the bungalow. They talked about irrelevancies as they ate, until the sun painted the evening clouds with swirls of orange and yellow that progressively faded into splashes of pink and beige, shifting like a kaleidoscope until darkness enveloped the world around them and stars filled the sky.

Jack pushed away the coconut shell he was using for a bowl. "So, back to the main reason you're here, which I know wasn't to taste my award-winning cuisine."

Zahra smiled.

"You're curious about how I can help you."

"Yes," she replied, sitting up in her chair.

Jack opened his mouth to explain, but found himself searching for the right words to say. This part was always the hardest.

"Basically, the way it works is, well, you won't be having your baby."

Zahra's eyes grew large with confusion.

"I mean you won't be giving birth, so to speak. Your fetus will be extracted and then grown in vitro, where I can monitor its development while keeping it safe."

"Oh," Zahra said. No one had mentioned that to her, although it seemed like a key piece of information. She didn't know whether to feel discouraged or glad about it.

Jack noticed. "You should be happy," he said. "No morning sickness. No labor pains. And most importantly, no birth."

She nodded half-heartedly. "I suppose. Guess in the meantime I can help out around here until the baby is born–or 'done'–whatever you call it, right?" She shifted about uneasily in her chair. "I'm a decent cook, you know. I just haven't done it in a while, since they started making us eat the goop. I used to fish a lot, too. With my dad before the rivers dried up. Of course, I can clean up well and I'm very handy at...."

Listening to Zahra struggle to find something to cling to in light of having her baby extracted, Jack didn't have the heart to tell her the true sacrifice that needed to be made. Rising out of his chair, he grabbed a lantern. "Let's go for a walk."

Together they left the bungalow and followed a meandering trail through the dark jungle. Palmettos swiped against their arms. Sea grapes bobbed on their heads. A rhythmic boom like cannons firing from an old British galleon pounded in the distance. Rumbling. Tumbling. The sound of crashing waves. The music of the sea.

The pounding grew louder as they approached the beach. Jack quelled the lantern and took a pair of special binoculars out of his pack. Staring through the eyepieces for a moment, he handed the spectacles to Zahra. "Look there." He pointed in the direction of the moonlit waters.

Through the lenses, nighttime appeared as day. After panning for a moment, Zahra saw something moving in the sand.

"Do you see her?" Jack asked.

Zahra peered harder and adjusted the focus until she could distinguish the large dome-shaped feature. "It looks like a turtle," she answered. "What is it doing?"

"She's laying eggs," Jack said. "Sea turtles come here every year to do so. They pull themselves out of the ocean and crawl several yards up on the beach, where they spend the night digging a nest."

Zahra watched in awe as the massive creature with no arms or hands used its fins to dig a crater in the sand.

"That's incredible. What does she do after she lays the eggs?"

"She covers the hole and leaves," Jack said.

"She doesn't stay around afterward or return when they're hatched?"

"No," Jack said.

"Do you think she ever sees her babies?"

"Perhaps. I'd like to think so. But she can't stay here with them, waiting for them to hatch."

Zahra eased the binoculars down from her face. She could tell by Jack's tone that this wasn't a simple lesson about sea turtles. The gravity of the scene sank in. "I can't stay, can I?"

Jack shook his head.

"But I can help get food and—"

"It's too dangerous."

"But I wanted—"

"A baby. I know."

"But...but I want to hold it. Love it."

"And hopefully you will. It'll just take some time to get him or her integrated into the system without the Coalition knowing the child is not a clone. My people have ways of getting children in. We do it every day. But first we have to get you back in. If your bug was being actively used, then the government already knows you're pregnant. They'll be looking for you when you return, so we'll have to change your identity. That process must be started right away."

Anguish and despair crossed Zahra's face. Jack took her hand. "You're going to have to trust me on this. My people and I, we'll do everything in our power to place you and your baby back together. I promise. It's the best alternative you have."

Zahra sighed in frustration. "But I don't understand why I can't stay."

"Think about it," Jack said. "What if every mother I helped stayed here? This isolated place in the middle of nowhere wouldn't be so isolated anymore. It would become a community. One bungalow would turn into twenty. Satellite surveillance would certainly pick up on the increased activity. We'd cease to be off the grid, and my work would be compromised. That's why; for the safety of the mothers and babies–for the future of mankind itself–you have to leave."

After a quiet moment of thought, Zahra acknowledged with a nod.

Jack put his arm around her. "Come on. I'll take you back and show you the lab. You'll be happy to know your baby will be in good hands."

Approaching the hut, Jack veered south a few hundred yards before stopping by a pile of dead branches and palm fronds. A tug on one of the branches resulted in a quiet hiss of air as the debris swung unnaturally upward, revealing a hidden passage with stairs leading into the ground. Cool, dry air emanated from the opening, slicing into the thick layer of humidity outside. Instead of being constructed of bamboo, straw, and deadwood like the bungalow, the walls of the stairwell were immaculately clean, white, and pristine. The stairs, smooth and clear, were almost like glass. Jack and Zahra descended. Soon, a room filled with high-tech equipment, monitors, and medical supplies came into view. Set into the far wall was a row of holograms, barely distinguishable. As Jack flicked a switch to make them clearer, images of embryos in different stages of development appeared. Underneath each figure was a name.

David.
Miguel.
Renee.
Nishiko.
Hope.

There were at least three dozen more.

"These are real-time images of the babies I'm tending," said Jack.

As Zahra observed them–some pink and barely formed, others almost to maturity–Jack spread a clean sheet across one of the tables and patted his hand on the slab.

"Hop up here. Let's see how your little guy or gal is doing."

Jack helped Zahra lie back on the table and asked her to pull up her shirt. Then, fitting a small device into his palm, he waved his hand slowly across her abdomen. A moment later, one of the holographic images changed.

A fetus appeared, no bigger than a kumquat.

"Is that my baby?" Zahra asked.

"That's it," Jack said.

Zahra beamed with joy. "It's beautiful."

Jack brought up some data and studied the numbers a moment. "Everything looks good, too. Stable. Healthy. There should be no problem with the extraction and transfer. In fact, we can probably get started tomorrow, as soon as–"

An odd dinging noise interrupted his words, like the sound of soup cans being clanged by a spoon.

"What's that?" Zahra asked.

Jack turned to see two canisters tumbling down the passageway, bouncing and ricocheting off the steps. As they fell to the bottom and rolled along the expanse of the main floor, a white gas began to seep from their ends.

"They're here!" he said.

"Who?" Zahra asked, but she knew. Coalition troops. Government agents. Borgs.

As a dense fog filled the air, an army of footsteps could be heard tromping down the stairwell. An array of long red beams sliced through the smoke, searching for targets.

Moving quickly, Jack pulled Zahra off the table and rushed her to the back of the lab. Reaching into a cabinet along the way, he jerked out two sealed masks.

"Put this on! Hurry!"

Flipping a panel on the back wall, with smoke surrounding them, Jack pressed a series of buttons that engaged a deafening air horn overlaid with sharp, pulsating beeps. The clean white lights of the lab flashed red. The electronic instrumentation where the holographic babies floated in mid-air began to crackle and spark as flames burned through their circuits. Pressing more buttons, Jack commanded a section of the wall beside him to slide up, revealing yet another hidden passage.

"We've got to go!"

"But what about the babies?" Zahra asked.

Jack didn't answer. He yanked her through the opening just as a borg broke from the smoke and started leaping toward them with superhuman agility. Lasers shot from its eyes; the gun it held seemed to be an extension of its body. Jack triggered the door to close just as the creature reached for them. In the background, the beeping grew louder and faster as an audible countdown sequence commenced.

Five...four...three....

As Jack and Zahra fumbled through the darkness toward safety, the cold wall of the tunnel their only guide, an explosion echoed from behind, shaking the earth around them.

The next morning, Zahra awoke to the sun reflecting off the moving waters of the sea. Jack sat beside her, gazing at the horizon, his arms resting on his knees. A few hundred yards away, the robot named Oro roamed, combing the sand like a treasure hunter looking for lost gold.

"I'm sorry," Zahra said, her voice raspy and gruff. She cleared the phlegm clogging her throat. "It's my fault they came, isn't it?"

Jack kept staring at the sunrise.

Zahra couldn't blame him. He had lost a great deal. A lot of hard work. A lot of lives. Pieces of the future.

Oro began to expel a series of whistles and clicks. Jack snapped out of his trance, springing from his seat and jogging down to where the robot hovered. Zahra followed. As she approached the spot where Jack now knelt, an object came into view–a piece of metal, flat to the ground and circular in shape like the cover to a manhole, except painted dusty brown, blending with the sand. On top of the object were several solar panels, buttons, keypads, and a display. Jack tapped on the keypad until information appeared on the screen.

Name: Christopher.

Condition: Normal.

Time Remaining: 7 days.

Zahra was stunned. Looking about, she was barely able to discern two more lids nearby.

"Are these...?"

"Babies, yes," Jack said. "A few of them, anyway."

Zahra's mouth was agape.

"But...I thought...weren't they in the lab?"

Jack scrolled through more data. "No, I only monitored them from the lab. They actually gestate out here, buried in the sand where no one can find them."

"Like the sea turtles."

"Yeah. I suppose so."

Resetting the display and standing, Jack turned his eyes toward the south. The ocean breeze curled the hair about his head. "I have a backup station not far from here. It'll take me a few days to get it up and running and to download the necessary information from Oro's memory. Unfortunately, some of the babies will be ready before then. I sure could use your help."

Zahra flushed. "Really? You want me to stay and help?"

Jack nodded. "There's something else, too. Given our circumstances, I won't be able to perform the procedure on your baby as soon as I had wanted. Maybe not at all. It has to be done fairly early in the pregnancy for the best results. So you may be having a natural birth, in which case, if you stay long enough, I can see you through your term."

Zahra was ecstatic. "Of course! Of course, I'll stay."

She turned and faced the ocean as Jack proceeded to check the other two capsules. Oro had already left in search of more. As Zahra watched the waves crash and roll onto shore, serving up clams and fish that the seagulls and pipers devoured with delight, she couldn't help but wonder what the future might bring for her and her baby–for all the babies–amongst the turbulent sea of man.

A MARKETING PROPOSAL

Sara M. Harvey

For immediate release:
The perfume bottle gleams proudly on the shelf, as if such an object were able to bear such a human emotion. But this bottle and its contents are far from ordinary and its disposition indeed prideful. The bottle: glass hand-ground by Nepalese monks from the finest silica sand and shaped by reformed French prostitutes whose mouths has erstwhile engaged in a similar activity that left them uniquely suited to the trade of glassblowers. Its contents: some of the rarest stuff ever to be named and used by humans, a substance once only given by the whim of the sea, worth its weight in diamonds, the foundation of the world's finest perfumes and lately found in the most startling of places—the bellies of young human children. Like a drop of nectar, like a nitid dollop of honey—-of ambrosia—caught in that meticulously made bottle, waits the ambergris.

To explain the provenance of this exquisite substance and establish its value to you, the esteemed investor, a bit of definition might be required. Once found only in the intestines of the sperm whale, ambergris is an oily, bile-like substance created by the digestive tract in order to protect the body from puncture by the ingestion of sharp objects—something for which the sperm whale is well known. Something for which small children are also known. After a period of cleansing and refinement, the waxy grey substance blossoms into a translucent, opalescent fluid suitable for personal scent application alone or as the perfect blending medium for other fragrant oils. It has also been found that human-created ambergris is a much finer substance that yields a clearer base and retains none of the unpleasant odor of fish that so plagued the whale-derived original.

The initial discovery of the new form of ambergris occurred in the belly of a four-year-old factory worker after her death by suffocation beneath a pile of fallen textiles and sewing notions. The company sought only to retrieve its aspirated property and upon opening her torso, happily stumbled onto the greatest find of the century (the finder's fees alone have allowed the opening of nearly a dozen new mills and sewing rooms, employing over two hundred laborers). The dwindling fine perfume industry has rebounded with vigor.

Between the ages of two and twelve, children naturally produce the substance in minor quantities, but selective breeding and improved care conditions have quadrupled or more the harvest of the silvery wax. The finest cuts of vernal meat, a delicacy appreciated across the solar system, is a mainstay export to both terrestrial and interplanetary markets. As an additional benefit, the children put on a good deal of glossy fat that melts into the most delightful soap and lotion base, marketed under the trade name "Oil of Innocence." Losses have been further mitigated by the use of lesser cuts of meat and bone meal for the propagation of further broods. Investments made with the Guild de Parfum Internationale (GPI) can only grow and thrive like the children under our care!

At first, there was great consternation about the raising of these children, forced as they are to swallow tacks and plastic caltrops to induce the production of ambergris and then kept as immobile as possible with the most modern corsets so as not to dislodge the balls of the precious substance once developed. Added restrictions of movement allowed for the proper development of the silken subcutaneous fat, the Oil of Innocence, derived from these children. But regulations have been put in place to ensure not only the health and safety of the children in the program, but their happiness as well. Every child admitted into the program is given a semi-private suite shared with three others of appropriate age and gender in one of the dozens of "happiness ranches" placed into low orbit above the

United States and Europe. The reduced-gravity living conditions allow for optimal emollient production while reducing costly and unnecessary bone density and muscle tone, all the while maximizing the comfort and enjoyment of the children.

Other complaints centered around fear-based advertising campaigns warning parents and guardians of the dangerous possibility that their children might be stolen and forced into service. Such a thing could be hardly farther from the truth; only children legally signed over by their parents or guardians or those children without legal standing are allowed into the program. In the case of a legal sign-over, the parents or guardians are paid handsomely and offered incentives to consider their future offspring for this highly successful program. The welfare system has been all but dismantled for lack of use. Twenty percent of every dollar invested goes directly to the care of these precious children that would have otherwise suffered at the hands of an unjust and unloving society.

While under the care of the devoted staff of the happiness ranch, the children are well fed and well attended. Their intestinal shunts are checked several times daily and the ambergris formations removed every forty-eight hours as directed by the manual supplied by the director of health management of the GPI. As children's bodies naturally stop producing ambergris, they age out of the program, some as young as nine others as old as fourteen. They are then divested of their accumulated fat stores and tender vernal meat. As with the ambergris, this fat is handled only by the top-ranking chemists in the GPI, thereby ensuring consistency in texture, clarity, and quality. The meat is divided by cut and quality and shipped fresh to distributors. The GPI is also currently investing in a captive breeding program to create a more consistent product, as previous poor care and nutrition of many of these children results in ambergris that does not comply with the Guild's rigorous standards. However, once implementation of the program begins, the Oil of Innocence and vernal meat can be easily brought up to code.

Current production of both ambergris and Oil of Innocence does not quite meet peak demand, something that the marketing team has been careful to balance. The scarcity and rarity only heighten the allure and continue to drive prices upward, resulting in a fine profit margin for the GPI, and its shareholders, and other smaller producers (please note that the GPI cannot be held responsible for improper care or lower quality standards of companies not under its domain).

The GPI does not sell its by-products for profit, and anyone peddling vernal meat must be specifically licensed to do so. A company not complying with Interplanetary Regulatory Code #24-d is always prosecuted to the fullest extent of the law. The GPI is committed to a greener tomorrow and promotes a sustainable business plan. It employs cutting edge technology in bio-engineering, solar and wind powered facilities, along with the reclamation of resources. The result is a business that is as fit and happy as its delightful residents.

In conclusion, your investment dollars mean more than an investment in perfume-making—one of the oldest trades in the world, revered by pharaohs and kings. They are an investment in the future of mankind. Imagine a world where childhood disease and poverty are but a distant memory and all children, regardless of their situation at birth, can become productive members of society, driving the world economy in a personal and unique way that gives meaning to lives that would be otherwise be debased, if not destroyed, by poverty. These children are saved from sweatshops and the gruesome sex trade. They are given a safe, healthy home for the duration of their lives and a legacy that lives on long after they pass.

As if that was not enough, all investors in the highest echelon, the Angels of Mercy level, will be gifted with a lifetime supply of the fragrance of his or her choosing; this offer is non-transferable and is void where prohibited.

Imagine your capital becoming a hand-wrought bottle of the highest quality filled with the earth's greatest treasure: 100% pure, unadulterated, virgin ambergris.

The Guild de Parfum Internationale represents centuries of service to the world and was founded with the mission of integrating art, science, and the community for the betterment of all.

MEAT WORLD

Michele Lee

We should meet.

The message blinked on Ian's screen, impatiently waiting for an answer. But he had none. Still the words blinked, until at last the automated messaging system clicked on.

Did Alan know that he was sitting here, reading those words over and over? Did Alan know that they brought the vice grip of fear to Ian's chest? Meet? In the meat world? Where there were diseases and wild animals, where everything was uncontrolled and unpredictable and completely unmanageable?

The words blinked again and more appeared on the screen.

Lily's systems reported her permanently flat-lined today. So maybe he should meet with Alan. At least once.

They talked about it all the time. All the time. From the mundane ideas, as simple as sitting on a couch together where they could reach out and touch each other, to cruder—more delightful— possibilities. But it was easy to talk when you never really had any intention of following through.

It was hard being in love with a man who lived a continent away. But the world was a dangerous, dangerous place and Ian didn't know if the risk of what was out there was worth the momentary touch of another person's flesh.

From pictures Ian knew Alan's place was designed both to match the landscape and to stand out from it. It towered up, as domineering as the Himalayan mountains around it and equally as jagged.

But Alan's tower was slick and snowless and absorbed the light that shone across its lengthy angles and crags. The sun and the wind and the warmth of the earth below gave Alan all the energy he needed for his gardens, the water filtration systems and the cameras they used to communicate.

There was even a lake nearby. The sun rose gloriously overhead every morning, or the storms rolled over its mirror-like surface, almost as lovely in their violent fury. Alan sent pictures of the lake every day, but Ian wondered if he'd ever actually set foot in the green expanse of the land around the lake. Had Alan shed his clothes and stepped into that water, water Ian imagined would be warmed by the sun that burned cruelly above it?

Had Lily left her fortress and ventured into the meat world? She lived in the Far East, where daily bots were exploring the overgrown jungles and steppes and sending back pictures of towering pagodas, stone temples to dead gods, slowly losing their fights against strangler figs and acidic bird droppings.

Lily had found part of a city just last week. Corpses of gas-powered cars and rusted steel buildings lay side by side with broken, artificially-generated stone streets and hints of bridges. She had been so excited, just last week. Now she was...gone. Where there had been a voice, a chess game on Thursday and Sunday nights, and a lovely, musical laugh, there was now a long, flat building, nestled on the plains of Asia where the bots returned with their spectacular information about the world around them, to emptiness. A sterile, gleaming emptiness with every bot doing exactly what it was supposed to do—chronicling the world of humans—for a human who no longer lived.

Alan found Ian while he sat watching Lily's complex with a disturbing mix of emotions that seemed to fluctuate between admiration and devastation. Alan didn't offer any words of wisdom or condolences. Their grieving was equal. And they were both more comfortable with silence than with the sound of voices.

They reached toward each other, and despite being thousands of miles away, their hands found each other through the sensitive, electronically charged gel of the Sensoboxes at their sides. Alan's hand felt firm and warm—the box mimicked it through constant readings—but it felt of the smooth perfection of gel, not skin.

When Ian realized he couldn't remember the last time he had felt skin—real, imperfect flesh—a stab went through him.

Yes, he whispered to the cameras and microphones and sensors that transferred every breath and temperature spike to Alan's system for better communication. Yes, we should meet.

At some point, logic stated that Ian must have encountered other people, real messes of flesh and juices and skin. People didn't just spawn themselves, and while machines, no matter how intelligent, replicated themselves, it wasn't in the same biohazardous way.

After spending some time puzzling over it, Ian referenced his exterior brain, as he called it: the core of the complex's systems that retained every bit of information from his explorer bots and recorded every aspect of his own life, down to his hourly chemical fluctuations.

It took a few moments to return results: a picture and a name. There were four people in the picture. The older pair of people, a male and female, were smiling. They looked vaguely familiar in the way the more obscure halls of the complex looked familiar. He was aware that he'd been there at some point before, but couldn't recall events, just vague emotions.

The soft smiles on the adults' faces brought an unfamiliar feeling of happiness and emotional attachment.

The two children in the picture were male, their smiles so bright they appeared artificial.

Who are these people?"

On his command the names appeared, labeling each person. Richard Gregory Adams. Adrienna Delilah Adams. Ian Maximilian Adams. Sean Richard Adams.

"Why don't I remember them?"

The picture muted and a medical report rose to the front of the screen.

Ian Maximilian Adams. Daily scan approximate date: SY 5.035153 indicates weakening of areas of the brain. During sleep cycle old tissue removed and restructured. Ian Maximilian Adams shows a regretful reset of information, but remains at satisfactory functional levels.

"What year is it now?"

The answer flashed immediately on the screen. SY 5.035163.

Ten years. Ten years ago something had gone wrong with his brain and the machines had fixed it, stealing away his memories in the process.

"Who are these people?"

Richard Gregory Adams, partner of Adrienna Delilah Adams, father of Ian Maximilian Adams, father of Sean Richard Adams. Adrienna Delilah Adams, partner of Richard Gregory Adams, mother of—

"Enough. Where are they now?"

Richard Gregory Adams, deceased, winter SY 5.035089. Adrienna Delilah Adams, deceased, spring SY 5.035087. Sean Richard Adams, deceased, summer SY 5.035079.

The computer waited for his next query, but Ian couldn't think. Dead. They were all dead. For over fifty years.

"Where are the other people?"

Error, please better define search parameters.

"The humans, the other humans. Where are they?"

Names spun past across the screen, too fast to read. But they all had the same word after them. He could only read it because they were all the same, blending into one long column. Deceased. Deceased.

"Where are the living people?"

The screen blinked.

Ian Maximilian Adams, living, desert south central North America.

Alan Jonathan Winters-Cane, living, northwestern Himalayas, Asia.

Ian's breath abandoned him.

The logistics were a problem. There were deserts, mountains, oceans, and forests full of lost cities between them. But there were also long-retired—but theoretically still functioning—aquatic vehicles and land rovers in the sheds at the back of the complex. Ian set bots to work on testing and securing one for his trip.

Did Alan know they were alone with the quiet, busy rush of machines on the face of a once well-populated planet?

"What happened?" he asked once he was breathing deeply enough to speak again. "What happened to all the people?"

The rushing screen of deceased flew by again.

"No," Ian screamed. "How did they die? Map it."

After a few moments, charts came up. Accidents, bodily failures, natural disasters, diseases. Deaths, surely, but nothing to explain the massive loss of all the people Ian had always assumed were out there, secluded in complexes and buildings filled with sterile machines that met their every need. Machines that farmed for them, that cycled the air and made it breathable for them. Machines that mined fuel and raw elements from around them. Machines that formed a protective wall between people and the world. Machines that slowly chronicled the reclaiming of the planet after the people retreated to the safety that being away from their own kind represented.

Did Alan know?

Would he have shared this fact with Ian if he had learned it? When he requested a meat world meeting, was it because he knew they were the last of their kind?

Did Alan want him because he was Ian, or because he was human?

Ian forced thoughts like that aside.

"I have a plan," he sent to Alan. "I will be there in a week."

"A week?" Alan answered. "How?"

"A vehicle."

"You're going to drive?"

"Yes."

Alan didn't answer. His silence was so full, so complete, that Ian demanded Alan's system account for him immediately.

"Alan—"

"Yes, hurry."

Heart rate: elevated. Shows signs of stress.

Alan, Ian asked. You do want me to come to you, don't you?

I don't know.

* * *

Ian left as soon as the vehicle was fueled and packed with a secondary core system that would monitor the toxicity of the air around him and Ian's own biological systems. Alan's response to further communication attempts had been painful silence.

I don't know. Was Alan going to let them end like that? Was Alan going to let their whole race end like that?

Ian's brain let off such a mix of emotion-invoking chemicals that the vehicle froze and tried to talk Ian into taking a sedative.

"No, I want to feel these things," he protested. The machine injected him with a sedative cocktail anyway, and much of the rest of North America passed in a dreamlike state for Ian.

Despite the wondrous beauty of the world around him, it was easier to just sleep the trip away. Still, Ian fought it.

Remain calm, the machine answered. Stress levels more than thirty percent above normal range will be responded to with forced sedation.

When had the machines begun making decisions for them? Ian couldn't help wondering if, despite the overall result, the machines were better at it than the humans had been.

He'd set out with the intention of seeing the world, literally. He'd planned to touch, taste, and smell, to experience what the wondrous planet had to offer first hand, rather than through bot images and sims fed into his brain.

But the machines around him, traitorous hunks of metal and plastic, forced him into sedation, into a hibernation-sleep, so the trip passed and Ian awoke with only dreamlike memories. He couldn't tell what was real and what had been introduced to him in his REM cycle by the machines' soothing programs.

His moods regulated for the safety of his blood pressure and organs, Ian wanted to rage, to mourn, to feel something, but he couldn't. Senses and emotions were denied to him for the sake of his fragile human body.

He revived as the vehicle approached its destination.

Alan's home was a fortress, a thumbing of the nose at the natural landscape around it. A mechanical scream broke the silence as Ian approached and sent a dizzying array of birds and small mammals running through the land around the vehicle.

"Proximity alert. Warning. Proximity alert."

Startled, Ian connected to Alan, his feed buffered through his home, though it was so far away. After a moment, Alan's worried face appeared on screen.

"Is that you, Ian?"

"Who else would it be?

Alan didn't answer. Maybe he didn't know.

"I don't think this is a good idea, Ian. You could have a disease. Or be bringing foreign microbes and bacteria here that could harm the area."

"Are you joking?"

Alan looked pained. "No. Do you have any idea how many people have died from diseases?"

"Alan, do you have any idea how many people are left?"

"What does that have to do with anything? You could hurt me, Ian. You don't want to hurt me, do you?"

The alarms were still blaring. A side access port in the building opened and scout bots scurried out and surrounded the vehicle.

"Please turn off the security system, Alan."

The look on Alan's face was alarming. Ian might as well have asked him to stop breathing.

"No, no. They are there for a reason. We're isolated for a reason. Your vehicle is crawling with viruses and bacteria and fungi. Any one of them could infect my skin or my lungs, my body or my food and water supply. This was a bad idea, Ian. Go away. Just go away."

"Alan, but...we're the last—"

"Go away!"

"System armed. You have ten seconds to leave the premises before action is taken."

"Alan!"

Ian's scream, bound in the walls of his vehicle, couldn't even be heard by the bots surrounding him. He felt the silver burn of a pinprick, and then he couldn't focus. Warmth surged into his veins and he couldn't feel, either.

"...last...." he murmured.

Outside, the bots began firing.

Alan watched the vehicle retreat and hit the button that fed tranqs into his system again. Once Ian, entombed in silver, vanished into the landscape, he breathed a sigh of relief. The list of vile poisonous microbes on and in his vehicle was still processing. Had Ian come to kill him? Or was it just in carelessness that he had dragged a bio-war's worth of danger with him?

At the thought, Alan felt a gagging sensation growing at the back of his throat and hit the tranq button again.

And if they had been able to touch, what would have happened when Ian had to leave again? How would it have hurt when Ian left for home, abandoning Alan to the cold, lifeless halls of his fortress?

Alan changed screens to avoid another stab of stress at the growing list. It felt as though a tear might have escaped the corner of his eye but the tranqs soothed away the bad emotion, restoring the pleasant nothingness Alan knew and trusted.

What ridiculousness had compelled him to even suggest a meat world meeting? It was bad, impossible, and—worst of all—dangerous.

Too dangerous ever to be considered again.

Ian woke in his own bed to a gentle beeping.

"What happened?"

Daily scan indicates stress-induced weakening of the brain and heart. During sleep cycle old tissue removed and organs restructured and reinforced. Ian Maximilian Adams shows a regretful reset of information, but remains at satisfactory functional levels.

"What caused the stress?"

Ian Maximilian Adams embarked on an exploratory external excursion.

"Well, then. Let's not do that again, shall we?"

At the bedside, the monitoring machine beeped a soft, lonely rhythm that Ian had long ago learned to find comforting.

ALIEN SPACES

Deb Taber

The trouble on line one wasn't all Ginny's fault, but Chaz blamed her first and I wasn't about to say any different. What the hell. She was new, and she wasn't supposed to be wearing her ring.

Company policy handed down from On High: no jewelry or makeup of any kind to be worn when working on the production lines. It can flake off, fall in, maybe do a do-si-do, and contaminate the product, which the customer never looks at anyway, seven times out of ten—in base eight, that is. But who's to fight word from Her Highness? Not me, not most days. Ginny, on the other hand, was all starry-eyed Newlywed Game and couldn't pull a couple of epithelials off her rosy fingers to sit with the rock-heavy ring in her pocket for an eight-hour shift. No wonder her parents had named her Virginia. Snow White might have been better.

"Stacia, get your fingers the hell out of the product," Chaz shouted at me.

I dropped the ring into my left hand and held it out behind my back for Ginny to pick up, if she wasn't catatonically stupid, while giving Chaz a latex-gloved one-finger salute with my right.

"You've lost us one," he grumbled.

"You've lost six more. Seven, eight, nine...." I said.

"Stop!" shouted Chaz.

I had to reach past Ginny to hit the E-stop and she jumped back like I was going in for a feel. Chaz stared down at the wet concrete around his feet. The nine aliens he had failed to catch had tumbled off the production line and splatted like water balloons on the ground. Aliens, not A.L.I.E.N.S. Another command from On High: Thou shalt not capitalize thy acronyms; it is base, common, and nowhere near as funny to sell people A.L.I.E.N.S. as it is to sell them "aliens." I'd asked her once what base she was referring to, and she'd said, "Thou shalt not question thy superior mathematicians," then tamped out her cigarette in my coffee and demoted me from uploads back onto the line, where I could screw myself fishing Ginny's stupid ring out of the product.

One ruined aliens would have been no big deal. They get pulled off the line for flaws all the time, and if we don't pull them here, we hear about it from uploads, packaging, and the boss lady herself. Even the nine units Chaz lost shouldn't have cost us too badly, but broken aliens have to be stored in prophylactic tubs until they can be recycled back into the processing vats. Chaz was so cocky that he hadn't bothered to put a bin at the end of the line.

So thanks to him, we had the components of nine Advanced Living Inter-Exponential Nominal Spaces soaking into the concrete floor and spreading their interdimensional physiomathematics out into the foundation of the building. I used to think that sounded like fun.

It's not.

A crowd gathered around Chaz while he was still sputtering at me, so I hurled the ring at Ginny—no, she wasn't smart enough to take it from my hand—and grabbed a couple of rags.

At least we'd only been working on a batch of Zombies. You've seen the ads, right? They look like cut crystal and store dead people's brains. Well, not their brains, exactly, but a mathematically accurate replica of the living person's synaptic activity that lights up like a Macy's Christmas display. Absolutely useless to dear Aunt Mabel who is already six feet gone to Alzheimer's, but you can store a little piece of what's left of her thoughts when she passes. They aren't cheap, but hey, that's what you pay to get over the guilt of not visiting her in the home, I guess.

Zombies eat brains. It's what they do. And while I wasn't convinced that any of my coworkers had much to offer the Zoms right there, the jellied forms were sucking the concrete for anything resembling synaptic activity, and that meant the building's brains.

Lights began to flicker and the production belts started and stopped and jerked off track as their mechanical noodles tried to figure out what to do. A stench like formaldehyde and hot ketchup permeated the air. I wasn't sure if Chaz was being brain-sucked, since he always looked like he thought with his ass, but I could see the air around Ginny starting to crackle and light up with the glimmer of triangular sparks. I shoved her backward, partly because I'd been wanting to do it for a while, and partly because the Zoms weren't good beyond a certain proximity and I didn't think she had the synapses to spare.

Chaz finally grabbed a scoop and began shoveling the major bodies of the Zoms into the bins, but the stuff that had already soaked in was going to call for more drastic measures.

"Guess it's damage control time," he said, looking at me.

"No way, it's your mess," I said.

"You take this to her, Stacia, and I won't tell her why your nickname around uploads is Stash," he said.

I tried to figure from his grin which stash he knew about, but unlike the Zombies, I don't eat and transcribe brains. One of my hobbies could get me an orange jumpsuit vacation with a bunch of burly blue uniforms to play with, but the other would get me in real trouble.

I found the founder and creator of aliens, inc. in her office, as usual. A couple of lackeys smirked as they let me into the golden sanctuary on the second floor where she lounged on an obese purple couch. The whole office was done up in retro opium den style, updated with modern movie posters and her computer. The keys on the computer were etched with obscure mathematical symbols highlighted in gold leaf, fitting in pretty well with the overall theme.

"What are you doing here, Laurel?" she said.

"I'm Stacia. You fired Laurel last week."

"Hmm. I wonder why I did that. Have they sent you to be

next?" She took a studious puff of something from a long cigarette holder.

"Whoa, I'm just the messenger. It was Ginny's ring."

"Virginia was wearing a ring?" she said.

"I told her not to."

I'm aware of it when I sound like a whiny five-year-old, but I was taking Chaz's shit for him and I wasn't about to take Ginny's too.

"So what information does Mr. Levins have on you to convince you to take the blame for him?" she asked.

"Chaz?"

She nodded, her dark curls bobbing deliciously close to the smoking end of her stick. "I know where all my employees are positioned, of course. I know who was at the end of the production line where the trouble occurred, yet here you are in his stead. So what does he have on you, I wonder?"

"Nothing," I said.

"Mmmmhmmmmm." She smiled at me.

Next time I would do more than just flip Chaz off. I pulled a one-by-one zip bag out of my pocket and handed it to her. She looked at the pale blue powder inside, tested it with her little finger and touched it to her tongue.

"Not bad work. Good product, but not as pure as it should be. You miscalculated the conversion back into base ten," she said.

"No miscalc. Base thirteen isn't as pure, but it gives the user more of a David Lynch-Edward Gorey thrill ride than the pure high of ten. Want to try some?"

If I could get her high—well, higher—maybe she wouldn't fire me or search any farther for the real stash I was keeping hidden.

"Thank you, no. I never get high during business hours," she said.

She waited for me to laugh, but I can hold it when I have to. I didn't even glance at the hookah still smoking on the table beside her lounge.

"So, can you control the damage?" I asked her.

"Do I want to?" She held up the little baggie of blue powder. "I am sure you can find the skills to take care of the problem. And when your shift is over, you'll come back here and we will see if your base thirteen is as interesting as you say."

"I don't use," I told her.

She grabbed my chin and tilted my head down to look into her eyes. I wasn't sure if she was going to crack my jaw or give me a kiss, but she just flicked her eyes back and forth around the edges of my face and kept the crushing grip long enough to burst a blood vessel or two. Then she took her hand away and sighed.

"You've been clean for far too long for a mathematician. I'll see you after work," she said.

Pain mingled with the taste of that sick tomato stench in my mouth in a way no breath mint could beat. I tried to spit the flavor out on my way back downstairs, but it just got worse as I got closer.

The production area was a mess. Chaz was scrubbing at the wet concrete with handfuls of powdered desiccant. The air had stopped crackling, but the belts were still going crazy and it looked like we'd lost a worker or two, unless I'd just been previously ignoring their tendencies to drool. I sent Chaz off to take care of the droolers—he deserved it, damn him—while I snagged a calc and got to work. I was starting to suspect that the demotion from uploads hadn't been all my fault. Clearly, they needed someone on the floor who could add more than pi plus two.

The spill was an irregular 915-sided polygon with a 2-D periphery of 143.825 inches. At least Ginny had managed to get that much while I was with Her Highness, though I was a little iffy about trusting her count. But when I questioned her she gave me the closest thing to a dirty look I'd ever seen on that princess face, so I took it as a good sign.

I extrapolated Ginny's figures into base six, the operant base of nominal space biology, recalced for the 10_6 dimensions of their geometry, and multiplied by the standard light refraction in each of those dimensions. I etched the figures onto the spill with a chemical compound stylus designed to cause physical reactions when combined with the right math.

There was no time to double-check on the calc as I went. My arms tingled with the electrochemical antithesis of human synaptic activity, and I could feel my brain fighting to hold onto the calculations that wanted to swirl away into thick, wet sludge. My whole damned shirt was soaked in sweat by the time I got the figure for the final division to compress back into plain old base ten 3-D, but sweat is better than drool.

My numbers fused and bled into clear jelly. The three-pointed sparks let out grinding-gear squeals as they popped and disappeared, and the concrete went back to standard-issue grey and dry. Only the stink stayed around to continue ruining my already waste of a day.

"Ginny, how did you get a job here if you can't do the math?" I asked her.

She turned her big weepy eyes on me and her chin wobbled—actually wobbled, no kidding—and I told her to forget it. I didn't really want to know. Ginny was a pretty thing, unlike me, and Her Highness liked all kinds of pretty things.

With everything back to the chaos that passes for normal on the production line, the rest of the order went off okay. Despite the mess that comes from broken Zombies, the finished products are pretty stable. Once the final firing is complete, they'll only take brain patterns you put into them, and their light show is stored entirely in the here-and-now, no extra dimensions required. Our next order was much bigger. Seventeen thousand Oubliettes.

Oubliettes are different.

Plain and simple, all aliens are extra space. Zoms just take things out of dead space and put them into something alive. With Oubs, the space is a little more tricky. Oubs are bigger than Zoms, about five by five, and that's inches for anyone who went with the Stateside Metric Conversion. Not that I care meters from yards. I'm just glad she didn't decide to take up her own system of measurement or I'd be calcing in vernoplexes or something equally useless. So a five by five Oubliette is actually five by five by five to the naked eye, but inside it is a whole lot more, and it's all thanks to the jellis and She Who is Almost Always High.

The calc is first-grade basic: she went on a deep sea diving trip—and I mean trip in more ways than one—and discovered a species of sea creeps that looked like jellyfish, only they bit instead of stung. But they didn't have any teeth, not that she could see. Not until the moment of the bite. So she dug around and figured out they existed in six dimensions instead of the requisite three, and then she ground their bones to make her bread. No bones in reality, at least not in our dimension, but close enough.

With the right math, the jellis' extra dimensions are open to us, and their insulative properties are bar none. So the Oubs sit here in three-dees, but shovel something in through their hungry mouths and it comes out in four-five-six. That's the theory, anyway. All we know is that what goes in...goes. Memories, tuna cans, your mother-in-law, whatever. If you can con her into one, that is.

We started working on those Oubliettes, but an Oub can't have the tiniest flaw because its only purpose is to seal something away so tight that no one will ever find it again. Most people use them for bad memories. Shrinks, abuse victims, probably the abusers, anyone who wants to put something away where it'll never come back to haunt them. Hell, I used one once for something that happened in fourth grade. I'd tell you what it was, but sorry. Gone.

The Oubs started streaming down the line, and Ginny's job was to hit them with the air hose and knock off any dust leftover from the molds. Mine was to snip their teeth. Yes, that's literal teeth. Something about those sea creep beasties, when they're pressed into the geometry that holds them in our three dees, they come out ready to bite. The compression that holds them here keeps the teeth nice and solid and sharp.

The creeps bit me about every fifth snip. Each Oub has three teeth—two top, one bottom—and they gnash with a regular rhythm, so if you get them when they're closed, one snip of the cutters takes out all three. The problem is if you miss, you end up with one or two broken teeth and a cube of jellied goo flying at your jugular even though the damned things have no physical way of launching themselves off the line.

After an hour of snipping, my jugular remained intact but my left forearm, which I used for protection, was starting to resemble a scratching post. It didn't hurt much, since the Oub takes the memory of the pain with it when it bites. I guess no one will ever really know what an Oubliette bite feels like, but I have a healthy imagination, and I was running short on bandages.

"Here, Ginny, you snip and I'll blow them off for a while, just until the bleeding stops. Shouldn't take long," I said.

"I don't know how," said Ginny, looking at the cutters like they might turn on her too.

"It's easy. Just get the rhythm of it. And if you miss, keep your other arm ready. They aren't smart, they won't fake you out or attack anywhere other than the throat, and it won't hurt your arm a bit."

"Then why don't you keep doing it?" said Ginny.

"Because Her Royal Highness doesn't like blood on the line—human blood, anyway. It muddles the physics and can distort the shape of the spaces," I said.

"Why do you always call her that?"

"I don't. I call her lots of other things, but she monitors down here at minimum with visuals, and even if she doesn't have audio, I don't doubt she can read lips, so I'll keep those other names to myself, thank you."

"I just meant, why not call her something else? Someone here must know her name," said Ginny.

"Yeah, what do you call her?" I said.

Ginny kept her mouth shut and looked at the cutters I was waving in front of her.

"Just snip," I said.

I entertained the thought of grabbing one of the good Oubliettes off the line, marking it as faulty and shoving the evidence of my private enterprise down its gullet before she could get it out of me. Her Highness would never be able to reach it there, but neither would I, and I needed it more than I needed my job, or anything else for that matter.

What I had was just math. Simple numbers, calculations. Not the physics and geometry of jellis and their spaces, but a whole different way of viewing number systems that opened up more possibilities than a few extra angles and planes ever would. It started with the calculations I used to keep my mind from going numb at the factory. Just little bits of thought in symbolic logic, transcribing the formulas for processing the creeps into alternate base systems. Binary, base five. Thirteen had its obvious appeal. Even she had probably done it up to around base 58 or so, knowing her. She liked to play. But when you get beyond base ten, you have to start thinking in symbols other than the numbers we commonly use. At about two hundred, I ran out of alphanumerics, and geometrics ran dry a short time later. By base 375, I had to think my calculations through in complex pictures, and that's when the floodgates opened. Insight. Epiphany. Oh, God, it was good.

And I couldn't have done it without her aliens.

The little blue powder I made was nothing. Ground up jelli leftovers processed with a little abstract math and designed to let the user hallucinate herself into another dimensional perception for a short time. Limited strictly to the sea creep oeuvre, so all things watery and fishy with teeth. I'd done it myself, back when. A lazy, floating high with grotesque and pretty shapes all around. Escape.

My nirvana, on the other hand, required more than just the castoffs of her aliens and a little imagination. It enabled me to cross the dimensions with simultaneous physical presence, to hold the symbols of my body in one plane of my mind while calculating movement elsewhere in another. Thoughts in time, self in space and all that poetic mumbo-jumbo backed by sea creep physics and defined calculation. For this, I filched the Oubliette rejects and saved them from the processing vat.

Not all of them. The molds had to be imperfect in a certain way. I needed chunks with a sheer plane on two sides at an obtuse angle, and the rest so full of cracks and divots that it increased the surface area by a minimum of fivefold. With the correct figures drawn with a stylus on their surface, I could be here in the factory snipping teeth out of Oubs, while at the same time exploring anything, anywhere, in this physical plane or one of the jelli dimensions. Simultaneous living, like lucid dreams but with bite. Who needs a clone when you can be yourself anywhere and everywhere you want to be, and still take care of the daily grind?

"Stacia, I don't think this one is right," said Ginny.

I felt that shiver in my bones that told me I was about to look at the real deal. I'd been dry for three weeks, stuck in one existence only, and I was craving the taste of a few dimensions more. The energy of jellis is finite, and I'd been using hard.

"Hand it here," I said.

She reached toward it gingerly.

"Forget it," I snapped, and grabbed the thing. "I told you, they only go for the throat."

The cracked Oubliette vibrated in my grip, straining to suck the life out of me but ignoring my easy-bleeding hands in its desire for my jugular. Who knows, maybe they don't understand hands in any dimension. What I don't get is how they understand throats.

I inspected the surface of the Oub. Scarred and pitted from too cold a pour. I pushed at a crack and broke a small section off with my thumb. Two sheer planes, obtuse angle, looked like at least a fivefold increase, though I'd need a closer inspection to be sure. Perfect.

"Inside's good. Just toss it in a vat and we'll get it back to processing after work," I said.

I chucked the thing to her while I squirreled the broken piece up my sleeve. After all, she was near the reject bin, not me.

The girl couldn't catch. I don't know if it was fear or lack of brain function, but she watched it arc toward her and the only movement she made was to raise her left arm to her throat. Fortunately, I had counted on her chickening and put a spin on the throw that sent the Oub off at a thirty-nine degree angle and into the bin.

"Heads up," I told her.

I took the cutters back and started up the line again.

"About time!" Chaz called down to me.

"Bite me," I said.

"They will," he said.

He was right.

I didn't get the chance to give my chunk of faulty Oub a closer inspection after work. At least, not in the way I had intended. Her Highness decided I might try to rabbit—good decision on her part, bad on mine—and sent one of her office twits to secure me before I even had time to grab my keys. He left us alone in the thick air of her sanctuary with a look almost as smug as her own.

"Laurel," she said.

"It's Stacia. You wanted to see me."

"I remember."

She was laughing at me. I waited until she looked like she was just about to ask me to sit down, then I dropped my ass onto the nearest pouf. I wasn't quite sure how close I was to being fired, but I wanted to make the worst of it, just in case.

Do sit down," she said, one-twelfth of a second too late.

"Thanks," I said, mostly without the irony.

"Are you ready to have a little fun?"

"Look, I've gotta get home pretty quick today, and I'm not really interested in getting high with you right now. Maybe at the end of the week or something, but I've got the line to run tomorrow and you don't want me doing that if I can't tell my head from a hole in hell."

"What a pretty speech, Stacia. Now, come here."

She grabbed my arm and slid a sharpened fingernail down a vein. I hardly felt the cut, and what I did feel sent a tingle of something from my throat all the way to my toes. It wasn't fear. I looked at her, and her amber eyes were swimming with sharks. Anticipation. I was hungrier for this than I could have imagined.

My blood finally realized it could make a run for it, and a trickle of red started to flow from my wrist. She dipped an agile tongue into my blue powder and pressed it against the break in my skin.

"There you go, pretty girl," she said.

I snorted. Pretty. Sure. As if I hadn't seen my own face before. She still held my arm, but as I slipped into the dreams of other dimensions, my other hand felt for the chunk of faulty Oub that had made it from my sleeve into my pocket, where I always kept my stub of a stylus. I could scratch out the calcs I needed in my sleep, so if the pocket factor didn't smear them, I was going all the way.

Everything doubled. I looked around, testing the equations, feeling the moisture on my very present skin. Yes, my body was with me; it wasn't all hallucination. The broken piece was perfect.

In a world of six dimensions, direction gets slippery. I'd been here before, but if there were landmarks, they tended to move or else I never made my way to the same place twice. Funny thing, though, is that when you're in six dimensions, you're *in* them. Body and brain, too. I laughed, and my double in her sanctuary laughed with me.

I *was* pretty, damnit. At least when I was here. The old pits and scars on my skin—stupid acne and chicken pox, nothing tragically grim—stretched out with color and light. My bones danced beneath my skin in a motion that was at first unsettling, then exciting, like an internal roller coaster ride. Sure, the blue-powder high could imitate this, but I was real, and my bones did dance, and my brain stretched out in three-to-the-third ways, and I could understand almost everything. I knew where the stuff we shoved down the Oubs went, and I had something to find.

I know what you're thinking, but it wasn't her name. I didn't care if she was Princess Prunella Prusita of Prussia. And it wasn't my own long-forgotten memories I was after. Shit, I'm smart enough when I'm not causing trouble. I know that if I let them go, they were better off forgotten.

No, it wasn't me I was after. I admit, I'm a nosy bugger, and it pissed me off that someone who must have had a brain at some point would have chosen to trade hers in for the blush on her rosy cheeks and a rock on her finger.

I bone-danced through the thick liquid atmosphere, scenting my way with a sense that was something like smell, taste, and touch combined. I caught a whiff of some of Her Highness' castaways—her trail reeked of poppies, talcum, sour mayonnaise, and the textures of fire and silk—but I shied away from them. Like I said, I didn't want to know. She had dived into the remaining blue powder back in her office and was sprawled on the floor beside that iteration of me, quivering silently except for the occasional "Oh!"

I wanted to slap her, but the drug had a moderate paralyzing effect, so I flopped like a fish once and held still.

Even in the shifting spaces of six dimensions, human junkpiles were filling up fast. Every looping, swirling step I took seemed to reveal more castoffs that breathed in and out of existence on the ever-changing landscape. Something like seaweed tangled in talking heads—someone's memories of a conversation. I didn't stop to listen. It was the usual soap opera junk. No wonder the Oubs were so popular. We were too big of shits to keep our crap to ourselves.

A sweet cloud nearly sent me staggering, but there was something familiar about it. There, surrounded by the taste and texture of school glue, summer rain, and frozen blackberry margaritas, was an idealized image of Chaz, clearing his throat nervously and practicing in front of a mirror to ask some unlucky chicken out on what I presumed was a first date. Blackberry margaritas. How frou-frou of him. And he couldn't even handle a memory of himself being less than Mister Suave.

That thought sent an unpleasant tingle through my liver, and I turned away before I saw what I'd shoved down an Oub's gullet years ago. But space here doesn't work like I'm used to, and I ended up stepping into the middle of my own pathetic meltdown, the puppy crush I'd had in some way-back-when over a guy who couldn't even remember my name. I wondered if he'd thought it was Laurel, too.

The feeling of a hand on my shoulder spun me around so fast that only the liquid atmosphere kept me from crashing to the ground. Gravity pulled me in three directions, not the least of which was my stomach pouring out through my throat, but I shoved the bile back down and got ready to rip her a new one for feeling out my pockets and following along.

But it wasn't her.

Ginny's pale eyes looked back at me. Not a glamorized memory of herself, not a distorted reality. Just Ginny, but with a pissed-off look in her eye and furrows around her mouth and forehead that I wouldn't ever have guessed she could have. She was still beautiful in the fine-boned way that made me think men might offer to carry her over mud puddles, but she was sharper and more alive than I'd seen her at the factory.

"What are you doing here?" she said.

Her breath smelled like cider vinegar and sandpaper and oranges.

"Hey, Ginny," I said.

She frowned harder, literal lightning bolts flashing from the furrows around her jaw. I needed to figure out how to do that.

"Do I know you?" she said.

"Kind of. We work together. Well, the you who got rid of you and I do, I guess."

Ginny shook her head. I got it. The dimensions carry thoughts through time better than speech, if you know how to listen, and I'm a quick learner.

"So then you know you're not real," I said to her. "Just an echo of the other Virginia's mind."

I heard a flurry of snicking sounds that seemed to come from a shower of sparklike teeth around her hand. A moment later, a crumble of broken Oubliette—two planes at obtuse angles and surface area increase that was probably at least to the power of seven, the pits and cracks were so deep—rested in her hand.

"It doesn't work like that," I told her. "I don't split what I was and what I am; I didn't shove myself down a hole. I can still go back and be what I was. You can't."

But what if my calculations were wrong? If only part of Ginny was here and only part stayed behind at the factory with her sparkly new hubby and her dimwitted brain, what were the chances my calcs were wrong, that I had left some pieces behind...and what if they didn't take me back? I didn't like the math.

"It's not quite like you think," said lightning-Ginny. "She—I—did shove me down the throat of an Oubliette. I didn't want to look back. But I had this with me as I went through. It was my first day at the factory, and I thought—"

She didn't have to finish. She'd been fascinated by the math. I tried to reach out extra-dimensionally to ask her why she'd shoved herself in the hole. It seemed kind of rude to ask out loud.

She laughed at me and shoved me out of her mind with a noxious cloud that felt like an outhouse had been dumped over my head.

"We're not friends, Stash," she said, and melted away.

It was six weeks before I caught a break and was able to squirrel away another piece of broken Oub in my sleeve. In the meantime I kept my head low and tried not to stare at Ginny on the lines. I must not have done a very good job of it, though, because she sidled away whenever I got too close. Sometimes, I thought I caught a hint of the smell of oranges.

This time I was able to start my trip alone in my crappy apartment; being a grunt on the line doesn't put me up in the opium couch income bracket. I turned up the air conditioning because I figured it'd keep me awake enough in this world to pull myself back if anything happened. I don't know what kind of "anything" I was thinking of.

The cold felt good, though, in contrast to the liquid heat of the jellis' world. So maybe I just wanted to balance things out.

Wandering the dimensions seemed less appealing this time around. Heaps of junk flooded in and out. Body parts and garbage and disembodied voices, old electronics and possibly even the corpse of a mother-in-law or two; it all came and went among the local version of kelp and the rolling hills that tilted in the multi-gravitational pull. I learned to walk right through the junk, rather than trying to zigzag around things that were there one minute and gone the next. The same piles showed up again, in different places, and there were always, always, more. I felt sick, but when the bile rose it tasted sweet and hot, like cinnamon candy.

I recognized the citrus-vinegar-sandpaper scent, now heavily laced with pinpricks and mold, before Ginny touched me this time. The spark-teeth snicked their mouthless chomps around her, but this time nothing was revealed in her palm. They just bit at her flesh, causing black little burns that healed as fast as they appeared.

"Are you doing okay here?" I asked her.

"Do you care?"

I had to think about that one. Yeah, it worried me. I didn't care much for the Ginny at the factory, was still pissed that she'd shoved this smarter, livelier version of herself down a hole. But Ginny-here could carry on a conversation. There hadn't been much of that around, lately.

"You can't stop people from shoving things down the holes," she said. "You must know that."

If I'd have thought about it, I would have known, but I'm not the save-the-world-from-itself type. She is.

Was.

I shrugged. "More room for me there, I guess."

"And what about here?" asked Ginny.

"What about it? I'm guessing that's your cause, not mine."

Ginny smiled. Suddenly, having the lightning shoot out of her face didn't seem quite so fun. Her teeth bared, and it was like looking full in the face of what the jellis thought of humans. There were no words, no scents, not even feelings to describe it. All I can say is that they didn't like us one bit.

Not that I blamed them. It would reek the royal wasteland to have some other-dimensional shit shoved into your world until there wasn't space to move, and it looked like we were definitely stretching into all six of their dimensions. But what could a jelli do?

"I guess you'll find out," said Virginia, with a smile like burnt corn.

* * *

I waited for something to go wrong the next day. And the next, and the one after that. Hell, I was a nervous wreck on the line, so bad I couldn't even muster the attitude to flip Chaz off when he chewed me out. He was right. I *did* have my head up my ass. Or the ass crack of a six-dimensional world that Ginny-there seemed to think was about to bite back.

I calced the scenarios, then calced some more. Probabilities, liabilities, statistical analyses. I ran them in my head while the product ran down the line, silent as Ginny and maybe not without drool. I kept waiting for our stuff to be tossed back through, for the dimensional rifts to vomit back six years worth of slowly growing garbage heaps. Every odd scent that I caught on the air made me stiffen. I managed to screw up on the line so many times I wondered why she didn't demote me until I realized there was nowhere lower I could sink. Chaz even stopped scolding me and treated me like the walking dead. I caught him eyeing me as I handled the Oubs and knew exactly what he thought. Let him think it. At least he was still thinking.

That was more than I could say for most of the rest of the crew. It dawned on me that I'd never checked into using my employee product discount except to try once at getting my perfect imperfection out of a finished, fired Oub. It hadn't worked. But I checked the records and nearly everyone else, herself included, was tossing bits of this and that down the jellis' unwilling throats. For all I knew, it was just old mattresses and tax returns, but from the whispers and recriminations that had thickened the air in that other world, I doubted the material junk was what they shoved inside.

And still, it didn't explode; nothing came back through. Nothing but the occasional scent of oranges when Ginny walked by.

For weeks, I couldn't find another faulty product to sneak out of the lot, not even when the orders for Zombies and everything else fell away and all we were making was Oubliettes. When I finally did get a hunk that was just right, I hesitated. Oh, it went into my pocket, sure. But it stayed unmarked by my stylus for another week.

The look in Ginny's eyes grew more vacant. So did Chaz's and the rest of the crew's. The people I drove past on my way to work forgot to start again when they stopped for a light. Shit. It's not like any of this was new.

When she called me back up to her office by my nickname, I figured it was all over. But no, she just wanted to get high. I wished then that I had stumbled across her name in the jelli world so I could spit it back in her face and see if it stuck. Instead, I handed her a blue powder-filled baggie, shook off her croons of not wanting to get high alone, and sped my way home with my hand on the horn. Taking it off seemed pointless.

"All right," I told lightning-Ginny. "I get the big plan."

"I'd hardly call it a plan," she said. "It's just stupid people doing what they do."

"You have to give it back," I told her.

"Me? What have I got to do with anything?"

"You're here, and you can take yourself back. You have the physics, the chemistry and the math."

Ginny shook her head. "I could take half myself back, or whatever percentage of the me I was before I shoved myself down this hole."

I was dying to ask why she had done it—taken the intelligent, reasoning part of herself and tossed it away—but I was afraid to hear the answer.

She smelled that on me and smiled.

"Because I was smarter than you are, Stacia. I saw all this coming a long time ago. When I first saw what the Oubliettes would do. Toss away whatever you don't like in your life, in yourself, and go on about your merry way. I was never much for being merry."

"You are now," I said, throwing the sweet-without-the-sour scent of her "real" self at her.

Her face darkened and her eyes and nostrils flared. The lightning that always crackled around her grew sluggish and purple, and it bit me with a stinging burn that lasted only nine-tenths of a second before it faded away.

"Go back there, Stacia. You're not wanted here."

I couldn't help it. I had to laugh, and the laughter came out of me in molten lava flows that burned through the in-and-out-again junk piles that surrounded us. The bitter smell of singed hair and seaweed filled my stretching lungs, but it was all shifting too quickly for me and the fire rolled off in one of those unnamable directions and the atmosphere was thick and liquid again. This was a world where everything bit, and no one ever felt the pain.

"Nothing here is wanted. That's kind of the point," I said.

She clenched her fists, but her anger was useless. She was only half a person or so, here or there. That's all she ever would be. That's all anyone ever would be, throwing themselves away exactly like the garbage they were, leaving two half-worlds with piles of junk in one and empty shells in the other. I was whole—twice whole, in fact, at the moment. I laughed again and watched the lava flow before I brought myself fully back home. I stood both my bodies face to face for a moment—something I'd never bothered to do because I of all people knew I wasn't much to look at.

I took in that ugly mug with its scars and its overbite, its too-pale eyes and uncombed hair. Our clothes hung like sacks because I'd never cared what size I wore, and when we grinned at each other our teeth were yellow and dirty. But we were there, both of us. Both of me.

It didn't matter if the rest of the world decided to throw itself to shit. I was as intact as I cared to be, and I could keep my own company.

FATHER'S FLESH, MOTHER'S BLOOD

Aliette de Bodard

The group waiting at the gates of the house looked innocuous enough: two scholars, dressed in the grey robes of their profession, and an escort of neutered men holding repulsor screens to protect their masters against the howling winds of New Zhongguo. Nothing seemed out of the ordinary.

But, even sitting inside, watching the scene though the lens of a roving remote, Leyou saw that the scholars held themselves a little too eagerly, a little too hungrily. And the cloth of their robes was impeccable, with not a trace of the omnipresent red dust on the large sleeves and carefully embroidered hems: their robes were new and never-worn, barely out of the imperial weaving mills. If Leyou were out there now, he'd find that the scholars smelled of cinnabar and bleach—an odor too deeply sunk under their skins to be scrubbed away.

Cutters.

With a gesture on the control pad, Leyou turned up the sound and listened to their conversation with the gatekeeper.

"I'm deeply sorry, honored sirs," the gatekeeper was saying. "But I've never seen the man you describe."

"I see," the younger cutter said—a boy, barely old enough to have sat for his examinations, his wide, innocent face oddly out of place. "But still, he might have passed your way."

The gatekeeper made a respectful gesture of denial. "This is the

Graceful Aining's house, not a pleasure place. There are no scholars here."

The elder of the cutters looked amused, a predatory smile spreading across his pale features. "We know what games your mistress plays in her bedchamber. It's her own business, as long as she pays her dues to the Ministry and doesn't run afoul of the law." His voice was skeptical: as one of the rare women on New Zhongguo, Aining fell under the purview of the Ministry, and the cutters would no doubt have preferred her in some high official's harem, where they could be assured of controlling her.

Not a chance, of course. Aining might appear well-bred and soft -spoken, but beneath the manners was a will as unbending as the essence of metal.

The gatekeeper's voice was stiff. "My mistress is no fool, honored sirs. She would never harbor a fugitive."

"Who said he was a fugitive?" the elder asked. "We're merely looking to have a...conversation with Bi Leyou, that's all."

"A long and productive one," the younger one said, and his earnest, naive smile was more frightening than that of his elder.

Leyou turned off the sound, keeping a distant eye on the situation. The gatekeeper would see them off; they had no proof yet, only suspicions. Otherwise, they wouldn't have bothered to ring the chimes. They'd have battered down the door and invaded every room until they found him—and dragged him out, back into his husband Kong Pin's embrace.

That was why he'd run away. He'd borne Kong Pin's foibles, the growing darkness in the household, the pain and the misery of being a spouse—powerless and moneyless, bending his head to reproaches and blows. But then Kong Pin had got it into his head to become respectable, to have children to bear his name, children who wouldn't be born in incubators, but borne in a womb and birthed in labor and pain and pride.

That had been the breaking point.

To bear children, you needed to become caihe: to be remodeled as a half-man, your breasts raised from your chest, your hips widened, your womb carved out by robot surgeons and knives—a machine, that's what the cutters would break Leyou into, nothing like what Heaven had meant when creating men and women.

So Leyou had run away—into the darkness of the streets, finally finding himself here, in a wholly different kind of embrace, in a shelter he'd never conceived of, not even in his most far-fetched poems. And he wasn't going back; he just couldn't.

Outside, the cutters had finished their conversation and were taking their leave politely. But the elder one glanced up at the house with a dark, amused light in his eyes; they'd be back, and soon.

Leyou had to be gone before that happened.

He found Aining in her studio, putting the finishing touches to a model of a palanquin. Her broad hands wielded the brush with surprising deftness and precision, transferring the coat of paint from the thick, black hairs of the brush to the motor compartment.

When she was finished, Aining laid the model on her desk, next to that of the spaceship—the one that bore the chakra wheel symbol of her homeworld, Trimurti, and a dusky-skinned pilot in the cockpit, like a diminished memory of Aining herself.

"You're up early," she said with a frown.

Leyou knew there was no point dancing around the truth. Aining wasn't New Zhongguan; she didn't impart her opinion subtly and carefully, or pass on secret messages through her silence. "The cutters came," he said. "I saw them."

Aining was silent for a moment, her lips drawn as tight as a brushstroke. "But they didn't see you. You wouldn't be here if they had."

"No," Leyou said. He fought a growing hollow in his stomach. "But they'll be back, Aining. I need—"

Aining made a quick, stabbing gesture with her hand. "I know what you need," she said. "But travel documents aren't easy to obtain. It takes time."

"That's what you said two moons ago."

"And it's still true. Leyou, you can't afford to be so impatient." She came closer, leaning her large frame over his shoulder for a brief kiss on his neck, which tingled like a memory of need.

But even that did nothing to close the hollow in his stomach or banish the nightmare images of blood and pain hovering in his mind. "There were cutters on your doorstep, Aining. Not scholars or officials. *Cutters.* You know they won't give up. They'll be back—they have to—"

Aining turned away from him and said nothing for a while. "Even if it were true," she said, "—and trust me, cutters are like the rest of us, easily mistaken—what would you want me to do about it? I've already told you." Her voice was weary. "Your papers will be here in a week. That's the most I can do for you."

"I know," Leyou said. "Heaven strike me, I know." He knew that she was taking risks by keeping him so long, that the cutters would latch onto any excuse to take away her fragile independence, that she pitied him and wanted to do right by him. But still…. "You said you had other means. The others—"

From time to time, a man or a half-man caihe would come to Aining's house with the sick light of the hunted in his eyes. Aining would receive them in her studio for hours on end—and the following morning, they were gone.

Aining massaged her forehead thoughtfully. "Trust me, Leyou. That way's not for you."

"I might not have any choice left," Leyou said.

"You're a harsh man," Aining said. "An unbending one."

"What does this have to do with anything?" Leyou asked. He'd thought of leaving, more than once, but Aining was his only chance of a normal life: he could find another city, another identity that the Ministry wouldn't hunt so relentlessly. He could start afresh.

But Aining was his only chance; and she was his drug, too, haunting his days as she did his nights, the memories of their bodies mingled together bittersweet, a breathtaking experience that could not last. A New Zhongguan who was no high official had no business bedding a woman—Heaven forbid that his seed might take, implant tainted offspring in the womb.

Aining made a sound halfway between a sigh and a snort. "Leyou, you worry too much. I've run this household for far longer than you've been on the run. Everything will be fine."

"I know," Leyou said, exhaling. "I know you're doing your best. I know you could get killed for what you do."

Aining snorted again. "They'd never kill a woman, Leyou. We're far too precious on New Zhongguo. More precious than jade, more precious than water. Rarity does that to you."

"They can still—" Leyou started; and stopped. "There's plenty of things they can do to you." He knew a lot of them, from his days in Kong Pin's household: all the ways you could hit and not leave marks that showed; all the casual cruelties, the rough sex that made him want to scream; the slow and methodical way Kong Pin's other spouse, Ren Xuan, would apply white ceruse makeup, layer after layer until the bruises on his cheeks and forehead had all but vanished.

Aining's face twisted. "Leyou—" She reached out, stroked his shoulder gently. "You shouldn't think about that."

Leyou shrugged. It was the distant past, another life he'd set aside. It couldn't hurt him, not anymore. He wouldn't let it.

"Gods, sometimes I wish I could get my hands on this man," Aining said darkly. "Some lives are worse than death. And some people are quite busy making sure they stay that way."

"It's nothing," Leyou said. "You worry too much." It didn't come out as he'd wanted; it made her sound overwrought and stressed, whereas he'd meant to say was that she couldn't right all the sins of the world, that she couldn't better everyone's lives, no matter how hard she wanted it.

Aining smiled. "See, now you're the one saying it. But they'd never hurt me that way, Leyou." Her face hardened. "They'd get me with child, yes, but they'd make sure I was pampered."

"And imprisoned," Leyou said.

"A woman's life is better than a man's," Aining said. "You people starve in the streets and go weak with sicknesses and are worn to stubs through braving the storms every day. I'll take the gilded prison, any day. But then I've always been pragmatic." She moved her hand away from Leyou. "But you *do* worry too much, you know. Get the cutters out of your head. I'll see you out of here, safe and sound. It's a promise."

She sounded unconcerned, but then she hadn't seen the cutters. She hadn't seen the promise in the elder one's eyes, the dark amusement in their bearing. She wasn't the one waking up to nightmares of knives, blood welling up from the red line they'd drawn on the skin—and Kong Pin, standing in the background, watching it all, his breath heavy with pleasure....

"Honored mistress," someone said at the door.

It was the gatekeeper, escorting a cloaked figure: a caihe, the hunched set of his shoulders familiar.

Aining's face shifted slightly, her rough features melting in a startling grimace of sadness—as if she had just lost something dear. "Oh dear. Come on in, you poor thing."

Leyou knew better than to overstay his welcome; she'd throw him out soon enough, anyway.

"I'll be in my room," he said, making his way out. He bowed briefly, perfunctorily, to the caihe, who bowed in return—frowning, as if not sure where to place him.

Now that Leyou was close, he could see the folds of fat on the caihe's face, the traits that were too soft, as if the skin had melted in some great oven—the swaying hips, too wide to be true, the breasts, overlarge, hanging like rotten fruit.

To think that the Ministry of Rites took the body of birth—the precious, hallowed gift of Heaven and of the parents—and wrecked it, molded it into...this.

That was how far they'd fallen.

He walked back to his rooms in a bleak mood, determined to find some distraction, to listen to some opera or live poetry broadcast. In the end, though, he settled for the first book he could find: the Annals of the Autumn Landing, which described the colonists' ancestors' arrivals on New Zhongguo and the first battles to be fought for supremacy over the planet of red dust.

He was perhaps thirty pages in when his screen beeped: a private communication, sent to one of his old inboxes. Most of those, he knew, would be Ministry plants; if they could trace him to Aining's house, they would be justified in invading it to drag him out.

The shortened information disclosed nothing more than the sender—the Hermit of the Perfumed River—but that information was enough to give Leyou pause. The Hermit of the Perfumed River was the pen name of Ren Xuan, Kong Pin's other spouse: a name he had disclosed to no one, not even his husband, for Kong Pin did not approve of spouses writing poetry, thinking it a most unfeminine act.

It was a ploy. It had to be. Xuan had revealed the name, he was working with the cutters....

But it seemed too convoluted, even for Leyou's paranoia. There were other means to catch him, less elaborate—not this message, the very existence of which seemed suspicious.

He took a deep breath and downloaded it.

It was short and to the point, most unlike Xuan.

Leyou. I'm outside, in the back street. I'm alone, promise—let me swallow a thousand needles if I lie. Please. I need to talk to you.

Xuan, here? Impossible; he had always loved his comforts, reveling in Kong Pin's protection—his shield against the outside world, against the storms that blew dirt on spun silk, that desiccated the skin and painted new wrinkles on a man's face like thousands of small wounds.

But still....

He thought of Xuan, of his easy smile, of the broad face creased in thought over a particular verse, and felt an abrupt, sickening nostalgia for the life he'd left: the life that might have been brutal, subjected to the whims of another, but one which wasn't that of a cloistered fugitive, living in perpetual fear of the future.

Before he could think, or regret, he was walking out of his room.

There was a small courtyard at the back of the street. It was unguarded, a discreet exit for Aining's refugees. Nine pine trees

surrounded a stylized turtle on a ceramic tile, and thin filaments—
the remnants of a wisteria plant that hadn't weathered the latest seasons of storms—dipped toward the water as if in thirst.

Leyou stood for a moment, hesitant. But if Aining wouldn't help
him, he'd take comfort where he could.

The door slid under his touch, as if eager. Outside, there was
nothing but howling winds and dust that prickled his eyes. Carefully, he advanced into the street, wary, ready to bolt back inside if
the need came.

A dark silhouette waited for him, leaning against the ochre wall.
"Xuan?" Leyou asked.

The silhouette moved, and there came the hum of a repulsor
screen. Gradually, the wind's howls faded to nothing, replaced by a
quiet gurgle of running water.

"I'm glad you came," Xuan said.

The voice—the voice was high and hovering on the verge of
breaking, with that particular falsetto, a metallic accent. And the
face....

"They got to you, didn't they?" Leyou asked, fighting not to run
back inside. His eyes traced the contours of a face that had once
been as familiar as his own—now fattened with folds of flesh, the
harsh traits smoothed out, the eyes receding into beadiness.
"They—"

Xuan sucked in a breath between his teeth, a gesture of dis-
agreement. "It's not such a bad life, Leyou."

He did not say, "better than that of a fugitive," but the words
hung in the air anyway.

"And you've come here to preach the laws of the Ministry to
me?" Leyou asked. Everywhere he looked, he saw only the unfamiliar, the artificial. Xuan's breasts were small and too straight, his hips
stuck at an awkward angle, and his belly was slightly round. Surely
he couldn't be carrying already, not in a way that would show?

Xuan stared at him for a while. "I could preach. But I don't think
that's what you want."

Leyou fought the urge to vomit. "No," he said. "I didn't expect you'd go for it. All because Kong Pin wanted some respectability, a proper *harem*—"

Xuan cut him off. "I know what you believe in."

"Everyone believed it, once," Leyou said. "Before the Exodus." *Father's flesh and Mother's blood should not be thrown away, or debased. Take what Heaven in its benevolence granted you....* But things had changed, decayed.

Xuan snorted. "Well, not all of us have the heart and liver solid enough to run away. You're not even asking why I'm here."

"Sorry," Leyou said, his eyes still glued to Xuan's face. He needed to see past this, he really did. It wasn't just any caihe; it was Xuan. Xuan with whom he'd laughed and held drunken poetry contests late at night; Xuan who would stay up chopping mushrooms and vegetables to make a restorative meal after Kong Pin had had sex with them. "Why are you here? I imagine it's not to give me away."

Xuan snorted. "To each of us their own choices. But you should get out of here, Leyou, you really should."

"I don't understand—"

"That's because you haven't heard the stories," Xuan said, shaking his head, one of his hands moving to brush the small breasts on his chest, as if still unused to them. "This house is bad, Leyou. It's cursed."

"By ghosts?" Leyou shook his head, amused. "We never believed in spirits."

"Maybe you should start," Xuan said. He paused, obviously at a loss for words. "Look, Leyou. I enquired, and it wasn't hard to find information, even from inside my quarters. The men that come here never come out."

"That's the point," Leyou said. "She helps them get a new life— forged papers, a new identity—everything they need to start afresh."

Xuan sucked in a noisy breath through his teeth again. "I don't think so. When I say they don't turn up, they don't. Ever. Not under a different name, not in a different place. They just...vanish."

Leyou remembered the grimace of sadness that had crossed Aining's face when seeing the caihe. "What do you mean, 'vanish'?" Someone was holding a shard of ice above his heart, the point just piercing the muscle—he was just starting to feel the pain, the coldness....

Xuan spread his hands. "I can't tell you more than that, because I don't know. You could ask her, I suppose. But my advice remains: I'd get out of here, as fast as you can."

Some lives are worse than death....

The shard was going in, slowly, irretrievably. "What do you think she does with them?" Leyou asked.

Xuan did not answer. But it was obvious, wasn't it, what he thought?

It couldn't be true. Not Aining, Aining with her heart as fragile and as beautiful as jade, who felt for every one of her refugees....

Xuan folded his arms back into his sleeves; clearly, he had said all he wanted to say and was taking his leave. But something in the stiff manner in which he moved tugged at Leyou's heart in a familiar way. "He's still at it, then."

Xuan's face was expressionless. "It doesn't matter, Leyou."

"It does," Leyou said. Kong Pin's household was a thousand small things that pushed against you until you broke, and Xuan was now alone in it. "I shouldn't have left. I'm a fool."

"To each of us our own choices," Xuan said, and he really did sound as though he believed it—and, for a moment, Leyou saw his old friend beneath the mask of the caihe, pretending not to care for the others' sake.

"That's why I had to run," Leyou said, finally, looking away from Xuan. "That's why you should, too. He'll never be happy with what he has, not until he's broken it. And being a caihe won't make things better."

Xuan was silent for a while. "I'll carry his child," he said. "The seed that will continue his lineage, worship his ancestors. He won't dare break that. He won't—"

He'll look at you and hate you, Leyou thought. *He'll see the* same I do: a creature neither man nor woman, a *made* thing. Every day he'll hate you for not being the wife of his dreams. And every night, too, after he's entered you and seen, again and again, that you're not a woman.

But he couldn't say that to Xuan, couldn't make him break down.

"It might be better," he said, wishing his lie not to show in his eyes.

Xuan shook his head, with a sad smile. "It might. Thank you, Leyou."

"I'm the one who should thank you. For the warning."

Xuan made a dismissive gesture. "That's hardly a problem. Kong Pin won't be back from his office for a while yet, and you could do with some directions." He smiled, a little stiffly. "You always could. Don't worry about me. I'll be fine."

Of course he wouldn't. This—everything—it was as wrong as Heaven under Earth. It was unfair, and there was nothing he or Xuan could do about it.

"Be careful," Leyou said, finally. "You know your limits."

Xuan snorted. "Do I ever."

He never did; that was the trouble. He'd just walk as if nothing was wrong, even with broken bones. "Please," Leyou said. "You should make other plans...."

"You too, Leyou," Xuan said. "Think about it."

Leyou looked up at the house towering above him, a darker and crueler place than it had been in the morning. "I know," he said. "I know."

Leyou walked back into the house, more rattled than he'd wanted to admit to Xuan. Xuan was the quintessential stay-at-home, perfectly suited for the role of spouse save for the impulses of men like Kong Pin. For him to have come all this way, to have braved the wind and the dust, he had to believe strongly in what he said—and, knowing Xuan, that meant a lot. He wasn't a man given to fancies; being a caihe hadn't changed him.

Leyou wandered for a while in the gardens, another of Aining's follies: orchid flowers and plum trees in a setting of rocks and waterfalls—as if anything as delicate as flowers could withstand the climate of New Zhongguo for long.

But he couldn't so easily forget what Xuan had told him.

They just...vanish.

Aining made it all sound so simple when she spoke of it: like a simple process, sending them on to their new lives....

New lives. He was so naive. No wonder they'd thought him unsuited for high office, no wonder they'd shut him in manual labor until he'd happened to catch Kong Pin's eye. They didn't get lives at all.

No. He wouldn't believe that. Aining had taken him in, sheltered him....

But why else would she refuse him? Why else would she look so sad, so haunted?

Some lives are worse than death.

No. She had to be sending them on to some better place, some hidden place that even Xuan couldn't find out about. She might not want to send him, but that was only because she wanted him there, to be bedded and stroked whenever the urge took her. Had to be. Selfishness was one thing, but the other....

He took a long, steadying breath, but it was too late. Xuan had planted doubt too deep.

He looked at the house again, the myriad quarters and courtyards and rooms filled with Aining's models and paintings: the house he'd never explored, never wondered about. And why should he have? He'd had Aining—a woman, who wanted to sleep with him; a woman who loved him and would keep him safe from harm. All he had to do was wait.

But he couldn't wait anymore.

Inside, the wide-paneled corridors were much as they had always been: elegant, tasteful, decorated with eight-sided mirrors and pictures of mountains and waterfalls from Old Earth and the occasional picture of Aining in women's robes, her large face smiling broadly at the camera—almost ugly compared to the frail, delicate beauties that decorated the panels...Lady Xi, the Distinguished Bride, the Favored Concubine.... He used to think that didn't matter; the beauties were all in the distant past of pre-Exodus China or shut in some inaccessible harem. Aining was here. But now he looked at her eyes and wondered how one could read guilt, or remorse, from pictures and holovids.

He couldn't, of course.

The house was eerily quiet; from afar came the distant sounds of chanted sutras in the droning voices of neutered men. The floor moaned under Leyou's feet, as if eager to denounce him. The pictures seemed to grow ever closer, oppressing him with a memory of what the world should be like, of what it had been like before they fled—before Old Earth was engulfed in the fire of alchemists, which had seared every plant and every rock until nothing grew evermore—before women became rarer than water, rarer than jade or pearls.

At length, he reached a corridor, as quiet as the others, but in which Aining's scent hung, citrus and ginger and something else.

He walked to the door at the end of that corridor, a huge pane of metal tightly closed against prying gazes. As he got closer and closer, seeing his reflection in the glass grow larger, his arms and legs shrinking and expanding on the rhythm of his walk, the citrus and the ginger slowly faded away until he smelled one thing, and one thing only: a sharp tang against his tongue.

Blood.

There were stains before the door, scrubbed away, covered by bleach and vinegar, but the smell wouldn't go away. It still hung in the air, as thick as a funeral shroud.

Some lives are worse than death.

No. No. Aining wouldn't....

The cold part of him—the part that Kong Pin had shaped with closed fists, with bruises, with cracked bones—went on walking. Past the door, past the stains, past the blood, into a smaller corridor, almost an afterthought. Aining's smell was fainter there, forgotten.

The smell of blood, though, remained, working its way deeper into his clothes, under his skin.

The corridor led into a courtyard he had never seen. It, too, was deserted. It was a quiet place with an overgrown pine tree over wilting flowers and a small octagonal pavilion at the center.

In the pavilion was a funeral pyre. It was empty, scrubbed clean, but this somehow made it worse, like a gaping maw awaiting victims.

Raising his gaze, he saw the seated figure of Guanyin, bodhisattva of Mercy, smiling her enigmatic smile at him. A quotation from Buddhist scripture wrapped its way around the base of the pyre: *Life is worth so little, oh Man! Remember this lesson, when the time comes to set it aside.*

To set it aside.

Under the smiling bodhisattva was a row of urns, neatly aligned, labeled with Aining's decisive brushstrokes. *Lin Pao, son-in-law of Gan Tian and Zhu Pao. Respectful spouse of Gan Jihan. Came to an end on the fifth day of the second moon, in the fifteenth year of the Tianshu reign. Fai Guilin, son-in-law of Yu Chiang and Ming Sun. Respectful spouse of Yu Bei. Came to an end….*

Oh, Celestials, Xuan had been right. She was killing them. With love, with mercy, and with compassion….

Nausea welled up in his throat, raw and inescapable, a dry heaving that racked his esophagus, sending him to his knees, tears welling up in his eyes.

Each and every one of them, from the first to the last.

Oh, Celestials….

He did not know how long he knelt there, breathing in the smell of blood and old ashes under the wide, mocking eyes of the bodhisattva, the row upon row of mute testimonials to snuffed-out lives.

Somehow, he made his way back to his room, to the pathetic dearth that had been his life for the past few moons. The bed smelled of old sex: dried stains of his seed upon the covering and Aining's scent, hanging just out of reach, stirring nausea again in his gut.

Cutters or not, he needed to get out of there. There was no telling what she'd think of next—when she grew bored of him in bed, when her conscience stopped warring with her instincts. The protective mother, opening her arms wide: come, you poor child, come. Let us make an end of it....

He was easily packed, his few clothes crammed into a bag, his chopsticks and writing pad hastily thrown on top of everything else. At the door of his room, he paused for a moment, looking at the discreet, tasteful decoration—and, feeling for a moment, the touch of Aining's hands on his spine, sending a shiver of pleasure to arch his back, her eyes open wide as he took her, the little moan as he spent himself inside her, the smile as she lay on his chest, the feeling that everything was right, was as Heaven had meant it to be.

Once he'd left, he wouldn't ever sleep with a woman again—wouldn't ever find anyone like Aining.

And what did it matter? She was mad, dispensing the final mercies instead of trying to help. No, he was well gone, out of her reach. Out of her hands before she turned him into another urn to add to her tally.

He shouldered his bag and went out.

It was the noon hour, and the wind blew the red earth through the gardens, plastering it over the crimson walls. Leyou wrapped his scarf around his face and trudged through the howling storm toward the waiting gates. The gatekeeper probably knew what Aining was up to, but if Leyou could overpower him—if he could get out of here before Aining was finished with her grisly task downstairs—

He trudged through the gardens, blinking repeatedly to clear the sand from his eyes. His legs ached already; one did not brave the storms casually, but he had no choice. Xuan had been right: it was high time he left.

Because of the winds, he didn't see or hear the group at the gates until he was almost there.

The cutters, standing smug and self-satisfied behind their repulsor screens. And, behind the cutters....

Kong Pin's thin, haughty face—the face of a man who never let anything of his escape, never surrendered any of his toys to another's hands—and Xuan, hovering in the background, his face a mask, his eyes fearful. And behind Xuan, a posse of Ministry guards, more than enough to raze the house if the fancy took them.

Get out of here, as fast as you can. You fool.

The breath slid away from him, leaving only ice in his lungs.

He had to run. Now now now.

But running would give him away. They'd catch him easily enough, drag him back to the Ministry, to the tables and the knives; they would break him according to Kong Pin's wishes. They would—

With a supreme effort of will, he kept himself still, quieting the mad beating of his heart. Slowly, carefully, he turned away from the group at the gates, as if he had merely forgotten something in the house. He walked away, one step at a time—against the winds, fighting the urge to turn back, to know if they were following.

One step after the other, the house growing nearer and nearer: the inner courtyard, the hallway leading back to his room....

Their voices drifted to him over the noise of the storm.

"...search every room...," the elder cutter was saying. "...find him, one way or another...."

"...trap him...."

"...bring him home...." Kong Pin's voice, low and cultured, as if this were nothing, just another inconvenience that would soon be resolved.

Leyou climbed the stairs to his room two at a time, just as the sound of dozens of booted feet echoed under the ceiling of the hallway.

"Leave two men in every room," the elder cutter was saying. "Our fugitive will soon run out of refuges." He laughed: a dry, cruel sound, like a hunter finally running down a deer.

More booted feet. They were spreading through the house, invading Aining's sanctuary. He stood on the threshold of his room, unable to bring himself to move. At any moment he'd feel their hands on his shoulders, the soft pop of the tranquilizer syringe as they slid it into his neck.

Kong Pin whispered in his mind, *Come back, Leyou. Let me have you, let me take you, let me remake you....*

There was no escape.

Aining.

She'd find a way—she'd always find a way. Surely she loved him; surely she wouldn't let him die. Surely....

He ran, then, his legs propelling him into the empty corridors, always ahead of the men spreading themselves through the house, of the voices calling to each other in calm, professional tones.

"Second courtyard secured...."

"...no one in the kitchens...."

The door, when he reached it, was locked, as it had been before. He banged his fists against the metal, every hit echoing in his chest, on the rhythm of his frantic heartbeat. Surely they'd hear, surely they'd find him out—come on Aining, come on....

The door swung open at the same time as one of the men screamed a cry of triumph.

"Here!"

But Leyou was already in, slamming the door back on its hinges, finding the lock by touch more than by sight and engaging it with a flick of his hands.

Only then did he rise to face Aining.

The room smelled, not of blood of or death, but of bleach and opium. Machines hummed on the tables—all round and smooth like eggs, obviously of offworld manufacture—and strange liquids sloshed in beakers, a hypnotic display of colors swirling behind the glass, as if trapped.

Aining had retreated to the end of the room, watching him with hooded, unreadable eyes, her pink robes weighed down at the sleeves with the unmistakable shape of knives.

"They're in the house," Leyou whispered, even as the first blow—dull, distant—broke itself against the door. "The cutters. Please...."

And then he saw the bed at the back. Someone lay on it: a woman Leyou had never met, with almond eyes surrounded by a sea of bruises that spread from forehead to cheeks to chin. A simple red robe covered her; her small breasts rose and fell to the rhythm of her slow, even breath. For all the bruises, she looked like a maiden caught in innocent sleep—

No, wait.

He *had* seen her before, but she had not been a woman then—a caihe, one of Aining's refugees, destined for a grave at the back of the garden....

The universe lurched out of focus again, Heaven slowly sliding under Earth, the world's axis snapping like a bent twig.

No no no.

"You make them," he whispered. He looked from Aining to the woman, from the woman to Aining, and then back again, as if something, anything, might change.

Aining's face was a painted mask, frozen into place. "You people know nothing about gender changes," she said with a contemptuous toss of her head. "Rank amateurs. You take men and bend them out of shape until they break; and then you go on to make them pregnant, as if this could make everything right."

Not only pregnant; he thought of Xuan, of the stiff way he moved, of all he was enduring, wordlessly. "You—" Leyou whispered. "You could have turned them back into men," he said, finally, because it was the only thing that came to mind. "Into what they were meant to be."

Aining tossed her head again. "Does it matter, if the change is perfect?" He saw in her eyes the reflection of his haggard, horrified face. Of course it mattered. How could she not see it? How could she pretend herself better than the cutters?

She shook her head, amused. "As men, they're filed in the Ministry of Rites' files. Women are much harder to track. And they'll have better lives."

"In some gilded harem—"

"I already told you. They'll be more precious than water, more precious than jade. They will be cared for—they might even be loved, for who doesn't love jade, or water?" Her voice was mocking.

The blows against the door were redoubling in intensity, though the metal pane did not seem to bend in the slightest. Still time—time to stare at Aining, at the enormity of the caihe who wasn't one anymore.

"You have a choice," Aining said. She, too, was looking at the door. "You can walk out of here into their hands, or—" she raised her hands; the sleeves went down, outlining the knives in their sheathes "—you can put yourself into mine."

"I would be—"

"Entering a different life." Her voice was slow and gentle but firm. "But you must have known this one was over as soon as you ran away."

"I—" Leyou looked at the door again, then back at the caihe— the face remolded, the breasts enlarged and firmed, the hips slightly flaring out. No more natural than what he had been before, done with consummate skill, yes, but the womb inside was still machine-made, the breasts had still been carved out of flesh by knives; the broad, rough face was still a construct.

He stared at the door, thinking of Xuan's stiff moves, of Kong Pin and of the cutters and what they would do to him. Kong Pin couldn't afford a woman; he would be safe, or as safe as he could, if he could only—

"I can't change," he whispered, knowing it was the wish of a spoiled child.

Aining's face was sad. "I know," she said. "That's why I never offered before. But you have to, Leyou." She held out her hands to him, as inviting and wide as they had ever been. *Come to me, come to find your shelter….*

"Not that way, " he whispered. "You don't understand. It's never going to be the same. I was born a man. You can't change that. You can't ever change that. No one can." The Celestials, per-haps, but if they had wanted to do anything, they wouldn't have let New Zhongguo come about.

Aining's eyes narrowed. "Don't be a fool. The body is exactly the same. The humors in the blood will be regulated the same way." She turned, slightly, to look at the caihe on the bed. "In time, the heart and mind will follow. That's all we are, Leyou. Flesh and muscles and blood. There's nothing more than that."

She couldn't see. She'd never been able to see. "You don't understand," Leyou repeated. "There's more to it. There's the way Heaven made us, the way our parents gave birth to us—"

"You're a fool, Leyou. I can tell you, it changes nothing. A gender-changed man is no different from a woman. I've seen it so many times." Her voice was wistful. "It takes time, but it can be learned, step after step. And it gets better as time passes."

How would she know? Her refugees never stuck around for long enough. How would she....

He stopped, then. He stared at her broad, rough face, at the hands he'd always thought too thick and ungainly compared to that of the ancient beauties. He tried to imagine her with her hair in a topknot—not the elaborate construction she pinned with jewelry, but a simple, masculine design—and he finally understood what had been under his eyes all along.

"Aining—please tell me you were born a woman. Please—"

Aining said nothing.

He had slept with her. He had believed himself so fortunate—felicitous, blessed by Heaven and the God of Lovers, tied to her with the red thread of fate, or of sex at least—he'd believed he had enjoyed something far beyond his station.

Lies. All lies. She was nothing more, nothing less than a caihe: remade, remolded, a creation of man and his arrogance—worse, for you could tell a caihe apart from a man, but with what she offered, there would be no visible difference. The flaws, the cracks would all be in the minds, the subtle differences wouldn't be spotted, and they'd all live a lie, everything subtly twisted out of shape. They wouldn't be able to tell the impostors apart from the real women, wouldn't see who had been made by Heaven and who had been made by men and machines....

"Leyou—" Aining started.

He was moving then, toward her, his hands reaching for her, and at the last moment she must have seen that it wasn't love or desire on his face, for she tried to turn away. But he was already upon her. His weight carried her to the ground, and his fingers closed around her neck—the large, ungainly neck that wasn't that of a woman, that had never been.

He had strong hands from years of manual labor, and she barely had time to struggle. Her mouth opened and closed, but no word could come out of her crushed windpipe. Her face turned a dark blue, and her eyes bulged out of her orbits; she kept looking at him as he squeezed, and he saw the surprise and the disappointment etched on her face slowly fade away into the blankness of death.

You're a harsh man, Leyou. An unbending one.

Not unbending, no. But harsh enough to do what needed to be done.

He stood for a few ragged breaths over her body, trying to find the words of a prayer, but finding nothing in the growing silence of his mind.

Life is worth so little, oh Man! Remember this....

The door shuddered and buckled in. They would soon be inside: the cutters and Kong Pin—and Xuan with his body carved by knives, Xuan with his falsetto voice and his breasts that were too small, the living image of what Leyou had once feared so much.

They'd come in and see him, standing over the body of a woman he had loved and killed.

He didn't know what they would do. They might execute him for her murder or carve him and give him to Kong Pin as a caihe, knowing this to be ample punishment.

But with Aining dead, they wouldn't see. The machines would be polluted toys, the woman on the bed just another of Aining's playthings. They wouldn't understand the knowledge that promised a greater debasement, a more elaborate and subtle twisting of the laws of Heaven, even more out of place than New Zhongguo.

And that was a thought he would take with him, a warmth he would draw comfort from, all the rest of his warped life.

There *were* worse things, after all.

A STONE CAST INTO STILLNESS

Maurice Broaddus

The text of the tear-smudged page was barely legible, but she stared at her Certificate of Procreation notice. She re-read it with a hollow ache, a derisive laugh dying on her lips. She vidded the insurance company in charge of bonding her caste and was bounced from bureaucrat to bureaucrat, never connecting to an actual person. Each time, she explained her situation. Each time, there was a pause as the drones calculated and conferred, scanned their data banks, and with all due deliberation, responded the same way.

"Your Certificate of Procreation has been issued." The electronic voice emulated a soothing, nearly human tone. The image matched her race and sex, drawing on her information to provide a relatable image.

"I know. There must be a mistake."

"You have your certificate?" The AI system must have had a snark subroutine running to produce its snide tone.

"Yes, but...."

"Then there's been no mistake. Thank you." The vid disconnected.

Each time, the same reply. According to her medical records, she was pregnant. No amount of her arguing a computer glitch could sway them. She would have been due today. And, by law, the poor—even the working poor—only had one chance at a family.

The bare room faded to its usual grey walls. She had once thought it a suitable punishment for criminals to have to sit alone, with just their thoughts and loss, in a room of grey. Such was the way to madness. Hell was a kind nothing. She wrapped herself in her blanket; the room never seemed to warm her despite her adjustments to the settings. The hair on her legs scraped against the fabric. Catching a whiff of it as she fidgeted, she hoped it hadn't captured her unwashed odor and wondered if she truly smelled that sour. It reminded her of her work: packed into rooms like slaves during Middle Passage, one atop another; the press of bodies stroking consoles and coaxing data along; the air thick with body odor and heavy floral perfumes to cover the body odor.

Luckily, she was no longer as sensitive to smells as she had once been.

On the couch, she activated her eye panel, a high-res viz screen dropping into place and allowing her net access through the eyepiece. It was the first time she'd connected to the net in weeks. She flicked through net stations, over a million different sites, and nothing was on. Sometimes she saw things and she didn't think they were dreams. Images of older days with the space of parks, of the green of lawns, of white picket fences and a corner to raise a family. Sometimes she heard things. An infant's coo. A baby's cry. The laughter of a child. And she knew those were tricks of an overwrought imagination.

Her door chimed.

"Come in," she said, not bothering to stir from the couch, an empty soul trapped between where it was and where it wanted to be.

"How're you holding up?" her friend asked. The fabric of her stiff grey dress hid whatever figure she had, rendering her shapeless. They shared the same caste, though her friend lived on the bottom side. "Would you like something to eat?"

"No."

"I can make pelmini. Or how about a boeuf bourguignon, or maybe a light yosenabe?" She stood at the console ready to program in flavors to give the experience of taste to the nutritional paste. As a cook designate, the chip assigned and implanted into her allowed her to create a virtual symphony for the palate, even if the food wasn't actually there.

Like her visiting friend, the woman was in the working caste, chosen early in life to be wired, programmed with skill sets, thus there was no need for formal school training. No need for a name. Drones used numerical designations, but rarely when not in the employment cycle.

Unlike her friend, she was fortunate enough to have been implanted with an AI chip, a virtual mid-tech at the general data warehouse with 234 floors of glass-walled cubicles jacked into the systems. Some had menial tasks, like plugging logic chips into everyday products, making toothbrushes that could monitor the number of strokes and keep detailed dental records for the medical corporations. Every day sifted through the endless streams of programming code; a cog in the machine, denied further upgrades.

Having accumulated several weeks of vacation, she burned through them with abandon. An early return to work would only have her depression diagnosed, and either she'd be put on mandatory treatment or have her situation cured by being taken off the employment cycle. Damn the corporations and the madmen who ran them.

"I said no," she said, her words a little too harsh. Nothing sounded good to her. Nothing had any taste. She'd lost thirty pounds in four weeks, yet her medical records didn't reflect concern, probably assuming the loss of baby weight.

Her friend had that look in her eye, her unspoken "What do you have to be sad about? You live in the towers, in the gleaming" expression that usually signaled her departure. True, she lived in the gleaming, one of the huge towers that saw sunshine when the sun passed between the other buildings. They were what passed for middle caste, and life there certainly beat the camps of the bottom side, where people slept on pallets in the streets and were interred, disowned, and disappeared. Those in the gleaming had huge homes, a nearly twelve-by-twelve room; hers was on the ninety-ninth floor. The politicians boasted that the gleaming's residents were among the richest poor on the planet—while the politicians themselves and the rest of the wealthy resided in lunar colonies. Her friend left without another word, off to her proscribed tasks, passing her husband as she exited.

"I interrupt something?" He tugged at the cardboard-stiff grey collar of his grey frock as if the itch of temperature was what made him uncomfortable. He adjusted the environmental control settings.

"The usual."

"Honey, I've got something for you."

"What?"

"First, you have to promise to hear me out." Keeping his back to her, he moved toward the console, obviously concealing something, doing little better than a child trying to conceal a toy to be sneaked into his bedroom at bed time.

"Where would I go?" She frustrated him, she understood. He didn't know what to do, remaining patient when she screamed herself awake at night. She loved him....

...but the sound of his voice irritated her. His touch made her recoil. The idea of him lying next to her repulsed her. The act of love -making struck her as vile and primitive. What were they thinking? Thinking themselves so young and rebellious. Flopping about like beasts in the sweaty entwinement of bodies, the mess of swapping fluids, for what? To appear vital? Defiant? Safely anarchist? They flirted with monogamy, not even a quad-couple or a marriage pod, despite the less-than-subtle inquiries by her friend. They engaged in actual sex while their friends, their social strata, participated in the rite of the joining of seed, a ceremony witnessed by friends and family, fully sanctioned by the government. Another thread in the tapestry of the medical bureaucracy.

"I know you've been depressed lately about...."

He couldn't bring himself to say it. Ever since that night, he had never spoken of it. The loss. But his eyes hadn't met hers since then, afraid that to look at her would disclose his own anguish. Even now, he focused his attention on the data cube as he fumbled about the panel, downloading whatever it was he wished to surprise her with.

At one time, they'd had such hope. Money didn't matter. Jobs didn't matter. Life was theirs and they had each other. But as things were wont to do when the bloom of youth faded, their marriage reached a plateau. They continued to love each other in a staid, obligatory way, too wrapped up in their own concerns, joined by their could've-beens and missed opportunities.

Then she found out she was pregnant.

The news terrified and rejuvenated them. Once again they thought outside of themselves, dreamt of possibilities, planned futures. The immature, irresponsible boy he was most of the time seemed to grow up overnight. Through midnight promises and soothing kisses, he talked with great vulnerability and openness about his father—the kind of man he was, the father he wasn't—and vowed to not be like him.

"…so anyway, I got you a VirBab," he said.

"A…VirBab."

"A virtual baby. It's all the rage on the West Coast."

She knew what it was. The latest trend in Hollywood and among the ultra rich who had no desire to dirty themselves with parenting or spoil their bodies with carrying—much less birthing— a child.

"A VirBab," she repeated. The words hung in the air as if their syllables, the very language itself, held no meaning for her.

"Look, we program in our DNA sequences and it knits a baby." He brought over a portable scanner and placed her limp, non-resisting hand on it. The console projected an image. Magnifying the image, two cells joined. The cells creased and folded, appearing to tuck, then double, as they went through their division and replication cycles. "It's programmable. It can gestate at a normal pace so you can watch it develop at each stage. We can even connect you to it so it can monitor your diet and even trigger cravings. Or you can speed things up and it can be a toddler now." Punching in a few commands, the cells morphed through recognizable stages until a face took form, increasing in delineation until it had aged to nearly a year.

The curl of its tiny fists. The cherubic cheeks as if it chewed a mouth full of cotton. The bald head. The large, expansive eyes that followed her with intense interest.

Her husband smiled, too used to getting by on his charm and easy manner. "Can you imagine? We can skip those troublesome teen years."

She hated her husband in that moment.

He was such a...man. Trying to fix something—the hole inside of her, that eternal ache—that couldn't be fixed. A void nothing could fill no matter what she threw at it. A black hole of a wound that bled emptiness that couldn't be staunched. A longing to be swallowed whole and shat out and forgotten. He couldn't get to that place of loss, to know the sting of soul death, a part of herself extinguished in a gesture, a careless word. With the sight of her future and hopes swirling like so much shit down the toilet. Where the most precious love of her life got ripped away and she cried when she realized that person wasn't her husband. He didn't understand the pain, the pain that echoed the hurt of that night.

The pain tore at her insides, waking her from a sound sleep. The terrible cramps, a desperate seizing, a death clutch. Pain so bright and sudden, all she could do was grasp the bedsheets in a voiceless scream and wait for the initial wave to pass.

"What's the matter?" His voice was unshaken and calm. So damned proper and stiff upper-lipped. She wanted him to be scared like her. Scared with her.

She clutched her belly. With half steps, a slow, measured gait, she felt her way through the dark and pain to the bathroom, knowing the fluid trailing down her leg wasn't her broken water. She sat on the toilet waiting for the spasms to stop. Tears trailed down her face, though the pain had already ebbed.

"We can't...." her mind grappled for an excuse as she stared at the ethereal face. "Afford this."

"That's my other surprise. I'm on the employment cycle."

"What are you slotted as?" she asked.

"Artisan."

"Oh."

"It pays. Not especially well, but it's something. Enough to get us over the hump."

There was always a hump. They were trapped in the cycle; the system's claws dug into them and dragged them down. He beamed at her in sick triumph, a little boy who'd proudly given his father a lumpy, cracked ceramic bowl and called it an ashtray, despite his father being a non-smoker; craving his father's approval for a job well-attempted. She knew her role and nodded.

Pleased with himself, he left her with their child. Undoubtedly, he imagined them forming a virtual bond like mothers did.

One day she knew she'd forgive his insensitivity.

She didn't know what to do with her anger. She wanted to hurt someone. She wanted to hurt herself for her body's weakness. She wanted to hurt her husband for his help. He might as well have offered to slit her open and remove her now-useless uterus and label her defective. She wanted to hurt the doctors. The insurance company. The whole damned system and its endless, soul-crushing bureaucracy.

Her legs unfurled from under her, her attention riveted to the ghostly image as she approached it. The baby's eyes followed her movement with abject fascination, a look half quizzical and half lost. A ghost in the machine. Her hand brushed against the image. It shimmered for an instant, as if a signal interfered with it. Her fingers danced along the console panel like a concert pianist playing an unheard melody, opening up dialog boxes and revealing the streaming code that controlled the life of her child. Code easily enough altered.

In her dreams, her beloved child consumed terabytes of data in a hunger so insatiable her breasts ached at the thought of feeding it. A gentle caress sent it data mining, a terrible tantrum of tearing at infrastructures and laying waste to the heart of global corporations. Momma's perfect little angel.

"How's mommy's little man?" She went about the task of program modification.

"Momma." Its voice drew her attention. It cocked its head as if mimicking her. Was that the flicker of cold rage in its porcelain eyes? Maybe it knew her secret hopes and dark dreams. Children longed to please their parents. She averted her gaze and renewed her code manipulation.

"Mommy wanted what was best for you, but everyone gets sick. Catches a virus. Not every virus can be scanned for, vaccinated against, or reported to medical records. I'm so proud of my little man. How much data you hold and how quick your data streams are to self-replicate. You are like a big complex virus holding and hiding many viruses, aren't you?"

"Momma," it cooed. A wan smile crossed its face. Maybe it had passed virtual gas.

"I'm so proud of you. I can't wait to show you off to some of mommy's friends. We'll start with the medical insurance database."

The melancholy cloud lifted from her a bit, a blanket drawn back in the face of a new day. She had much to do in little time.

They grew up so fast, after all.

LOVE KILLS

Gill Ainsworth

"I am your mother's uterus."

The words blasted through Jake Peterson's brain. He turned to the exhibit: a fleshy glob of human tissue within a Plexiglas cage. The glob contorted, then elongated, and slurping sounds erupted inside Jake's skull as if an earthworm slithered between folds of his grey matter. Then the mass of cells morphed into his mother's uterus, a shape he'd seen a million times even though he always tried not to look. He increased his pace—not running; running would get him dismissed, but fast—to get past the numerous stages of his development that demanded his attention.

Sweat collecting over his whole body, he reached the end of the exhibition with the final display's statement, "I am you at birth," still rattling between his eardrums. As he walked up to his boss, he wiped his forehead with the back of his hand.

"Jake. Everything's okay?" Mr. Hofstein asked.

He nodded. "Every exhibit's performing well."

"Good. There's already a queue at the entrance." Hofstein smiled, and his face crinkled into something that reminded Jake of his Stage Seventeen development. Not quite human but getting there.

"I've got a man at the entrance making sure people enter one at a time at two-minute intervals. You're to stay here. Just in case. You know...."

Jake knew. Not on his watch, but it had happened, and every day presented another possibility. He gritted his teeth. "Yes, Mr.

Hofstein," he said, and prayed it would be another ordinary and boring day. Like all employees, he knew about the guy who'd been told, "I am *your* sperm." The poor fellow, even now, would be wanking away, providing sperm sample after sperm sample in case an "I am *your* ovum" failed to turn up in his lifetime. *The poor guy must be sick of porno mags,* Jake thought, imagining a life restricted to white sterile rooms and...well...Jake couldn't envisage what magazines and erotic devices they provided. Certainly more than would be available on the top shelf of a newsagent's or sex shop.

"I am your mother's ovum...I am your father's sperm...I am you, a fertilized egg at two hours gestation...." The familiar words shimmied through Jake's head as punters viewed the exhibits. Today would be like any other day. Of course it would.

So why was he still sweating? Why was his heart palpitating? As a nought-point-nine on the Psi Scale, he had no prescient powers. And he couldn't block or interfere with those who had: the "volunteers." Being a point-niner made him the ideal Zone employee, gave him a well-paid job for life.

"I am you, a fetus at Stage Four development...I am you, a fetus at...."

Hours passed, and Jake almost began to relax.

Almost.

"I am you at birth." Jake looked up. The woman exiting was beautiful. Blonde tresses that curled into her waist, firm backside, shapely legs. *Bet the fellow jerking off would ditch his specimen bottle for that piece of crumpet!* But her messages had been normal; the bloke wouldn't get the pleasure.

"I am your father's penis...."

Sperm, Jake thought. *Sperm, not penis.* He watched the exit, waiting for the next person to appear. A male, about the age his father would have been—early forties—with greying hair and sporting a tweed jacket stepped into the daylight.

A plant? Some scientist blocking the system, trying to get a heads-up on the technique? Jake didn't think that was possible, but what did he know? And besides, they had a male; what they needed was a female.

"I am your...." The syllables blurred to sperovum, glangina and other non-comprehensible words. Jake glanced at his watch: only an hour before The Zone closed. He looked up, gazed at the surrounding landscape. Tufts of thick, wiry grass clung to the hillside. They reminded him of a trip to the seaside when he'd been a kid of three or four. Mile upon mile of sand dunes topped with salt-resistant fronds of grass hardly bending in the wind. He'd breathed in, tasted and smelled the crisp tanginess of the wind. Stooping, he'd tugged at a clump of grass and the sharp blades had cut his fingers. Suddenly feeling alone, he'd screamed as drips of blood left red craters in the soft yellow sand. Then his mother had scooped him into her arms, dabbed at his tear-streaked face, and wiped the blood from his fingers, and he snuggled into her warm mummy-smell. He hadn't been alone, just isolated. Like The Zone was isolated. Only for The Zone, isolation was the prime consideration, one that didn't come cheaply on an overpopulated planet.

"I am *your* ovum."

Panic gripped Jake's chest as the phrase exploded in his head.

Please, not on my watch! He blinked, shaking his head to rid himself of the words violating his mind, but they didn't—wouldn't—go away. They ricocheted between his eardrums. And then guards swarmed the exit.

A woman came out. At least seventy, neck dry and wrinkled like a lizard's, hair dyed chestnut—surely she couldn't be a fertile.

For the first time, Jake was glad he'd only scored point nine on the Psi Scale; at least his thoughts were his own.

As she walked past him, following the signs to "Electronic Devices Reclaim," Jake turned to her. "You're a special lady," he said in an attempt to soften what was to come. "Please follow—"

"My Alfred! What about my husband?"

"He'll be directed to you," Jake replied, forcing a smile.

The woman returned his smile. But hers was one of acceptance...understanding. Meekly, she followed him toward Damiana House. Not that she had a choice; guards, weapons drawn, stood behind and to their sides. The only safe way was forward.

* * *

"Call me Fleur," she said that first day. And she was. A silk flower. Cream and auburn beautiful. Too delicate to touch. Greg—Jake hadn't known his name when he'd stood guard at The Zone's exit, but now he did: Greg, Greg whose baby-blue eyes seemed too innocent for porno magazines—sat at the other end of the room.

"I didn't want to visit The Zone," she said. "But Alfred—he's gone now, isn't he—" she didn't wait for an answer "—wanted to see the exhibits. He wanted to know how they could tell what you were. How you were." She wiped at the silken skin beneath her eyes. "I knew; I tried to tell him. But what would he understand about listening to astrocytes?"

Astrocytes? Jake thought.

"I know, the science is a little advanced for an old lady like me," she said, and Jake shuddered at the realization that she had read his thoughts, "but my children have degrees in the biological sciences." Again, she wiped at the parchment skin below her eyes.

Children! This time Jake tried to cap the thought, but he was too late. Stroking a silver-grey eyebrow with her middle finger, she sighed. "Twins." She turned to Greg. "About your age."

Identical, please let them be identical.

Fleur looked back at Jake and shook her head. "No. Filial. A boy and a girl." Then her eyes widened, forcing her crows' feet into oblivion. "You think they'll force Beth and Benjamin to have a child together!"

"No. It's double recessive; the chances of them both displaying the gene are almost nonexistent," he said, quoting the handbook. But he did think they would. Or tried not to think it. But Greg, now glaring, and Fleur, wide-eyed in horror, told him otherwise. All the better; it would make his job easier. He swept the girlie magazines from the coffee table and leaned forward, his elbows resting on the edge of the table. "Look, I'm sorry," he began. "This is difficult for me. But I have no choice. Unless I want to end up as recycled food, that is." At Fleur's horrified look, he grinned and added, "And I wouldn't wish Jake Gristly Thigh Pie with Kidneys on anyone." A smile twitched at the corners of Fleur's mouth, so he continued. "As you two seem to know pretty well everything I do and think, I'm going to be honest. The bad news is, your husband's probably dead by now, Fleur."

"He is. I felt his absence within minutes of leaving The Zone." For a moment, her eyes shone as she fought back tears, and then her face became closed to all emotion. But, in a brief glimmer of almost-perception, Jake saw a sparkle—he couldn't class it as anything else—dash across her features. "And Benjamin was reading the e-mail I purportedly sent to say we're going away for several months on a second honeymoon. When the door closed—" she glanced toward the lead monstrosity that shut out the world "—Beth hadn't picked up her message, but she will when she gets home tonight." A brief smile washed across her face. "They're safe, at least."

Nodding, Jake said, "And they will be. You can thank their sexes for that. Which means, yes, they will force them to have a child if you two—" he glanced at Greg "—don't cooperate. That puts a big load on you both." Palms open, Jake raised his hands to shoulder level. "Sorry. I can't help it."

Greg stood up, paced the small room twice. "Look!" he shouted, and slammed his fist on the table. "You're putting Fleur in a dreadful position. I don't care about me; I have no family, but you're asking Fleur to be unfaithful to her dead husband!" He began pacing the room again, kicking at the magazines, tearing pages from staples with the soles of his shoes. "It isn't fair! It's damned well not fair! Why can't you just take her eggs, my sperm and—and—fertilize them!"

He collapsed on the sofa, apparently spent.

"He doesn't mean it like that," Fleur said. "He's worried, that's all. I mean, I'm hardly the best catch in the world for a thirty-something good-looking guy like Greg." She smiled, and Jake found himself loving her for her quiet acceptance. "And we know it isn't your fault, so push those thoughts from your head. We accept, and we're both willing, not for us, but for my children. Aren't we, Greg?" She walked over to him and placed a hand on his knee. "I'm going to accept the fertility treatment and we'll both try." Her gaze deliberately avoided the magazines scattered on the floor, all open and presenting provocative images.

"Thank you," Jake said. "If it's any consolation, they'll attempt in vitro fertilization before, well, you know...."

"Before forcing Beth and Benjamin to have sex," she finished for him, and once again Jake found himself loving the little old lady. If he'd had the right genes, he would have carried her to a bedroom there and then to help her.

"And the P bonds?" she asked.

How's she know about the—

"From you. When Greg mentioned IVF. They tend to break, even under the most careful in vitro handling. It's in that handbook of yours."

"It won't come to that," Greg said, placing a hand over hers.

Jake answered a knock at the door. "Mr. Hofstein—"

"Peterson," Hofstein said, interrupting him, "you're here because you're a point-niner, a deaf mute, and for that very reason, I expected results weeks ago."

"Results?" *How can I make two people of different generations fuck each other silly?* Jake looked around at the white ceramic walls: clean, surgically clean. "Mr. Hofstein, I have it under control. They're sleeping in the same bed."

"And they're having sex?"

"Yes," Jake lied, remembering the long silences from the room next door before he would eventually fall asleep. *They might talk telepathically, but they can't have sex that way.* "We've been through three pregnancy testing kits," he said, and saw himself urinating on them all, chucking them in the bin when the blue strip didn't show. Someone would be detailed to look through the rubbish, pick out such things and forward them to the lab.

"Mr. Hofstein, would it help if you brought in a twelver to oversee them?" Jake looked down at his feet. Now that he'd voiced the question, he despised himself for it. Fleur and Greg deserved someone who could empathize with them, not someone who would "listen" to them.

"Policy states that they must be supervised by an under-one. Have you any idea of the powers those two have?" He stared through Jake as if he were nothing more than an amoeba. "They're both fifty-plus. Off the scale. They'd know when someone was eavesdropping. How d'you think that could possibly help? If they used their powers together, they could throw you or anyone else through the window! And the glass is lead-bound! This whole fucking place is encased in lead." Hofstein kicked the wall, and then he seemed to relax a little, almost smile. "Look, son, don't gaze at me like an imbecile. Just accept that they can do things you've never heard of and get your act together. It's my job on the line, too, and neither of us wants to join the food chain as Stroganoff. The Zone needs fertiles, and so do we if we want to keep our jobs."

Jake nodded.

"Good. I'm glad we've got that settled." Hofstein patted Jake on the shoulder, then turned and strode away along the concrete path.

Jake shut the door and slithered down the wall onto his haunches, his head resting on his hands. *I joined The Zone because I didn't want to end up being recycled. Oh, fuck, fuck, fuck. I don't want to make them have sex. I can't make them. I'm not bastard enough.* He buried his head in his hands.

Gentle fingers touched his shoulder, and he looked up to see Fleur. Dressed in a see-through negligee, her delicate bone structure shimmering through the fine fabric, she appeared to be twenty years younger. Her aged, lined face was now smooth. And when he thought about it, he realized she'd become more agile and graceful as well as more youthful. The hormone therapy had helped, but her hair, now silver, shone under the electric lights, giving her a sophisticated premature-greying look. She didn't say anything, but even Jake could read the thoughts written on her face.

"Look, it's all right." He resisted an urge to take her into his arms and comfort her. Instead, he stroked her cheek. Warm, soft. "I have no family. Nothing. If I do one thing in this life, it has to be something I feel good about. And maybe...." He shrugged.

She shook her head, and her hair washed across her shoulders. "No. It's up to us. And I'm not saying this just for Beth and Benjamin. I'm saying this for you and Greg, too. For all of us." At that, she turned and left him. Then muted sounds of sex permeated the wall dividers.

Happiness didn't flood Jake's being, but relief did. Maybe, just maybe. He had upped Greg's Viagra dosage, and Fleur might be mature, but she had gained that sexual appeal older woman could exude. He tried not to imagine running his own fingers through her hair, and then he wondered whether erotic thoughts would help Greg. He headed for the lounge and the dirty magazines and thumbed through them, imposing Fleur's face onto the models.

The fair-haired girl in a picture became blonde, then platinum, then silver shimmer. Her face, youthful, took on a mature wanton desperation. He ran his fingers over her breasts, found himself stirring. Down to her crotch, and then up again. Trance-like, Jake moved into her picture, and her body enveloped him.

And then the door burst open and Greg stood there, a huge grin on his face. "You know what?" he said. "I would never have thought, but—"

Jake put his fingers to his mouth. "Don't. It's tempting fate." Massaging his groin, he headed for the bathroom.

Jake hadn't urinated on this one. Fleur's hormones had caused the blue line in the window. *They've done it!*

As soon as he'd thought the words, both Fleur and Greg appeared in the doorway. "Indeed we have!" they shouted in unison. Fleur ran to him and kissed him on the cheek. Again, Jake marveled at how lithe and youthful she was.

She grabbed his hand and then reached for Greg's. Suddenly, they were dancing around in a circle. "It'll all be over soon," she shouted, "and then we'll go home."

Jake and Greg nodded.

Fleur grinned. "You're a pair of skeptics, you two. And you both know better than to try and lie to me." She came to a halt mid-step, throwing Jake off balance. "Once they have what they want, they'll be happy."

Jake disengaged his hands. "I have to notify Hofstein. And I need a blood sample, Fleur."

The knock at the door came within minutes of Jake's communication. He opened it and handed over the test and blood specimen. The next thing he knew, or so it seemed, they wheeled Fleur off for a termination. The fetus wasn't a fertile, wasn't viable psi-wise.

I was me at Stage Nine development, Jake thought, *and then they hacked me to pieces.* The pregnancy might have been useless to them but they'd still examine every perfect, undamaged cell. Thin slivers of Fleur's baby, dropping away from a microtome blade, then stained and fixed on a slide. Eyes peering at them under a microscope. He put a hand up to his mouth and swallowed hard to stop the vomit forcing its way into his mouth.

He and Greg spent two days in silence as far as Jake was concerned but, every time he glanced at Greg, he found his thoughts mirrored in Greg's face. Then the e-mail arrived: *the usual four weeks of abstinence are waived due to Fleur's "youthful" physique.*

She returned with staples in her abdomen and a determination to succeed.

"She isn't concerned for herself," Greg said when Fleur had returned after her third termination. The pain had been etched on her face—yet another lost child, a dead husband, and her twins under threat—but somehow she seemed even younger. Nearer forty than her real age of seventy-two.

"She's concerned for you and me," Greg continued. "This messes up too many times and you're out of a job." He ran a hand through his hair. "Me, I'm stuck here anyway. She won't believe that, of course. She's convinced they'll let us out into the big wide world once she's had a fertile." He walked to the window, pulled back the curtains. "As if. There're more guards out there than the Yanks had in Guantánamo Bay." He let the curtains fall back.

"Maybe," Jake said. But something itched at the back of his mind, a phrase, one of the statements an exhibit had made. Something to do with the day Fleur had appeared at The Zone exit. He sorted through his memories, saw himself gazing across the open countryside. And the words in his head had refused to abate. *I am your mother's ovum...I am your father's sperm....* No, that wasn't it.

And then he remembered. The "sperm" exhibit had said "penis."

"Fleur! Come here!" he shouted, and then he turned to Greg. "Sit down," he ordered as he placed the latest magazines on the table, each opened at a page approximately halfway through. The naked girls stroking themselves smiled up at him erotically. But that wasn't the point; the point was that the pages were open. Or maybe the blatant sexuality was the point. Maybe thinking of sex masked his real intentions. And if they knew, maybe his experiment would be fruitless. By the time he'd finished, Fleur and Greg both sat on the sofa, looks of confusion on their faces. *Good,* he thought, not caring if they "heard" him.

Turning to Fleur—he'd decided she should to go first—he asked, "Can you turn one of the magazine pages?

She looked at him quizzically, then her brow furrowed; old, long-past wrinkles suddenly reaffirmed themselves. Jake held his breath. Nothing happened. "Good," he said, knowing his words would show themselves as lies to her. "Okay, Greg, your turn."

Pages whipped open and closed. Magazines began to land on the floor, one stacked neatly upon another.

Jake looked at them both. "An exhibit malfunctioned on the day Fleur went through. I think her assessment was wrong."

"Alfred didn't die for nothing." Fleur stood and gathered up the pile of magazines. As she put them back on the table, she glanced at Greg. "There is a way of making it work, and you know it."

Greg shook his head.

"You can. For my children, for my dead husband, you can! You have to. I'd do anything for...." She sank onto the sofa and covered her face with her hands.

It had been a long time since Jake had seen Fleur's tears, and that didn't help. He found himself jockeying with Greg to comfort her.

Her breath caught in her throat as she cried herself out. And then, as if by sheer willpower, she stopped. "Please, Greg." She stood and moved to the window, that funny accepting smile of hers twitching at the corners of her mouth as she waited passively.

Greg closed his eyes, and his lips tightened. "No way. I won't do it!"

Ripples passed through Jake, stirred the hairs on the back of his neck, and a smell, almost familiar, tickled his nostrils. Suddenly he was at the seaside, blood dripping from his hand. Ozone, the smell was ozone, waves breaking on the shore.

Then Fleur collapsed.

Jake ran toward her but, before he'd taken two steps, a bolt of electricity whacked him in the chest like a steel cricket bat. The impact flung him to the other end of the room, his shoulder thumping against barely concealed lead.

A crack as his joint dislocated.

Lightning streaks bouncing off his skull.

Greg! He's protecting her.

No, Greg was concentrating on Fleur, oblivious to everything else. Jake looked at Fleur. Her features contorted with pain.

And then it ended, the tingly smell of ozone gone. Fleur began massaging Jake's damaged shoulder, her movements remarkably strong as she pushed and pulled his muscles to her will. Heat spread through his body, and then her movements became thoughtful, ones of an ex-lover who still cared but didn't want involvement. The pain vanished.

"I'm sorry," they said in unison.

Forgetting about his damaged shoulder, Jake shrugged. "Who?" he asked, and Fleur left the room.

"Let's give her a couple of weeks," Greg said. "Get me one of those pregnancy things."

Jake whisked a stick from the sideboard and offered it to Greg.

"No, wet it first. Tap water'll do. Then place it on the coffee table."

Jake complied and then went to stand next to Greg, waiting and watching. Slowly, the strip became blue. "Is that all she wanted?" he asked.

"No. She wants me to kill her. And now I guess I'll have to." Greg stomped out of the room and Jake heard a door slam. Not the double-room door. Greg had chosen a night to himself.

Shaking his head in confusion, Jake also retired to bed. He dreamt of Fleur, the silk flower, blossoming, turning to seed and....

He woke in a cold sweat. The plant had become twisted, deformed, and at the top of each stem was a head. Fleur's. Only instead of her hair, each head had been covered with a fine silver halo of stinging nettle hairs that had turned into spears tipped with poison. He crawled out of bed and into the bathroom, splashed cold water over his face, and then he became aware of raised voices.

"I won't! I was wrong last night."

"You have to. You turned the pregnancy test blue. They'll expect some sort of result."

"False positive, that's all."

Jake entered the room to see Fleur shaking her head. He moved back to the doorway. Ozone, albeit a faint trace, tickled his nose.

"False positive be damned," Fleur said and, as she said it, Greg's body thudded against the opposite wall.

"Whoa, whoa." Jake held his hands up in gesture of peace, and then wondered why they were shouting at each other when they could converse silently.

"I'm...I'm sorry. I can't help it," she said, running to Greg. "That's why I didn't play your magazine game, Jake. I have no control." Her hands began massaging Greg's muscles. "I'm like a sound system with two settings: off and pulverizing-eardrums loud." Her fingers did one final walk over now-relaxed muscles. "There, is that better?"

Greg grinned. "Pain gone, thanks. You should be a faith healer."

"Humph. And if I'd done that, there'd be no Beth or Benjamin;

there'd be a bunch of psi freaks instead. Here, get up." She offered a hand and pulled him to his feet. "Ben got his nose broken in a rugby match once. I had to sit back and watch him in pain. And afterwards, I couldn't even allow myself to straighten it, or sort out his septum. Even then, questions would have been asked." She stared at Greg, who paced the room, kicking at the strewn magazines. "You promised," she said. "Don't make me force you, please."

He shook his head. "No. I've slept on it. I can't do it. Psi freaks, you said, and you're—"

Crackling ozone and a thud as Greg's body slammed against a window. For a second the glass bowed, and then it sprang back, depositing Greg in a heap on the floor.

He pulled himself upright, and Fleur walked to the door and waited, smiling. But this was a smile of determination, not acceptance.

"Forget it," Greg said. "I won't."

"Do I have to knock you black and blue? This is about me saving my children! And you, you ungrateful bastard."

Greg shook his head, and again his body slammed against the window. Jake ran to help, and suddenly he found himself spread-eagled, pinned to a wall. "I mean it," Fleur said. "It's the only way."

Greg struggled to his feet, and again his body slammed into the window.

Fleur. Flower?

"Some flowers have prickly hairs," she said.

Like stinging nettles.

She gave a half-hearted nod. "Like stinging nettles with poisoned spears for stingers."

Greg pulled himself to standing. "I don't want...." He ran a hand through his hair—an act of defeat, Jake guessed. "Fleur, you know what this'll mean."

Fleur grinned.

"You win," he said, his face a mask. "Stand over there." He pointed to the window. "Jake, move away from her. I want a good three meters of clearance."

With the grace of a ballerina at the peak of her career, Fleur complied. And then she said, "Greg, I love you like a son. That perhaps sounds a bit…. But it isn't. Sex with you could have been like that, but it wasn't. And this is so pure, so clean and—"

Ozone cut through the air and she doubled up in pain as Greg pinned her to the glass with his gaze. And then she seemed to force all her muscles and ligaments into place, turned, and walked out of the room.

"Done," Greg said. "I've just killed her, but at least she won't end up being recycled now. That's something to give her comfort in the months to come." He, too, left the room.

"I'm sorry, Mr. Hofstein" Jake said. "You've tested her blood samples, seen her scans. This is the real thing and there's no way I'll let you take Fleur into—"

"Get the fuck out, you shit," Greg shouted from the hallway. "You'll get the end product, but Fleur you will never have!"

Hofstein stepped onto the sill, and Jake's nose tingled with the familiar smell.

"Duck!" Greg screamed, but Jake was already dipping and jumping sideways away from the door.

Seconds later, Hofstein flew three meters into the air. He landed on his shoulder and skidded across the concrete path. Shirt in tatters and blood running down one arm, he pulled himself up. Another invisible blow. The thud of Hofstein's chin hitting concrete echoed off the lead walls. His left ear now oozing blood, Hofstein tried again. Then, almost comically, he did a half-somersault into the air and came down on his right knee as if proposing marriage.

"I told you to get lost, so do it. Now! Or next time you'll land on your fucking head!" The door slammed shut spontaneously and Greg grinned. "You've learned, eh?" he said, looking Jake up and down. "Seems you don't need Fleur's healing powers this time." His features sobered. "She deserves to be surrounded by people who care for her." He walked off into Fleur's room and Jake followed.

Fleur, a mound of pregnant flesh, lay on her back, her breath coming in short gasps. "They talk to me," she said, and then stopped to catch her breath. "All my babies talk to me." She clutched Greg's and Jake's wrists, one in each of her hands, and pulled them toward her. "See, Greg, you did it. A hundred and fifty -three little babies nurtured within their own wombs." She smiled. "Each aware. Each a little personality with an individual voice."

Letting go of Jake's wrist to cover her mouth, she coughed a polite, delicate cough. But when she withdrew her hand, a streak of blood smeared her lower lip. She moved her hand to her left breast, and Jake noticed her fingers were also tinged with red. "Inside here, by my aorta, is a boy. And these little lumps—" she prodded her right side where, it seemed, a pair of conjoined breasts pushed up from deep within her "—are both girls." A tear ran down her face. "They aren't viable. My body can't support them. I know it and so do they. The Zone'll harvest their parts, though. My babies forced to live forever inside Plexiglas wombs."

She looked up at them both. "Do you think they—? No, of course they didn't." She stopped to suppress a cough. "The exhibits are conglomer—" The cough she'd held back exploded out of her, spraying fine droplets of blood into the air. Greg gave her a tissue, and she dabbed her mouth. "Conglomerations of cells. No voices. No personalities. Just sponges that absorb thoughts, energy from the astrocytes." She took hold of Jake's wrist again, her fingers pressing into his tendons, her nails digging into his flesh. "The exhibit didn't malfunction. Scientists. You were right." She coughed. "I felt their implants distorting the system." For a moment, that accepting smile crossed her face. Then it vanished as a paroxysmal coughing spasm gripped her body. When she'd finished, she locked her gaze with Jake's. "Let my babies die. All of them." Her finger went to the delicate skin beneath her eye and began stroking it, inadvertently wiping away tears.

Silk flower. You haven't done that for so long. And then he looked at her properly. A frail old lady, far frailer, far older than her actual years.

Her lips twitched into the smile Jake loved so much, and then she shut her eyes. Eventually, her breathing slowed to a more regular rhythm.

"She's asleep," Greg whispered, and they tiptoed out of the room.

"Did she mean it?" Jake asked once they were in the lounge.

"Yes." He ran his hand through his hair. "She doesn't want her babies to be exhibits, which they will be if The Zone gets its hands on them. All this money; they aren't going to throw away what little they've got out of it, even if it isn't what they'd hoped for. Bastards!"

Jake prepared to duck, but the ozone smell didn't come.

"They all seem to agree with her from what I could hear. David—he's the one by her heart, the strongest—was quite adamant that he didn't want to live like that."

"They can talk? No. Not possible." He stared at Greg as if he were crazy, and then the meaning of Greg's words hit him. "No, oh no," he muttered. "I couldn't. I couldn't just stick a pillow over her face and...and...."

"You!" Greg grabbed a magazine and physically tore it into pieces. "It's me she asked. When she spoke to you she was screaming at me, begging me. I've killed her anyway. There's no way she can survive. You heard her. A hundred and fifty-three psi babies growing inside her. All over her fucking body! Five are in her lungs." Another magazine landed on the floor in shreds. "And she didn't just mean the fetuses. She meant Beth and Benjamin. They're her babies too; grown up, but still her babies." He stood, sending the remaining magazines flying through the air with so much mental force that Jake's nose tickled and the hairs on his neck rose. "She thought I could control it. Because I controlled the magazines that time. Ha! But changing cells! I haven't got a laser beam straight to her ovaries." He began kicking at the magazines that had come to rest on the floor. And then he bent down, picked one up and began shredding it manually. "God, what a wonderful woman. She blocked that from me, you know. That she believed in me. So I wouldn't feel guilty if it turned out like it has." More strips of paper fell to the floor. "I only found out because she let her defenses down." He nodded toward her room. "Just for a second. During a coughing fit. I could never do that. She's so much better than me. Her strength. Her healing powers. She doesn't deserve—" He threw the half-shredded magazine down and left the room.

Jake buried his head in his hands, hating himself for what he'd allowed to happen, for being weak, for not protecting the lovely, delicate silk flower. Over and over, his mind wrestled with the events, trying to work out where he had gone wrong, where he could have stopped it. His job had been to look after them, but he hadn't even managed that. Fleur was about to die at the hands of a loved one: her almost-son.

And then, in an odd moment of intuition, he felt someone standing over him.

"It's done." Greg's voice was no more than a whisper. "She went peacefully in her sleep. They all did. Brain hemorrhages. To-morrow. We'll let *them* know tomorrow, when it'll be too late to get viable samples." Greg walked out, and silent tears rolled down Jake's cheeks. He wanted to see Fleur, pay his last respects. But he felt a traitor, felt his presence would sully her memory. He stayed put, allowing his grief to flow.

Jake walked past The Zone exit. Guards, their weapons subtly concealed, surrounded him.

"I am *your* sperm." The words proclaiming a fertile sliced through Jake's grey matter.

He glanced over his shoulder. The man exiting The Zone didn't resemble Fleur, but even as a point niner, Jake knew it was Benjamin. Maybe the squashed-flat nose that looked like it had been through a particularly rough rugby scrum gave it away. Or maybe living with Fleur and Greg for over a year had somehow heightened his senses. He hung back, praying he was wrong, praying that the next person to exit wouldn't be a fertile, and the guards seemed happy to let him wait the few minutes he needed.

"I am *your* ovum."

Jake's heart shriveled when he saw the woman exiting The Zone. Chestnut-colored hair. Not dyed. But didn't women try to recapture their original hair color? And then another column of guards appeared, this time overtly displaying their weapons, and the man and woman were escorted toward Damiana House. To their deaths?

He wondered if Greg could bring himself to do it, and whether he would. He closed his mind to thoughts of Benjamin and Beth, used more mental tenacity than he'd known he had, and imagined himself slithering between slices of mushroom. Jake Stroganoff. And then he imagined slithering between slices of Fleur. He smiled, and in his mind he saw Fleur smiling back at him. Her simple, wonderful smile of acceptance.

FOR RESTFUL DEATH I CRY

Geoffrey Girard

The Changing Health Care Environment [pp 9-22] [1]

A four-story C3 still inhabited by dozens of the undead. You've wandered each floor to make a quick head count, double-checked their number before hauling in any equipment. Enough cloth to wrap all the bodies, canisters for the old fuel cells. Charges and nitroglycerin for the building. Other teams have already been through to strip out the copper wire, op fibers, and any viraglass. Now it's your turn. In two weeks, the crushers will roll in to recycle whatever worthwhile concrete and timber remain above, then flatten the rest to finish burying the recently departed. Not many here. One hundred and six.

Fourth floor is already clear. All the cartridges—helium-cooled reactors the size of a fist—are secured in the truck for future disposal. All bodies brought to the lower level. Each one neatly cleaned and wrapped and positioned to RSC code. You've taken a couple days. There's no real rush. They've been here some three hundred years. What's another week? There were eight residual C3s in this zone. All but one was work you could do alone, and did. Peteyr and Jefferson helped with that other one. This is the last before you're expected north to join up with them again and a larger team for the big New Cleveland job. A pair of tombs with a hundred floors each. Dark and terrible crypts from another time. It'll take ten of you all summer.

---

[1]All headings taken from *Assisted Living: Needs, Practices, and Policies in Residential Care for the Elderly* (Hardcover) by S. Zimmerman PhD (USA Author 1378-1472 AH), published 1422. Credit: Madrid Archives (Intelligence Council Permit tp/0801867053 10/06/1931AH]

Creating a Therapeutic Environment: Models [pp 53-77]

God watches as you bring another into the room. He does not take his eyes off you. Sits in his *LifeChair®* exactly where you parked him two days before. White beard and tubes. His cartridge core throbs, like his eyes, with the dim glow of something still clutching at life. You will do him last.

The chair's rear monitor flashes that God's name was Evan Cooper. That he was born August 1, 2114, and admitted to the Truefund Continuing Care Community on July 18, 2209. All monitor dates still use the Middle Western calendar, completely unaware re international adoption of the Hijri civil calendar in 1850. The chair's monitor tells the names and addresses of all known relatives. Sons, grandsons, and great-grandsons. They are all dead now. Every one. Those who thought they were preserving something they loved, helping tens of thousands of Evan Coopers live comfortably just a little longer. Maybe a cure would be found, they thought. Or maybe they just didn't have the courage to let go. Either way, you smile, they're all gone and here we are.

They couldn't even wait until your birthday, you say into his ear. The monitor says he was a surgeon of some kind and served in the U.S. Navy fifteen years and played piano and mountain climbed competitively well into his eighties. He is a deity, an abomination, from the last Golden Age of man. An age that briefly conquered hunger and ignorance and disease and even subjugated death. For a time.

You will do him last. Maybe he'll kill you then.

Resident Characteristics [pp 144-172]

This next is a woman again. You know this only because her chair's monitor claims so. Otherwise, sexless. As wrinkled and besprent with wisps of ashen hair as the one you call God. Folds of grey skin hang over her skull in a hundred individual deep-rutted flaps. The body is nude; any clothes once worn have decomposed two hundred years ago. Only the wires and tubes remain, joining her and the chair. Joining present and past. Withered breasts are only two more flaps. Some sort of lavender fungus grows up the right side of this area into her face. It looks like a deep, fuzzy bruise. You drink. Her lips are gone.

Worlds before, she was a mark of scientific realization and hope. Proof that man could humanely and economically support itself beyond a single century. Nanotechnology, bionics, gene therapy. More cures and miracles awaiting discovery each year. But then came the Sickness and the wars. Again, man took a step backward. A second Dark Age and another two hundred years to scrape back to something recognizable as society. Three generations later, move back into the old cities to continue Man's rebirth.

Hope is a waking nightmare.

The Physical Environment [pp 173-197]

One tube for tracheal/bronchial secretions. One for nasopharyngeal torques. Another wire for cerebral venous return. Twenty more, thin as yard-long needles, to deliverer nanobarbiturates and antiseptics and cathartics and nitroGen® and minchloral hydrates. Nanomagnets to fight atrophy. Sensors to monitor everything from hemoglobin levels to decubitus ulcers and thrombosis of the extremities, to self-prescribe and repair with synthetic calories and marrow and synthluminum and phosphorus and methylcellulose. You learned all of this in a two-week course at RSC headquarters. Only spent an afternoon on this part. All you'll do is take the wires and tubes out. Most of the training was spent on the art of dismantling nuclear cartridge cores and a refresher class in building demolition. Also two days to review proper burial laws.

Some deep and terrible sound escapes her rotted maw. No tongues. Something the curative chairs hadn't protected. Froth trickles over the rusted nubs of pins drilled into her lower jaw. The smell. You drink. The cartridge core lies in the lower back of the carrier. Its ever-present glow casts a golden hue on the dirty floor. When you remove it, she will finally die.

The Process of Care [pp 198-221]
You remove it.

The direct-cycle generator locks. The deep and terrible sounds grow more intense. You step around to the front of the carrier again to watch. The regulations are simple. If she lives without the aid of forbidden sciences, she lives. You've seen it happen only once. A man lived for twelve whole minutes, even lifted up from his chair and walked a few steps before collapsing. Methantheline bromide, paregorics, pectins stop. Ventilation and cortex spurs stop. Her eyes widen. Sharpen. Glisten like black jewels in the shadowed lobby. *In the Name of God, the Merciful, Compassionate.* The body shudders. Dies, really dies, at last. Three hundred years.

State Policy and Regulations [pp 9-33]
Continue the authorized prayers. *Oh God, forgive our living and our dead.* Secure the cartridge. Ten MWe of silicone-coated fuel particles, enough to power a small community for several years. Or a single chair for a lifetime. More than a lifetime. If left alone, one might conceivably run another five hundred years. Another thousand. Quite beyond, you assume, what the masterminds of the late 21st century had ever considered. Imam Shafi or some other cleric once said *That which does not destroy, makes stronger,* and you often wonder why that is a good thing. Stronger for what? For still more pain.

Tilt her forward to take hold of the cords and tubes that snake behind. Disconnect. The C3 buildings are feared, worshipped. Cursed places. Most have been burned to the ground, vandalized for centuries. You've buried some who died terribly at the hands of the newly budding humanity. The new administration wants a more humane removal of these abominations completed within two years.

The pallid skin and chair have fused in several spots and you reach for the dissolving paste. Lay her flat on the prep board. Cover the genitals and then wash the body. Exposed bone at both knees and all the fingertips. Vermin have gnawed her feet. Fresh cloth laid over the corpse, water poured over all, siphoned away by the board. Reach for another *kafan* to wrap the body. White cotton cloth. Prayers again as you align her with the other bodies. All heads facing west, per RSC code.

Restoration Services Corps. One of a hundred relief agencies created to continue civilization's loping resurgence. Almost a million strong now. Public works crews involved in everything from building new roads and schools to contamination removal. Any citizen between fifteen and forty can enroll and employment is up to 70% for the first time in a generation. At first, you just worked cleanup crews, reclaiming old cities back from the dead to become part of the promised future. You soon volunteered to study demolition. It paid a little more, but that's not why you did it. Eventually, RSC attentions finally turned to the nuclearly-hazardous C3s and you volunteered again.

Upstairs once more for another chair. There are now forty-three. Many still move about randomly through the halls and rooms, and several move in slow circles and patterns that have etched narrow ruts into the floor. A single pearl-colored ball nestles beneath the chair and swivels like a giant eye. Watching. Deciding where to look, *turn*, next, based on some model programmed centuries ago. On this floor, one of the ancient carriers transports a full skeleton. Nothing but bones that hunch in the seat and dangle over the armrests. Each time it passes, you gaze at its thick, discolored ribs and the dark empty skull sockets. Each time it passes, you could swear it's laughing. Drink. Tell yourself it's only the shrieking of a departing *LifeChair*®. You take hold of another and lead it to the ramp. Not sure what time it is. Tired. Ten more before you call it quits for the day. No one at the RSC will expect more. Or less. No one is waiting for you back in Ottawa. The difference between today and tomorrow and yesterday and tomorrow is microscopic. The difference between him and her and you and I is microscopic.

Key Topics in Assisted Living [pp 1-8]
You lie beside them. Try to sleep.

Maybe some terrible disease from another century still lingers within their decaying flesh. Maybe one of the reactors will trigger and explode the city block. Maybe the roving skeleton will collide into the nitroglycerin cart. Maybe the building will collapse. You turn in the darkness. The light from God's chair illuminates the floor. What were they thinking? This farce of life. Is now any different? You run fingers across your own shadow on the floor. Think of her. Reach for the canteen of still drink. Seven years since she was assigned to another. You still think of her when you try to sleep. Stare up at the black rafters overhead. Columns on the upper floors are already drilled and packed with nitroglycerin and TNT. Smaller columns and walls are wrapped in detonating cord and geotextile fabrics. When the lower level is completely filled with bodies, you will push the button and four floors will collapse and turn the chamber into a tomb.

God makes burbling noises just above.

Fuck you too, you say. Try to sleep.

Aging in Place [pp 224-40]

In the morning, more bodies. The difference between now and then is invisible. The difference between them and God and me is invisible. Did you know each other, you ask God, while preparing another. Did Evan Cooper ever share breakfast or a game of cards with—you check—with Patrick Gilronan? Does it hurt you to watch an old friend finally die? Or are you happy for him? Each job, the jobs you work alone, you try to pick One. One Evan Cooper. One God. To mock, entice. To anger. You will do him last. And just maybe….

In Harrisburg, a female named Hsu-Ming Lim long ago managed to claw your face before dying. There remain faint scars on your left cheek. In Dover, a man whose monitor was broken spit something like black tar at you. Some foul substance three hundred years dead.

Still, you live.

Staffing Problems and Strategies in Assisted Living [pp 78-91]
You think of jumping again. But you're only a dozen meters up. And it is still a sin. *O ye who believe, do not kill yourselves for truly God has been to you most merciful. If any do this in rancor, soon shall we cast him into the fire.* A sin for eternity. You look out from a pair of stripped window casements on the west side of the building. The sun sets low over the ruined city, the sky cast in ancient blood. You see a dozen other worksites. The charade of rebirth. How long before it all just burns to ashes again?

Think of pushing the detonator now. Right now. Of ingesting dissolving paste. Slitting your wrists, throat. Tripping one of the reactors. All of them. Think of jumping again. Night's wind cool on your face. And it is still a sin. *Nor take life, which God has made sacred....* You will sleep again, and rise again, and work again. The difference between days is imagined. The difference between us is imagined. The dead city in darkness below will rise again. Lift up, coughing dust and rot, like something breaking free from its grave. Like a hundred cities before. Man will sleep again, and rise again, and work again. The King is dead, long live the King. Crawling like a dead thing from infinite dark ages toward the promises of hope and salvation.

Forever.

Connectedness in Residential Care: A Qualitative Perspective [pp 292-316]
Tomorrow, you tell God. One of us dies tomorrow.

His grey eyes burn brightly. He hates you now, too.

You sleep like the dead.

Admission and Retention Policies [pp 304-7]
At the first hint of morning, you rise and work all day. You do not stop for food or drink. You do not stop when it grows dark again. You clean and wrap the dead by torchlight. Ignore the skeleton still rolling about on the third floor. Exhausted. Double-check the

TNT charges. The detonator sits waiting. Maybe sleep and finish the burial in the morning. No, you're sleepy, fatigued. There's more chance for a mistake now. More chance for a misstep. An inadvertent death. All floors emptied, you move to the basement for the final time.

God sits waiting for you. Just you and me now. Only more burbles and sounds in response. Smack his face. He jolts in his chair. Live? Die? Stop fucking around in the middle, and pick just one. The cartridge core lies in the lower back of the carrier. Its ever-present glow casts a golden hue on the dirty floor.

When you remove it, he will finally die.

You remove it. The direct-cycle generator locks and you step around to the front of the carrier to watch. His eyes widen. Sharpen. The body shudders. Moves to lift from the carrier. Tilt him forward to get a hold of the cords and tubes that snake behind. Disconnect. The Death Angel. Say the sanctioned prayers. *Oh God, if he was a doer of good, then increase his good deeds, and if he was a wrongdoer, then overlook his bad deeds. O God, forgive him and give him the strength to say the right thing.* Give him the strength. Evan Cooper falls forward. *Leans* forward. Lay a hand on his chest to push him back down. You'll be dead in just a minute, you tell him. He waves your hand away. You laugh. First self-propelled movement in centuries. Now what, God? You lay the cartridge aside for later. Take a seat, drink some more. Watch as he struggles to escape. Five minutes. Struggles to breathe. Ten. The struggle to get up. To live. Your knees curl up like you are a child sitting around one of the settlement fires. Another drink. Wipe your hand with the back of your mouth. God grips the armrests for leverage. Inhuman exertions. Or, all too human. Pushes himself forward. Naked skin rips. He leans forward again. There's no real rush. He's been here some three hundred years. What's another few minutes? The charade of life. His eyes remain fixed on yours. He *does* want to kill you. The furrowed face shakes in agony, exertion. One leg moves forward on its own. Bones splinter and crack. Still he rises, crawling like a dead thing toward the promise of resurrection.

God stands. Evan Cooper stands. For the first time in more than three hundred years. You're sobbing now. And laughing. The canteen of spirits is empty. He staggers toward you. The difference between you is wholly clear.

Do not move when he collapses upon you. When the jagged claws dig. The fists drop. The unearthly weight. Ancient. Urgent. Something metal in its hand now. It comes down. Again.

Emerging Issues in Residential Care/Assisted Living [pp 317-33]
Wake. After the blast. After the four-story C3 tumbles. Covers all. No light filters from above though the debris. The glow of a single active *LifeChair®* casts across the basement. Half the chamber is collapsed, buried. Seventy-three bodies remain in long rows on the ground beneath you.

Evan Cooper. A surgeon. He is not among them.

Half a million pounds of rubble now separate this tomb from the rest of the world. In a week, the RSC crushers will roll in to recycle whatever worthwhile concrete and timber remain above, then flatten the rest to finish burying the recently departed. There is no chance of ever being found.

You look down upon the long rows of dead from your chair. Your back and sides burn and ache. Slit open. You're nude. Only the wires and tubes remain, joining you and the chair. Joining past and future. To disconnect them now yourself would bring death. Suicide. Sin. Hell. For eternity.

Or maybe only another thousand years.

A choice you might make tomorrow.

In the Name of God, dear God, the Merciful, Compassionate....

HYDRAULIC

Ekaterina Sedia

Lewis watched through the endless, almost solid, curtain of rain as a velorickshaw pulled in front of the Amicio's restaurant across the street. It was difficult to see the faces of the man and the woman who exited the cab–the streams of rain washed over the window of the coffee shop in which Lewis held his vigil. The reflections of the neon signs and marquees in the wet pavement blurred and flowed, a poisoned palette of broken colors and promises.

He folded his newspaper, left money on the stained Formica surface, and ran outside. The vertical jets poured over his head and shoulders, getting inside his rain slicker and running warm down his back. He jogged across the street and cautiously peeked through the window of Amicio's.

The man talking to the maitre' d was indeed his subject–Jack Eslinger, suspected of illegal battery recharging and possibly worse. Probably worse–otherwise, FBI, the branch of the Bureau of Licensing and Intellectual Property (BLIP) wouldn't be interested in him. The woman at his side looked toward the window, and Lewis retreated, but not before catching a glimpse of long grey eyes between the rim of her storm hat and the scarf that swathed the lower half of her face. Those eyes sent his heart pumping; no matter that her face was hidden–he recognized her, recognized her as one would a first love. Callie Swainson.

He stepped under the awning of the shop next door and lit a smokeless cigarette. Breathing deep a cool stream of nicotine and rain vapor, he let his eyes search the neon signs and the holographs, the billboards that bubbled and detached under the battering rain. It didn't take long to find her–there, over the red-lit doors of the ArXade, was a 3D poster advertising their latest VR release. On that poster, Callie wore a school uniform; she crouched down to adjust her sliding knee-high, her knee almost touching the ground, her smooth thigh draped in a tartan skirt; a flash of her white panties, a serious look in her grey eyes under her dirty blond bangs. "Jailbait," the title read. Lewis cringed–not another rape-a-schoolgirl romp.

Why did she keep licensing herself to these creeps? He considered buying the game nonetheless. He dared another peek at the window, in time to see Eslinger and the star of the video industry settle at a table. She didn't remove her scarf even as she ordered. Lewis sympathized–he remembered hearing that she'd had a problem with a stalking fan couple of years back. He guessed that this was why she hid her face and didn't have any games out for a while. Lewis smiled, thinking that her game releases were the true measure of time, of recall. When people talked about the events of 2012, he first thought of her third-person shooter and not about the decision of Congress to sever all ties with the rest of the world. 2015 marked Callie's first interactive NC-17 gig, and not the year when Israel was finally engulfed by its hostile surroundings. And 2017 was when he first made love to her–to her image, but really, it was her he was thinking about–and not the year when they switched to the rain-powered economy.

He looked through the window again, to see his subjects settled in for their meal, and then jogged back to the coffee shop. Eslinger's appointment was nothing more than a date, and Lewis would've felt disappointed if it weren't for seeing Callie. He had to fight an urge to walk up to her and say hello; but of course she wouldn't recognize him. And she had to be weary of the men who treated her as if they knew her because they had bought her licensed image.

Lewis didn't expect anything to happen until Eslinger was done with his meal, so he touched the corner of his left eye, switching on his retinal implant. He flicked through the staticky channels and wished he brought a movie from home. Or a game—but of course, the console would be too bulky. He turned off the implant, and the static in his left eye disappeared, letting the grey and neon of the outside melt back into his vision. He watched a group of teens run down the streets, laughing and splashing, kicking over the mushrooms sprouting through the cracks between the cobblestones of the pavement. He listened to the low but resonant hum of the electric generators, their membranes strumming under the constant gushing of the rain, their vibration charging the giant accumulators and smaller portable batteries that bore the words "Warner/AOL/Disney, Federal Property, DO NOT RECHARGE."

The air outside grew darker by the minute, and Lewis glanced at his watch impatiently, then to the windows across the street. The door squealed open, and on the threshold stood Callie, her face in shadows, her body hidden under the ample slicker but unmistakable. He knew her as one would his lover.

There was no Eslinger in sight.

She stepped to the curb, her arm flailing for a velorickshaw. Lewis left his table and stepped outside, his lungs filling with water vapor. When he was a kid, they used to have smog; now they had rain. Tit for tat. He was just trying to find a better observation spot, but his legs carried him over to the curb where Callie stood. It was foolish, it was reckless, but he approached her.

Her dark eyes flashed reflected neon at him, and she took a step back, fearful.

"Sorry, ma'am," he mumbled. "Didn't mean to startle you; just wondering if you're okay."

"Of course." Her words were muffled by her scarf, but he recognized the rich bitter chocolate of her voice. He was a bit more accustomed to this voice saying, "Yes, please," and "Please, no!" and he blushed at the memory, annoyed that it was not mutual. She glanced at the restaurant doors. "Why wouldn't I be?"

A rickshaw peddler skidded to a stop, dismounted from his bicycle, and held open the cab door for her.

"Just a moment," she said. "I'm waiting for someone."

Lewis remembered Eslinger and stepped away from Callie.

She breathed a sigh of relief as the doors opened once more and Eslinger's long, lanky frame and the smaller, denser silhouette of the proprietor shook hands in the lit doorway.

"Come back any time," the proprietor said.

Lewis slid into the shadows of the restaurant wall as Callie and Eslinger climbed into the cab and were off in a firework of splatter, but not before Lewis noted the cab number. Tomorrow morning he'd find out whether Eslinger went straight home; but with Callie there, he had little doubt that it would be the case.

Upon his arrival home, Lewis was greeted by the mewling of his cat, complaining bitterly of his owner's long absence.

"Yeah yeah yeah," Lewis said. "It was horrible, I know. C'mon, I'll feed you."

He proceeded to the kitchen and was somewhat surprised to discover that the normally ravenous beast had left his food untouched. He gave the cat a concerned glance. "You're okay, pal?"

The cat meowed and rubbed against his soaked trousers; the cat's fur had an unfamiliar green tinge to it, and it left a grass stain on Lewis's trouser leg.

"The hell?" he said, and picked up the now-purring cat. His fur was definitely turning green. Lewis thought that this phenomenon deserved an investigation, and put the cat down. He turned on the retinal implant, and soon was searching the Fed-Net for information. He found out that indeed many cats in the area had turned green; the scientists claimed that many animals were acquiring algal symbionts in their fur, since the moisture in the air was high enough to support their growth. The authorities recommended the use of full spectrum lamps to facilitate photosynthesis, and urged the pet owners to reduce feeding. Lewis switched on the desk lamp. The cat immediately curled in the circle of light. Lewis shrugged and went to the kitchen to get a drink, the lines of text still scrolling across his retinal implant.

The next morning Lewis learned that the velorickshaw had delivered the couple to an address near the marina. That wasn't Eslinger's house, Lewis told himself. It was hers. He needed to do some reconnaissance, and he got ready. He tried to keep the smile off his face, but it cropped up now and again. He knew where Callie lived. Not that he couldn't have found out otherwise, but his colleagues at BLIP would want to know why he needed her address. Now, it was strictly business. Before he left, he poured a handful of spidercams into his pocket. You just never knew when you'd need one.

He dismissed the rickshaw a few blocks before her house and walked the rest of the way. The sky was cloudy, but it didn't rain, and the passersby craned their necks at the sky, where a few government crop dusters bearing an AOL logo herded the clouds.

Lewis stopped to watch and wondered if Canada would complain again about the U.S. Weather Service stealing their clouds. The warming and the increased evaporation did not affect the area north of the border quite as much, and their clouds were fewer. Tough luck, Lewis thought. We need the rain.

He stopped outside of Callie's house, activated one of the spidercams, and hooked up to its video and audio feeds. When he had first started out, this experience had made him dizzy–his right eye looked at the normal landscape, while the picture in his left weaved and changed as the cam moved about. But not anymore. Clouds crowded the lens of the cam as it climbed along the wall, and then the bricks of the house as it searched for an entrance point. It found one through the chimney, and Lewis felt as if he had gone blind in his left eye for a few seconds. Then there was a hearth and a tiled floor, white walls devoid of pictures or posters, chipped paint on the chairs. And then there was Callie's foot–long and white with short, bleak toenails.

The spidercam skittered away, its heat sensors warning it from too close a contact with a person. It searched the apartment to make sure that there were no others present, and then returned and settled on the wall, as small and unobtrusive as a real spider, and watched Callie.

She sat in a deep chair, her legs crossed, her head tilted over a book, half-concealed by her long, dirty-blond hair. Lewis wished that she would look up into the camera so he could catch a glimpse of the perfect face he knew so well. But she remained transfixed until the phone rang.

Lewis looked up at the sky and walked over to a small patch of artificial trees. He sat on a bench, damp and slick, and returned to his observation. Callie picked up the phone, and the cam picked up the sound–poor and crackling, but discernible. Lewis wondered why Callie still used a phone, like old people. He guessed that she didn't have an implant, either.

The phone was ancient, with a black and white video panel, grainy like an old photograph. Eslinger's long face was sketched on it in oversized pixels. "Hi," he said.

"Hello. Are you coming by?"

Eslinger's small image cheerfully held up two batteries. "I need to do some recharging. Maybe later, 'kay?"

She nodded. "I miss you."

Lewis cringed on his bench. He could not believe that this guy was so dismissive of her, so blind to his luck. Lewis was going to find out what he was up to, and hopefully would send him away for a long time, to a place where it rarely rained.

"I'm sorry," he said. "I'll try to stop by later, and we'll talk." With that, the video screen went blank.

Lewis had to go, to find Eslinger and track his steps. The BLIP had been suspecting that he was running an unauthorized generator. Not the rain one, but the kind that fed on the upward drafts of air. A convection contraption would be easier to keep hidden and harder to monitor–that was why they were illegal. Lewis had to track Eslinger to the generator. Yet, his feet refused to carry him away from Callie.

He focused on the image in his left eye just as Callie settled back into the chair. Her gaze swept up the wall, and her grey eyes met Lewis' for a moment. Then, she emitted a brief scream and tossed the book in her hand at the wall. The hurled paperback obscured the sight of her, and static danced across his implant.

"Fuck," Lewis said.

He caught up to Eslinger near Chinatown–another agent notified Lewis that his subject had taken a velorickshaw there. It started to rain again, and Lewis was grateful for the generous shroud of rain and mist that hid his presence from his quarry.

He felt at home, like a salmon bounding upstream, across the waterfalls and jagged rocks.

Eslinger walked ahead in an easy loping stride, his feet barely making ripples in the puddles that accumulated in the pockmarks of the pavement, his long silhouette melting into the greyness of the rain, then reappearing again. He turned a corner by a pagoda that still bore shreds of yellow, red and green paint, and ducked inside a narrow doorway.

Lewis noted the number of the building and kept walking,

reluctant to attract attention of a young man who made camp on the doorstep, his vinyl poncho stretched over his head like a tent. An opium pipe cradled in his hands emitted a thin stream of blue smoke, almost invisible in the mist. Lewis shook a cigarette out of his pack and dropped a spidercam. He found a pawnshop up the street. The spidercam transmitted the view of the doors and the young man smoking his pipe.

There were hardly any Chinese left in Chinatown, but one of the survivors stood behind the counter of the pawnshop.

Lewis regarded him with his right eye. A young, round-faced man smiled at him. "Can I help you?"

"Just looking," he said and let his gaze sweep across the walls and shelves crowded with junk–umbrellas, toys, silk flowers, sculptures made of discarded batteries and bottle caps.

A giant metal skeleton leaned in the corner–long legs, a torn rubber membrane flapping like a lone broken wing. Lewis recognized the remains of a convection generator.

"Scrap," the young fellow at the counter said, not moving.

"Don't have any working ones, huh?"

The young man shook his head vigorously, whipping his long skinny braid. "No sir. No illegal merchandise here."

"Where then?"

"Wouldn't know."

At length, Eslinger appeared, accompanied by another man.

The youngster with the tent and the opium pipe stirred and ran to the back of the building, soon reappearing with a well-worn bike harnessed to a covered wagon, a cross between a rickshaw cab and a children's toy. He helped Eslinger and his companion load the wagon with dozens of portable batteries, jumped into the bike seat, and disappeared into the mist. Eslinger followed on foot. The spidercam skittered after.

Lewis looked at his watch; the spidercam had at least an hour of life left in it. Time enough to dry off.

The man at the counter gave him a tense smile. Lewis bought a lacquered box and headed home.

The cat was greener than the night before, sprawled under the lamp. It wheezed when Lewis entered and made no attempt to get up.

"Fuck you," Lewis said and threw the dripping wet slicker on the floor. Nothing ever was truly waterproof, and he changed out of his shirt wet at the seams. Callie was on his mind, and he rummaged through the stack of her games. An interactive sex flick did not seem appropriate at the moment, and he settled for a third-person adventure game. It was old–the motion was still a bit jerky, a bit unnatural, with just a hint of mechanical creepiness, but he was willing to disregard it now. He dropped the pretense of work and disconnected from the cam in favor of rescuing Callie from a group of demons that meant to do unspeakable things to her in the cutscenes.

He fought the monsters and rescued Callie, and she was grateful. Then they were ambushed, and fought, and ran, and she cried. He told her he loved her and meant it. It was just a game, but he felt that there was a deeper truth in it: Callie was caught up in something bad, even if she didn't realize it yet, and Lewis was going to open her eyes. Eslinger would go to the federal prison on the floating island of Orlando, Florida.

And Callie… he tried not to set his hopes too high, but it was difficult–he was setting up camp, and she was cold in her gauzy shift. She pressed against him for warmth, her breast flattening against his chest. It rained, and her dress flowed over her lines, casting them in luminous shine. The cutscene played.

She never faced the spidercam. It became a game–watching the cam's feed, waiting for her to turn toward it. But every time she did, the cam was smashed, showing only her long eyes flashing fear.

Sometimes Eslinger showed up, but he'd become a nuisance rather than the reason for Lewis' surveillance. He was a convenient excuse to watch Callie reading, Callie taking a shower, Callie washing the dishes. For two days, Lewis did not move from the park bench, didn't go home. He watched. Eslinger was visiting. He brought batteries.

Callie pushed the door open with her rump and entered the room backward, carrying a tray with a steaming kettle and two cups.

"Thanks," Eslinger said from the couch. "You didn't have to."

"You must be freezing." She set the tray on the table and sat next to him, burying her face in his shoulder. "I worry about you."

"I'll be fine."

"I worry. There're spiders here. Maybe we should move. To the wheat belt, maybe. I hear there's less rain."

"And less electricity."

Callie thought for a moment. "I could do with less electricity."

Eslinger shifted. "It'll be okay. Now, let's get your machine hooked up."

He went rooting through a large plastic bag he had brought with him, extracting a monitor and a plastic box.

Lewis had seen computers like that–outdated, but they still cropped up here and there. Not everyone had an implant.

Callie crouched down and watched. "You're saying we can put a movie on the FedNet?"

"Not Fed. Just a net."

"I can't believe it's still around."

Eslinger's narrow shoulders jerked in a shrug. "Why wouldn't it be? Just because it's illegal?"

She snorted a laugh.

Lewis watched, his body hunching over instinctively. That,

right there, was enough to put Eslinger away for a long time. He tugged on his eyelid, saving the footage.

The machine was assembled, sitting on the floor amidst the entwined wires, hooked up to one of the batteries with stolen energy in it, connected to the illegal net. He saved again.

Eslinger fiddled with a camera–just a thin tube pointed at Callie. She seemed nervous, her shoulders tense, her arms wrapped around her in a childish protective gesture, her fingers kneading her shoulders.

"Ready when you are," Eslinger said.

Lewis found the cat under the lamp again. He barely looked like one–a puddle of green slime with some fur and a lone tooth. The mass quivered and tried to meow.

"Oh for fuck's sake," Lewis said.

He tossed the disk on the table, not quite ready to watch it yet. He stretched on his unslept-in bed that smelled of mold, and closed his eyes. On the dark side of his eyelids, stitched with red veins, he saw Callie's face again, the melted face of a doll tortured with a magnifying glass. It was the first thing he had seen when he'd entered after the agents who had busted down her door, and the only thing he remembered. Concave cheek, one corner of her mouth lifted on a knot of pink scar tissue, her teeth bared in a leer all the more horrible for the fear in her eyes.

He sighed and got up, pacing back and forth, past the puddle of light in which his ex-cat was slowly disintegrating, turning into ooze. Whatever was on the disc couldn't be much worse than what he'd already seen. He turned on the player.

"Is this thing on?" the horrible Callie said with a fretful look to her left.

"Go ahead," Eslinger said off camera.

She looked straight at Lewis. "I'm Callie Swainson. This is not the way you remember me," she started. "I'm sorry. I wanted to show you, but they keep reusing my old images. Everything about me has changed, but people only see the old scans and motion captures. I'm almost sorry there're no live action movies anymore."

"Tell them what happened," Eslinger said off-camera.

"A man who liked my games met me in person, and he was upset that I wasn't the way he remembered me. He threw acid in my face." She fidgeted a bit, her fingers twisting the hem of her cable-knit sweater. She didn't seem upset, as far as one could judge from her hideous face, just nervous. "I just thought that you should know. My company wouldn't let me tell anyone. They were afraid that it would cut into the profits from the licensing fees—"

There was a bang, and the camera swept toward the entrance.

The door swung open and hung off one hinge as the men in BLIP uniforms, yellow and black like wasps, crowded the camera. Lewis turned off the video. His heart felt like it had turned to ash and crumbled, leaving a large Callie-shaped hole in his chest. The hole yawned, empty, and even the thought of Eslinger in detainment and his forthcoming imprisonment in a place where there was almost no rain did not satisfy it. Only the real Callie could, and he wasn't sure if he would be able to go back to her pure, unspoiled image, if it would be strong enough to displace the hag in the seized video.

He turned on his implant and watched once again the cutscene from the game he had played a few nights back. The heavy droning of the rain grew more distant, blending with the background music in a percussive counterpoint. The ex-cat bubbled and lolled on the desk with a soft kissing sound. Callie's face, magically mended and whole, took up the entire implant, blotting out the sight of the room, of the cat, and the flooded world outside.

A FUTILE GESTURE
TOWARD TRUTH

Paul Jessup

UrsaUrth was a broken rock of a planet whose last days were cold and ruinous beneath the dying light of the sun. Mankind had flourished, conquered the galaxy, and then, like a firefly, quickly vanished. Retreated. The recoiling cold of the universe far too frightening for their frail bodies.

On this rock of UrsaUrth and under the light of the wheezing sun crawled a junk boat through the green and gold waters of the Glass God Sea. It bobbed on the churning waves in drunken and disorderly movements, searching for something of its own amongst the debris. It was a massive barge, as large as the largest city that Tarel had ever seen.

It was composed of bric-a-brac thrown and cemented together, relic world pieces pushed into odd and new formations. Pyramids, glass walls, domed ceilings, each part and piece crawling with vine and grass, living things with green leaves outstretched and seeking the failing nourishment of light.

Tarel stood on deck, hand on his sword: Dama, Durhalla, the singing sword of the Rootworld ruins. Naked sun outlined his body as he watched the waves and saw, beneath the green-lit water, the glowing silver bodies of the glass gods. Miniature, transparent, filled with humming wires and ancient circuitus magick. The gods parted, swimming aside, letting the barge through their sacred lands.

From behind came clamoring shouts from the crew, and then a familiar shuffling sound. Tarel turned and saw his sarcyst moving toward him, her feet scuffling the floor in her strange manner of walking. She wore a black patchwork dress, revealing nothing. Her skin was scarred, her fingers holding a cane with a knotted tip that she used to help her walk.

It was hard for Tarel to tell her age. He knew she was barely in her second decade, but her eyes and her flesh held scars older then he. In the manner of the magecraft, the left side of her skull was shorn, and placed against her skin and under bone were the sorcer-altubes, sparkling with a hot neon intensity. As she approached, her eyes flickered like black beetles in her skull, and her remaining hair danced along her shoulders like raven wings.

He remembered when she had hired him. Felt like ages ago. When the eenoks came from the trees and stormed the ancient city of the Dreaming Monks, and he fought them off and had taken her to safety. At the time he had wondered why she hadn't magicked them away.

He had seen her cast spells since then. There was no wonder in their workings. Only misery and a hollow victory. And her weeping on the ground.

They said nothing, only stood next to each other and let the sea carry their thoughts away, far away, to the southern shores of the world where the fish rose to land and prayed to the crushed light of the orange-faced moon.

The next morning Tarel woke to a shaking hammock, his ox-thick body twisting in the fabric and then dumping on the ground. Two sailors stood above him like rough statues carved from the face of a cliff, their eyes dagger-thin and piercing him with unspoken questions. They wore black coats that scraped the ground, the ends muddy and ragged. Mismatched copper buttons were affixed to sleeve and chest, with a scant few missing and leaving gaps in cloth, baring skin.

"That girl. The one you protect," one said. "She can cast, yeah?"

Tarel nodded. "Yeah."

The larger of the two leaned down and extended a granite hand. Tarel clenched it, was pulled up. Rose light streamed in from the windows, tinting the room in a pinkish red. "We need her help. The captain, the others. They're different in a way. Terribly different. Can you talk to her for us?"

Tarel shrugged. "Talk to her yourself."

The two sailors exchanged a look of fear. Their bodies quivered, hands shaking, eyes darting back and forth. "Well, we would, but well, not sure if we trust her. You know?"

The other blurted his words out, his tongue clumsy behind his lips, smacking each word against his teeth. "She might burn us from the inside out or transport us to the crumpled shores of the moon!"

Tarel hid a smirk behind his hand. "Don't worry. It's not like that at all. Now, tell me what's wrong. Maybe I can help? She's still sleeping, and we should let her rest. If things are as bad as they seem, she will need all of her energy."

Tarel stood over Lamlarra's sleeping body. So restful, so quiet. He didn't want to disturb her. It would be like smashing a statue or breaking glass over his fist. He told the sailors to wait outside, and they listened to his suggestions only out of fear of her eldritch powers.

She tossed. Turned. Muttered something. Instead of waking her, Tarel felt the desire to write a poem. He'd found out years before that he had a taste for poetry, and even though he could never keep the words in his head for more than a minute, he felt that he liked the way they rolled around in his mouth before they expired and were lost in his memories. They were like wet stones, skipping across the placid lake of his mind.

He would've written some of these down, had he the power and mind to read or write. But his mind was clumsy in this aspect, and so gave his poetry the art of distance and expiration. It became, like all humanity in that moment, a futile gesture toward truth. A vanishing, dying truth. That of civilization's end, of world's end, of time's end, when the universe cooled down and finally, finally, gave an end to life.

"There is a sorrow to the sun," he began, "a deft weight that binds us."

He paused. Chewed on his tongue. "No," he said. "No. That's not quite right. The birds who scream? Does that sound like a better start? So many promises with words. Yet we must choose them carefully, lest the wrong words at the beginning cause discord in the end."

Lamlarra stirred. Her eyes danced, then opened, peeling apart and letting the sparkling black of her irises soak up the light of day. "What did you say?"

Tarel looked over at her, resting his chin on his hand. "Nothing. Just composing words. Are you awake?"

She sat up, looked around the room. The pink light coated everything, tinting the colors into a fleshy hue. It made all seem living, all seem breathing. The junk walls tasted the air, tested it for sentience. The creeping vines across the window whose leafy fingers tried to push past glass and through cracks in the junk now scratched, carefully, like a dog that wished entrance.

"Awake enough. I dreamt of white horses in the rain. And riders wearing masks. You?"

Tarel stood against the wall. His back ached, his spine raw against his skin. "Haven't yet. Slept or dreamt. There is something you should know."

A raised eyebrow. Singed. Ring of scars around her eyes, spiral shaped, dancing out across cheek. Eyes flickered, from black to grey. The beating of raven wings on stone. "They fear me, don't they? They want us to leave. Like the last time. Fearing that I cursed the waters. Is that it?"

She pulled out a small vial that she wore suspended around her neck. Clear blue glass wrapped with twine, and that twine then noosed around her shoulders. Inside of the frosted blue glass was a shriveled up female form, no bigger than a thumb. Curled up, tightly woven into a spiral shape. Lamlarra kissed it gently. Tarel never understood her attachment to this fetish. Maybe, he mused, it was a god of her choosing?

"I'm sorry," she whispered to the doll, "Maybe later, maybe soon, we can get to the oracle, and then, maybe then we could see the Wellworld, and drag you from the vats, newlynew and shining again."

Tarel looked discreetly the other way, admiring the piecemeal wall that combined several stone cobbles, a plate of stained glass, and a mismatched dome over their heads with scattered paintings across it. After she was done whispering, he spoke again. "Your fears are unfounded this time. It seems that the captain and a few choice members of the crew have become, well, possessed. They wish to procure some of your services in the area of magecraft."

Lamlarra locked eyes, wings fluttering through the naked void between them. She shoved the delicate shriveled doll into her skirt and pursed her lips. "No," she said sternly. "No, I will not remember. Not again. You can't force me to do this. You can't force me to help them. I'm sick of magick, sick of all this pain that covers my soul like soot."

Tarel weighed the air, saw the ghosts that flickered between them and felt the sharp sparks flickering from the tubes placed into her skull. The light from them changed the air, changed the tint and shadow of the room. Away, away went pink and flesh and in came the sick of neon green and bright bleeding red. "Look, look, look. There might be other ways that you can think of, right? Ways not involving magecraft? Ways that I can't muster in my own meager mind. I can fit words together, yes, it is a talent. But I can't fit logic together; it is always a puzzle for my mind. And besides, how can we move forward with a captain infected?"

He leaned in closer, to accent his point. "Are you willing to break another promise?"

She frowned, her lips see-sawing and her eyes betraying the complexity of her thoughts. Logic might not have been Tarel's forte, but reading people was a poet's charge. And there, in that moment, he read a partial victory.

She relented. "I'll go and we'll see. But I do not promise a thing. And if I am to remember, than I shall do so only for the promise I made toward another. Even though it burns me and breaks me each time."

Tarel nodded. "Good, then."

He knew that this was a hollow victory at best, and his mind did not dwell on it for more than a scant second. He hated his persuasive talents in moments like this, and dreaded what was to come. But he would watch. He would always watch. And someday, he might even remember all that he had seen.

At night Tarel had nightmares. Pieces of memories came back to him, draining him in his sleep. And with these dreams came sharp pain in the back of his head, as well as a numb feeling crawling across his sword hand.

Some nights he awoke and saw Dama, his singing sword, closer to the bed than he had originally placed it. It sang in the darkness hours and vibrated playfully. He saw reflected smiling faces along the blade, and then a picture of cities ages ago, when the sky was filled with light and the burning tails of sky ships.

The song always put him back to sleep, and then in the morning the memory of all dreams would vanish. All that was left was that song, like a sailor drowning in Tarel's thoughts. Terrible, and he was unable to look away, unable to save it. And then the images of that city and memories of a time that was not his own.

Outside stood the two sailors. Changed. There coats were half eaten, their eyes hollow lamps that burned no light. Splattered across their faces was a liquid glass, filled with neon blinking circuitry and the intelligent dust of magick. The glass gods had infected them too, it seemed.

Lamlarra stood back, framed by a junk doorway arched and carved with ancient runes. With each surge of a wave more glass gods flew across the prow of the ship and leaked onto patchwork planks. The eyes of the sailors stared at them numbly.

Lamlarra hissed between her teeth. "Tarel, I can't do this. Not so many times. It will be once, and then I will be spent for the greater part of the day. We must revive one or none. This many would kill me."

Tarel thought for a moment. The two sailors lurched forward, the circuits blazing. The lips of one opened and spoke. "You need not fear the gifts we bring. Look there, lo! Look below the ship and into the waves. See what we can give you? Eternal life, eternal everything. In our care you need not eat or breathe or age. We shall upkeep all. In our care, you need not even think! For we shall do that for you as well."

Over the side of the ship and within the waves were the transparent and haunted faces of men and women, trapped underwater, swimming and floating with the current, hair long and trailing behind like flickering veils. Their eyes had no light, and they seemed to be no better than corpses.

Tarel grimaced. "And what if we decline your noble offer?"

The sailors barked and moved forward. "We are made from the darkest magicks, from when the sun was still young and burning. True, true. Since then we have eroded a bit, our AIs have gotten too listless, too imperfect. Such is age! Ah, ah. Such is age. But needless to say, our magick does not require a beating heart. It does not require a living man. Your corpses will do just fine."

Without a second thought Tarel unsheathed Dama, the singing blade. He felt Lamlarra grasp the walls of the arch, knew that she was saving her strength and her magick for what was to come. The blade hummed in his hand. He looked over at the sailors and felt—

Dizzy. Shadows became stark cutouts. He remembered something in that moment. The way the light glinted off the glass gods, covering faces and hands. He remembered being in the Rootworld ruins. It felt like so long ago, when the walls had come to life and the roots had come down, scattering dirt across his face.

And from the shadows crept tall, ancient things. Silver- and brass-boned with thin fingers that prodded and sharpened and ate into his skin. Tarel remembered with fear, remembered being covered in light film that breathed for him, his thoughts not his own.

A pain. In the back of his head. He touched and felt stitches there, and something moving beneath his scalp. Tiny things, no bigger than a thumb. In his distraction he let his guard down, and the sailors rushed forward, howling, brutal, blades raised as the glass gods commanded their puppet bodies.

Tarel had not the time to reminisce, nor to feel fear at the things that moved beneath his scalp. He let the blade sing and swerve in the air and felt his arm burning and a sharp pain, then a numbness that swept across his fingers and to his elbow. He looked down as his arm moved without him, and saw tiny tubes blinking orange and neon and connecting under skin, under bone. It pained him, and pulled on him, and he felt a draining of his blood and marrow. Sharp pains cavorted beneath the surface of his thoughts, and then a blinding light.

Memories rose to the surface as he fought. The sword darted and bit into flesh, a living snake of steel. It ate through the sailors, chewed through them, and Tarel could only stand and stare as his body danced without his knowing.

The memories that rose to the surface were the important, powerful things he had long since forgotten, now bubbling to the surface, horrific and real in their intensity. The details of the memories overwhelmed him, all the tiny particles of information drowning him in their complexity.

He felt the creatures move beneath his scalp some more, and then heard the tiny ticking from millions of microscopic engines performing surgery in unison. They cut into his mind matter and began to draw on the energy of these memories, erasing them as they were tapped.

The blade devoured. And when it was done, the sailors lay dead on the ship with the glass gods unblinking and destroyed into messy splatters. The sea surged, the bodies in the waves looking out, staring at them. Hungry. And Tarel felt a tickling in his brain, and then forgot again the memories, forgot about the things under his scalp, forgot all about the combat except for the blade sliding into each body.

Again, again. Objects slid into impermanence, and the truth of the matter became a shadow in his mind. The combat became something external, something cardboard. It had happened to someone else. Some other time.

He was exhausted. Lamlarra stared at him with the same blazing look she always gave him after he fought. A look of distrust, of pity and of fear. The bodies in the waves seemed to move in unison, moving toward them. The sword vibrated in wait, hungry.

"We should see if the captain is still aboard the ship," Lamlarra said with a calm fear in her voice, "and revive him so that we may escape other terrors that wish to intrude."

Tarel nodded. His head burned. A fire in his skull. Always after combat it was like this. Always. As far back as his memory led him to believe.

This is a discarded memory. It is one absorbed and eaten by Dama, the singing sword, when Tarel first succumbed to its bite and gnawing powers:

The road was long, with corpses scattered to either side and the trees filled with a loose fire. Skulls hung from the necks of giant flowers whose petals were sharp and pink and looked like conch shells.

In the center of a circle whose circumference was death sat Lamlarra. Her eyes watered. Her hands trembled. In front of her was a tiny, spiral-shaped girl. Mewling. Calling out for help. Tarel stood. Watched.

Lamlarra shouted, "Help her! Her! I told you to help her! She was dying. What cruel twist of fate is this? My magick is worthless."

She picked up the deformed little girl and held her in her arms, wiping her cheeks with the back of her arm. Tarel looked down, saw his sword hand covered in blood. Felt as if this was familiar somehow. As if this had all happened before. Over and over and over again. From the trees came a whispering, the voices of leaves.

Reflected in the harsh red light of the sun, Tarel saw Lamlarra's genii. A ball of mist and smog, whose very existence was electrical and magnetic. He felt his sword pull on his arm, reach toward the shambling cloud of misery.

"I will make her portable," the genii mused. "Maybe then, in a year or so, when you have proven your worth to me, maybe then I will restore her to you."

Lamlarra sobbed. She stared up, looked into the strange smokeling beast. "I have given you so much. My memories, my life. With each spell I cast I feel you draining me. Devouring me. Why have you seen fit to do this?"

The smoke ripped through the air, pushed back her lips and her teeth and forced itself into her mouth. It was done conversing. It was done talking. It had returned back to its home, drilling under skin and lip and tooth, spearing through her pores and dwelling beneath the flesh. A thousand living particles, each speck of dust imbued with an intelligence woven from the oldest of magicks: bacteria, LISP and silicon.

Rope was wrapped around the captain, who sat in his chair with eyes flickering through the spectrum of colors. His face and arms were coated with the glass gods, and his teeth were sparkling, electric. Lamlarra perched in the shadows, her eyes wary. Outside of the cabin the dead were piled loosely, with more coming across, rising out of the waves, their vengeful eyes seeking.

Tarel's sword twisted and sang in his hands, hungry for another round of combat. He sat against the door, hoping that the glass gods would soon give up chase and leave them be, allowing them to sail the junkboat across the sea.

Behind the tied-up captain were the ancient magicks that controlled the ship. Light, glowing numbers that danced with prismatic colors. A chest of ruined electronics, talking to the angels of satellites that hung close in low orbit, guiding them from pier to pier and relaying the weather into cute miniature graphics.

Lamlarra spoke. Her voice burned with each word. An endless fire of language. "Let us go. You have many bodies. And many more will come to you. Just let us go. Leave the captain's body."

The captain's face twisted, became more angular. They saw the glass gods crawl across his features, rewriting them on a molecular level, changing each piece until it fit with whatever new design they desired. "You mistake us for those who care about the toiling of mortality. This sea is ours, has been ours since our creation. Before we came it was a desert, sun-starved and vacant. We gave it life, gave it a purpose. And we grow it daily, feeding from the air, creating new molecules. Growing, spreading. Further and farther. We will not let you go. We will take you apart, atom by atom, and use you to rebuild, to create new glass gods. We are the eating sea, the devouring sea, and we will swallow the world whole."

Lamlarra sighed. "My genii has whispered to me of your true nature. You are the slush things, built by the eld of man before the sun began to flicker. Originally built for terraforming. Your purpose on UrsaUrth is misdirected."

The captain screamed and howled, and the glass gods tore off chunks of his flesh. Using this, they remade the ropes, remade them to be looser so they could wiggle arms and legs free. The captain ran toward her, screaming, his face warping into a conch shell shape, his limbs elongating into spider-thin architectures, his whole form mutating, joining with the ship to create a web of flesh and glass god. Tarel's mind itched, his memories burned, and his singing sword stung out, struck out, slid through and burned away the glass gods inside of the captain's shell.

The body fell. Crumpled. Messy. A pile of bones with meat stuck to it, rotten and made into strange angles by the glass gods. The neon lights flickered no more, the glass gods feeding off of his body now perished and extinguished.

Tarel's mind still burned. He leaned against the wall, dizzy, his sword hand tingling and numb. He muttered something incoherent and struggled against passing out.

Lamlarra sighed and drew a circle on the junk floor with white chalk, staining her fingers and hand with the dust. Her lips twisted in her head, moving and chanting. Tarel watched with a dazed sense of reality, everything in the junk room burning with the odd light of her sorceraltubes.

She had tears in her eyes, her lids closed, her cheeks turning red and blushing. Her fingers performed complex symbols, mudras in the air that enacted a sign language based on ancient programming code.

After a moment, her hands dropped. Her eyes popped open, wide. Her lips twitched a little, and Tarel saw such sadness reflected in her pupils. It crept out and swallowed him with the misery she experienced. Her lips mouthed the words, *I'm sorry, sister, so sorry* as the genii poured forth from every pore. His black and gold specks created a shadowy gaseous cloud, with floating, hollow red eyes glaring. Each particle of his being flew about, sticking into a strange shape based on flocking patterns designed well over a millennium ago.

"Can't we pick another memory to associate with the summoning sigils? Why does it have to be that specific one?"

The genii hovered in the air for a moment. "Memories are as they are."

Lamlarra pointed at him, her chalky finger outlined by the red light of her tubes. "Don't ignore my question."

The air hummed with a feeling of electricity; it was alive and burning the insides of their throats and sticking thickly to their eyes. The genii looked at her, watched the tubes on her head dance and sparkle. "I see. I can read your thoughts, and I see what you desire me to do. You realize that what you ask of me is a form of genocide, correct? These are the last of the glass gods. The planets were been created to terraform are now cold and empty husks waiting for the universe to unwind itself into nothingness."

Lamlarra grinned, her face twisted in pain, her eyes wet with tears that shone against her cheeks like rare jewels. Wet sapphires born from the surface of the moon. "Does genocide matter, then? If the world is to burn out, if the heavens are to become cold and empty, how does anything equal any importance?"

Tarel rested on his sword, using it as a cane to prop up his body. His hand felt naked, burnt. His skin was alive with the crawling sensations. This time it felt worse than ever before. Combat had almost killed him. His head hurt. He touched the back of his skull with a hand that felt gigantic, and pulled back sausage-shaped fingers coated in blood. And almost fainted.

His sight swam. The genii spoke, but its words made no sense. The language did not add up; the symbols of the language held no meaning. Sure, he recognized the words in one way, but in another they fell apart and become clumsy cardboard abstractions.

He collapsed to the ground. The air pulsed with heat. And then, then, he drifted into dream.

When he came to, the Glass God Sea was gone. The stars grinned grey and heavy above him, and the ground was a desert of sand and dead things. There was an architecture of burnt corpses and the failing neon circuits of the glass gods. The sea itself was just shadow, was just light.

They were still on the junkship. He was on the starboard port, it seemed. The crushed orange glow of the moon illuminated everything in a harsh, strange twilight hue. Lamlarra stood next to him, her hand on her heart, her face looking pained.

"How do we move still? There is no sea."

Lamlarra shrugged. "The bottom of this boat is built on ancient technology. It walks. Or rather, glides. Over the bodies beneath us."

Tarel nodded. The back of his head still throbbed, and his fingers felt blistered and ancient. "I think we both overstretched our capabilities."

Lamlarra walked over to him, put a delicate hand against his shoulder. Scars ringed around each finger. "I don't want to remember."

He saw a tear leave her eye and splash on his shoulder. He stood up, his body embracing hers. He held her, held her against the stars and moon, against the sea of corpses around them. She held close to him and sobbed against his ribs. He was three heads taller than she, and she fit so comfortably inside his arms. He realized that he could encase her with his body, he could protect her from the elements. She could carve a hole into his chest in the shape of a door and burrow in and live there forever, keeping his heart company in the cold and empty hours.

They were silent, then. The air stayed heavy and stank of corpses. They did not move or speak. Not for an hour, not for a day. Not until they saw hills dotting the horizon, live and real with flush jungles and the sparkling lights of ruined cities waiting to be explored.

And then, then, when they talked it was a simple thing. A thing composed of empty words, comforting words, and a promise that someday the sun would be cold and the world would be cold and neither of them would be cursed any longer.

BLACK HOLE SUN

Alethea Kontis & Kelli Owen

User Profiles:
Erica "Sunshine" Lukac
Age: 15
princessunnie@gmail.com
Twitter: SunnieLu
Following: 22 Followers: 17

Seth Williams
Age: 17
notgoth555@gmail.com
Twitter: notgoth555
Following: 0 Followers: 1

****

From: *Princessunnie@gmail.com*
To: *notgoth555@gmail.com*
Subject: Messages to the Black Hole

Hey, Captain Blackheart!

Mom was shopping today— she's having some weird cravings with this new baby. She and Ron haven't decided on a
name yet. I'm calling him Surprise. Sunshine and Surprise.
won't we be a pair? Anyway...she bought a ham at the store
(do you know how hard it is to find a ham when it's not
Thanksgiving?) and I remembered that funny story you told

me about the crazy homeless woman trying to shoplift that ham. I hadn't thought about that in forever. And then I remembered something else you said that day at the park— about how you were always crap at emails but if I kept sending messages to the Black Hole that you'd read them. So...hi! And I hope you're okay. And I made an A in English— can you believe it? And i painted my toenails blue. And I think Mom and I are going to see Memory of Angels at the Roxy on Friday night and you're welcome to join us even though I know you won't. But I had to ask anyway. You're always my first Impossible Thing before breakfast.

Hugs, grass blades, and bubbles!
xox
Sunnie

****

Seth's laptop announced new mail with a thin metallic ping. In the two years since his mother's suicide, "Seth's muted shock has transformed into full-on victimhood, with a twist of anti-social behavior." The counselors should have just called him emo and filed the papers.

He hadn't spoken to Sunshine since the funeral. He would never again trust the female of the species not to crush him. He had severed all ties to them: his grandmother, his father's sister, his best friend. But Sunnie's contact with him continued as if nothing had happened.

It didn't surprise him anymore, but it was starting to annoy him.

Seth highlighted the email and hit delete. He hadn't read any of her attempts for the past year, and he wasn't starting now...but he couldn't bring himself to block her address or flag it as spam. Deleting each email was just another form of self-immolation, a virtual way for him to remember that he had some control over this semblance of reality he called life.

****

From: *princessunnie@gmail.com*
To: *notgoth555@gmail.com*
Subject: Rise of the Squirrel Nation

Ahoy, Cap'n Blackheart! The wind's blowing from the south today and the squirrels are restless!

I was thinking about you today. Okay, technically I saw you first and that made me think about you— you turned down the hallway to Principal Harrison's office when I was walking to the bathroom during forth period. It looked like you were being escorted. Well, I hope it was for something good. Chopping off all Dr. Nesbit's ties is still my favorite prank of yours. That was so freaking awesome. You have mad skillz, my friend. Don't you ever forget it. Does Principal Harrison's office still smell like wheat paste and shoe leather? I still maintain she's running an underground elf sweatshop. No way a principal's salary buys that many manicures.

You didn't seem to be wearing Prank Face, though, so I hope you're okay. You know I'm always here if you want to talk. Our old swingset on the corner of James Park hasn't been demolished yet. Dad says it's going to be condos. I hope a ton of kids move in there and cry to the management because they don't have any swings to sing about and jump from and have secret meetings on. Would serve them right.

No, it definitely wasn't Prank Face. I still remember all your faces. I still have that radar for you too—the one that tells me whenever you've just entered and left the room. I didn't just notice you in the hallway— I knew you were there. i guess when you grow up with someone from birth you never forget that. At least, I don't. Do you? As of today my birthday is officially six months away. It feels like forever. I'm still planning on staying up til midnight and singing that song from the Sound of Music because then it will be true. I will be sixteen-going-on-seventeen then. You can come sing with me too, like we used to on the swings. Don't worry. I won't tell anyone you really have a mushy center.

Miss you, prankface—
xox
Sunnie

****

The email notification sound was Sunnie. It was always Sunnie. He'd seen her in the hallway; this email no doubt said what her open mouth hadn't been able to before he'd turned his back on her. She was always offering an opinion and a bubble-blowing, flower-picking, glitter-covered shoulder. He didn't want to hear it. He was sick of hearing it. She wouldn't have recognized the new counselor at school. The highly educated head shrink they'd brought in just for him. He didn't want to hear it from them either. His mother was dead. Dead. Couldn't they all just accept it and move on?

Whatever.

Seth highlighted the email and hit delete, but his stomach flipped as the email disappeared from the list. He didn't mind if it hurt; he just didn't want to care. For a moment, he missed life the way it used to be. The way it would never be again. The moment passed.

****

SunnieLu: Surprise Baby is craving apples today: Granny Smiths! Not Honey Crisps! Surprise and I are going to have a chat later abt quality.

****

Seth remembered Mama Lukac and her love of all things Honey Crisp. Her mouthwatering pies. Her amazing cobbler, still warm, with ice cream. The way she'd rant about the perfection of that apple and how all others paled in comparison. Such seriousness over a simple thing; it had always made him giggle. He missed Sunnie's parents some days, but seeing her mom only made the abyss of his own pain deepen. It reopened scabs and scars he desperately to heal over.

He was glad to know her mom was pregnant. The Lukac house

had been so sad when she'd lost the baby. So quiet. He knew that kind of quiet now, understood it. It had happened the year he and Sunnie were in third grade. That was the first year they'd been allowed to swing on the swings by themselves. While he sat there, blissfully lost in memory, there was an update.

****

SunnieLu: Missing a childhood friend is like missing baby teeth. You know there'll be more but right now there's just a hole that can't enjoy apples.

****

Seth closed the laptop.

He walked through the living room, slicing through the quiet with an invisible machete. His father mumbled something at the television, which was currently displaying a commercial for some insurance company. Seth wasn't sure if the program, the commercial, or life in general had Dad upset this time. He'd learned shortly after his mother's suicide to avoid that tone, and then his father as a whole. He grabbed his backpack—containing everything he'd need to survive in the event he decided to never come back—and left the house without a word.

At the bus stop he pulled out his phone and checked his messages. There were several unopened posts on Twitter. For a school-day morning, Sunnie had been busy.

****

> **SunnieLu**: Wow. Chicken Little told us once that the sky was falling. We should have listened. Wow. Wow. Oh my god...

****

Seth pushed his overgrown hair back from his eyes and stared at the nonsense tweet. Huh? Sunnie wasn't one of those overly dramatic girls that constantly annoyed him at school. She was Sunnie. She was fun and bubbly. What the hell drama could make her talk like this? Maybe Mama Lukac's hormones were messing with more than apple cravings. Maybe she'd gotten a C on her History test. Maybe it was about a guy. God, he hoped not. Then he really would have to cut her loose.

****

SunnieLu: We're in a bad made-for-tv disaster movie. Quick—change the channel! I'd happily live in Tubbybabyland forever. As long as I got to live.

****

As long as she got to live? What the hell? And Tubbybabyland was the worst show on TV. It should have been cancelled back when they were ten. Things must have gotten really ugly over at her house. Then Seth remembered his father. Maybe it wasn't just her house....

****

Breaking News: The change in gravitational lensing of Sgr A was first noted by Norwegian Astronomer Borak Krugeur in 2008.

Breaking News: Officials now stating initial figures were off and the trajectory of Sgr A has been recalculated at 94 days.

****

Confused, Seth silently cursed his choice to turn twitter off on his phone from midnight to six in the morning. He'd obviously missed something fairly important and now had to play catch-up on the news. He kept scrolling.
****

SunnieLu: *sob* oh god there will be no surprisebaby. i'll never meet my brother. never turning sixteen seems stupid now. it was a dumb song anyway.

****

No capital letters meant Sunnie was really upset. Shit. Sunnie's mom must have miscarried again. But why wouldn't Sunnie have a birthday? The baby wasn't due until two months after.

****

Breaking News: Leak of Sgr A causing panic across the globe. Major cities in U.S. declaring martial law effective immediately.

****

What.

The.

Fuck.

Seth snapped his phone shut and looked around the neighborhood. Several cars that should have been long gone—their occupants well on their way toward workplaces and daycares—sat untouched in driveways. The previous night's frost clung to windshields that hadn't been scraped. Not a single vehicle ran idle in its driveway, fogging up the early winter morning. He raised an eyebrow, spun on his heel, and headed back to the house. Once again, school was the least of his concerns.

His father was still glued to the television, unshaved, in the T-shirt and sweat pants he'd slept in, half a cup of coffee sitting forgotten on the table in front of him. He didn't notice Seth. Just like he hadn't noticed for the last two years.

Seth tossed his backpack toward the corner of his bedroom and flipped open his laptop. He checked the emails first, retrieving Sunnie's last few from the garbage folder. The first was just Sunnie being Sunnie. He smiled at the childhood references she'd made in the second, but he was still pissed about the school counseling. Dad had told them it was unnecessary—especially after finding out they were going to charge it to his insurance after the first three sessions.

But nothing explained the bizarre tweets. Out of habit, Seth clicked the toolbar link for the suicide support forum he'd lurked on since his mother's death. He trusted regular people, not anchors or actors, to tell him what was going on. He scanned the thread topics as the dark blue and tan page finished loading.

- *Holy Crap! Less than 3 months?*
- *Sagittarius A*
- *Oversimplified or hyperbole?*
- *What's the point to healing now?*
- *Galactic suicide*
- *Reporting End of World*

Seth clicked the last one.

General Discussion— —-> Reporting the End of the World

Bob0626 User #45 Posts: 1274	Fox News just reported some comet or something is heading this way. I've checked the other channels and they all seem to be talking about this Sagittarius thing. Does anyone understand what exactly they're talking about? It sounds like it was here the whole time, so why is it important now? And holy crap, why are they freaking out?
4Jesse711 User #923 Posts: 88	It's not a comet, it's a black hole. And yes it's been here. But it's moving. For whatever reason it's moving through the solar system and it's going to knock the planets out of alignment. The sun too. What it doesn't suck up will be out of orbit and the temperature will plummet, putting us in a deep freeze and killing everything on earth. Yeah... it's serious!
NeverForget Moderator Posts: 3762	Get offline. Go see your family and plan how you're going to live the last three months. The time for mourning is done. You've got 94 days to live. I wish I had gotten over my daughter's suicide earlier and done more with my life now...

Ninety-four days.

Until the end of the world.

Seth shook his head to clear his thoughts.

Police's "King of Pain" suddenly earwormed him.

There really was a little black spot on the sun today.

Ninety-four days.

And then nothing.

****

> **SunnieLu**: My parents stopped calling me Sunshine because I remind them of everything we're going to lose. I'm not even sure who "Erica" is anymore.

****

"Jesus!" He eyes rose from the laptop to the tattered picture on the cork board above his dresser.

****

> From: *notgoth555@gmail.com*
> To: *princessunnie@gmail.com*
> Re: Subject: Rise of the Squirrel Nation
>
> Dear Sunnie,
>
> I saw

****

He didn't know how to finish the sentence and deleted it. He stared at the blank form. A million thoughts ran through his head. Sunnie, the park, apples, playing pirates, climbing trees, his mother's brownies....

Mom.

Dad.

Ninety-four days.

****

notgoth555: @SunnieLu Ground Control to Major Tom

> **SunnieLu**: call me now it's all right. it's just the end of the world. ♫ http://blip.fm/~hhw9w

> **notgoth555**: @*SunnieLu* Really? You know I suck at the lyric game... check your email.

> **SunnieLu**: @notgoth555 *gasp* *sob* Land ho!

****

From: *notgoth555@gmail.com*
To: *princesssunnie@gmail.com*
Subject: (no subject)

Erica,

Wow, I haven't called you that since the first day I met you. The day you broke my blue crayon and then cried about it and got *me* in trouble with our kindergarten teacher... Mrs. Ford, wow. Remember her? Anyway, you ARE Erica. Whether you know who that is or not, that's you. It's always been you. My best friend. My confidant. My discarded wingman. And I'm sorry.

Now pick yourself up and brush off that funk you're twittering! This isn't new. This has been happening our whole lives, we just found out, that's all. As it happens, everyone just found out. We've been dying since the day we were born. You could have died tomorrow. You could have died without knowing. Now you know. Now you can live. On the other side there could be sunshine and flowers, who knows. We'll find out. Right now, we just need to cram in as much fun as we can.

I know it's been a while, but the world isn't gone yet. Our park won't be demolished by the developers. If we've only got ninety-four days, I need you to know something, to hear something.

Meet me at our swings...

S

****

Sunnie didn't close her laptop. She didn't grab her hoodie off the bed. And she left the front door wide open.

Contributor Bios

MAGGIE SLATER writes in Portland, Oregon, where she lives with her husband and two old, cranky cats. She has seen her work published in a variety of small venues, most recently in *Fantastical Visions IV*. She currently moonlights as a reviewer for Tangent Online and is the assistant editor of Apex Publications. For more information about her and her current writing projects, visit her blog at maggiedot.wordpress.com.

GENE O'NEILL has seen 100 plus short stories and novellas published in various magazines and anthologies. Recently his collection, *Taste of Tenderloin*, published by Apex Book Company won the Bram Stoker award. Upcoming soon are a pair of novellas from Sideshow Press (*Sideshow Exhibits*) and Bad Moon Books (*Jade*). In August Bad Moon Books will release his novel *Deathflash*. Currently he is working on a new novel in his Cal Wild Mythos, *Journals of the Collapse*.

JENNIFER PELLAND lives outside Boston with an Andy, three cats, and an impractical amount of books. Her collection *Unwelcome Bodies* was released by Apex in 2008 and contains her Nebula-nominated story "Captive Girl." She has stories coming out this year in *Dark Faith*, *Close Encounters of the Alien Kind*, and *The Naked Singularity*. Because that doesn't leave her busy enough, she also belly dances. Visit www.jenniferpelland.com for further information.

NATANIA BARRON is a writer with a penchant for the speculative; she is also an unrepentant geek. Her work has appeared in *The Gatehouse Gazette*, *Thaumatrope*, *Crossed Genres*, *Bull Spec* and *Steampunk Tales*. Her current novel projects run the gamut from steampunk to heroic fantasy. She is also the founder of The Outer Alliance, a group dedicated to queer advocacy in speculative fiction. Natania holds a BA in English/Writing from Loyola University Maryland and an MA in English with a concentration in medieval literature from the University of North Carolina at Greensboro. In her spare time she cooks, bakes bread, drinks coffee, crochets, blogs, plays guitar and ukulele, and gardens. She lives in North Carolina with her family.

ANGELINE HAWKES holds a B.A. in Composite English Language Arts from Texas A&M University-Commerce. Angeline's collection, *The Commandments*, received a 2006 Bram Stoker Award nomination. Her story, "In Waters Black the Lost Ones Sleep", appears in the 2007 Origins Award nominated Chaosium anthology, *Frontier Cthulhu*. *Shades of Blood and Shadow*, her collection from Dark Regions Press, will be followed with *Inferno: Tales of Hell and Horror*. Bad Moon Books will publish *Out of the Garden and Other Tales of the Barbarian Kabar of El Hazzar*, a novel-length compilation of her barbarian fantasy series, in 2011. Christopher Fulbright and Angeline will see publication of their novella, *Black Mercy Falls*, from Bloodletting Press in 2010; and novel, *Scavenger*, from Elder Signs Press in 2011. Angeline has seen the publication of a novel, novellas, collections, fiction in 35+ anthologies, and over 100 short fiction publications. She is an active member of HWA and the Robert E. Howard UPA. Visit her websites at www.angelinehawkes.com and www.fulbrightandhawkes.com.

GLENN LEWIS GILLETTE began his career In the early 1970s with a pair of publications in *Analog*. More recently, his work has appeared in *Mystic Signals 2* and *Apex Magazine*. More of his short fiction can be found at Flashfictiononline.com (March, 2008, issue), the Bardsandsages.com print anthology (April 2009), Morriganezine.com, Edgeofpropinquity.net, Mbrane SF, and Themonstersnextdoor.com. You can read more about Glenn and his writing at www.glgwrites.com.

JAMES F. REILLY is a horror fiction writer who lives in Massachusetts with an intolerant wife, an angry toddler, and four animals he despises. He also runs the popular horror movie review site, Horrorview.com, which takes up far too much time for something that doesn't pay him a dime. Visit Reilly's website at www.jamesfreilly.com, where you can read more of his short fiction, send him hate mail, and wait in anticipation of his bi-annual blog postings.

ELAINE BLOSE is a freelance writer who loves to travel overseas and domestically. When she is not traveling she resides in Ohio on the family farm and helps her elderly mother with a whole menagerie of animals. She is currently working on her first novel.

An engineer by day, ROBBY SPARKS moonlights as a writer and filmmaker by night. His short fiction has appeared in *Apex Digest* and in the anthologies *Harlan County Horrors* (available from Apex Publications) and *Harvest Hill* (available from Graveside Tales). His award-winning films have been shown at film festivals, and some of his camera work can even be seen on *Adventure Chefs*, a new reality show that mixes *Survivor* with *Iron Chef*, available on I-tunes. Robby would like to express his thanks to Misty, his wife, for her aid in his creative endeavors.

SARA M. HARVEY lives and writes in Nashville, TN with her husband and three dogs. The second book of her Penemue fantasy trilogy, *The Labyrinth of the Dead* (Apex Publications), will be released in the summer of 2010. She also loves perfume. A lot.

MICHELE LEE writes horror, science fiction and fantasy from the relative safety of her haunted house in the oldest section of Louisville, Ky. When she isn't writing, she reviews books of all genres, spends too much time on Twitter and grows monstrous vegetables. She can be kept track of at www.michelelee.net.

DEB TABER is Senior Book Editor at Apex Publishing and a copy editor for any and all things in need of copy editing. Her fiction has been published in *Apex Digest, Shadowed Realms* and *Fantasy Magazine* and will appear in the forthcoming *Art from Art* anthology (Modernist Press). Her nonfiction has appeared in a variety of print and online venues including Tor.com. When not writing or editing she can be found designing lighting for theatre and dance performances throughout the Pacific Northwest. She blogs on very rare occasions at debtaber.livejournal.com.

ALIETTE DE BODARD lives and works in Paris, where she has a job as a Computer Engineer. In her spare time, she writes speculative fiction. She is the author of the Aztec fantasy *Servant of the Underworld* (Angry Robot/HarperCollins), as well as numerous pieces of fiction published in venues such as *Asimov's*, *Realms of Fantasy* and Gardner Dozois' *The Year's Best Science Fiction*. She is a Campbell Award finalist and a Writers of the Future winner. Visit her website at www.aliettedebodard.com.

MAURICE BROADDUS' dark fiction has been published in numerous magazines, anthologies, and web sites, most recently including *Dark Dreams II & III*, *Apex Magazine*, *Black Static*, and *Weird Tales Magazine*. He is the editor of the anthology *Dark Faith* (Apex Publications). His novel series, *The Knights of Breton Court* (Angry Robot/HarperCollins UK) debuts in 2010. Visit his site at mauricebroaddus.com.

GILL AINSWORTH, a British writer, lives in leafy-green Kent in South East England with her husband and children. She is an assistant editor with Apex Publications. As well as having numerous scientific publications to her name, her fiction has seen print in the United States, the United Kingdom and Germany. Her writing has won several awards and, jointly with Jason Sizemore, she was a Bram Stoker nominee in 2007 for their anthology, *Aegri Somnia*.

GEOFFREY GIRARD has appeared in such anthologies as *Writers of the Future*, *Gratia Placenti*, *Damned Nation*, *Harlan County Horrors*, and *Dark Futures: Tales of Dystopic SF*, and the magazines

Murky Depths, The Willows, Aoife's Kiss, Beyond Centauri, and *Apex Digest* (which serialized his horror novella *Cain XP11* in four issues). His first book, *Tales of the Jersey Devil* (a collection of thirteen tales based on the myth), was published in 2005, with *Tales of the Atlantic Pirates* and *Tales of the Eastern Indians* following. Find more info at www.GeoffreyGirard.com.

EKATERINA SEDIA resides in the Pinelands of New Jersey. Her critically acclaimed novels, *The Secret History of Moscow* and *The Alchemy of Stone* were published by Prime Books. Her next one, *The House of Discarded Dreams*, is coming out in 2010. Her short stories have sold to *Analog, Baen's Universe, Dark Wisdom* and *Clarkesworld*, as well as *Haunted Legends* and *Magic in the Mirrorstone* anthologies. In 2010, Kathy won the World Fantasy Award for her editing *Paper Cities: An Anthology of Urban Fantasy.* Visit her at www.ekaterinasedia.com.

Residing in Pennsylvania with her two children, a needy cat and some hippie, KELLI OWEN spends her days paying the bills and her fleeting free time writing, reading and/or editing for several popular midlist genre authors. She can be found in *Dark Futures, Dark Faith*, the upcoming Nick Cave Anthology, and her novel, *In the Shadow of Darkness*, is due out this winter. Visit her at www.kelliowen.com for more information.

ALETHEA KONTIS is a geek, a princess, and a fairy-godmother-in-training—not necessarily in that order. She is a big fan of life, liberty, and the pursuit of happiness, and believes that everyone has the right to be awesome. (Yes, *everyone.*) Princess Alethea recently escaped her own life of tyranny being held captive in an Ivory Tower. She now lives Somewhere Over the Rainbow, in the land of butterflies and fairies. She is still searching for the perfect magic wand, and she writes better than your grandma.

PAUL JESSUP is a critically acclaimed writer of really weird and strange stuff. He's been published in more magazines and anthologies than he cares to admit, and has two books out right now with one more on the way—the first a surreal space opera named *Open Your Eyes* (Apex Publications), the second a collection of short stories named *Glass Coffin Girls* (PS Publishing). The third is *Werewolves*, an illustrated novel with crazy cool art coming out in July 2010.

ALEX ANDREYEV is a Russian digital artist currently living in St. Petersburg where he holds the position of creative director of a major advertising holding. Alex's work displays a clear surrealism influence with fantastic composition details such as flying trains, long-limbed alien monsters, and houses on the edge of the world. Visit alexandreev.com for more information and samples of his work.

JASON SIZEMORE is a Stoker Award-nominated editor and the owner of Apex Publications. He hails Big Creek, KY, a tiny community nestled deep in the backwoods of the Appalachian Mountains. After earning a degree from Transylvania University (yes, it exists), he went on to a mind-numbing career in software development. On the side, he edits and publishes anything that can be categorized 'dark genre' that he can get his hands on. For more information visit www.jason-sizemore.com.

CPSIA information can be obtained at www.ICGtesting.com
264761BV00002B/117/P